D1100331

PHYLLIDA SHRIMPTON

HOT
KEY
BOOKS

First published in Great Britain in 2018 by
HOT KEY BOOKS
80–81 Wimpole St, London W1G 9RE
www.hotkeybooks.com

This is a work of fiction. Names, places, events and incidents are either the
products of the author's imagination or used fictitiously. Any resemblance
to actual persons, living or dead, is purely coincidental.

A CIP catalogue record for this book is available from the British Library.

ISBN: 9781471406881
also available as an ebook

1

For my daughter Rebecca Katelyn Mooney
May you always turn your face towards the sunshine.

Silence.

The bluish light to the day gives away the early hour, and I hug my knees to my chest as if I should be cold.

Sitting on the grass verge of a narrow country lane I become aware, with the gradual creeping light of dawn, that I must have been here for some time. It comes to me slowly, in the same way that I search for recent dreams when I first wake.

I can't remember . . .

The shrill call of a wild bird and the urgent flapping of its wings shatters the still air, nudging me to question why I'm here and not at home where I should be, in my pyjamas and tucked under my duvet. All around there's nothing but sparse winter countryside, no house, no shop, no building.

I'd been shopping in town.

A low mist spreads over the fields, disappearing into the grass around me, like in a horror film when dry ice creeps across the set, just before something scary happens. A light glittering of winter frost is sprinkled over everything, but I don't feel cold.

Why don't I feel cold?

My purple Converse shoe is on its side, half in and half out of a puddle, and the remains of the night still linger in the darkness of the water around it. I stare at the shoe, and the laces trailing in the dirt, still caught in the grip of overnight ice, and I wonder if it's washable or ruined.

The purple will go well with the T-shirt I just bought, if they're not completely wrecked.

I'd begged my mother for these shoes, until she'd finally given in and bought them for me. Now the Converse star stares back at me, its single eye unblinking.

It was Saturday. I was with Beth. I bought a T-shirt.

We'd both agreed that Nathan Peterson, my boyfriend of seven weeks, would think that I'd look extra cute in it. Or is it seven weeks and *one* day now? Is it Sunday morning? It was almost dark when I was walking home.

Beth. Shopping. Walking home.

I grab at the fragments of my memory as they float past.

I'd spent most of my bus fare on a fabulous pair of earrings . . . I texted Mum to tell her I was on the bus home – a small lie . . . I had to get off the bus early because I didn't have enough money for the whole journey. I took a shortcut down King's Lane and it was evening, almost dark . . . and now it's not.

So, why am I still here?

I reach around for my phone, but it's not beside me. The bag with my new top in is about five feet away, half buried in the long grass, and my handbag is next to it, shining with wet and frost. I look again at my shoe in the puddle, and then at my feet . . .

I'm wearing both shoes.

The sound of a car engine pushes through the quietness of the morning, and I drag my gaze away from my feet, towards it, wondering what the driver is going to think about a fifteen-year-old girl sitting out here, in the middle of nowhere, alone.

Yellow headlights flicker intermittently between the winter-bare roadside hedges, then blur as they hit patches of mist. The engine chugs slowly, and it hits me that I should be nervous about what sort of person is driving *that* slowly . . . but I'm not.

'Thank God!' I mutter under my breath, standing up, as the white, blue, and yellow of a police car comes into view and two policemen get out. They look briefly at my purple Converse in the puddle, then make their way over to me. 'OK, so, I have *no* idea why I'm here . . .' I tell them, laughing a little, to cover my embarrassment.

The dark-haired one reaches his hand towards me.

'I think we've found her,' he says, rather rudely reaching past me and brushing weeds and grass aside.

I turn to see what they've found.

And there I am.

My legs are bent upwards with a bone sticking out where my right ankle should be, making my foot hang from its tendons, facing backwards in its stripy sock. My chest is pressed into watery brown mud at the bottom of a ditch, but my head is turned, facing towards us at the strangest angle. My long, dark hair is spread out in the mud, and I can't take my gaze off the bluey whiteness of my skin, and how I'm staring blankly up towards all three of us, a milky bloom spreading across the green of my eyes.

I am statue still, unable to move, staring back at myself with total disbelief. A thin scream, high-pitched and desperate, fills my ears and I realise that it's coming out of my mouth without my consent. The police don't react to the noise I'm making, as if there's an invisible soundproof wall between us.

'Noooo, this isn't happening!' I shout at them, grabbing desperately at the arm of the nearest one, but my hands disappear into the black of his jacket.

I can't feel any of the trembling that comes with fear, or the rush of breath that comes with panic. No tears are running down my face. I just feel kind of . . . disconnected, as if I'm watching this happening in a film. 'OK . . . so it's a *dream*,' I say out loud, another small laugh escaping from me, like I've just laughed at a joke that only I'm pretending to understand. I circle both men. 'It's a DREAM!' I shout in their ears, willing them to fade away and let me wake up. I scream again, and pinch myself, really, really hard, only I can't feel my fingers because I'm in a dream.

I'm not in a dream.

I hear the dark-haired one radio back to the station for reinforcements and an ambulance, while the ginger one runs over to the car and comes hurrying back with a small machine in his hands.

'I'm not sure you're going to need that, mate,' the dark-haired man says sarcastically, as his 'mate' kneels down beside my body in the ditch, and starts to get the machine ready. 'I *said*, I'm not sure you're going to need the defibrillator, Gary,' he repeats, alternating his gaze between me and Gary.

'Why?' Gary pants, squinting up, the red of his face competing with his hair.

'Because her fucking head is on backwards,' he says.

This is really happening.

I am dead, and I've absolutely no idea how it happened.

'Shit,' I hiss to myself. Hardly articulate, but it's all I've got to go with right now.

And the pinching and the crying and the trembling, it would seem, are for the physical body, and as I watch and listen to everything unfolding in front of me, I realise, with a kind of detached and awful shock, that I no longer have one of those. My body is in that ditch, and, to quote that police guy, my 'fucking head is on backwards'. My body and me have somehow got separated, and now I'm trapped in a soundproof bubble, and no one knows I'm here.

I watch the hustle and bustle of my roadside death: the ambulance with its wailing siren, the various police officers, investigators with their grim faces, tape stretched across the road, measurements taken, information recorded, pictures carefully snapped, and phone calls made. My phone is checked but the battery is flat, my bag is examined and so is my body. A large man with russet-brown skin stands close by holding a photograph of me, his lips squeezed into a downward turn.

This whole thing is all about *me*, but for once it's nothing I want to hear.

Apparently the trauma to my body is consistent with a road traffic collision, a 'hit-and-run', meaning that I have basically just become an . . . incident.

I, or rather, my body, has got rigor mortis, which has reached its maximum at around twelve hours after death, and has probably started the next stage. This basically means that I'm stiff, and am now going to head towards that floppy traditional dead look. Right now, I'm like a dolly chucked on the ground and broken. My rigor mortis, and the fact that evidently the angle of my head is not compatible with life, means the paramedics can determine, categorically and without doubt, 'life extinct!'

I shout at them all again. 'Hey! . . . I'm not a *dinosaur!*' What does that mean exactly? My body is still on the planet, and I'm still here, seeing and hearing. I am not extinct! Although I am quite obviously not alive.

I watch the empty ambulance drive away, leaving my body behind, venturing on with its mission to save lives, as it has been unable to do with mine, its siren now hushed, all hope of saving me gone. I wouldn't say I've 'lost' my life exactly, and I haven't exactly 'lost' my body but I have, for sure, somehow lost the connection between the two.

My rigor mortis also means the procedure for scraping me out of the mud, and shoving me into a body bag, is totally degrading and less than graceful, and I watch with an expression of contorted disgust as they force my unwilling limbs inside and pull up the zipper.

Finally, long after the mists have dissipated, and the crystals of frost have been evaporated by the winter sun, and the sounds of the road and nearby town have filled the air, I climb into a black van, next to my own bagged-up self, and together we set off for wherever dead people are taken.

I can only describe it as *unusual* . . . looking at yourself from this angle.

My body is now lying down in the hospital mortuary covered by a sheet. My stiff limbs have been forced, and manipulated, into a more appropriate position, so I look a little less grotesque at least, and my closed eyes thankfully mean that I'm not staring back at . . . *myself*.

I've never studied my face from above like this, let alone porcelain smooth and still . . . eyes shut. I have always seen 'me', looking out from a mirror, a photograph or a screen, looking at my face full on, eyes wide and shining, and alive.

Always looking good, so I thought.

Bizarrely I can't help admiring how well I'd put my make-up on. Still perfectly applied in the places where it wasn't smudged and spoiled. Black mascaraed lashes fan my cheeks; they look quite long – thank God for waterproof! Forest shimmer green and pearly cream shadow, painstakingly applied with little brushes, now looks odd against my skin where all the natural colours of my life have slipped away, like paint down a plughole. The empty grey of my face looks creepy against the still blackness of my once beautifully straightened hair, and the twinkle of gold and fake diamonds, peeping from my ears, look wrong as if they're clashing with death.

I hear my mother before I see her. There's an agonised noise coming from the depths of her body, like the groaning of an animal in pain, and I can hardly bear to listen. The sound heaves over and over, and it's getting louder, travelling down the hospital corridor, escorted by the echoes of three pairs of shoes tapping against polished vinyl. A fat man with thin white hair poking fluffily upwards over his ridiculously large forehead opens the door with a gentle click and a respectful expression. With his hand still on the door, he hesitates. 'Are you sure? We have already . . . identified her.' I'd already seen how the police had matched my ID and my strangely angled face, with a photograph held by Brian, the man with the russet-brown skin, and embarrassingly they had made a note of my birthmark, a kind of coffee stain of Australia on my right buttock. But I guess my parents couldn't believe without seeing, because they enter the room anyway.

'Mum . . . ? Dad?' I run to them, reaching out and watching my hands disappear mistily into their live bodies, like grabbing at steam. Although I already know it's pointless, I try wildly flinging my arms about in front of their faces, yelling at them to notice me, until, frustrated, I give up.

They hear and see nothing.

Mum and Dad hold on to each other, as if by letting go they'll somehow fall, down into the black abyss that is horror, fear and death itself. My mother's normally shoulder-length brown hair is scraped back into a fat hair comb, but a large chunk has escaped and hangs in mousey-brown tendrils down the side of her stricken face. Dad's black- and grey-peppered hair looks short and smart as always, but merely serves to frame his haggard face. From memory it looks as if they're wearing what they were wearing when I left the house yesterday morning, only now their clothes look crumpled and almost too big for their bodies.

The impenetrable metal of the entire room cups their raw emotions, like a bowl holds water. If I can be glad about anything right now, it's that they didn't have to see me as I had seen me earlier.

A thin, strangled sound now chokes in Mum's throat as she looks down at the dead me, and a trickle of saliva glimmers on her fingers as they try desperately to hold in her grief. Tears course down her cheeks and her nose starts to run, joining the saliva on her fingers. She shakes her head and says 'noooo' in one long and ugly drawn-out sound, almost identical to the way I had when I first saw me.

The man with the ridiculously large forehead reaches for a plain box of tissues and pulls one out. As he hands her a tissue, she reaches for it but her eyes never leave my face. Dad has clamped his teeth and lips together and I notice how the muscles in his jaw flex over and over. He says nothing but gives a nod of affirmation to the man with the forehead. The faces of my parents have become distorted by tension below the surface of their skin, as if they're merely rough sketches of themselves.

Grief, I have learnt today, is the colour grey. All around us is grey. The walls, the equipment, the skin of the dead, and the skin of the living. The reddish brown of Mum's jacket and the green of Dad's chunky-knit jumper look barely sepia against this room of grey.

Having confirmed with that nod that the lifeless mass of slowly putrefying cells lying in front of them had recently been me, the living, breathing, body of Lily Richardson, fifteen years old, daughter of James and Amelia Richardson, twin sister to Ben Richardson, they are allowed to leave. Or rather, they are encouraged, gently, to abandon their child, so that the accurate cause of my death can be determined, and recorded.

Dad turns stiffly, still holding Mum's hand, as he leads her out of this shiny room where death remains in the reflections of the stainless steel. Mum pulls against him, her free hand reaching for my hair, and her eyes caressing my face. 'What happened, Lily? Who did this to you?'

'I don't know, Mum,' I answer sadly. 'I wish I knew.'

She lets out another low horrible mourning sound, which drags itself out of her mouth again, while Dad puts a protective arm round her shoulders, turning his face away from both of us, his movement causing the tears balanced on his lashes to spill.

'I love you,' she whispers, walking through my invisible outstretched hands as they leave.

'I love you too,' I call out, as I follow them, but my words don't reach their ears, only the echoes of their footsteps on the vinyl fills the corridor, until Dad's voice bounces off the walls around me. 'I'll find the bastard that did this to you, Lily . . . and I'll make him pay. So help me GOD!'

Brian is waiting for them. He's obviously been assigned the task of supporting my family, and I'm thankful that he looks . . . *reliable*, like a big rugby player with kind eyes. Just . . . maybe, fingers crossed, he'll be strong enough to keep us all together right now.

As they walk to the car, I realise their last possible shred of hope, that the body in that room might not belong to me, has evaporated. It shows on their faces, robbing them of several years while the colour of Brian's skin only serves to highlight the lack of colour in theirs.

Leaning with his back against the passenger door, Ben catches sight of Mum and Dad, their expressions confirming everything there is to know. His eyes peep out from beneath his black hair, which flops over his face, then they snap tight shut as if this will protect him from something he isn't prepared to understand. But he does understand. With one hand on the wheel arch of the police car for support, he vomits repeatedly, until his understanding splashes against the wheel and his shoes, and gets caught in the folds of his jeans. By the time our parents reach him, my twin brother is left with nothing but the silent retch that is pain trying to get out.

Nathan's mum was making Sunday dinner, while the frequent sound of canned laughter came through the door from the lounge, where Nathan was watching television.

She chose a bottle of red wine from the wine rack, and added a small glug of it to the juices surrounding the meat as it bubbled in a pan on their kitchen range. Then she got two large wine glasses and filled both. Taking a mouthful, she reached for a small terracotta pot and crumbled a little sea salt into the dish. 'Are you going out today?' she called to Nathan, glancing at the clock.

Nathan paused the programme he was watching, leisurely stretched out his long legs along the huge feather-stuffed cream sofa and yawned. 'No, tomorrow night. A few of us are going out but we don't know where yet. Why?'

'Because I'm making your favourite, sticky toffee pudding, but it won't be ready for a while. I just wanted to make sure you'd still be here to eat it.'

'Sweet,' he called back. 'Thanks, Mum.' Then he flicked the TV back to life, knowing that his empty stomach was going to appreciate his mother's cooking more than his ears were appreciating her intermittent singing from the kitchen.

She took another sip of wine, before grinding a pepper mill

liberally over the top and stirring all the ingredients with a wooden spoon before tasting it. Nodding to herself, she took another sip of wine and hummed the tune to an advert on the television, loudly singing the last few words of it, '. . . washing bright tabs dot com,' just as Nathan's dad walked in from helping a neighbour.

He hung up his jacket in the coat cupboard, but the smell of the cold evening air still clung to his clothes. He lifted the lid of the pot to see what delight she had rustled up for his dinner, then gave her a kiss, causing a lock of her long auburn hair to come loose from its black velvet ribbon.

'Nathan? Dad's back. Set the table for dinner, love,' she called, then she lifted the wine bottle towards his dad and smiled, saying, 'Beef in red wine,' and with her other hand she passed him a round-bowled glass. He cupped the glass gratefully, the very good wine slipping down his throat easily, leaving hints of blackcurrant on his tongue.

Nathan appeared in the doorway, taking up most of the frame, his quiff of light-brown hair, creating the illusion that he was slightly taller than his dad. 'Smells good,' he said, smiling and giving her a look of approval, then he poured himself a pint of milk from the fridge and downed half of it, before making his way to the dining room to set the table.

As the day progresses, I watch my family's reactions shift and change in ugly turns.

They have stayed in the kitchen surrounded by cold cups of tea and Ben's half-eaten sandwich from the night before. Bacon, turned white from cold fat, pokes out of slices of white bread, now stiff and stale, reminding them of the exact moment that Ben knew, without a doubt, that something was very wrong.

We've always had a thing between us, me and Ben. A 'twin thing', like we've always known without words what was going on with each other. Ben was capable of eating the entire contents of the fridge in one sitting, yet that sandwich had stuck in his throat last night, when he just *knew*.

Next to the sandwich is an empty silver-edged frame. A pair of scissors lies alongside a large photo taken of us all at Christmas. Everyone was smiling at the camera and the light had caught our eyes along with the strands of red tinsel that I had draped over Dad's neck. Mum was wearing a reindeer headband, her antlers waving at us, and Ben had my fingers above his head like rabbit ears. We had just finished dinner, totally full to a point where we thought we might split, when Granddad Peter had taken the shot. I remember him, slightly drunk, his purple Christmas cracker hat lopsided on his head, and how his false teeth had shot out of his mouth onto the table when he laughed at something. Ben and I had gagged at the sight of them, landing dangerously near to the honeyed parsnips. We were a normal family, nothing amazing about us, apart from our normality.

The photograph has a hole in it where I used to be, and all that is left of me are my rabbit fingers above Ben's head. I'm now in Brian's file somewhere, used for the purpose of identifying me. No doubt my family had hoped, at the time, that I'd just got distracted by friends, or a party, or *anything* other than what had actually happened. Now they all stare out from the glossy paper on the table, and, as in real life, I am no longer with them.

I'm totally helpless and I can't think of anything I can do to get anyone's attention. I can't be heard and I can't move objects, or pick up a pen to write a ghostly note. I've tried . . . I've really tried, but I'm literally trapped in some kind of virtual world, watching my family getting steadily more demented about my untimely death.

Uncle Roger, Dad's brother, rushes into the house trailing the shapeless and very useless Aunty Ruth. Aunty Ruth has always been what Mum politely calls socially incompetent, but Dad says if she was any more stupid, Roger would have to water her. And now, here she is, in a voluminous orange blouse, saying nothing except, 'Cup of tea, Meil? Cup of tea, Jay?' in her grating voice, shortening their names in her ever-irritating way. She chews the nails of one hand and dabs at her insipid grey eyes with the other, whispering 'Poor Lily-Pad' over and over, until Roger snaps at her.

'You're not helping, Ruth.' Aunty Ruth has a nickname for everyone and everyone hates it.

Uncle Roger dives into help mode by getting all practical. He phones my granddads and I can hear their cries of disbelief, strangely metallic down the receiver, and I feel bad for them when he finishes the call, leaving them alone with nothing but their news.

I am on the outside looking in. I can see the shaking fingers and hunched shoulders of my family, the whites of their eyes growing a network of red veins and shining with salty tears, yet I'm not reacting in the same way. I suppose all of that belongs only to the living machine that drives the adrenalin and pumps the blood and beats the heart?

I can't feel how the pinkness of their skin is made warm by their flowing blood, and I know that I will never again feel the weight of their arms round me, or the softness of their kisses on my cheeks. I know every feeling by memory, but I can't react with saline and chemicals like they are, and it seems wrong, and so unfair, that in a single breath it was all over.

'Another sarnie, Benji?' Aunty Ruth asks Ben. She scrapes the remains of yesterday's bacon sandwich in the bin and looks at him with agonised eyes, as if the extreme sympathy in her expression should support him with any grief that he may feel.

'No,' Ben answers, bristling, as always, from her name for him. She tries again. 'Biscuit, Benji?'

'He doesn't want any bloody food, Ruth,' Uncle Roger hisses at her, which causes her to flinch like she's been stung, and resume the nail-chewing and eye-dabbing. He lights a cigarette, placing his packet back down on the table but Mum unexpectedly reaches for one, and barely raising an eyebrow Roger leans over and sparks his lighter into life at the end of the cigarette, which is now balanced shakily in her lips.

'Ew, Mum, no?' I gasp at how strangely unfamiliar she looks with the curl of grey smoke coming out of her mouth, and how, for sure, she would have gone mad at me or Ben for doing it.

Dad, who would always, without fail, waft the air whenever Roger trailed his smoky aura into our house, looks at them both. '*Really?*' he says with a heavy note of sarcasm, and walks over to the back door, opens it and points outside, as if ordering a dog out. They dutifully prop themselves against the open door frame to the kitchen, and I notice how Mum sucks on her cigarette as if it is the only way she can now draw breath. Aunty Ruth shivers and reaches for a thick and bobbly beige cardigan, while Ben is eyeing Mum and the open packet on the table. He either hates the idea . . . or wants one.

'Don't do it, *Benji*,' I whisper into his ear. 'I'm *still* here.' Then we all jump as Ben suddenly hits the table with his fist, and with his teeth clenched, in a burst of vented anger, he swears. 'Bloody *hit-and-run?*'

Brian had informed them of the initial judgement, but exactly what happened last night is a horrible, unanswered question on everyone's lips, including mine. I'm pretty sure though, that if we *had* to choose the cause of my death, we would all choose hit-and-run, rather than rape, murder and a roadside dumping. Not that it's much consolation. Dad joins in and repeats his threat from this morning. 'I'm going to kill the bastard who did it, then tear his limbs off and shove them all down his throat.'

Ben simply sits, rigid, hand still clenched, staring at those cigarettes.

It isn't fair. Someone out there will carry on with their life, while mine has stopped because of them. I want justice. I want the police to find them and ruin their life and the lives of their family as payback for mine, preferably before my dad gets arrested for dismembering someone.

But most of all, I want my life back.

Although I can move around with my family, I can't seem to actually leave them, so I've no idea how Beth is coping with all this. I want to wind the clock back and be back in town, shopping with her, having a laugh . . . being alive. I don't even know if Nathan knows yet. It's as if I am caught in the family zone and can't move away. I know Ben will tell his friend, Matthew, but he might not think to tell Nathan straight away. I want him to wrap me in his arms right this minute, to kiss the top of my head and tell me that this nightmare will all somehow be OK. I want him to tell me that he loves me, dead or alive.

Stunned disbelief, like a person whose face has just been slapped, has filled the room all day, and when finally Uncle Roger goes home with Aunty Ruth, who despite his chastising, has left huge piles of sandwiches covered in cling film in the kitchen, my family detach themselves and head robotically to various parts of the house, to lick the wounds that they probably believe will never heal.

Dad plants himself on the sofa with a bottle of whisky, and Mum crawls into bed with sleeping tablets and gin, as if they are merely clinging to the debris that is the remains of our family.

I follow Ben into his room. Does he still know me, without words and beyond walls? 'Can you tell I'm still here, Ben?' I ask him. No one really understands how close we are, except us, and as I study Ben in his state of jagged devastation, I wonder if he believes that I'm now severed from him, or whether somewhere deep inside, he can feel me with him still.

He puts a can of beer, swiped from the fridge, on his bedside table and with fingers shaking he holds up one of Uncle Roger's cigarettes, and lights it.

'Don't,' I plead with him, but he carries on, drawing on it, ignoring his obsession with fitness and sport. He takes a drag, then another, and carries on until the whole cigarette is nothing but a squashed and yellowing stub in the lid of a deodorant can. It makes him choke, and his choking turns into a sob, yet he wipes his face angrily, turns on some music and ramps up the volume, as if loud noise will replace the thoughts in his head.

He reaches for his phone and texts Matthew to tell him, without softening the blow, that his sister is dead, then waits for the screen to light up and ring with Matthew's personal *Mission Impossible* tone, signalling his reply, which, as it happens, is instant. Personally I don't think that 'Shit man, that's intense' is adequate at this point to support Ben through his grief, but within moments a second text comes through. 'I'm coming over.' After texting back a single word, 'No,' Ben switches his phone to silent and flops back on the bed, cocooned by the music yet clutching at the can of beer as if it is the only thing that will keep him afloat.

My brother, such a huge part of who I am – was? – or whatever, has become a kind of agony where my heart should be, and I can't bear that the very essence of who we, as twins, were, might have been ripped and ruined. I am trapped in an awful cavity between life and death and all I can hope for is that my twin brother will find me.

Nathan's mum's beautifully restored vintage car, the shiny blue curves of its old-fashioned bodywork topped with a cream convertible roof, was parked in the garage for the second night running.

She planned to get her car washed early before work on Monday, because Nathan's dad, Alex, would have left the house by then, and Nathan was on half-term so would still be asleep. She really didn't want to tell Alex that she had hit a deer, or whatever it was, coming home from the late lunch with her friends on Saturday. She didn't want to explain the mud on her precious and normally pristine car, because she would then have to explain why she had cut across the countryside to avoid the main roads and the chance of more cars.

She didn't normally drink more than two glasses if she had to drive, but Morag had bought another bottle, and she had eventually given in to her friend's pressure to '*Go on*, have another'. In the end, although she had been quite careful and felt totally fine, she had probably been over the limit by the time she drove home, but as someone else had been pouring the wine she wasn't exactly sure *how* much she had consumed.

She'd been looking for some mints on the way home, while avoiding the potholes at the same time, when she heard the *thunk*. There was nothing to indicate what she had hit as she looked into her rear-view mirror and her side mirrors, seeing only the inky black puddles and the darkening outlines of the trees and the nearby hedge. She had stopped, briefly, but couldn't see anything from her seat, and when she had tried to get out to look she realised very quickly that her high heels, the increasing dark and bad weather would make it a futile task to hunt for an animal, and even then what could she do? She could hardly shove an entire deer into her car and take it home. *No, better to let nature take its course*, she thought, then drove home, desperately hoping her car was OK.

They didn't have secrets from each other in her family, but she was terribly embarrassed that she had lost track of her safe driving limit. She decided to keep quiet about the animal, and the mud, and wash her car on Monday.

When the shreds of what had once been his family had dispersed, Lily's dad, James, sat on the sofa clutching a bottle of whisky, and listened to the sounds in his own head. It was the noise of jarring disbelief playing over and over, stabbing at his soul.

The two tiny babies that his wife had presented him with over fifteen years ago had completed his whole world. So vulnerable and perfect, he had held one in each arm, just looking from Ben to Lily, and being totally amazed and thrilled that they belonged to him. Amelia had smiled tiredly at him, flushed with exertion and pride, and he had loved her. In that moment he knew he was going to be a good dad and his heart had been a seesaw of joy and fear at the prospect ahead.

Amelia would joke with him over the years that he was almost caveman in his need to be the hunter-gatherer of the family. His key function in life was to provide and protect. They were so happy with twins, one of each, they had decided to stop there. From little pink wriggling things to strong, healthy teenagers, he had revelled in every stage. He had watched them over the years, how they fought with each other, defended each other and loved each other. Many times when they were little he had found them in the same bed, curled up, warm little hands clasped as if they needed each other even when they were asleep. He had admired his children for everything that they had become, their achievements, their talents, their personalities forming as they grew, and yet he hadn't been able to keep Lily alive.

He took a large burning gulp of whisky and dialled a number on the phone. The steady rhythm of the dialling tone filled his ear and he swigged at his whisky again. The drink stayed in his mouth as a tired voice on the other end simply said his name. 'James?'

James was unable to swallow past the huge lump in his throat, and the liquid trickled out of his lips and down his jumper as he spoke. 'Dad?' he mumbled into the receiver, and waited while his father gathered himself.

'I'm here, son.'

They sat like that for some time, receivers to their ears and only silence coming down the line until James quietly said, 'I've failed, Dad.' He took another gulp of whisky, then another, then more, hoping with every second that it would numb the pain, even just a little. 'I didn't keep her safe,' he confessed into the receiver, the faceless bulk of his daughter's killer lurking in the corner of his mind. 'I can hardly bear . . .' The rest of his words wouldn't come out, but he thought about his wife and all the similarities there were between her and Lily and how she would now always be a stark reminder of the beautiful woman his daughter should have become. And Ben, so similar, the black hair and the shape of his face, but now with an empty space forever beside him. He put his face in his hands while his father's words floated up from the carpet, where he'd dropped the phone.

'It will get better, James. It may not seem like it now, but it will. Trust me. Hold on to that thought.'

But James continued to hide behind his hands. He had failed. Life had proved too fragile and he'd broken it.

I stay with Ben all night.

I don't know *how* to go anywhere else anyway. It's a scary prospect, being trapped like this, by some kind of virtual glue, in this universal chasm. I no longer need to sleep. I can't get into my own bed, or turn on the television, or eat, or hold a conversation, or go and see Beth or Nathan. I can't do anything and it's terrifying. 'I'm right here, Ben,' I tell him. 'I'm right, sodding, bloody HERE. *Find* me!'

But there's nothing . . . not a turn of the head or a twitch of the lips. I resort to poking my finger into his eye, then his other eye, then flicking the end of his nose, like I loved doing before, when he was asleep, but still nothing – my fingers simply pass undetected through his nostrils.

The gradually lightening sky brings Monday, and the first day of half-term, but for Ben time and agenda won't matter right now. A group of us were supposed to be going out tonight. Me and Nathan, Ben, Matthew, Beth and several others, but that idea sure is ruined now. Ben falls asleep eventually, fully clothed and on top of the duvet, early daylight filling the room and his phone flashing silent messages beside him.

I miss Ben already. A lifetime of knuckle burns on top of my head, or the stinging flick of a tea towel on the back of my thigh, or violently chucking me out of my comfy seat in front of the television, so that he could prove his size over me and sit wherever he wanted. I'd made it my personal mission to retaliate by sabotaging whatever he had been into over the years: toys, cars and more recently fraping his social media sites. I'd become an expert at firing elastic bands with amazing accuracy, or stealing his stash of sweets or money. The list was endless between us, and the merciless fighting was constant but we loved it. The tellings-off that we got from Mum and Dad were both frequent and ignored.

'I'm obviously the superior twin,' I told him often over the years, since I had made it down the birth canal first. Nearly sixteen years ago on 3rd June, I was born a full hour and a half before Ben finally decided to turn up. I could imagine myself pushing and shoving my way past him, in my eagerness to be first, and then we'd spent the next fifteen and three-quarter years behaving in exactly the same way, competing for the best of everything, from the first go down the slide at the park to grabbing at the biggest slice of cake. Yet in truth our love for each other was our strength. We fought each other's cause, when needed, with the determination of gladiators and we protected each other from the rest of the world like private bodyguards.

We were always in tune with each other. We *were* each other.

I look out of the window and down at the street below. A woman is pushing an empty buggy in the early-morning light, and holding the woolly-mittened hand of a small child. The walk is painfully slow, as the child stops to investigate everything. A leaf on the ground, something in the gutter, an aeroplane overhead. Her whole life is in front of her, exciting and inviting, and I'm totally envious of her. They disappear from my view, and if I still had a beating heart, I believe it would be heavy with missed chances. 'When did we stop noticing everything?' I ask Ben's sleeping body. 'When did the wonder of it all fade away?'

Ben stirs. He breathes in and groans, deep and croakily. Then he sits up suddenly, as if he has just been punched in the stomach, by the memory of what happened yesterday. A tear makes a single, watery track down his cheek and I watch it travel slowly at first, then race down his skin to plop off his jaw. He scratches his cheek where the tear tickled his skin, but he doesn't attempt to wipe the wetness away. Another tear makes a track down his cheek, then another, and another, until he presses his head back onto the pillow where they change their watery tracks to his temples and into the blackness of his hair.

'So you *did* give a shit all these years,' I joke. But, even so, I turn away. I can't bear to see him this way, because even without a physical body of my own I *get* his pain. It's just that thing we do and never question, an illness, a sadness or something funny. I still *get* his pain . . . but can he still get mine?

Ben punches the bed beside him with his fist and shouts a single angry 'FUCK' to the air . . . or to himself . . . or to me.

Nathan's mum took her car early to the place round the corner
to get it washed, then nipped home to finish getting ready for
work until it was done. She heard Nathan coming down the
stairs, and despite the fact that she was perhaps a bit late to
leave for work it didn't pass her by that he was up ridiculously
early for a school holiday.

'Who are you? And what have you done with my son?' she
joked with him, throwing him a quizzical smile. 'You *do* realise it's
half-term, Nate? You don't have to get up until at least bedtime.'
Engrossed in the flashing screen of his phone, he leant against the
door frame to the kitchen with an unfamiliar expression on his face.

She gave up waiting for a reply and turned to the ornate hall
mirror, putting her favourite red lipstick on, before slipping
into her shoes, which perfectly matched her jacket. Then she
pulled on her coat, which nipped in smartly at the waist, picked
up her half-empty coffee mug from the mahogany hall table
and smiled her famously beautiful smile at her gorgeous son.

'Mind, love, I'm running late,' she told him, as she pinched
his cheek gently so she could get past and into the kitchen.

'She's dead,' he replied.

'Who's dead?' Her mind was flitting in all directions. *Have I
got my phone? Where did I put the car keys? Someone's dead . . .*

'Lily,' he replied, as if hardly bearing to hear himself say it out loud. His voice cracked . . .' My Lily.' He clutched his phone, which bleeped in his hands yet again. It was full of messages shared throughout the night by shocked and saddened friends, the second after Ben had texted Matthew. Nathan imagined that at this moment *everyone* was saying the same thing. 'Shit! Lily Richardson is dead!'

'Oh my *God*!' She gasped. '*Your* Lily? How awful. How did it happen?' She turned to him and placed a tender hand on the back of his head while standing on tiptoe to kiss his forehead.

'I'll ring work and tell them I'm going to be late this morning,' she told him over her shoulder as she headed across the kitchen to put her mug in the sink. *Family always first*, she thought.

'They think she got run over down King's Lane on Saturday . . . that's where they found her,' he said.

Nathan's mum dropped the mug before she got to the sink and it smashed on the tiled floor.

Not only is being dead traumatic and upsetting, it's also deeply boring.

Monday drags itself horribly slowly, and I watch Mum swallow a pill with one hand while holding a cup of coffee and a cigarette with the other, the steam and the smoke swirling into the air as one. Caffeine, nicotine and benzodiazepine. 'Very healthy, Mum,' I tell her. I know it is bizarre to watch people grieving for me, and I'm possibly a tiny bit flattered. But I can see their pain and the fact that I have caused it, and I wish from the very depths of my soul that I could change things.

Dad is still in the lounge, crumpled and silent. Stubble is pushing its way through his chin and there's a dark stain of spilt whisky on his jumper. He looks a bit like Homeless Bob, the rough sleeper in town who everyone tries to ignore.

Everyone, it seems to me, grieves in different ways. They go quiet, they go loud, they talk a lot, they don't talk at all, they cry, they don't cry. And Mum and Dad are going through this beside each other rather than together. Mum's rattling with tranquillisers while Dad's locked within the confines of his own head and drowning in a vat of whisky.

I'm really worried about Beth and how she's feeling, and I guess Nathan will also know by now. Are they OK? Will Beth find another best friend and will Nathan keep counting the weeks and days that we have been together, as I still do, or will he stop at seven weeks and one day? I'm desperate to go and see them both but I still can't leave the house, and I don't understand why. As if being dead wasn't bad enough, being trapped in the house is adding insult to injury. It's not like I can feel the strength of the brick or the firmness of the doors; it's more like that thing you get in a dream when you want to run away from something but you can't. I had been able to travel with my own dead body to the hospital mortuary, and I travelled with my family to my house, but I can't go anywhere else.

I curl my fingers round Dad's so it looks as if I'm holding his hand. I want him to know I'm there, to squeeze back and be strong for me like he always is, but he doesn't believe in all that 'spiritualistic bollocks', as he calls it. Every time there is anything about mediums or ghosts on the television, he tuts.

If only he knew.

'Dad? Please find me.' I try to nudge him. 'It isn't bollocks. *Trust* me.'

In the forecourt of Spanners Auto Repair Centre, Fred had been hand-washing a car when a police vehicle drew up and a female officer got out. The brown hair of the police officer was scraped into a neat bun at the nape of her neck, and her rounded police hat was perched importantly on her head. Fred began to feel the first flush of excitement. He loved a drama.

He looked across the tarmac to the main repair workshop and saw through the office window that his boss was on the phone, so he took it upon himself to approach the police officer to ask if there was anything he could do to help, his head bobbing up and down in his strange, eager way.

The officer tried to ignore the constant bobbing of his head as she spoke.

'There's been a local incident that I would like to talk to you about,' she said, taking in Fred's dirty boiler suit and eyeing a much smarter-dressed man in the office. 'But,' she added quickly, 'I'll wait until he is off the phone, and until –' she jerked a thumb towards the mechanic under a jacked-up car – 'he can unpin himself and listen in as well.' She smiled at him, but mainly because he had a strip of black oil above one eyebrow and another along his top lip like a comedy moustache. Fred turned and hollered loudly over his shoulder, almost bellowing in her ear.

'Mike, come 'ere, there's a officer wants to see us.' And he made excited beckoning signals to his boss with one hand, while pointing at the very important police person he was standing next to with the other hand.

While they waited, Fred decided to tell her everything about himself that he could think of, battering her with so much verbal diarrhoea that PC Jenkins wasn't even sure if Fred was taking in breath between sentences. By the time he got to a relative of a friend of a friend who was a community police person, she had long since given up listening to him.

The other mechanic turned out to be a she, not a he, and PC Jenkins felt a tug of guilt that, as a fellow woman, she had made the subconscious assumption that you needed male genitalia to work with cars. The boss finished his call and both were now coming over, joined by a very thin young lad with oily overalls and black nails. As she told them about the recent fatal hit-and-run incident she watched genuine sympathy flit around their faces, while Fred unnecessarily punctuated everything she said with 'yes' and a bob of his head. They took on board the serious issue of looking out for any car that may have received a significant impact on the bodywork, and made a note of how to correctly report any relevant information to the police.

Fred, with assumed importance, escorted her to her next point of call, which was the petrol station next door.

'My niece got knocked off her bike when she was a kid but fortunately only broke her leg, and we've only been open for two hours today but already we've 'ad five cars in, and if any come in with summink suspicious about 'em, I'm the one what will notice. In fact, I'm doing a really dirty car now –'

PC Jenkins stopped him politely. 'Thanks, Fred –' she smiled at him – 'I'm sure you will. Now I've got to get on.' And she retreated inside the petrol station with immense relief.

Fred nodded happily at the back of her head as the door shut in front of him, then made his way back to the car he had been cleaning. He would most definitely keep an eye out for anything suspicious.

Pouring warm water over the last traces of mud on Mrs Peterson's car, Fred ran his cloth over its huge curves and chrome trim, restoring it to its normal pristine condition.

Nathan's mum had watched the discussion through the window of the petrol station, almost rigid with fear, having leapt in there when she saw the police turn up.

What on earth should she do?

Her limbs had transformed into jelly and she didn't realise she was making rapid breathy sounds in her throat until an old lady placed a wrinkly hand on her shoulder. She had almost knocked the poor woman off her feet, she'd jumped so much.

Had she really killed that poor girl . . . her own son's *girlfriend*?

How much wine had she had that afternoon? Surely not that much? What would the other ladies tell the police? Would anyone say she'd been *drinking*?

The implications of what would happen if she came forward were huge. Her own son, her own beautiful, funny, loving son . . . would despise her.

Even as she thought of it, she realised that right at that moment, Fred could be washing away all evidence of her ever having been in King's Lane. It won't change anything for Lily, she thought, but maybe . . . just maybe, no one will ever know.

When the police woman came into the petrol station shop she hid in the public toilet at the back of the shop for so long that five different people tried the handle before she dared to leave.

It doesn't take long for the police to work out what happened to me.

Although my use of social media, and any form of contact with friends had been frantically investigated, it was, as they informed my family, Beth who had been able to provide them with the information they required. She'd been able to tell them about my lie because I didn't have enough bus fare for the whole way home, and she didn't have any left to give me. She was able to tell them that I had been perfectly happy, that I definitely wasn't planning on meeting anyone else, and that we'd said goodbye at the bus station, because she was staying in town to meet her dad for dinner. She had no idea how far my bus money had got me or where I had got off.

CCTV showed me getting on to the bus that went to our village at 16.45 and the driver subsequently confirmed that I had bought a ticket only as far as Burmont Corner where I had got off, and walked, seemingly attempting to cut through King's Lane across countryside to home. My mobile showed that I'd last used it at 17.16 to send a text to Mum, telling her I was on my way home, and by this time it would have been almost dark. I'd then listened to music through my earphones, and had probably died sometime around 17.30, which was how long it would have taken me to walk to King's Lane.

Brian informed my family that, although an autopsy would be carried out as soon as possible, early indications all point to a straight hit-and-run as they had previously thought. He added that unfortunately it had rained heavily through the night before the cold snap had turned it to ice, which meant that the footprints and tyre tracks were impossible to determine, but the police were doing everything they could to find the driver.

'Why won't he just bloody own up to what he did?' Dad had grumbled angrily. Brian added kindly that I probably hadn't heard the vehicle because I was using earphones; I would have known nothing about it, and I wouldn't have been scared.

I didn't know anything about it, but I *had* been scared.

I finally remember.

I'd been getting very freaked out about how drizzly and dark it was becoming so quickly, and my heart was pounding, and my throat was tight from breathing in the February air. I was going to cut through King's Lane because it was quicker, but the puddles and the mud were making my feet wet and cold, and it was all such a really stupid idea. I'd hoped desperately that it wouldn't get dark until I got to a part of the walk home that was lit by street lamps, and also a little less deserted . . . but it did. Before I even got to King's Lane the surrounding trees and hedges were just a mass of silhouetted shapes against a darkening sky.

I was, as he says, listening to music on my phone, because I was trying to calm myself down. It didn't occur to me to think that it would have been safer to listen for *traffic* instead of to music.

The next thing I knew was that I found myself sitting on the grass beside my dead self in the cool blue light of Sunday morning.

What I do know, for sure, is that if I hadn't spent part of my bus fare on a stupid pair of earrings, I wouldn't have had to walk, and I would still be alive. I know that I quite simply died for that pair of earrings, which funnily enough was exactly what I had said to Beth at the time: *'I'd die for them, Beth; they're gorgeous.'*

I feel strange.

I don't know what it is because it's not like I actually have a living body to feel strange in, but whatever it is it is definitely a very odd thing.

Mum is falling asleep on the sofa, tiredness drawing dark lines around her eyes, and even though it's only been three days a nasty yellow stain is forming on the tips of her fingers.

I think I may be *disappearing*, because it's like a kind of *pulling* sensation is happening from the very middle of me.

As I can't physically hold on to anything, I fix my gaze hard on Mum as if what I can see might be the only thing that will stop me evaporating.

So this is it, I'm going.

I'm finally leaving this weird gap between life and death, and I really don't want to go, and I'm sure as hell not ready.

'MUM?' I shout at her, but her eyes finally shut and her mouth drops open. 'PLEASE, MUM?' My begging words are possibly the only thing left in the room, as the rest of me is dragged through some kind of virtual sieve.

'NATHAN!'

He's here, or rather, I'm there. I've actually left the house and I'm in Nathan's living room. I'm not dead . . . or at least,

I haven't disappeared. 'Nathan?' I kneel beside where he's lying on his couch, calling his name softly, and then more loudly. The TV is on in the background and a plate is on the coffee table beside him, showing the remains of something tomatoey. His house is wonderfully familiar. I've been here before of course, and each time I can't help but admire how big and luxurious it is compared to ours. Everything is unique and expensive-looking, and the heavy curtains hang from floor to ceiling in tightly woven golden threads, like something out of a style magazine. They're not fully closed, which allows the street lamp outside to cast its dim orange light across the room, over Nathan's face.

'Nate?' I study his face, putting my own face so close to his that if I was alive I would be able to feel his warm breath on my skin. I move round until I'm looking at him full on, right into his eyes, so that it appears as if he is looking into mine. His lashes curl at the end and I can see where the froth of blue shades like waves on an ocean gather around the endless black of his pupils. 'I miss you,' I whisper. 'It would have been seven weeks and three days now, Nate.'

His lips move. 'Lily?'

'You can *hear* me? Oh my God, Nathan! You can hear me!' I think I'm about to pop inside with the most unimaginable relief, that finally someone has found me. I stand up, then kneel back down, then put my head in my hands, then lean back to look into his eyes again, like I am doing a mad dance of extreme demented gratitude. 'I'm here, Nate.' I almost shriek in his face. 'Can you see me as well?'

'Where are you, Lily?'

I move my face, but Nathan's gaze stays fixed where it is. 'I'm here! Right here, in front of you.' I sink my hands into his shoulders, in my useless attempt to touch him, feeling the beginnings of an unwanted realisation form a frown between my eyebrows.

'If you're there, Lily . . . *If* you can hear me . . . give me a sign . . . Something, *anything*, so that I know you're OK.'

My smile freezes on my lips and my disappointment is huge. He can't hear or see me at all! He's just trying to communicate with the dead me. Maybe that's how I got here, that he managed to somehow *summon* me to him. But what's the point of him being able to pull me to him, if he doesn't even know that he did?

'How can I give you a sign when I can't *touch* anything, and I can't be *heard*?' I grunt angrily and poutily. We stay like this for a long sad moment, while Nathan continues to will the ghost of his dead girlfriend to his side, totally unaware that's *exactly* what he managed to do.

'A *pink* feather,' he says eventually, out loud, continuing his one-sided conversation. 'Any old ghost can do white feathers, but I want a *pink* one . . . a *bright* pink one.

I'm obviously not *any old ghost* because I can't even give him a stupid white feather, so I definitely won't be able to give him a pink one. 'Oh God, this is so FRUSTRATING!' I yell through clenched teeth. Everything about him is gorgeous: his face, the square of his jaw, the arch of his eyebrows, the way his heart beats in the nape of his neck. 'How about this? Can you feel this?' I ask him, leaning over and placing my undetected lips on his, kissing him softly, before moving away, just far enough to allow my lips to open and murmur, 'I love you.'

'I love you, Lily,' he says into the air beside me, touching his lips with his fingers, as if he just might have felt something. But he's looking up at the ceiling, as if I should be floating above him . . . as if dead people turn into invisible helium balloons, bobbing around above everyone's heads.

'I'm not up there,' I grumble. 'I'm here . . . right in front of your FACE!'

From above we hear the stairs creaking as if someone is walking down them. Nathan's mum moves past the open door and into the kitchen, where the sound of something like a glass being placed on the counter top and a bottle hitting its rim make their way into the lounge, and a few seconds later I see her walk back, holding a full glass of wine. I notice how she doesn't turn her head, or say anything to Nathan, but quietly creaks her way back upstairs. He, on the other hand, watches her pass by, his unfathomable eyes following her as she moves.

The spell is broken.

As she disappears from view, Nathan's fingers leave his lips and reach for the TV remote. He changes his position on the sofa and switches channels and, against my will, and far too soon, I feel the dragging start.

I'm back with Mum and she's awake, lighting a new cigarette by the back door. So Nathan *pulled* me to him and my mum *pulled* me back.

Basically I'm the spiritual rope in an emotional tug of war . . . and Mum is winning.

Lily's mum, Amelia, hardly knew what day it was.

Nothing seemed to matter any more. Her mind was trapped in a moment of disbelief, and nothing anyone did or said could snap her out of it. The evening her daughter went missing was a point in her life when time had stretched and warped like melting tar, black and ugly. Everything inside her had shifted when she'd phoned Beth and learnt that Lily had left her for home so long ago that she should easily have been home by then. It was as if all her organs had been wrenched out and pushed back inside her in a different order. She hadn't wanted to phone the police at first, it would be like admitting that something might actually be wrong, but she knew in her heart that her daughter would never have changed her plan; she would never have gone off somewhere without telling one of them.

She'd rung Lily's mobile of course, and after a few rings it had switched to her voicemail. Each time Lily's voice came through calling 'hi' she would breathe the words 'Oh, Lily, thank God,' until the recorded voice of her daughter interrupted, talking over the top of her desperate relief. Amelia had cursed her repeatedly for not picking up, or for probably having the sound turned off on her phone again, but she kept trying all the same. When it began to switch immediately to voicemail she knew that the battery must have gone flat. This time she cursed herself for using up precious seconds of Lily's battery in case she was in trouble and needed to call home.

When the police finally become involved Amelia had begun to tremble. It started inside with her jumbled organs, reaching all the way to her toes, until even her ears and scalp prickled with the fear coursing through her. She'd made Ben a bacon sandwich early on, and the fact that he was unable to finish it was everything she needed to be told. If her big ever-hungry son couldn't eat, it was because he was worried, and if he was worried it was because that strange thing that they had going on between them had told him that his sister was in trouble.

Her twins, her beautiful, wonderful twins . . . they understood each other without words, and then, because of that bacon sandwich, she had known too.

When Brian had come to the door in the early hours of Sunday morning she'd stared at his mouth as the words came out, even though his face had said it all first. She'd waited, listening as he offered her a string of words, such as 'sorry' and 'found' and 'daughter' and 'dead', and all the other words had become lost between his mouth and her ears.

When he finished what he had to say it was as if it all collected together and burst inside her head, and suddenly she needed to protect Lily from what he said. If he said different words, the meaning would be different. She remembered striking out at him, trying to tear him down, forcing him to tell her a different kind of truth, but even the desperate, animal-like instinct of a mother couldn't save her child now.

In the vacant hours and days that followed she didn't know where she slotted into life any more. She played her daughter's voicemail message over and over again, lost in that precious moment when she said 'hi' down the phone. If she tried to think of tomorrow, it merely frightened her that it was another day further away from when her daughter had been alive. If she tried to think of today, she couldn't bear that she was living in a moment where life, as she knew it, was broken. If she tried to think of yesterday, her insides twisted with the ugliest feeling of guilt and remorse that she had ever told Lily not to bother ringing for a lift home from town if she spent all her money.

Amelia believed with all her heart that if she had been a *good* mother she would have told her daughter that if, for whatever reason, she did spend all her money, and couldn't pay for a bus home, then she must ring her, because a *good* mother would have driven to the ends of the earth to get her precious daughter and bring her home.

She struggled with every hurdle that every day inevitably brought with it. She pushed food into her mouth because her body insisted on it, but it no longer had a taste. She smoked because it was something to do with her empty hands. She drank wine or gin to numb the ache inside her and every time she looked into the face of her husband she saw his pain and every time she looked into the face of her son she saw the likeness of Lily.

She was misplaced in her own home because her family belonged to yesterday.

Fred was enjoying his role as detective and was taking it very seriously.

He had reported the Morris Minor that he'd been cleaning, even though the police woman hadn't seemed that interested. 'It was very muddy and Mrs Peterson never lets that car get muddy.' he told his boss, 'She was very rude to me,' he complained.

'I'd have been very rude, Fred, if you'd accused me of killing a kid,' his boss replied, with his face in his hands.

Fred bobbed his head. 'Yes, yes,' he said, 'but I didn't accuse her; I just asked her if she *had*.'

'Fucking hell, Fred!' His boss groaned. 'Mrs Peterson is a pillar of the community, not to mention a tight bit of arse.' He stopped for a second to leer at an imaginary thought.

'She's out of your league,' the mechanic called over from the coffee machine. 'You dirty old bastard,' she added under her breath.

'I'll apologise to her the very next time I see her. And you are not allowed to talk to anyone else, Fred. Understood?'

'Then how can I be a detective?' he asked and his head didn't bob.

'You can only look for cars with dents on the front. Like they've hit something heavy.'

'No mud?'

'No mud, Fred, only dents . . . Well, maybe the odd eyeball or set of teeth embedded in the paintwork,' he added, and sniggered at his own joke, while the mechanic tutted loudly into her coffee, and Fred walked off, looking dejected and desperately disappointed.

Uncle Roger has spent a lot of time at our house this week.

He's made himself the self-appointed head of our dysfunctional household for the time being, and he's making me feel a bit nauseous in the process, as he glides around speaking to Mum and Dad in a soft voice as if he's going to make things worse by speaking at a normal volume. I know they have to organise all the stuff to do with me, the dead stuff, but he's bugging me now. I'm sure it's because Aunty Ruth is so tedious this must be the most exciting thing that's happened to him in, like, forever. He's taken to leaving Aunty Ruth behind, bringing packets of fags with him instead so he can hang around the back door offering them to Mum as if he's doing her some kind of favour.

Today my parents have to take part in a press conference and local television report to raise awareness regarding the mystery of my death, and try to glean some clues or tip-offs from the public. They put on their smart clothes, which go some way to creating the clever illusion that they are still normal people. If anything, Uncle Roger seems to be thriving on this, strutting around with an air of importance, his hand possessively on Ben's shoulder, nodding in agreement as Dad tells the camera how this tragedy has torn them apart, and if anyone knows anything, they should come forward and help with the investigation.

Then . . . Dad looks hard into the camera and begs whoever did it to come forward themselves and take rightful blame for the total devastation they've caused. His mask of 'normal person' slips and a beetroot hue fills his face as he starts yelling, 'C'mon, you BASTARD, you know you're out there.'

'Way to go, Dad,' I tell him. 'You've just sworn on TV.'

The cameras skilfully switch to a speech from the police who confess that at this stage indications are it was an anonymous hit-and-run collision and they still have no clues regarding the type of vehicle involved, but the vehicle would most likely have an area of significant impact caused by the collision. They add that they are currently investigating CCTV footage from various local points, including petrol stations, and staff at local garages and repair workshops have been asked to look out for any vehicle that may come in for repair. Then they make a plea to the public to come forward if they have any information regarding the case.

It began like the distant sound of water rushing through a tunnel and this time I knew what was going to happen, but I didn't know where I was going to go.

I'm in Beth's bedroom. Predictably my entrance is completely undetected by her, but she has obviously been crying, because her lips are all puffy, her nostrils are quivering, and her eyelids are the colour of a ripening plum. The drying tracks of her tears are staining her cheeks as she lies motionless on the bed, staring at my social media page on her screen. The light fitting above her hangs in strands of pink crystals, which cast tiny glimmers of speckled pink light on the bed and on her skin. A cold cup of previously hot chocolate sits untouched on her bedside table with its wrinkly disc of milk skin floating on top. A plate with a half-eaten piece of toast is beside it.

'Beth, oh my God! I've missed you!' I squeal and run towards where she's lying on the bed.

Beth is my best friend. She's half Jamaican with the most enviable warm copper-coloured skin. Her hair has the partial wiriness of her dad's Jamaican origin but with mad long curls, yet the amber streaks of her mum's hair. Her cheeks are sprinkled with the liberal freckles of Irish descent and her Cupid's bow lips are the envy of the whole female population of our school year. Together we had turned heads, we knew it, and we loved it. Even with the stains of her tears all over her face she is still gorgeous, like a weeping film star.

On the screen is a photo of us, taken the night a bunch of us stayed at a friend's house. We were wearing onesies and hugging each other so that our cheeks were pressed together, but our faces were pointing at the camera. Our lips were stretched into happy smiles, our futures stretching before us.

I guess because she's thinking about us she's managed to pull me to her, like Nathan did the other night. I feel like the genie of the lamp – *your wish is my command.*

'It's about time you got past my mother to bring me to you instead,' I tell her, trying to lean on the bed beside her, but predictably falling right through. I settle for pressing my cheek to hers, like in the photo. When she turns her head, for a happy second, I think she has felt me, but like with Nathan, it's just a cruel coincidence, as the door pushes open and the little mop of her dog, Charlie, comes in.

He wriggles and sniffs and tips his head up me. I crouch down. 'Hello, Charlie, good boy,' I tell him, amazed there is a chance he can detect me, but he keeps jumping back, the curls on his black and white fur bouncing excitedly as if I'm something to be wary of.

The dog knows . . . Why does no one else?

'Don't be scared of me, Charlie,' I beg him. 'You used to love me.' His rejection hurts, and in that split second a tiny but ugly realisation comes to my mind. *I don't belong.* To Beth I'm just an image, staring out of a screen from a world that belongs to another time. She can simply close down that screen and carry on with living in the moment. The thought grows until it crowds my head, with its sticky green fingers, trying to push away the love I have for my best friend and replace it with *resentment*.

Charlie yaps at me and Beth looks through me then down at him. 'Shhhh, Charlie, there's nothing there.' And her words hang in the air like soiled clothes on a line. Charlie backs away, still yapping, but Beth throws a cushion at him and he lies flat on the carpet whimpering for two seconds, before jumping up and starting again. Then Beth gives in, closes down the screen and reaches for him, murmuring comforting things in his ear, and, again, the spell is broken. Her thoughts are with Charlie and no longer with me.

'No, not yet. I don't want to go yet . . . I'm sorry. You're still my best friend. I'm not . . . *nothing*,' I call desperately to her, as I begin the uncontrollable process of disappearing from her room. I have only enough time to kiss Beth's cheek before I'm completely dragged away, but I see her rub her cheek where my kiss had been, as if something had touched it.

These little fragments of the life that I should be living are killing me more than death itself.

So I can't be touched, I can't be heard, and I can't be seen, but occasionally perhaps a tiny act of love can somehow find its way through death's lonely barricade.

As soon as the television report comes out, it's as if our doors have been flung open to the baying crowd.

Mysterious food parcels appear on our doorstep. Pies and casseroles and puddings, which have been anonymously baked, are slipped kindly near our front door, as if bereavement should give my family the appetite of contestants in a food-eating challenge. Flowers are propped up in abundance against our front wall and passers-by keep stopping and looking with sympathy . . . or relief that it's not *their* family. The phone rings constantly and Uncle Roger keeps diving for the handset, like it's a competitive sport, talking down the receiver in hushed, important tones. 'Yes, she was hit by a car . . . unknown driver . . . She wouldn't have known anything about it . . . They haven't found him yet . . . Yes, I will pass on your condolences.'

A journalist comes to the house trying to get some juicy news to top up his press release, and Dad stands in the doorway helpfully answering any questions he can. The journalist guy, however, makes a fatal error, *microphone pointing at the bereaved*: 'The driver hasn't been found yet. How does that make you and your family feel after the tragic death of your daughter?'

Dad's jaw drops a little and his face begins to flush as an uncomfortable silence creates a gulf between them.

'Uh-oh,' I mutter from my position beside him.

The young journalist swallows loudly, the saliva making a slight gurgle in his throat.

Dad's voice begins answering this question, like the low rumble of thunder before a massive storm. 'How does that make us *feel* . . . ? How does that make us *FEEL*? Have you ever done multiple choice?' Dad asks him, actually waiting for an answer, while the poor journalist nods feebly in return. 'Because I'm not sure what the answer is. Is it . . . a? Relieved . . . because teenagers are so expensive, or is it b? Concerned . . . because someone has got a nasty dent in their car . . . or c? Totally fucking DEVASTATED! How do you *think* we're feeling, you moron?' he shouts, as the door slams in the poor guy's face. Then Dad lifts the flap of the letter box up and shouts 'Dickhead!' through it.

How to make friends and influence people, Dad.

I give him the thumbs up for standing up to these invasive, pathetic story-mongers, then Ben appears and pats him on the back. 'Impressive, Dad,' he says with a grin, then he too gives him the thumbs up.

Sitting in my bedroom and holding my hairbrush in her hands, my mother loosens the dark hair that is wrapped round it, a part of me still.

I want to hug her. I want to tell her I was sorry for leaving our closeness behind in my childhood. For sighing every time she told me to do my homework or tidy my room. She spent my and Ben's whole life shaping us into the confident teenagers we'd become. In addition, she'd spent every day making our food, washing and ironing our clothes or hunting in her purse to give us extra money when we asked for it. She had shown she loved us by basically being our bank, our waiter and our cleaner.

I'd been so preoccupied with growing up that I can't remember showing her exactly how much I loved her and, too late, I so want to now.

She lifts the hairbrush to her face and, with her other hand strokes the trailing hair across her cheek and lips, so slowly. My smell must still be on my pillow because, placing the brush carefully down, she picks up my pillow and pushes her face into it, breathing deeply.

'I'm so sorry,' she says, surprising me, with words made no less painful by the softness of the feathers and down.

The words of her apology are muffled.

'What on earth are you sorry for, Mum?' I ask.

'I should never have told you not to ring me if you spent all your money,' she replies, as if answering me. 'It's my fault you walked home . . . I'm sorry.' She continues to rest her cheek on my pillow as if it were me.

'Can you forgive me?' she implores and I answer with my head on her shoulder.

'In a heartbeat, Mum . . . if I had one . . . but it wasn't *your* fault.' My words of forgiveness are unheard by her, and my mother's shame is left to fester.

A sticky print of lip-shaped strawberry balm still clings to the glass by my bed. Mum replaces the pillow full of lost words on my bed, and kisses the glass and it's heartbreaking to watch.

If only I could have just one more day with my mother. One more moment. One more hug.

Uncle Roger calls up the stairs. 'Amelia? I've just popped in to see if there is anything you need?' He's standing at the bottom of the stairs, car keys in one hand and a packet of cigarettes in the other.

Good old Uncle Roger . . . always here to help.

Mum wipes the cuff of her sleeve across her face and clears her throat.

'I'll just be a minute,' she calls back, checking her appearance in the oval reflection of my dressing-table mirror, blowing her nose with a tissue from a little square box, and putting a smile on her face. Then kissing her fingers, she pushes her kiss into my pillow and leaves the room.

The coroner's report has been completed and it confirms that I hadn't had alcohol or drugs, which obviously I knew but it had to be done for the record, and I hadn't been raped or attacked. It confirmed I had received a significant trauma to the right side, indicating a collision with a vehicle coming from behind and that I suffered a compound fracture of the tibia and fibula of the right leg. The force of my body hitting the ground resulted in a fatal cervical fracture to the third vertebrae, hence the horrible angle of my head when they found me. An interim death certificate was produced allowing my funeral to be arranged, and an inquest would take place over the next few months.

Basically the tyre caught my lower leg and the knock from the car caused me to catapult into the ditch awkwardly, breaking my neck on impact with the ground. I would have been dead in an instant.

Uncle Roger, in his self-imposed role of Chief Dead Person's Family Coordinator, announces round the kitchen table what he thinks should happen now.

'I think a burial is the best thing,' he says, nodding slightly as if he is most definitely right. 'We will have somewhere to visit,' he adds, as if he thinks I might be hanging around a creepy cemetery for all eternity waiting for guests to grace me with their presence. My parents nod their approval, to Uncle Roger rather than each other, as if he is the chairperson of this meeting.

'What, no discussion?' I ask, looking at them all. 'There *are* options you know.'

Uncle Roger makes a fat bullet point in a little red notebook that probably should have the title 'WHAT TO DO ABOUT LILY' on the front, then writes the word 'burial' next to it.

'Hang on.' I look round at them all. 'I don't want bugs and worms using me as part of their circle of life. I don't want to be eaten until I'm nothing but a skeleton.' I feel a kind of burst of energy inside me at the unfairness of having no say in what will happen to me. What if being buried will somehow trap me underground forever in this limbo state, decomposing in a grave, unearthed hundreds of years later in favour of a modern housing development? The idea makes me shiver with the horror of it. Perhaps a cremation will somehow 'release me', allowing me to go wherever it is that you're supposed to go for all eternity. That sounds like a much better idea . . . if deciding to be cremated while you're conscious of it could be considered a *better* idea.

Uncle Roger makes another fat bullet point, then taps the pen against his lips. 'Where shall we have the wake?'

'I don't want to be buried,' I say, annoyed. 'Go back to the previous bullet point; it didn't have a unanimous vote!'

This meeting is about me; yet I'm the only one here who isn't getting a say in what should happen.

'She doesn't want to be buried.'

We all look across at Ben. 'Doesn't?' Uncle Roger asks, noticing Ben's use of the present tense.

'Doesn't,' Ben repeats. 'You wouldn't understand . . . It's a twin thing.'

'Yesss, Ben!' I shriek, jumping up and down amongst them all, inappropriately excited, considering the event. 'Yes!'

A flush blooms across Ben's jaw, which is always his version of a neon sign advertising how angry or upset he is. I can imagine what is going on inside his head. *I am a twin. I was a twin. I used to have a twin. I am now one half of a whole.*

We're not broken, Ben. You can still do it.

Uncle Roger answers with an unacceptable hint of annoyance creeping into his tone. 'But . . . we will need somewhere to go to talk to Lily, after –'

Ben interrupts angrily. 'You think she's going to answer? You think she's going to be sitting on her gravestone waiting for visiting hours . . . ? She will *want* to be cremated.' Ben pronounces each word carefully with a small gap between each one to ensure Uncle Roger doesn't miss the point.

'Way to go, Ben!' I shout and make to high-five him, but he doesn't high-five back. He just leaves me awkwardly hanging.

'And . . .' Oh, he's on a roll now. '. . . she will *want* to have something dramatic done with her ashes.'

'Oh, you're *good*, Ben,' I tell him, then immediately question how I could get so enthusiastic about my body being *dramatically* scattered in a million little pieces of burnt-out flakes.

Uncle Roger loses his invisible balance on his invisible podium, tapping the pen on the table agitatedly, looking between Mum and Dad for support.

'Cremation!' confirms Dad, peering over at the notebook and pointing at the word 'burial', indicating he should scrub out the first point on his notebook and change it. How I'm going to be 'dispatched' has just become a messy scribble followed by a new first bullet point . . . 'cremation'.

Ben flicks his phone into life and plugs his headset into one ear as if his work here is done.

We can still do it, Ben. We are still twins.

Nathan's mum had a really bad week.

She phoned in sick on the day Nathan told her the news about Lily, but the trauma, the guilt and the lack of sleep that followed managed to convince everyone that she really was ill. She had watched the news reports on television from behind a cushion or shielded by the duvet, while swallowing down the nausea that threatened to fill her mouth.

They still hadn't found the driver . . . of course . . . She was right there, hiding, like a cowardly child watching a horror film.

She looked awful and she felt worse.

Nathan's dad was worried about her and how she seemed incapable of supporting their son after the death of his girlfriend. In addition, he was more than a little surprised that, although ill, she had started drinking her way through the entire wine rack.

It's the first day back at school after half-term, but Ben hasn't gone in. Instead we are all at the funeral parlour doing the expensive part of dying.

The woman who sits in front of them greeted my family serenely in the foyer then showed them smoothly in to her room as if she was on wheels. From behind her polished desk she continues to perform her job with appropriately placed ripples of expression and perfectly placed pitches to her voice as if she's been to the Bereavement School of Voice.

I had been able to stay in the family zone, following them to the funeral parlour, as if I was simply on a day out, the irony of my presence undetected by them all, as I learn for the first time ever what actually happens in these places.

The room has been decorated with the utmost care to not use a colour or ornament that might offend. Flowers in pleasant pastel shades are placed in large vases, not so much to be admired, but to stop the room looking empty of life, and the lady asks a series of questions with a gentle smile, as if death is an inevitable procedure, and not the utterly devastating, heart-crushing event that it obviously is.

What sort of obituary, if any, did they want for the

newspapers? How many cars did they feel they would need? Would they want flowers or monuments? And what sort of coffin would be most fitting? She peers over her glasses while managing to slide brochures and ideas easily in front of them, making the whole process as quick and painless as possible, whist keeping the ever increasing prices as insignificant as she can.

When they get to discuss the flowers, the inevitable 'daughter' and 'sister' are suggested, which for some reason seems silly to me. Like I need a floral label in case they forget who's in the coffin on the big day. Huge hearts made out of white lilies, quite apt . . . or cheesy, one or the other, are suggested next, but these aren't what I want either.

I visualise the blackness of the funeral procession: slowly moving cars, made no less shadowy by the suggested array of blooms twisted into words and shapes, designed to inform the sympathetic faces lining the pavements who the passenger in the wooden box had been.

I imagine something different. I want sunflowers!

'*Sunflowers.*' I whisper their name in this room of desperate choices. Would they remember how much I loved them? I had wanted sunflowers at my wedding. Their big yellow heads nodding happily against cream and lace. My funeral would be the only big occasion I could have now and I wanted those glorious heads, as yellow as a summer's day, to take the black out of my final goodbye. I notice how the furrow on Ben's brow deepens.

'*Go on, Ben, you can do it.*'

But they move on, and talk about what is going to

happen with my ashes, to which no one seems to have an answer, dramatic or otherwise. They all sit with shining eyes, surreptitious fingers pushing back the salty water, trying to make it stay inside their faces. In the end they decide to take me home in a pretty blue urn while they make a decision at a later date.

'Like a kind of funeral doggy bag,' Ben says to the lady across the desk, shaking off any threatening emotion and smirking at his own joke. I smirk with him.

The choice of coffins is vast, from the most beautiful heavy expensive wood to the cheapest cardboard, although it would seem that it's bad form to consider *cheap* on an occasion like this. The lady describes those ones as 'individual' or 'eco'. Everyone leans forward, their eyes instinctively starting with the top of the range, and she skilfully diverts their gazes to the selections more suitable for cremations.

'Sort of . . . better for burning?' Ben chips in again, then shrugs his shoulders when Dad shoots him his best 'shut up or get out' look, and Uncle Roger digs him in the ribs.

The kind lady looks up from the brochures. 'People often find it easier to relieve the stress with humour,' she says with a smile, and by doing so unwittingly sucks any residue of humour right out of the room. She continues in her professionally rehearsed and sympathetically melodic tones: 'There is also a company that makes coffins out of recycled newspapers,' she adds, almost as an afterthought, and Dad wrinkles his nose at the very thought.

'Yesterday's news?' he scoffs. 'Not for my little girl.'

But his little girl likes the idea. A lot!

Mum chews on a nail on one hand and twists at the hem of her cardigan with the other. 'Oh, I don't *know*,' she mutters, obviously trying to imagine her only daughter being placed in one of these things, no matter how expensive or . . . *individual*.

'White,' Dad and Uncle Roger say together, looking at the page where the lady's highly manicured hands have opened the brochure to the white and shiny coffin section. Dad's finger is caressing one of them, as if stroking the photo gently will make it lovelier for me. Mum nods quickly, obviously pleased that someone has made a choice.

I know they want to put me in the nicest heavenly postal package their limited income can pay for, and I suppose white and shiny is kind of nicely . . . virginal, which, as it happens, due unfortunately to age and circumstance, is exactly what I am, But I'm not a white coffin kind of girl.

'The recycled one,' says Ben suddenly. 'The yesterday's news one.' He waits for them all to process the fact that he's actually serious. 'It can be whatever colour we like. People can pin notes and pictures to it if they want to, like sending Lily off in a kind of giant pinboard full of messages.'

I can see their brains working, taking in the vision of a pinboard coffin, imagining how it would look, and thankfully none of them can deny that it is, in fact, a BRILLIANT idea. 'And she has to have sunflowers . . . instead of . . . that crap,' he says, waving his hand towards the glossy pages, ignoring the surprised looks at his distain of the brochures. 'She loves them . . . remember?' he adds, using the present tense again.

Mum nods and a tiny sound resembling a laugh sneaks out as if to say, how could she have forgotten?

66

'Yes,' she agrees, 'sunflowers . . . of course.' And she smiles, spookily in the direction that I'm standing in, and I smile back, noticing that most of her mascara has smudged its way under her eyes where she has constantly wiped them.

'It might not be traditionally funerally, but it will be the sort of thing that Lily would want,' Ben finishes.

'It's *funereal*, Ben,' I correct him. '"Funerally" isn't a word.' But I will have my sunflower day after all because my dear inarticulate twin brother can still do that *thing* we do.

'Can you even get sunflowers in February?' asks Dad, looking questioningly at the lady.

'Yes, of course,' she tells him, 'you can get anything you want these days.' What she means is you can get anything you want these days, *if you pay for it*.

Dad looks out of the window at the bleakness of the February day and I guess he is imagining yellow heads against the grey . . . 'I like that,' he says softly.

And so my funeral is arranged for the last Friday in February. This is apparently a good week for booking funerals, as normally, according to the lady, there is quite a queue of people waiting to be cremated. It would never have occurred to me that us dead people might have to wait in line, almost like waiting for God's bus, only this time the fare has cost my parents a few thousand pounds!

I wonder if this time I'll make it all the way to the afterlife.

I'm laid out in the funeral parlour and I can be visited.

Mum and Dad chose to go, presumably so their last image of me will be better than the one they must be currently left with, of me in that mortuary. I knew Ben wouldn't go. It would probably mess with his head because of our 'twin thing'. We don't need to see; we only need to *know*.

Thankfully Mum had decided that I should wear the dress she was going to buy me for the school prom in July. I'm quite obviously not going to go dancing in it now and it's a real shame because, even dead, I look great in it.

I'd pointed it out on the same day as the battle of the purple Converse shoes back in January. My hands clenched together with delight when she finally agreed to buy the shoes, saying we could go back to get the dress in February, when she next got paid. She had, as promised bought it with her February pay. Eyes heavy, and with a tight throat she'd smiled bravely at the shop assistant who carefully folded the dress, placing it in an expensive and attractive bag. 'It's a lovely colour,' the assistant had said through vibrantly painted lips with an aggravatingly cheery voice as she handed the bag over. 'Is it for something special?'

'My daughter,' Mum had answered, and she walked quickly away as the girl called out. 'I'm sure she'll look lovely in it.'

I do look rather lovely in it . . . all things considered. The dress is long, and slender, with spaghetti straps, in a dark shimmery green, which would so have picked out the matching flecks of green in my eyes and made me look exotic. Mum had bought it because she had promised she would, so that I could look beautiful for my final day.

The green of my eyes is long gone, stolen by the milky cloud that appeared on the first day. It is mercifully hidden by my eyelids, now closed and tinged with the fleshy pink of make-up cleverly applied by the guy that makes dead people look not so dead. It's not how I would do it, but I suppose it's not too bad.

Standing over me, Mum pulls out a box from her bag and carefully lifts the lid, revealing a beautiful Chinese silk scarf, hand-painted with a spray of pink flowers. Buried in the folds of time is the fragile scent of her own mother, and she lifts it to her face, breathing in all the memories it holds. Combining these delicate traces of who we both were, she lays the scarf across my cold shoulders.

She takes a moment to look at me, dressed, painted and fully embalmed, then places her old St Christopher necklace inside the gaps of my stiff cold fingers. 'The patron saint of travellers, love,' she whispers, 'for your journey.' She jumps a little at the icy coldness of my marble-hard skin as she kisses me lovingly for the last time on my forehead. Tears fall out of her watery eyes and land in my hair.

'What is my journey, Mum?' I ask her. 'I don't know where I'm supposed to go.'

My parents are standing right beside me, sending me off on

my way, and they can't hear me asking for their help. Will I always be caught in this lonely gap between life and death, or will my cremation force me through into the next life?

'Sleeping beauty,' Dad says, breaking into the silence. He's looking intently at my carefully made-up face with its delicate rouge on each cheek, faking the flush of my youth and my life. I can see the muscle in his jaw flexing again.

He used to call me that when I was a little girl. He would come into my room to say goodnight and I would pretend to be asleep, my black hair fanned out on the pillow and my eyes tight shut, trying to look my most beautiful. He would kiss me on the cheek and I'd miraculously wake up and laugh. Then he'd hug me and tell me I was his princess, but that I really had to go to sleep, so I would wake up just as beautiful in the morning.

I think we are both remembering this right now.

He leans down and kisses my icy cheek, his eyes closing as if making a wish. Then they both leave the room knowing that even their love cannot break this spell.

I'm in Nathan's house but Nathan isn't here.

Nathan's mum is sitting at their dining-room table hunched over the local newspaper. Why on earth would *she* be pulling me to her? She's talking to herself, but her hand is covering her mouth as if she's trying to keep the words that she's saying inside.

'I thought it was an animal. I didn't *know. I didn't know. I didn't know.*'

I lean over to see what she is staring at and there, printed in the newspaper, is a photograph of me staring back at her happily through grainy black-print eyes. I read the text beneath my photograph, which is telling her that the funeral of Lily Richardson, who was fatally hit by a vehicle that failed to stop on King's Lane on Saturday 18th February, will be taking place on Friday 3rd March

It's not a huge piece, but it does say that police still want to speak to anyone who may have information about any vehicle that may have been in that area around 17.30 on that Saturday. The article shows a map of the local area and a horrible accusing red arrow pointing to where the body, my body, was found.

'Oh shit!' she groans with a kind of angry desperation. 'I'm sorry.' And I suddenly realise with an awful clarity . . . that my boyfriend's mother was the person who killed me.

'Oh my God . . . it was *you*!' I accuse, barely able to believe what I'm learning. 'What will Nathan think when he finds out you knocked his own girlfriend down . . . then *drove away*?' I ask her, my voice sounding incredulous and desperate, but of course she can't hear me.

I know Nathan's mum quite well and she's always been really nice. She's pretty glamorous too, with her designer sunglasses and that old-fashioned car. And here I am, standing beside her, and I'm dead . . . because of her. My dad's threat – '*I'm going to kill the bastard that did it*' – echoes in my head. I too had kind of imagined the driver to be a man, who didn't care enough about his crime to come forward. Instead, the 'bastard' is Nathan's mum and she is the one not coming forward . . . hiding like a coward. I stand motionless by the highly polished table and stare at her for a long time.

All around the room are photographs with smiling faces. Nathan and his dad fishing, Nathan and his mum and dad on holiday, his mum and dad's wedding day, pictures of Nathan growing up, the very cute thing that was Nathan as a baby. There are even photos of children from Belarus, affected by the Chernobyl disaster, who the Petersons had hosted in previous summers, Nathan's mum's arms protectively round their skinny little shoulders.

The perfect, caring, loving family.

All the happiness of Nathan's family is now frozen in those photographs, the beautiful smiles hiding an ugly secret.

'It's not fair,' I almost spit at her. 'You're alive . . .'

When Nathan turned sixteen his mum and dad were at his party. Most kids would want their parents out of the way but Nathan's mum and dad were cool. Nathan's mum was probably the only mum on the planet who could get away with actually joining in. She'd mingled amongst us, enviably wearing a black dress that made her tiny size eight look better than most of the girls at the party. She had tossed her auburn hair that fell halfway down her back and made most of the boys in the room fall a little bit in love with her, before saying something funny to Nathan that no one could hear, and he'd laughed out loud before kissing her on the cheek and joining me where I stood with his friends. She'd watched him for a moment with nothing but the purest love and adoration in her eyes.

I remember how she'd run her hand down my long hair at the party, and caught a carefully made dark curl in the palm of her hand. 'Beautiful! You are beautiful,' she'd said. I remember how I had modestly tried to tell her she was talking rubbish, but she'd replied with a gentle telling-off: 'Never throw a compliment back at the giver, Lily. You should graciously accept their praise and enjoy how it makes you feel. It is a gift.' I'd thanked her, because she had, indeed, made me believe that I looked beautiful.

Now it's as if the vision in front of me is an effigy – a wretched and repulsive representation of the woman she used to be. I watch her take another drink, huge stinging gulps that contort her face and make her shiver as if she is forcing them down like medicine.

'When my dad finds out it was you, he'll rip your head off and put in on a spike in the middle of town so that everyone can hate you too.' I push away her flattering words from the party as if that kind person no longer existed. 'Until then . . . I hope you're so consumed by guilt that your insides are sucked dry until there is nothing left of you except your rotting conscience.'

Then I catch sight of Nathan's recent school photo, his handsome smiling face looking at me from its wooden frame. If his mother's awful secret is found out, Nathan's own life will be ruined. He would forever be the son of the woman who killed his girlfriend.

'But it's still not fair,' I tell him. 'Your mother has got her life and she has got you – both of which I'll never be able to have.'

Her mobile phone flashes into life to the tune of *The Muppet Show*, its amusing tones so totally inappropriate for the moment. I peer at it over her shoulder, to see who's texted.

Morag: 'Don't forget lunch again this Saturday. I'm going to be wearing my drinking pants, so can you drive me? LOL!'

Nathan's mum and I stare at the screen, until I say, on behalf of both of us. 'I think you'll find there is no LOLling' going on here, Morag.'

Nathan's mum's finger hovers over her phone as she tries to think of something to say. She types and deletes several times until she finally she manages to send 'I won't be going. There's been accident. Nathan's girlfriend Lily was hit by a car and she died.' Before replacing the phone on the table and wiping her hot hands shakily on the legs of her trousers. Within seconds, her phone lights up, vibrating on the polished table and chiming its ringtone at the same time, but she leaves it where it is, staring at it, until Morag's name eventually disappears from the screen and the telltale beep of a voicemail notification comes through.

'Go away and leave me alone. You're the one who kept pouring the wine regardless of who wanted one.' She accuses, under her breath. Nathan's mum grabs the phone, typing 'It's in the weekly. Check it out.' Morag obviously has a copy of the weekly in her house because minutes later a text appears: 'OMG I'm really sorry. If there's anything I can do? I hope they find him xxx' It's almost like everyone assumes that reckless hit-and-run drivers are going to be men. Not a middle-class woman, a mother . . . someone who everybody likes . . . someone who was drinking wine that day by all accounts!

She runs her fingers over the arrow on the photograph as if it's pointing directly at her, then pours herself another large drink and downs it in one.

I find myself being sucked out of this beautiful house with its ugly secret and the last thing I see is a large vase of flowers that are dying, their once-vibrant blooms curling and brown at the edges.

Ben is sitting on the edge of his bed wearing a crumpled-looking school uniform and staring at nothing on the carpet. I greet him, using the hour and a half I had over him in age. 'Hi, little brother. You will never guess who killed me . . . not in a million . . .' Ben suddenly shivers by way of an answer. 'It's only Nathan's mum!'

His reaction is a disappointing . . . nothing. 'And she's hiding behind a large bottle of alcohol like a beautiful coward . . . and no one knows it's her!' I add, but Ben suddenly gets up and pushes himself through me as he goes to check if the window is properly shut.

'What is it?' Can you feel me around you?' I ask, changing the subject, as he turns back round. 'Do I make you feel cold or something?' He sits back on the edge of the bed and I experiment by hugging him with my invisible arms to see what happens. Another shiver causes him to flop back on the pillows and pull the duvet over himself.

Wow! I guess he can feel me; he just doesn't know he can.

But almost before the duvet has settled round my brother I find myself leaving him and turning up with Mum, as if I'm the ball in an afterlife pinball machine.

The kiss that Amelia gave Lily at the funeral parlour still lingered on her lips.

She stood in her daughter's bedroom and felt as if she had been holding her breath for a very long time, but somewhere deep inside herself she knew the funeral of her daughter would be the beginning of something new. It wasn't the kind of new that promises a better life but a kind of anticipation at what might be at the other end of the tunnel she was in.

In the middle of the night when demons come out to play it frightened her that Lily had been so icy cold and hard, but during the safety of the day she was glad that her daughter could go on her way with a mother's kiss goodbye.

She hoped the day she dreaded most might quite possibly be the day that would release her from the image of Lily in that room, like marble and so alone.

The day is icy and grey and far too quiet.

No conversation, no television, no music. Just the sounds of showers running, shirts rustling, toilets flushing and the kettle boiling. The day of my funeral is here.

Both granddads are staying over and they've been given my parents' room and Ben's room; my family had, in turn, 'made do' in the lounge. I guess no one wanted to sleep in my bed for fear of crushing the space that is still the 'essence' of me. Granddad Colin is tall like Dad, but half his weight. Shadows have appeared on his face and he seems so much older than the last time I saw him, at Christmas. Granddad Peter has always looked a little like my mum, with his round face and easy smile, except for the goatee that as a child I was fascinated by, but today his goatee draws a white circle round his sad lips, which are slack and open like two raw wet chipolatas, and either his suit has grown or he has shrunk inside it. Both granddads move quietly around the house putting their shaky warm hands on any passing shoulder.

Ben goes to my room, gently closing the door behind him. He leans against the door and sucks in the air that I once had breathed, then moving to my wardrobe he takes a jumper from a hanger and holds it up to his face. 'It won't suit you,' I joke with him, but in amongst the fluffy wool he buries his brotherly words of love.

'You silly bitch.'

'Thanks. I can't argue with that though,' I answer, following him to his room where he places my jumper carefully under his pillow.

I'm convinced my funeral will be the catalyst that will force me wherever I should be going, but I really can't bear to leave, even if this kind of existence is worse. Even if it's just a halfway house with none of the benefits of either living or dying. Even if I have to watch everyone I know do all the things I should be doing, and how inevitably they will gradually push me to the back of their minds, living their lives, growing old, I don't want to go.

That little ugly seed of resentment that buried itself inside me at Beth's house, is taking root. When this day is over everyone will wake up in their new lives without Lily Richardson. They will still eat and watch TV, they will still go to school or work, and they will still laugh and go out with their friends. They will still live.

I try to remember if I know of anyone else who has died and right now, I can only think of Gran, Dad's mum. If there was anyone else, then I have forgotten them and it's a sad thought that soon, the best I can hope for is to be a recollection dragged from the back of people's minds. I hadn't thought of Gran in a really long while, but I did love her very much and for a long time I had missed her hugs, her smile, her smell of lavender, until one day the memory of her had simply faded away.

But she had left something of herself behind. In her will she gave me her most precious silver ornaments: tiny bells, bags and boxes, with intricate engravings and minute detail, all in shiny hallmarked silver, wrapped in pink tissue and placed inside a little old-fashioned chocolate box.

I suddenly want to dig out that box right now. To feel the pink tissue rustle against my fingers and imagine Gran beside me telling me how she came by each one. Over time, I added my own treasures to this box, each with a story behind them, but I can't help wondering who will love them now? Who will appreciate each trinket and recall the fragments of our lives still clinging to each one?

'Where are you now, Gran? Why can't I see you?' I ask her as I walk through the house turning slowly round, looking to see if she might have miraculously appeared because I'm thinking of her.

Dad walks right through me to open the front door and the cold February air catches hold of his breath turning it to ice. I walk out down the path to where Uncle Roger and Aunty Ruth are already in the street waiting with a small group of neighbours. Aunty Ruth is wearing a huge fascinator and its long black feathers keep poking Roger in the ear and the eye.

'For God's sake, it's not a bloody wedding, Ruth,' he hisses at her as she pulls out a compact and applies bright-red lipstick to her doughy face.

The dark and sombre colours of everyone's clothes are blending together, except Mabel from No. 44 who, as ever, is wearing her pink polka-dot raincoat and carrying her knitting bag. Mabel makes me smile.

Then all heads turn at the same time as the funeral director appears, perfectly Dickensian, round the corner of the street. He takes his steps slowly as if allowing the enormity of the situation to reach the bereaved in tiny stages. No one notices his face, this man who this morning probably watched breakfast TV while eating his crunchy nut cereal and chatting to his wife and kids. This man who might have texted his friends about a pint in the pub, or a game of squash later, or sung tunelessly to the radio while driving to work. All everyone can see is the charcoal grey of his clothes and the tall old-fashioned hat that is dipped over his brow.

The almost silent arrival of the hearse with its cargo of yellow flowers and dead girl causes hands to cover mouths and tissues to be fumbled with. I can hardly believe that I'm in there, and not in school in my English class, which is exactly where I should be on a Friday morning, doodling in a textbook and waiting for the weekend to begin.

My family emerge from the house, and the sight of that lone man walking slowly along the middle of our road makes my mum stumble. This man is bringing her daughter to her but he will take her away again and it isn't right. Her pain is almost too much to watch, but there is nothing I can do.

Suddenly a single dark-blue car appears at the other end of our road, bringing with it a vision so daringly opposite from the official funeral procession that it makes us all smile.

Clattering with age and a dodgy exhaust, but bright as a summer's day, the car containing Ben's best friend, Matthew, and Matthew's older brother, Jason, brings a heroic and wonderful gift to my funeral. The car is completely covered in artificial sunflowers. They are tied to the aerial and wedged into the windows and door frames, wrapped round the bumpers and taped to the hubcaps. It is beautiful, like a motorised bouquet. I see Ben laugh and give them the thumbs up and everybody relaxes a little because of it. I clap my hands together and lean down to the driver's window, as Jason unwinds it. 'Thank you, guys, this is really great,' I say just as Jason reaches his hand out of the window and chucks his fag butt straight through my chest. He gives a kind wink and a thumbs up back to Ben and joins the line of cars ready to head down the street.

The procession rolls its way slowly through my village like a jet-black snake with a yellow corsage until it turns in to the crematorium. The jungle drums of social media and phone calls have obviously done their job well, as the snake slithers to a halt at the crematorium, next to a man-made field of sunflowers. Loads of kids from our school are gathered outside, each holding a yellow bloom. Some are real, some are plastic and some are paper or printed pictures stuck onto cardboard. There are teachers and parents of school friends, and relatives, and friends of relatives, all holding their yellow offerings.

And there is Nathan.

I stand with him while I'm unloaded from the back of the hearse, and invisibly link my arm through his. 'It would have been eight weeks and six days, Nathan.' I look up at him, but of course his eyes are fixed over the top of my head and on my coffin.

A boy nearby nudges someone next to him and whispers. 'It's a good job it's not *her* funeral; they'd need a fucking big coffin and an Australian bush fire for *her* cremation.' He's pointing at Fat Lucy, who hangs her head, pretending not to hear, while they titter at her expense. I'm not without blame. I don't think I ever defended Lucy when the kids taunted her for her love of food and mocked her for the flush of crippling embarrassment that crept up her cheeks, highlighting her awkwardness in a deep shade of pink. I had unwittingly allowed the bullying that gave her such a miserable life. Now, however, I just see a young girl who holds a sunflower that she made herself. It is beautiful, crafted out of thin coloured paper in a 3D effect. This is a girl who has made an effort and carries her sunflower with tears in her eyes because someone has died too soon.

I am the one who should hang my head in shame. I wrap my arms round her and whisper in her ear. 'You are a beautiful person.' Lucy touches her hair and looks around her, as if she felt me brush against her.

I'm surprised at how big the crematorium chapel is and people are filling it. I'm very flattered. My form teacher kindly pushes Nathan towards the front and herds everyone else towards the back until there is a line of yellow at the back of the room.

My strange and wonderful recycled coffin, coloured a pretty forest green, with painted sunflowers round its edge and real ones on top, is placed in front of everyone. My family make their way to the first row, the seats that I'm sure everyone else is glad that, on this occasion, they don't have. There is a large photograph of me plus a lot of rustling, coughing and intermittent sobbing into tissues from everybody, and I look around at them all with what is probably an inappropriately big smile. 'Wow . . . this is awesome . . . ! This *all* about *me*!' Then the smile slips from my face. 'It was over so quickly.'

I want my life back. I'm not ready. I don't want to go today. I want a future.

Everything I could be doing rather than attending my own funeral plays in front of my eyes. I want to remember what it is like to have a huge plate of salty chips, or a squidgy cake, a cold ice cream . . . some hot chocolate. I want to go out with my friends, to party and laugh and dance. I want to go home and tell my parents I love them. I wish, more than anything, I had appreciated every single little bit of it.

If only I had the chance to die knowing that I had really lived. Maybe then it wouldn't be so bad.

'Let me go *home*,' I plead out loud, raising my eyes up to an unreachable God.

The chapel music stops, the sound of it floating away like bubbles into the high beamed ceiling and the heavy weight of bereavement gathers in its place. I had failed to appreciate the full impact of my recycled coffin until now, and I'm sure Mum and Dad are feeling the same, as after a short speech by the minister everyone is invited to pin any messages they may have to it. Everyone starts coming forward in an orderly line, each pinning a message or photo or flower to my coffin, and gradually it becomes covered with a collage of colour and text. I frantically try to read each one as it's pinned.

Someone's phone goes off and it must be someone from school because 'You've got a fucking message' is clearly heard coming from a pocket, followed by supressed laughter and a teacher whispering very loudly, 'Everyone turn your phones off *now*!'

I laugh too in my silent world. If I'd been alive, I would have laughed aloud.

Beth has the photo of me and her that she'd been looking at in her room with a letter printed with tiny and neat handwriting; she kisses it and pins it to the side of the coffin. Ben has cut out the design of my favourite Lady Gaga T-shirt and pins it to the top, and Nathan pins a corsage of lilies that he'd promised to give me for our school prom.

By the time everyone returns to their seats, my coffin looks like a huge colourful patchwork present, with a sunny yellow bouquet on top. It is a bright, cheery and desperately sad reminder of who I once was, and no one can hear me say 'Thank you.'

*

Something very odd is going on.

Wispy plumes of grey are swirling slowly behind Dad's right shoulder. There's another behind one of my uncles and another behind a friend's mum. My head teacher has one next to her and a few more are swirling slowly next to some of the kids from school, their tendrils coiling softly, undetected by them. I check the grates in the floor; it's a crematorium, so you never know, but it isn't smoke, just wisps . . . like clouds in a summer sky, changing shape with the breeze.

Are they people like me? Trapped forever, clinging to the people they love? Or maybe they are people who have moved on but are drawn back when a new death reminds the living of who they have lost . . . other spiritual pinballs like me.

The man who is conducting my ceremony is talking to everyone about how great I was, but right now all I care about is these strange wisps. I wander past each row of seats looking at them, until I get to One Shoe Sue, who not only has two of the smoky things by her, but she turns her head ever so slightly as I reach her side. She's the mother of one of the boys in my class, but everyone at school calls her One Shoe Sue, on account of the fact she has an artificial leg. 'She's here,' Sue whispers to Ted, her husband.

'I *know*,' he whispers back loudly. 'She's in *there*,' and he points to my coffin with a silly smile on his face.

'No,' she hisses. 'She's *here*. I can *feel* her.'

Does she really believe that? Can she really sense me? Or did she just say that because, let's face it, as a medium at a funeral it's a pretty safe-bet thing to say? I take a couple of steps, and Sue turns her head again as I pass. 'Can you hear me?' I ask right into her ear, but she doesn't answer. I wave my hand in front of her face but she doesn't blink.

'It's all right, love, you can leave,' she says.

'I'll wait until it's finished, if it's all right with you,' Ted jokes, but Sue scowls at him.

'Not you . . . *Lily*! Don't be afraid, dear,' she whispers. So, she can't see or hear me but she *knows* I am here. She's the one person who really believes I might still be around, and she's telling me that it's all right to go.

But unless the cremation process forces me to leave, I don't know *how* to go, and she hasn't factored in that I don't *want* to go.

Dad gets up and faces everyone, so I leave One Shoe Sue and her kind offer, and make my way back towards to the front as he begins to talk about me.

'. . . and the sunflower always turns its face to the sun to get the maximum light from each and every day, and when it finally dips its head at the end of its life, it drops hundreds of seeds so that next season it will be able spread its beauty further.' Dad clears his throat and I invisibly lay my head on his shoulder. 'I believe Lily was happy in her life . . .'

'Yep,' I chip in.

'. . . and that her sunny nature has touched all the people in the crematorium today –' he pauses while several kind people nod – 'so please take the seeds she is leaving behind and make the most of your own lives.'

It's a lovely speech, but I don't feel very sunny right now. I feel jealous that all these people have the chance to 'make the most of their own lives'. They can walk right out of here in a few minutes and carry on doing their own thing. The smoke swirling around Dad curls its way towards me and I don't know if I'm imagining it but it looks like a hand that is beckoning. But I don't know what it is beckoning me to. There is nothing actually there apart from a mist.

I don't like it, so instead I choose to ignore it, focusing instead on Ben who takes over from Dad.

Ben clears his throat, eyes scanning the room and resting briefly on the faces of people we know. 'Lily is my sister,' he begins, again speaking in the present tense, and I love him so much for doing that. 'I have known Lily for longer than I have known any other person in the world, and because of that I feel I am qualified to say that she was always a complete pain in the arse.' There is a rustle and a titter amongst everyone who is there and I gasp in mock surprise, taking an invisible swipe at him. 'Today . . . today, is my only moment to get payback without fear of retaliation.' He clicks a little button in his hand

and a picture of me comes up on the screen sitting on a potty. 'She will hate this,' he says, and he is so right. 'And she will hate this . . .' he says as the room fills with grateful laughter as another picture appears of me throwing a screaming tantrum at our second birthday party, while Ben looks angelic beside me. 'And this, and this,' he continues as more incriminating pictures appear, including one of me *picking my nose*. 'I'm pretty sure she's hitting me right now,' he laughs. And he is right.

'So, Lily, that was payback, but this is how it really was . . .' And on the screen, to the soundtrack of me and Ben singing 'We Are Young', which we recorded when we were about twelve, is a series of beautiful photographs. Our younger voices reach out across the room while photos of me and Ben, looking so alike, appear one by one from our childhood. We are playing, laughing or hugging in all of them and the final photo is from a family holiday last year, when we were tanned and happy and sitting on the balcony of our hotel, with the setting sun behind us, holding fruit cocktails towards the camera.

'I feel as if she is here –' he puts his hand over his heart – 'that she hasn't gone.' The last photograph stays on the screen after the recording of our singing has faded and Ben's last word is nothing but a squeak.

*

When it is all over, the Morecambe and Wise version of 'Bring Me Sunshine' plays out into the room. Everyone stands and they begin to shuffle out and some hands start tapping against legs in time to the music. 'Thank you,' I call out, as everyone I love passes me. 'Goodbye.'

88

My coffin doesn't trundle off behind the curtains; it stays, with me beside it, until the very last person has left.

The same boy who laughed at Fat Lucy nudges his mate, saying 'Girl on Fire' by Alicia Keys would have been much funnier, but Nathan pushes him and he loses his balance, falling sideways against some seats, which make an awful grating noise along the floor.

When they are all gathered outside and my coffin finally heads off down the tracks, the misty hand is still beckoning me, but I squeeze my eyes shut until all I am left with is the desperate hope that this crossing-over thing is going to be easy.

I'm still waiting.

I open my eyes slowly to find that the wispy fingers have disappeared and I am alone in the chapel with only the sound of voices outside for company chatting with that certain kind of relief that takes over once the worst bit has passed. After some time spent meandering around floral tributes to the dearly departed, they all start heading towards their parked cars and I find I can go with them. That same invisible thread that has linked me to my family pulls me again. Following Ben and my parents, I realise that either my coffin hasn't made it as far as the fire yet, or I'm never actually going to sit on a big pink cloud in heaven.

*

So now I'm at my own wake, unseen, unheard, in the function room of an old pub on the outskirts of town, where a buffet waits for the first hungry person to wonder how soon is too soon to be the first to pile their plate up and tuck in.

The best thing about being around people who can't see you is that you get to hear what they really think about you. Thankfully it's all good. Have I always been this great or have I somehow been elevated in status because I am dead, symbolically placed on some kind of pedestal? People are saying that I was beautiful, funny, kind and loving and a really, really good friend and a fantastic daughter. It is nice to know that I was or *am* so great. It's like watching the Lily Richardson Appreciation Show. The irony of death is that you obviously don't find out what you meant to people until it's too late.

Funerals are so totally wasted on the dead!

Dad shakes hands with Nathan, and Nathan in turn hugs my mum, predictably holding in one hand the first plate of food from the buffet. 'We're sorry we didn't contact you straight away, when it all happened, Nate,' Mum guiltily confesses. 'We weren't thinking straight.' She looks up at his lovely face and gives him another hug.

I want to give him a hug too.

'It's OK, Mrs R,' he says, and as he looks down at her he adds, 'I loved her, you know.'

'I know, Nate. We all did . . . keep in touch . . . please,' she urges him as he wanders away towards our friends, a sausage roll already working its way into his mouth.

'I will,' he mumbles through the pastry.

'I love you still,' I say, as he walks right past me.

*

It isn't a party exactly, but I want it to be.

I want to turn up the music and fill up the drinks. I want people to talk about it forever as Lily's fabulous wake.

Ben, it would seem, has somehow managed to drink quite a lot of alcohol, and is now cornering Dad. 'When will we get Lily's ashes back?' He sways slightly on his feet.

'I don't know,' Dad answers, with a flush of annoyance at Ben's timing, and he turns away to talk to someone else.

'But when do you think?' Ben persists.

Dad turns back, with that look he has when he's reached the limits of his tolerance, and he snaps loudly, 'I don't bloody know, Ben . . . possibly when they're a bit cooler!'

Ben is left standing alone, glass in hand and reeling slightly. 'Awkward!' sings a friend as he steps back into the group.

'I want her back,' Ben mutters angrily under his breath.

'I never left,' I say.

Most of our friends who have come to my wake are gathered together, and I am with them, listening and laughing along with their banter, pretending that I am simply one of them, chatting in a group in a pub. Suddenly a girl called Eve sighs at Ben, like he's some sort of lame dog. 'It must be *extra* difficult for you, Ben, being identical twins and all that.'

Matthew rolls his eyes at her and the rest of us giggle. 'Didn't you do biology at school?' he asks, but Eve just looks confused.

'What do you *mean*?' she whines, pulling a long brown plait over her shoulder and stroking it uncertainly, while we continue to laugh at her. Ben leans in, breathing fumes in her face.

'I don't think you understand the word "identical", Eve,' he slurs. 'As far as I'm aware . . . Lily had a vag-i-na –' as he says the word in clear syllables, he points to her groin – 'and I –' he points to his own groin – 'have . . . ornaments.' Eve's eyes roll downwards to look at his *ornaments*. 'Yep.' He nods his head up and down with a silly grin. 'I know . . . they *are* pretty awesome.' He winks theatrically at Eve who looks so confused that Ben properly laughs out loud for the first time in nearly two weeks, before he crumples into a nearby chair.

Nathan's mum did not come to my funeral.

Partway through the service I'd been pulled briefly to the corner of King's Lane, where I saw her standing on the edge of the grass verge, where flowers lay dead or dying amongst freshly placed bouquets. Red, pink, white and yellow cellophane wrappers crackled in the breeze and glistened in the light, holding their beautiful multicoloured offerings, tied with ribbons and lining the edge of the road. There were bunches pushed into bushes, lying on the grass or tied to trees and there, amongst them all, she placed a pretty terracotta pot planted with yellow roses, looking around her worriedly to make sure no one could see. But I could see.

'I'm so sorry, Lily,' she'd said, before wiping her face with a tissue and dragging some of her badly applied eyeliner across her cheeks.

Standing next to her, and staring down at the pot, it was all I could do to utter, 'You think a pathetic *flowerpot* makes up for my whole *life*?'

As the weeks come and go, my family and friends are left with the task of finding a different way of living in a world that carries on regardless.

The flowers that had lined the school railings have finally been taken down, Beth's mum has booked two weeks in Portugal for the summer, and after the exams Matthew has invited Ben to Paris for a weekend with his family. I'm pretty jealous about that one. I want to climb the Eiffel Tower too, and drink a huge hot chocolate in a real French cafe, or float down the Seine in an open-topped boat. I'd always wanted Paris to be the first step in my adventures around the world.

The seed of resentment with its once delicate roots is now taking hold and growing strong.

Nathan just looks more . . . sad and empty each time I get pulled to him. But it's happening less and less, as if he's closing down or something. I'm scared that that thing is happening, like it did with my gran where I am slipping to the back of his mind, like a forgotten item stored in the attic.

It's *her* fault!

If he could stop obsessing about the state his undeserving mother is in, he could spend more time thinking about me. I miss him.

I see Beth more than I see Nathan, when she catches sight of my photo or where I've been tagged in photos on social media and it brings my memory flooding back to her. Sometimes she has a different-colour nail varnish on, or her hair is twisted into a different style, or she's wearing an outfit we bought while we were together. The only thing I feel glad about is that she doesn't seem to have a new best friend. She hasn't replaced me yet.

Mum and Dad don't seem to talk about me much either, and this is the main thing that I really struggle with. It's as if my memory causes them too much pain. My bedroom is kept like a shrine, complete with the pretty blue urn containing my ashes, which is now placed on the dressing table, where Mum sits and cries a lot, but as soon as she comes out the door is shut. I'm rapidly becoming a painful secret, as if, to them, I am like misery, held inside Pandora's Box. I need to feel less lonely than I do right now. I need to be part of my family still, even if it's only by eavesdropping.

Ben gets angry with Mum and Dad quite easily, which I hate to see. He was always so laid back and likeable before, but now my beautiful brother seems to be morphing into someone with an attitude. He never seems to pull me to him when he's out of the house any more, as if once he's away from home, he's replacing me in some way. When I get pulled to Beth at school, or occasionally Nathan, Ben is always missing from the group. At the beginning I'd find myself beside him quite frequently when something was going on that involved me. Like, this one time, when he overheard two boys from the year below in the library talking about me.

'I heard that they're going to keep her ashes in their house,' one boy had said. 'I think they're going to put them on the shelf while they watch telly.'

The other boy had laughed. 'No. *I* heard that they're going to put her in the kitchen . . . but if they get it wrong, they'll think she's a jar of herbs. They might end up *eating* her.' Then they both laughed, doubled up and red in the face, until one of them found himself on the floor of the library with blood coming from his nose.

Fortunately I'm still on the dressing table, in my own bedroom . . . well away from the condiments.

The invisible boundary between life and death has just touched shoulders!

If I had breath, I would be holding it right now. I'm so scared that I'm going to ruin this fragile moment, where my brother appears to be looking into my world.

Because I no longer need to sleep, I've spent many nights in Ben's room, waiting in the shadows until my voyeuristic daytime existence could begin again, and now, suddenly in the middle of the night, Ben is sitting up and *looking at me*!!!

I can see two of him, one sitting up and one still asleep with his head on the pillow.

'Ben?' I ask, hardly believing what I am seeing, and taking a small step forward.

'I've missed you,' he says casually, as if I've simply been away on a camping trip.

I rush at him, like exploding popcorn, jumping excitedly up and down. 'BEN. I'm here. I've been *here* . . . all the time. The whole lonely, awful time.'

'Have you?' he answers quietly, and those two words have got to be the most anticlimactic words I have ever heard. He is too calm, like he's on automatic pilot or something.

'Jeez, Ben, aren't you pleased to see me? You've *found* me . . . ! I've waited weeks for this moment and you're acting like it's no big deal.'

'I'm only dreaming,' he murmurs. 'You are only a dream.'

'I'm so NOT a dream, Ben. It's really me and you'd better believe it.'

I reach my hand out very slowly towards him. Can I actually touch him? I'm almost too scared to try, for fear of ruining the moment. In all this time I've been unable to touch or feel anything and yet here he is in front of me looking into my eyes with the most awful sadness. So touchably close.

Are you OK?' I ask him as my fingers reach out for his, but just as he lies back down on the bed he utters one single word: 'No'.

'Ben!!!' I call out, grabbing for his hand, but it's too late, he's gone inside his sleeping body again, and my fingers grasp at nothing.

'Shit!' I yell. 'Shit, shit, shit.' My one chance at communicating from this vacuum, and I've missed it. 'Come and find me again,' I plead, staring hard at his face, and I can only hope with all my heart that he heard me.

I watch him closely for the rest of the night, just willing him to sit up again and talk to me. I find myself jumping eagerly forward with each movement he makes in his sleep, but the night rolls slowly on and my brother has nothing more to offer me than a brief snore and a loud fart from under the duvet.

When his alarm goes off, he wakes abruptly and looks around his bedroom as if now he's conscious he may be looking for me again.

'Still here,' I sigh patiently.

Ben gets up quickly instead of moving at his normal low gear, and he's dressed and downstairs in record time. I look over his shoulder as he taps at the screen of his tablet while slurping cereal noisily into his mouth. 'Can you see dead people in your dreams?' he types.

'Yes, you can,' I confirm. 'And yes, you did!'

He scrolls through everything that is listed beneath. Sites that tell him he can, sites that tell him he can't, sites that explain that seeing dead people in your dreams is just a reflection of your own 'need' to see people you love, and so on. He scans the headings in front of him, swiping and scrolling in and out of web pages, exploring everything including 'out-of-body experiences' and 'astral projection'. We read out loud together, because, even as the dead one, I also don't have a clue how we managed to meet in the night.

'Astral projection is an out-of-body experience achieved during lucid dreaming . . . That's it!' we both say at exactly the same time.

'A visitation appears because either the departed needs guidance from the loved one, who is dreaming to reassure them of their death, or the dreamer is in need of guidance or comfort from the one who has departed.'

Well, I don't need reassurance of my death because I'm absolutely sure that was me in the ditch, me in the morgue, me in the funeral parlour and me in the pinboard coffin. But . . . hey, I'm a visitation! Get me!

We both stare at the screen, neither of us knowing for sure which one of us is the cause of . . . my visitation, until Mum shouts through the door, making us both jump.

'Ben? What are you doing? You've missed the school bus.' She sighs loudly with annoyance, turning quickly and calling over her shoulder: 'I'll just have to take you. Get in the car.'

Ben downs a glass of blackcurrant juice so quickly that he's able to burp 'Thanks, Mum' impressively loudly at her. We both laugh.

When Ben goes to school, I can't normally go with him; I have only been pulled to him on a handful of occasions, like when he punched that kid in the library, or when the flowers got taken down from the school railings, or my seat got taken in English by Ada, a girl with berserk ginger hair and an attitude problem. Mum is still the stronger person at the other end of the Lily tug-of-war rope, but now I'm in the car with both of them, watching through the window with envy at all the kids who are making their way towards the school gates . . . having a normal day . . . doing normal things.

'Oh, there's Beth!' I call out and I continue to point to various other people I know. When Mum pulls up outside and Ben gets out of the car, this time I try really hard to go with him, but he's gone, shaking off any residue of family sadness and leaving it on the front seat of Mum's car.

'And there's Nathan,' I add, sighing as she drives past him, and we both wave, mouthing 'Hi, Nathan' through the closed car windows. He waves briefly at Mum but he no longer looks as chilled as he always used to.

Your mother did this to you. Your mother did this to us!

The night before, Nathan had been standing in the kitchen looking at the clock as the minutes ticked slowly towards six o'clock. 'Dad?' he said down the receiver of the phone, 'we *have* to do something about Mum. It's gone on too long. Something is really, *really* wrong. Not only is there no dinner . . . *again* . . . but she's properly drunk this time . . . like absolutely shit-faced drunk.'

His dad's voice came hopefully down the phone. 'Perhaps they had some . . . *do* . . . at work?'

'So you think she's been partying on down with a bunch of geriatrics, who've been raving in their incontinence pants at the care home?' Nathan asked, listening to his dad's telltale silence in reply. 'You *know* she's drinking at home, Dad . . . like, a *lot* . . . I've seen the empties.'

'I'm sorry, Nate. I *really* can't talk right now . . .' his dad said, ignoring his son's reason for phoning. 'Some shit has just hit the fan at work. I'm sure your mum's fine . . . a bit run down or something. Do you want me to bring you back a takeaway?' Nathan shook his head, feeling weary and dejected.

'Nah, don't worry, I'll nuke something.' He ended the call without saying goodbye, and rummaged in their big American fridge freezer to find something he could eat. Finally settling on microwave chips and a choc ice he pushed the packaging in the recycling bin . . . on top of the packaging for yesterday's pizza, which was on top of the packaging for chicken Kiev from the day before that, and when the microwave pinged he took his food to the sitting room, ignoring yet again the house rule to eat at the table. They hadn't eaten all together at the table since the day he found out Lily had died.

Since Lily had gone, the world as he knew it had scattered, like harsh breath on a dandelion clock, leaving shattered fragments around him where his girlfriend and his family had once been.

The numbers tick over to 06.12.

Just as the first glimmer of morning spreads across the sky and I'm about to give up on the hours I've spent *willing* Ben to come and find me again, he sits up in bed in exactly the same way as he did a few nights ago, leaving his body sleeping. This time he swings his legs over the side of the bed and stands up.

'It's happening again.' he says, uttering the words slowly. 'This is totally weird.'

'Yes, it totally is, Ben. And you're not dreaming.'

I walk over to him slowly, reaching my hand out to see if this time I can actually touch him. He carefully reaches his hand out at the same time, as if he thinks I'm just a visual bubble that might pop.

Our hands touch!

He curls his fingers round my own and it is like nothing I can describe. I could never in all my fifteen years have imagined that a simple touch could mean so many things. His hand on mine is everything that being lonely isn't, and I never want him to let go. I've waited weeks for a moment like this and here it is at last, the two of us sharing his dream.

'I've missed you,' he says softly, as if he still can't believe it, and I suddenly fling my arms round his neck, more pleased to see him than I've ever been, and almost too desperate for his company to speak.

'It's really you, isn't it?' he asks eventually, while I nod my head furiously into his neck. 'Awesome! This is actually real!'

'If you mean, is being trapped in a nightmare between heaven and earth real? Then yes, it's real. I am *really* here. I have been here all the time. I see everything!' I step back to look him in the eyes, laughing with relief. 'I even went to my own funeral, Ben. I watched it all!'

Ben looks down at me as if trying to compute such a bizarre idea.

'Nice speech by the way. Thanks for the potty photo.' I nudge him on the shoulder.

'That's OK.' He smiles in the way I know so well. 'Thought I might put it on YouTube. I do a special line in dead sister speeches . . . Sorry,' he adds, 'can't think of a nicer word for dead.'

'Dearly departed?' I suggest.

'Brown bread?' He grins.

'Someone who has bitten the dust.' I laugh.

'Or bitten the big one.' He laughs too.

'Come to a sticky end.'

'Counting worms.'

'Kicked the bucket.'

'Fallen off the perch.'

'Snuffed it.'

But his smile fades to a frown. 'So . . . have you come to say goodbye . . . ? Because –' he struggles with what to say next – 'apparently, according to the Net, I have to tell you that it's OK . . . to . . . you know, to go, Lily.'

'Trying to get rid of me already? Nice! Even if I wanted to, I don't know *how* to go, Ben,' I answer. 'It would appear it's not that simple.'

'The Net says that *the dearly departed* often hang around for some reason –'

'I don't know what the reason is then,' I interrupt. 'I don't have a clue why I'm still here. Maybe this is what it is like to die, but I don't really know because I've never . . . *snuffed it* before.'

'Perhaps you've got some kind of . . . I don't know . . . unfinished business or something . . .'

But I snort a bitter laugh loudly back at him.

'Thanks, Einstein, I'm *fifteen*. My whole life was an unfinished business.'

'Oh . . . Yeah, I get your point,' he says, an embarrassed smile sliding across his face, and he hugs me again. This is how we started our lives: twins, alone, squashed against each other's limbs, separated from the world only by the thin wall of our mother's womb. Now here we are again, separated only by the thin veil that divides the living from the dead. But he doesn't seem to be able to stay long, doing this astral-projection thing, or whatever it is, and the pull of tiredness from his living body washes over him again. 'I don't want you to go. I'm so tired, Lily . . . I'm sorry . . . I don't think I can stay.'

'Noooo, Ben, don't go. You've *got* to stay . . . I'm so alone,' I beg him, holding tightly to his arm as he makes his way back to the bed.

'I'll come back,' he reassures me. 'I'll learn how to do it properly . . . I'll get better at it . . . I promise.'

'Don't leave me here,' I plead, stepping between him and the bed and trying to push him away from it. He shrugs his arm and his hand releases its grip from mine, and then . . . I don't know why I did it, or even how, but I did it anyway.

Like when we were born, I beat him to it. I just lie down inside his sleeping body before he does.

Ben has gone.

And I have arrived.

Now here I am. Breathing in. Breathing out. Being.

I'm alive!

The feeling of linen on skin, and the coolness of air on my face, is amazing.

Ben's body, my body, reacts instantly in a physical way to the wrestling match of conscience taking place in my head. I can feel his heart banging wildly in reaction to the adrenalin that has been released. His skin . . . my skin, feels cold and yet sweaty, and my fingers are trembling. These sensations confuse me. One minute they feel like the most intense excitement and the next like the deepest ugliest guilt and I can't distinguish between the two.

I realise immediately that my ability to feel emotion has returned and I lie for some time with a whole range of emotions accosting me. This was not planned. I've just won the ultimate sibling battle. A split-second selfish act, leaving me totally unprepared for the mixture of joy, at being part of the real world, and the fear of what I have done to Ben.

I am not sure where Ben is but I imagine he's in the same kind of limbo that I have been in for the last few weeks.

'Ben? Are you there?' I call out, searching the shadows of the room. He doesn't answer, but I'm not surprised. I'm awake, so I probably won't find him again until I go back to sleep and do the weird not-asleep, not-awake thing.

'I'm sorry,' I tell him out loud, hoping that he's watching and listening, in the same way I have been all these weeks. But my words are small and hardly make up for what I have just done to my brother.

I pull the duvet comfortingly round me and by doing so I can smell the scent of deodorant and sweat that the heat of my body releases from the cotton and I breathe deeply through my nose, taking in the familiar odour of my brother. I study my hands by the red light of the alarm clock. Larger than mine, better nails. I feel my hair and how short it is compared to my own, which always got messy on the pillow and tickled my face. I feel a tiny bit of stubble on the end of my chin. I run my tongue over teeth, which are ever so slightly different from my own. One of Ben's incisor teeth is turned sideways; I can feel it with my tongue, angled and different.

I move a hand, feeling the fluffy wool of the jumper that Ben has slept with since my funeral, and there, amongst the fibres, is the fading scent of me.

What have I done?

It takes over half an hour for the racing beats of my heart, or rather Ben's heart, to slow down and follow a relatively normal steady pattern, while real life waits temptingly on the other side of the duvet.

I have to leave the safety of the bed and, although I toy with the idea of pretending to be ill and going back to sleep so I can let Ben swap back, in truth, I don't want to. And in my new 'not my body' heart I know I'm absolutely not going to. This is a chance to live for a day, and sorry, Ben, I'm bloody well going to take it.

The day has started for living people and I, it would appear, am one of those.

I swing my hairy legs out of bed and sit up at the same time. The air is cool and it makes me shiver. I move my feet from side to side on the carpet, the sensation of wool making its way to my brain through my feet and I wiggle my toes, inspecting the hair on each one, my new stomach recoiling slightly. *I've got the feet of a hobbit*. My toenails are surprisingly large and not that clean and I'm very glad that they're as far away from me as possible. I look around the room and manage to avoid the mirror. I can't look at him. Not just yet.

Still trembling I stand up, taller than I am used to. I am wearing navy shorts and a grey T-shirt and my arms are hairy. The adrenalin pumping rapidly around my body is making me feel a bit faint so I sit down again, feeling the plump duvet under me and the need to bow my head towards my knees until the dizzy feeling leaves.

My mouth is dry, and I suddenly really need a glass of cold water, but I can't go downstairs yet in case I bump into Mum or Dad. I have no idea how to be Ben; right now, I'm too wrapped up with being Lily *inside* Ben.

I make my way out of Ben's bedroom and across the landing to the bathroom for the water. I can smell toast coming from downstairs. Welcoming, warm and familiar. Wonderful.

I need to pee. The awful realisation of this fact causes me to study the toilet as if I've never seen one before. I now have boy parts and not just any boy's parts . . . these ones belong to my brother, and they are right there, dangling somewhere within the navy shorts. This is wrong on so many levels. I can't bring myself to even consider delving into Ben's shorts to empty my bladder but I'm going to have to do something.

I adapt. Suddenly aware, with an inner smile, that I'm automatically checking, as always, for Ben's favourite and boringly repetitive *cling film across the toilet seat* prank.

Anyway, I sit down, and I've never been more grateful for anything than the fact that everything tucks discretely downwards towards the toilet pan. This way I neither have to look nor hold.

Having sucked deliciously cold water directly from the tap, I dry my face and enjoy the feeling of the rough towel on my skin. Every sensation is enhanced, as if life itself is a drug, making me focus on every single thing that is happening: the cold tiles on the soles of my feet, the hungry rumble in my stomach, the scent of buttermilk and honey soap in the dish by the sink. Pulling Ben's T-shirt over my head, and carefully looking up at the ceiling, I remove his shorts and turn on the shower.

It's almost possible to forget I'm dead. It's almost possible to forget that I'm hijacking Ben. The water feels warm against my skin and the massaging effects of hundreds of drops of water on my shoulders and the back of my head is heaven. Taking my own pink sponge, I cover myself in soap, then wash it off in foamy rivers that cascade towards the shower tray and collect around my feet. Then I do it again.

I massage shampoo into Ben's hair, noticing once more how short it feels in my hands, then I turn my face to the water, enjoying the feel of it running off my head and face, forcing me to take gasps of air between water and soap. I could stay here forever. It is almost as if I will wash Ben away to the Lily that I am somewhere inside.

'Can you save some hot water for your mother?' Dad shouts, after thumping loudly on the bathroom door.

'I'm coming out now,' I shout back, but my voice comes out deep. 'Whoa.' I'm immediately surprised at the sound of it and it instantly reminds me of the imposter that I am. What I hear inside my head is ever so slightly removed from the voice of my brother, like when you hear yourself on a recording. I step outside of the shower and reach for a large grey towel, wrapping it round myself. 'Spoooonnge,' I drag the word out slowly, while making a turban for my head, out of a small blue towel. '. . . waaater . . . toooth brush.' I need to practise speaking. I don't want to look visibly surprised every time I open my mouth to talk to anyone.

'Are you all right?' asks Mum from just outside the door. 'Only, you're listing the contents of the bathroom.'

'I'm fine,' I call out, even though I am *so* far from fine right now. I try singing instead. Less obvious but no less freaky.

I clean my teeth with my own toothbrush, which is still poking its lime-green head out of the fish-embossed holder, along with the other toothbrushes belonging to Ben and my parents. When I dry my mouth, I feel once again the patches of stubble on Ben's chin and realise with a slightly sinking heart that I ought to attempt to shave them off.

I can't look at him.

Doing this while avoiding every mirror in the bathroom isn't easy, but filling the sink with warm water I dutifully rub soap onto the sparse patches of hair. 'Not exactly a beard, Ben,' I say out loud in my unfamiliar deep voice.

'Oh, it's coming along,' I hear Mum say, as she waits patiently outside the door. 'In fact, it's going to be the full Popeye if you take much longer in there.'

'Conchita Wurst more like,' I murmur quietly to myself. Five minutes later, my face is sore where I've made it bleed, so I tear a piece of toilet paper like I've seen Dad do, stick it to my chin and leave it there.

As I open the bathroom door, a high shriek in my ear surprises me, and I let out a high shriek too. Dad runs up the stairs two at a time to see why we are both screaming at each other.

'Oh God,' Mum breathes out, with a hand to her heart as if she's about to have an attack. 'I thought . . . you were Lily.' Her face is white, and I instantly compute that Ben would never put his hair in a turban, and his towel would be wrapped round his waist, not round his chest, like a strapless dress, as I have done. With only my face on display I know that our likeness must have really frightened Mum.

I escape to Ben's bedroom, rapidly having to change direction halfway there, as I automatically make for my own bedroom door. I can feel them both staring and I can hardly shut the door quick enough behind me, before I lean on it from the inside, trying to catch my breath.

I struggle to wrench a pair of Ben's boxers on, under my towel, as if I'm dressing on a public beach, hardly able to believe this is all happening. 'Oh, Ben, how the hell did we get into this mess?' I complain.

But I know what he'd say. 'I think you'll find you got into this mess all on your own.' And for once, he'd be right.

Picking my way through a pile of clothes on the floor looking for his uniform, I lift up a crumpled towel from yesterday and his school blazer, which has been thrown on the carpet. 'You're revolting, Ben,' I tell him, as I shake out yesterday's socks from inside the legs of his school trousers.

I can finally understand how it must feel when people say they're trapped in the wrong body. Ben's hobbity feet are covered by black socks, and his trousers and blazer feel . . . too shapeless, and don't represent who I am. I want my black tights and my short pleated skirt and my fitted white blouse. I don't know what I look like, but I know I don't feel very Lilyish.

'I can't face looking at you, Ben,' I tell him, knowing that if I looked in the mirror, I would see my own shame staring back at me. How long can I survive without looking? How long can I survive at all?

Taking some huge deep breaths, I head downstairs to the kitchen, noticing that, despite all this, my stomach belongs to Ben, meaning that I seem have inherited his insatiable appetite. China banging against china and the tinny rattle of cutlery meets me in the hallway, as Dad puts his breakfast things into the dishwasher. I need to act normal. I need to act . . . Ben-like. They can't know it's me in here, because they just won't believe it or they'll think Ben has gone mad or is playing a really cruel trick.

I hesitate outside, wiping my sweaty palms on the legs of Ben's uniform.

So, I'm going to walk into the kitchen.

I'm going to say nothing, like Ben does most days now, and I'll just start getting something to eat.

'Here goes,' I mutter under my breath.

I step into the kitchen, heart beating wildly as I walk past Dad, reaching for cereal with one hand and two slices of white bread from the bread bin with the other. His knees crack as he straightens up from loading the dishwasher and despite myself I catch his eye. I scan him in an instant. I see the way a little bit of greying hair sticks up at the side of his head, the way his ears kink at the top and his neck melts into his crisp white collar. His cheek and jaw are a freshly shaved kind of smooth, only now I can *smell* the wonderfully familiar scent of his aftershave.

Don't hug him. Don't do it.

I force myself to concentrate on pouring cereal into the bowl and putting the bread in the toaster. I must not give myself away; he'd never understand.

'I'm off to work now,' he says. 'I'll see you later.'

I hug him.

It's a scientific fact that people hug for approximately three seconds. We all follow some kind of unspoken social rule. I learnt this at school. I think about this fact, and I can't let go. I'm also aware that I haven't actually hugged my parents properly in a very long time. I read once that a twenty-second hug will release some sort of bonding hormone so I try it now. *Seven, eight* . . . A party of aromas join his aftershave: washing powder, toast, coffee and . . . him. *Eleven, twelve* . . . I feel his cheek all warm and squashy against mine. When I fall asleep tonight Ben will come back, and I'll never be able to do this again. But I'm doing it now, and I need to make this moment last me for eternity.

Dad is surprised at this sudden outburst, and I can hardly blame him. *Twenty!* He steps back, his eyes travelling back and forth across my face, trying to read my expression, to glean some sort of a clue for my sudden display of affection. 'You OK?' he quizzes me.

I toy with the idea of asking him to define 'OK'. Am I OK that I've pushed Ben into oblivion so that I can return from the dead? Am I OK that I can't tell him what I've done, or about how guilty I feel, or how scared I am, or how desperately I want to have one last chance at living?

'I'm OK, Dad,' I answer.

I feel that if I look at him for too long, he will be able to tell that it is me, because if eyes really are the window to the soul, then he will be able to see through them to the Lily inside. But as I unwillingly turn away with the distraction of taking a jar out of the cupboard in front of me, I can tell that for a few seconds he looked different, as if when I hugged him, I drew a little of the blackness out of his heart. He didn't ask me why I hugged him, he thought I was Ben, and he didn't need to know *why*, he just needed to know that I had.

'You don't like peanut butter,' Mum says, walking into the kitchen, just as I'm spreading my toast with peanut butter. I have already eaten my cereal, sugary, crunchy, cold from the milk, and its deliciousness suddenly churns in my stomach, and my knife stops mid-spread.

'Errrm . . . I want to see if I like it yet,' is my lame reply, and I take a bite. An event worthy of a fanfare is going on in my mouth right now, a toast-and-peanut-butter sensation and it's sticky and sweet and salty and lovely and my eyeballs roll involuntarily with ecstasy, almost retreating inside the back of my head.

'You look like you're *really* enjoying that,' she says, then adds, 'You look like . . . Lily.'

My throat constricts and I choke on my mouthful, regretfully putting the evidence down and covering my tracks. 'Nope, I still don't like it . . . *nasty*,' I lie, pushing the plate away.

She turns quickly towards the coffee machine and away from me. I scrape my chair back and pretend to throw my food in the bin, ramming as much in my mouth as I can before she notices.

'You'd better go; you'll be late,' she orders abruptly, placing a coloured capsule of coffee in the machine and pressing down the lever. She is cross that for the second time this morning I've made a tear in the protective wrapping she has spent weeks putting round herself. I swallow large gulps of apple juice, feeling it sliding coldly down my throat and cleansing some of the deliciously cloying peanut butter from my tongue.

This time I know I'm going to do it but I don't care. I lean towards her and my arms circle her body. Her initial surprise that her son, who has grown so distant lately, is hugging her, folds quickly as she gives in, slumping against my body. As Ben, I'm slightly taller than her now. Despite the smoke still lingering on her clothes, I can smell her shampoo and perfume, and I hold her scent within me for as many seconds as possible. *Thirteen, fourteen* . . . She sniffs and I realise that she is crying.

'Mum?' I ask her and she shakes beneath my question.

'It . . . still . . . hurts too much,' she mumbles into my shoulder. 'Just when I think I'm coping . . . there's always something to catch me out. She should be *here*.'

116

I kiss her cheek and it is salty wet against my lips.

I am here.

She reaches out and carefully removes the now-dry toilet paper from my cheek. 'Ow,' I squeal in a girly way and start to smile, but I see another fleeting shadow cross her face. She turns away, pushing gently from my hold and sighing wistfully. 'Go to school, Ben . . . I'll see you later.' And as I dutifully leave the kitchen, I hear her whisper. 'You're too much alike.'

I don't know *where* I am going, just that I am going.

My feet step along the pavement towards the school bus, toying with the very tempting chance I've got to see all my friends.

I want to go to school more than I've ever wanted to go to school in my life, but I can't rely on myself not to run up to Nathan and kiss him full on the mouth, or to fling my arms round Beth or to go round hugging random friends passing me in the corridor – even Mr Dougall would probably get a hug! If stealing Ben is selfish, then totally ruining his reputation with a sudden inability to contain a psychotic passion for everyone would be worse.

'You're at my mercy, Ben,' I say in my head, imagining the fallout of this weird situation if I were to behave like Lily while I've got Ben's life for a day.

But this day is too precious, and the decision of what to do with it is agonising. My heart sinks a little at the fact that my enjoyment must be limited.

I can hear Ben's shoes tapping on the concrete beneath me as I walk away from the direction of school. I zip his black coat up to the neck, covering the school blazer, and pull up the hood. It *is* cold but I also don't want to look too much like a kid who is bunking off school. Even if that's exactly what I am.

It's been raining and I can smell that gritty smell you get when rain has fallen on dusty ground. The sun comes out every now and then and turns the watery grit on the road into

118

shiny particles. It plays in puddles and bounces off windows. It warms the skin on my face just a little. Fabulous. I think of the little child I saw from Ben's window seeing everything life has to offer.

I want to touch everything, as if I am feeling the world by Braille. Dragging my fingertips along a garden wall, they feel the roughness of the brick and the softness of the moss in little lumps. They feel the dips where the concrete binds the bricks together, then rise and fall over the metal pattern of a garden gate.

I put my hand in Ben's coat pocket and run the pads of my fingers over some coins. If I can't spend this opportunity seeing the people I care about, then I'll just have to stuff my face with sweets. I walk past the nearest shop to a newsagent further away so I won't be recognised.

The shop has a smell. The smell is of everything. Of tobacco, of sweets, of boxes, newspapers, bottles, toys and cards. The smell of things we don't need but things we like. I ignore the suspicious gaze of the man behind the till, and head for the sweets. The packets, the tubes the lollies. My mouth is watering and I feel like a small kid counting my money, five pounds in total. I want them all. I want to feel popping candy on my tongue and hear it crackling inside my head. I want to taste chocolate and feel it melt. I want crisps, Coke, bubblegum, sherbet.

I make a collection of top-priority sweets and pay for them. £4.82. As close as I can get to my total. I hand over the hot coins that I have been clutching, and reach for my booty with the other hand. The man behind the counter looks at his watch. 'You're a bit late for school, son.' I glance briefly at him as I pull open the shop door.

'I'm a bit late for everything . . .' Then as the door closes behind me I add, hardly keeping the smile from my lips, 'but at least I've got today.'

I tip a small packet of Jelly Tots into my mouth and, screwing up the wrapper, I aim for the rubbish bin, scoring a direct hit before walking slowly down the road rolling the delicious gummy sweets around in my mouth. When I finish them, I eat each different packet, one after another. Tasting sherbet. Tasting chocolate. E-numbers, sugar, chemicals. Who cares? Crunching, chewing and swallowing, fizz up my nose. A massive burp comes from the pit of my stomach, making me laugh and choke at the same time.

Next, I head towards the green where people walk their dogs and children fly kites, then down the short lane that leads to some big open fields, away from anyone who could recognise me and challenge me about what Ben is doing out of school. Living in a village means that there is no urban anonymity to protect Ben from the whispers of sympathy, like wind through a leafy forest. 'There goes the boy whose sister died. They were twins you know. Ahhh.'

Clouds are rolling across the sky in grey lumps of different shades, blocking out the sun in patches across the fields. A blast of sharp wind blows in my face as soon as I reach the open field, and I stand and let it assault me, enjoying tiny spots of rain prickling my skin and clinging to my eyelashes and my hair. Normally I would have hated this, the weather wrecking my carefully straightened hair and ruining my painstakingly applied make-up. I would have grimaced and run for cover.

Now, I stand out here and let it give me all that it has. I can feel the strength of each gust racing through the trees and over the grass, bringing winter across the open countryside and slamming it into my body. It shows me that I am really alive.

I let my new friend the wind push me up a hill and closer to the sky, while memories play around me. Ben and me as children, rolling down this hill, screaming with laughter, and running back up again. Mum watching us from the bench at the bottom, clutching a bag with drinks and crisps and treats, ready for when we ran breathlessly back to her, our hands outstretched and our cheeks rosy. In those long-ago years this hill seemed like the top of the world. I believed as a child it brought me closer to heaven and if I jumped high enough I could touch a pink cloud where all the angels lived.

Where is God now? I ask myself. 'Where are you now, God?' I shout at a blue hole in the clouds above me. The driving wind rages in my ears, and whips my words away down the hill, and I imagine that it carries God's words with it, mocking me. *You . . . can't . . . find me.*

'Give me a few more hours, Ben,' I call out to the sky, 'just to remember what it's like to live again.' My insides sting when I realise that somewhere in death I learnt to really love the life that I had.

Walking to the other side of the hill, I stand looking down at the view. In the distance there are acres of winter countryside with the fleshless bones of trees poking through the land. At the bottom of the hill is our village, where the spire of the church rises between rooftops, pointing its ancient finger up to God.

From up here I can see the main road, which sweeps across

in a big arc towards the town, showing the route I should have taken by bus that day. And, drawing thin lines around the bare fields below me, are the country lanes where Nathan's mum and I made our fateful choices to take a shortcut.

I sit on a bench hugging my arms to my chest, either to keep warm or hold myself together, I'm not sure which, with the memory of the child I used to be still playing around me. The cold eventually makes its way inside my coat with its vice-like grip, until, shoving the hands that don't belong to me inside my pockets, I have to leave the top of the world.

Slowly pushing open the heavy wooden door of the church as if I'm not allowed to be here, I look around inside, not really sure what to expect, as I normally reserve church visits for special events only. But now, however, I can smell ancient history, and I realise that the unexplained feeling I always get in religious places, which makes me feel as if I ought to leave my personality outside on the steps, like shoes outside a temple, is actually *peace*. And peace comes now, greeting me at the door and draping its comforting cloak round my shoulders.

It is really quite nice!

The walls are white and the ceiling is high, with arches that reach into the middle and point skywards. A plaque on the wall says that this church was first built in the thirteenth century and I don't even know when that was, except it was a really long time ago, and that people have been praying for their souls, right here, for hundreds of years.

I run my hands along the pews and try to imagine the children who once sat here, who became adults, who became old people, and then died, laying their bodies forever outside under big crumbling stones until their children, and their children's children, repeated the process century after century. The lives and the loves and the dreams of all those people hang in the air within this building.

I should be crowded out by dead people everywhere but I'm not.

Where are all the dead people now?

The stained-glass windows throw their colours inside, telling stories I vaguely remember from the Bible. I am not at all sure where I fit into their promise of eternal life because when I was in limbo I wasn't wearing a halo or gliding around with a serene expression, but I'm pretty sure that taking over Ben's life is not a holy thing to do so I've probably lost my chance to get a halo now anyway.

Despite myself, I slip to my knees between the pews and shut my eyes tight, something I haven't done since I was a child. 'Are you there?' I whisper urgently into the age-old air, as if the church is going to be my spiritual telephone to the other side. I wait, while time holds its breath and the squawk of a bird outside ruins the silence. I don't know if I am talking to God or Ben, or basically *anyone* on the other side, but I try again. 'Tell me what to do!'

The bird squawks again, and I open my eyes only to see dust motes hanging loosely in the air. I wonder if God and Ben and all the dead people are answering me, but I can't hear them. Are they all on the other side of silence, like when I was in limbo and no one heard me?

I sit for a while longer looking for any possible signs that someone is there. A light brush against my hand or my cheek, as I had seen others feel when I was near them. I also search the

123

corners of my eyes for a wisp of smoke, like at the crematorium, but no . . . there is nothing.

'I'm sorry,' I say, apologising to Ben, 'but I don't care. I got to hug mum and dad one more time.'

The heavy door of the church is being pushed open, and I can hear people talking. I feel as if whoever is coming in will be able to detect my sin with their religious antennae, and I have never moved so quickly in my life. Two old ladies appear in bright-coloured jackets and patterned scarves, carrying a change of flowers for the displays, chatting and laughing with each other, and I try to glide past them without confrontation.

'Are you OK, dear?' one of them asks me with what I detect to be a mixture of concern and suspicion on her face. A teenage boy in church on a school day? I can see their point.

'I haven't taken anything,' I tell them, and guiltily hold my hands out, but I realise that ironically I look like the picture of Jesus shining out from the stained-glass directly in front of me. We face each other, Jesus and me, holding our hands out to each other, and I leave knowing that I *have* taken something. I have taken my brother.

*

For lack of anything else to do my feet and my morbid curiosity force me towards King's Lane.

It is quite a walk from here and I ask myself constantly what on earth I am doing, and why I am doing it, but I won't allow myself to change my route. As I get nearer, I feel the swell of my nerves fill me up inside until I step off the pavement, which edges the busy road out of town, exactly as I did nearly a month ago. As I follow my own footsteps, I imagine a scenario where, on that day, I had actually carried on walking along the safety of the pavement, taking longer, but making it home in one piece.

Why didn't I do that?

Ben's words from my funeral, now trapped in the fibres of my fluffy jumper under his pillow, replay again in my mind. 'Silly bitch,' he'd said. And he was right.

My feet trudge towards the corner of King's Lane, and I can hear the ground beneath my feet change to the crunch of mud and gravel as I make my way down the track. A large stone gets stuck in the tread of Ben's shoes so I lift my foot and pick out the stone with my finger just as a car in the distance becomes audible.

The final memory of me as living, breathing Lily starts ramping up inside my head, and, as the car gets nearer, my imagination starts kicking in.

What if the car turns into King's Lane? What if I can transport myself back into that single moment in time just before I got run over? What if I can change the course of events? If I can die, watch the world from limbo for several weeks, then get inside my brother's body so that I can be alive again . . . then surely *anything's* possible!

The sound of the car engine changes. It is slowing down. It is turning in.

I step off the road onto the grassy verge and wait, hands balled into fists, eyes tight shut and my face screwed up into an *I'm gonna make this happen* expression. The noise of the car is nearer: it is slowing down, it is turning, it is behind me . . .

The car will reach me, and I will step aside, and it will be

125

15th February again, and I will still be alive.

The car goes past me, the driver honking its horn loudly because I'm standing in the road, then roars down the lane as I step aside. I open my eyes, like you do when you're told to open your eyes for a surprise present. The rear-view of an old black estate car vanishes round a bend further down the lane, and I look down . . . at my boy's hands and my boy's body. Disappointment fills my chest and I find myself standing completely still for a long time on the edge of that lane, while my heart hurts with the most indescribable pain.

The flowers that lined the road when Nathan's mum placed her pathetic flowerpot apology are still here. It reminds me of a tree near Beth's house, where there's a permanent bunch of artificial flowers tied to it, dusty and fading in the sunlight, but every year on a certain day there is a real bunch placed alongside it, vibrant and sad and full of 'if only's.

This horrible muddy out-in-the-middle-of-nowhere place is still covered in flowers; dead, dying, they are all still here, but someone is adding fresh ones. They all have messages attached to them, many of which are now just a watery stain on the paper where the rain has washed the words away. Some have been laminated, preserved and written to me as if I would actually read them, which, ironically, I am doing. They make me cry, which I wasn't able to do in limbo, but crying is an emotion that hurts. It hurts your throat, it hurts your heart, and I don't like it.

'Who is still bringing flowers?' I say out loud, embarrassed that this place is still being remembered as the place where Lily Richardson died because she spent her money on earrings. 'This needs to stop! I am not in this ditch any more. I have not been hanging around this stupid place.' I kick one of the floral displays angrily and its dying petals scatter amongst the damp grass.

The large terracotta pot left by Nathan's mum has false pride of place, and I bend to examine the flowers, a rose bush with yellow blooms forced into life in a winter hothouse, yet prematurely rotting from overnight chill. 'They don't make up for anything,' I shout furiously, plucking at the ragged petals in my fingers, before smashing the pot into pieces in the ditch where I was found.

Just as I turn away to leave, I hear the engine of another car on the main road, indicating as if to turn in to King's Lane. This time I don't bother with my pathetic game of 'what if's, but as I turn round I see the blinking indicators of a shiny blue Morris Minor that has slowed down in order to turn, and which now suddenly revs its engine, flicking off the indicators and continuing on.

The driver has obviously had an abrupt change of mind.

Nathan's mum, sunglasses on, even on this dull day, hiding the eyes that saw me, drives away as fast as her ancient car will take her.

It's like Groundhog Day. How coincidental that we should meet in the same place again, and like last time she still can't see *me*.

In that moment I make a decision.

Gardening gloves and some little secateurs rested on the passenger seat of Nathan's mum's car. She made a regular pilgrimage to this place whenever she felt brave enough to come. Her panic over being back where it all happened was a constant inner battle. But the rose bush needed tending to. To let the flowers die would be like pretending it no longer mattered.

But it did matter. It would always matter.

She'd searched the papers and the news releases every week with no small amount of trepidation, but had noticed with a fragile relief that public interest in the case was beginning to die down. The police were unable to provide any further information at this point in time, and, as a result, the press had nothing new to report. For a while it had seemed as if everyone in the area had been talking about nothing else but the madman who had run Lily Richardson over and failed to stop, but then interest had eventually moved on to other things, as inevitably it would.

Each day she woke hoping that she would be able to breathe a little easier, but instead as each morning arrived it was as if she was suffocated that little bit more by the ever-increasing guilt inside her.

She clicked the indicator on at the approach to King's Lane and checked her rear-view mirror and the road ahead before beginning to turn right, but her body flinched violently and her lungs involuntarily drew a sharp breath as she saw the figure of a boy beside the road. Yanking the steering wheel down to the left, she swerved the car back onto the main road and changed up the gears as quickly as her shaking limbs would allow.

The boy grew smaller in her rear-view mirror as she drove away, but his gaze remained fixed on her car.

The eyes of that poor girl's brother followed her home.

Knocking on the door of Nathan's house makes my heart thump.

His house is big and detached, with a perfectly manicured front garden surrounded by a low stone wall, now aged with time and history. The front door to the house is made of wood and has a heavy knocker on the edge of it with a beautiful rectangular stained-glass panel in the centre made of greens and yellows. The total effect is very stylish. Just like Nathan's mum. But now its perfection hides a secret . . . Just like Nathan's mum.

The blue Morris Minor is parked at a rushed angle in front of the garage and its pristine paintwork shows not a single sign of damage. There is tray of plants on the passenger seat, some gardening gloves and a trowel. *So you absolve yourself with flowers and think that's OK?*

She looks awful, and jolts physically when she sees that the person on her doorstep is the boy in her rear-view mirror. I can see she is panicking and I imagine her heart is possibly thumping more than mine. I suppose I was expecting to see her looking like she always looks, glamorous and unaffected, but it takes only two seconds to notice that this is only a shade of the woman who used to be Nathan's mum. I was certainly not prepared to see her like this and the curl of surprise that forms inside me manages to morph into a spiky kind of satisfaction. She looks like shit!

There is a brown and silver tide creeping along her roots, sharply contrasting with the rest of her dyed-auburn hair. She is wearing a very large sweatshirt that somehow makes her look incredibly small and I realise that in Ben's stronger body I could easily hurt her.

'I'm Lily's brother.' The words come slowly and satisfyingly out of my mouth, leaving the remaining silence to continue my accusation.

'Ben?' she greets me in a strangled voice that comes out an octave above her own. She can't see me behind his eyes and a range of scenarios play out in front of me. Should I tell her that I am Lily and watch her turn into the lead victim of a horror movie? But this is real life, and although it would freak her out to hear me say those words it would not prove anything to the outside world.

No, I need to leave her dangling on this wire for a good while longer.

'Nathan isn't back from school yet.' She swallows, hoping that this might make me go away.

Her words cut into my thoughts and remind me sharply that Nathan is the one that would be hurt by me handling this clumsily.

As his mum stands in front of me, I can see that her rational mind is telling her that I couldn't possibly know who killed Lily, yet the hand that claws at her throat is giving her guilt away, and the skin on her face looks as if it has just become too big for her skull. She continues to hold the door partly in front of her like a shield.

'Can I come in? Maybe wait for him?' I ask, still unsure how I'm going to let this play out. Everything I want to say to her is trapped inside me, fizzing violently, as if my head is a cork holding it all at bay, and if I don't say something soon I'm going to explode.

'It's not convenient right now . . . I . . . I'm sorry,' she says, but just as she is closing the door and the moment is slipping away from me, I blurt out.

'I know what you did.'

One brief second in time. One error of judgement and the ugliness of that moment will spread across so many people, like black oil in a beautiful sea. For the single second that our eyes meet through the crack in the door, before she slams it shut, I see a kaleidoscope of fear and regret and pain.

And it makes me feel good.

I turn round at the sound of gravel crunching behind me to see Nathan coming up the drive. I have to physically restrain myself from leaping into his arms, unable to prevent a smile of pure joy making its way across my entire face. I look into his frothy blue eyes. 'Nate?' I almost squawk and I bounce a little on the balls of my feet with barely contained pleasure.

'All right, Ben?' he asks, more of a question than a hello, obviously more than a little confused why Ben is *so* happy to see him.

'*Don't you dare try to kiss him,*' I imagine Ben growling in my ear.

'Yes, thanks,' I say, grinning and immediately try to force my face into a more appropriate expression, desperately trying to keep my lips to myself and to think of a reason for Ben being at his house. 'Thought I'd come to see how you're doing.' But in an overly tactile way my hand involuntarily finds its way onto his arm, causing him to look down at it with one eyebrow raised. 'Oh, sorry,' I apologise quickly, but his gaze has already shifted to the glass panel in his front door where his mum's head is visible where she is slumped behind the coloured-glass panel.

'I don't think your mum is very well,' I add, knowing regretfully that Nathan is no longer interested in talking to me.

'What the . . . ?' he mutters as he rushes to open the door without saying goodbye, leaving me standing kissing my fingers where they'd touched his sleeve.

I leave the picture-postcard facade of the Peterson house with its ugly truth and broken heart and make my way slowly home.

Nathan's mum had shut the door and sunk to the floor, her back to the wall, and her head leaning against the thick stained-glass panel. The coir on the welcome mat prickled her skin and snagged her tights, but she couldn't move. She could hear Nathan and Ben talking outside and the taste of bile found its way into her mouth.

He couldn't possibly know.

When Nathan put his key in the lock she moved, but only to the stairs, where she put her head to her knees to stop the imminent threat of vomiting on the carpet.

Nathan dropped his school bag and crouched down in front of his mother. 'Mum?' He waited to see if she would reply but the only thing she offered him was the top of her head with its greying tide. 'Are you ill?'

She answered with her outstretched hand, which he took in his own larger hand. *So Ben hasn't said anything to him*, she realised with relief. *My beautiful son won't despise me . . . yet.*

'I love you, Nate,' was all she could answer.

Long after Nathan had taken her shoes off, helped her upstairs and made her a cup of tea, his mum had lain curled up in bed, staring at the wall and trying to undo the few awful minutes that changed her life for good.

Why hadn't she put her hand over her glass to stop Morag topping it up? Why the *hell* hadn't she just drunk coffee? Why hadn't she at least driven the normal route home?

She knew with absolute regret that if her husband and her son ever found out it was her who killed Lily, the love that her family had for each other would be extinguished.

Letting myself back in to our house I can hear Mum running down the stairs. As the door closes behind me, I manage the beginnings of a greeting, just before she pushes her hands on my shoulders . . . hard! It makes me lose my balance and fall against the door with a thud, banging the back of my head. She is hitting me with closed fists that are hammering at my arms and against my chest. Her teeth are clenched, and her face is twisted into an expression that I can only describe as bloody furious.

'Mum?' I yell at her with my arms bent in front of me to hold off the blows. 'Get *off* me.' Her arms get weaker until she is leaning against me, face red, eyes wet and an exhausted groaning cry coming from her mouth. Then she presses her forehead into my shoulder and unclenches her hands so she can hold me in a rough hug, finally sinking down until she is sitting on the bottom stair, exhausted.

'Where have you been . . . you . . . absolute fuck?' she demands between breaths. 'The school rang me to say you hadn't come in. I've been worried sick and you didn't answer my calls. I thought . . . not again . . . I thought . . .' Then she cries huge howling sobs until her head sinks and her knees are pressed into the sockets of her eyes.

This day that was supposed to be all about me has opened a barely healed wound for my mother. I sit down next to her, squashing us between banister and wall, guiltily knowing that I had not even thought about how she might feel. Wedged side by side on the bottom stair, I put my arm tightly round her shoulders and lean my cheek on the back of her head. 'I'm so sorry,' I say through the hair that has stuck to my lips, and my own warm breath comes back at me from her head.

'Am I losing you too?' she asks into my shoulder, and I think of Ben and how distant and angry he has been lately. A spike of irritation at Ben pokes me. Next time I see him I'll tell him to be more considerate about how he acts towards her in future.

I wish I could explain it all to her. But how do you tell someone that you had another chance to come back? That you couldn't tell anyone about it. That you just wanted *to feel the day.*

A sound behind me makes me look round. Good old Uncle Roger is standing in the hallway leaning on the banister with a tea towel in his hands. 'That was a bit selfish and irresponsible.' He frowns down at me, waving the towel at my face. 'This has really upset her. We were about to come looking for you, Ben!' 'It's going to take more than Captain Tea Towel to find Ben at the moment,' I mutter, but my cryptic sarcasm is lost on both of them.

It is as if the day is slippery and I can't keep hold of it.

Ben would normally be lurking in his room, watching YouTube or messaging friends, waiting for dinner, but I am restless with the need to do something before the day dwindles completely like sand through an hourglass.

I play with the idea of going to my own room, but Mum was in there earlier, and I'm not even sure I'm brave enough to cope with it. I feel that if I open the door to my room, I will expose my own heart, and my parents will wonder what's wrong with me.

I haven't eaten anything since the sweets I had this morning, and my stomach is rumbling loudly, complaining of its emptiness. Not counting breakfast, this kind of intense hunger is another feeling that I haven't had since just before sinking my teeth into the sugary doughnut I had with Beth on my last day on Earth. We'd tried to eat it without licking our lips, the sugar building up around our mouths, until Beth had accidently licked her lips, and I'd given in shortly afterwards.

'Can we have a takeaway? I'm dying for a Chinese,' I ask Mum, having to make do with only myself to appreciate my pun. 'And can we have the buffet for six that's got *everything* in it?'

'*Six*? But there are only *fo*— three of us,' she replies,

correcting herself quickly so that we can all try to pretend she didn't almost get it wrong.

'It's a great idea, Ben; we'll have a veritable banquet,' Dad answers, reaching for the phone, and placing the order for a home delivery. Then he opens a bottle of wine for him and Mum, and a can of cola for me.

This momentary break from the dismal heaviness that has been falling like dust over everything appears like a glint of sun between clouds. When Dad absent-mindedly puts his hand on Mum's shoulder as he pours her a drink she looks at him with the expression of a lost puppy who is being shown a sliver of affection.

Our *veritable* banquet, whatever that means, is like nothing I have ever eaten, or have ever really appreciated. Having watched people eat for weeks now, with only the memory of taste to make do with, makes me think of those people on the television adverts, who never eat more than rice, and the flies that invade their mouths, the baby with the huge eyes and swollen stomach, and the mother with the same look in her eyes that my mother has now, as if life has defeated her in some way.

I haven't exactly been starved of food in the way those people have, but being dead apparently makes you so much more philosophical about life!

Taste . . . it's such a luxurious and intensely delightful thing.

Grease dribbles down my chin as I bite into a pancake roll. It is on my fingers mixed with salt and sauce. My pleasure at combining this experience with the precious moment spent with my family is radiating from me. We are sitting round the kitchen table where I've managed to shunt my seat along, almost crowding the fourth chair so that the space next to me doesn't look too empty. Dad even laughs about something that happened at work and we all join in.

After dinner the simple act of joining my own parents in watching a programme on television has suddenly become a precious thing. No tablet, no phone, no earphones, just my family and its faint breath of life, and its pulse beating somewhere within its depths.

They don't question why Ben is suddenly less snappy and more willing to join in, and they don't notice me watching them from the corner of my eyes, but this is how it is until the day, inevitably, comes to an end.

Such a wonderful thing . . . *one simple day* . . . and each second that ticks by brings me closer to its end.

I kissed Mum and Dad goodnight and tried my hardest not to make it look like it would be the last time, forcing as much of my love as I could through Ben's body and into theirs, and, in return, trying to draw the very essence of my mum and dad into my virtual suitcase.

Now, back in Ben's bed, my thoughts wander along the various cracks across the surface of the ceiling to the enormous uncertainty of where I'm going to go from here. It is 03.21 and I have been fighting off sleep for the last couple of hours unable to actually let go of . . . *life*.

I can feel my eyelids growing heavy, making my eyeballs roll around behind them in their effort to keep my brain from slipping into unconsciousness, but they fail.

'Lily?'

Ben steps from the edges of my sleep towards his bed.

'Ben?' I answer, as if we are two nervous acquaintances who have just met after a long break.

'Lift your head up,' he says, 'I can only see your eyes. It's too creepy talking to myself.'

I raise my head until I am sitting, and instantly I can see

my own long dark hair hanging loosely down the sides of my face.

'You had another day,' he says quietly. 'Did it help?'

I think about this for a while. It was sad, beautiful, busy and desperately short.

Did it help?

'It was good, while it lasted,' I answer lamely.

'I saw you at Nathan's today,' he continues. 'I swear you almost made me kiss him!'

'I nearly did,' I answer, smiling at the thought.

'And why did you tell his mum that you know what she did?' he asks. 'What did she do?'

I inwardly groan. Should I tell him? Will he dive in and deal with it in the wrong way? 'I . . . I just happened to know that she did something. That's all.' The pitch of my voice is wrong, and Ben knows it too, especially as it's actually his voice. His sudden intake of breath is loud in the night as he gasps and slaps his hand over his mouth.

'Oh my God! She did it, didn't she? *She* was the driver.' He whistles through his teeth as the repercussions of what he has just realised sink in.

'Yep. Yes, she did,' I answer.

'Shit!' Ben pushes the word slowly out of his mouth.

'Too right it's shit. Mum and Dad are going mad with trying to find out who did it and all along it's Nathan's mum!'

'I'm going tell Dad in the morning,' he announces. 'He can tell the police.'

'What exactly is Dad going to tell the police? That his son met his dead daughter in the night and she told him "who dunnit"?' We stare at each other for a moment while he tries to think of a better plan.

'Her car! They can get forensics in to examine her car.'

'There isn't a mark on it. I can't see them confiscating her car just because you asked them to. And, more importantly, it will destroy Nathan.'

'If it isn't already,' Ben mumbles. 'He looks awful lately. I'm not surprised; his mother looks like she's ready to go trick or treating. Not the foxy mama she used to be.'

'Now that *is* weird, Ben. I don't care what she looked like before, but I'm glad she looks like shit now. Although Nathan might as well have "son of a killer" tattooed on his face if this gets out. Even if they leave town, social media will make sure his story follows him forever like a big fat label attached to his name.'

'His mum *has to* pay for what she did, Lily . . . People forget sooner than you think.' But his words are sharp spikes digging into my ego. *People forget . . .*

'I'd hoped for nothing short of a *decade* before I'm forgotten, to be honest.'

'I-I didn't mean that,' Ben stutters, trying to defend himself.

'I really will just be the yesterday's news girl, who was tucked inside the yesterday's news coffin and . . . removed. I will be nothing more than a horrific event that happened on King's Lane and all those guilt-trip flowers will only highlight the unfortunateness that happened there.'

'That's not a word,' he says, urgently trying to deflect my mood, putting his hands on his hips, visibly pleased that he thinks he can correct me for a change.

'Yes, it *is* actually, dumb arse,' I inform him. 'Anyway, I don't know what to do about Nathan's mum at the moment. The police won't believe us with nothing to back up the story; she needs to confess, but don't worry, I'll think of something.'

'No, *I'll* think of something,' he says and reaches for my hand to pull me off the bed, but my own hands, inside his body's hands, stay where they are, gripping the duvet, clenching at feather and cloth.

'C'mon, Lily.' Ben looks more than faintly cheesed off. 'It has to be enough. I can't stay here for the rest of my life while you skip around fields, eating sweets and talking to God. Aren't you supposed to *look for the light* or something?'

We both cast our eyes around his bedroom, both aware that there is absolutely *no light*!

I lift my hand away from its duvet grip, and my fingers become slim and feminine, but as Ben swipes for my hand I quickly yank it away and flop back on the bed inside his body. He grabs mistily through his own body, as if it's thin air, in the same way that I was unable to touch people when I was in limbo.

He swipes for my hair instead but I press my head back into his and, again, he swipes nothing, his fingers reaching through my face.

He can't get me.

'Is this funny?' he asks when a laugh escapes from me. 'I've just put my hand through my own face! It's like the bizarrest fight we've ever had.' He doesn't laugh with me.

'Now *that's* not a word,' I answer, feeling smug.

'Whatever. Anyway, you can't be me Lily. I am me . . . You are . . .'

'Dead?' My Lily eyes look out at him from his own face.

'Whatever amusing names we call it, Ben, I am nothing any more . . . and I . . . I . . . don't think I can go back to that.' My fingers grip tighter at the duvet and in that moment I know that it's true. I am too scared of that awful loneliness to go back to it. 'Can't we share?' I suggest, as if his body is a bag of chips.

'No! Think it through, Lily! It's . . . a more than totally weird idea. For a start, you'd never be able to do what I do . . . football, sport, everything. You're a girl.' He always uses the *girl* thing in his pathetic attempt to get one over on me because I'm the oldest and of superior intellect.

'Pitiful,' I sing at him, which is always my response. We have always been like a stuck recording with this argument.

He continues. 'You know what I mean. You're useless at sport and you'll just make me look like an idiot –'

'You are an idiot,' I interrupt. 'You've been ignoring Mum for a start.'

'Have I . . . ? Anyway, what if I have a girlfriend . . . are you going to share then?'

We both wrinkle our noses at the thought. 'That's gross,' I answer. My eyes, the only things I dare move, stare imploringly up at him and in return he stares back. As he does so, a look gradually comes into his face that I can't put into one word. Is it pity? Or empathy? Or annoyance? Or just plain old really pissed off that I'm refusing to budge? Knowing Ben, I think it's probably all of the above.

We continue to stare, like contestants in a thinking competition, until eventually I shut my eyelids and sigh deeply, breaking our silence when I whisper, 'I can't let go . . .' But Ben doesn't answer.

When I open my eyes again, he isn't here.

I briefly lift a hand and it turns into my own. Yes, I'm still in this bizarre night-time sleep-projection thing, but he most definitely isn't here. 'Ben?' I question the area where he was standing. 'Ben?' I call out a little louder into the shadows at the corner of the room, but there's nothing. He has gone. Convinced he will come from left field and rugby-tackle me away from the bed if I move, I stay put, yet he doesn't appear.

The telephone rings and I can hear Dad talking to someone. It's 08.40 and the minutes between my night-time crime and now have somehow disappeared in the lost time between waking and sleeping.

It is Saturday.

Has Ben given me another day? Is that why he disappeared? 'Thanks, little brother,' I call out from my comfortable pillow, as if I have just won a scuffle for the comfortable chair.

'Ben? Mathew's dad's just rung and he's going to pick you up a bit early,' Dad hollers up the stairs.

I suddenly remember with a sinking feeling what Ben does on a Saturday. He plays football. I've played a few times in PE at school and not only do I hate it, but I'm crap at it, and, what's more, if I have another day, I want to enjoy it, not spend it outside in the mud!

'I'm not going this week,' I shout back in a voice deep and croaky from not enough sleep. 'Can you phone them back and tell them?'

'You *are* going, Ben! You can't let your team down, and you can't pretend things aren't what they are. You told them you'd be there . . . and, trust me, you *will* be there.' I can hear his ranting voice coming up the stairs, his voice getting

147

louder as he reaches the landing.

I flop back on the bed and pull the duvet over my head, as he puts his head round the door. 'Get up! They'll be here in half an hour.'

'No,' I call out, my voice muffled by the duvet.

'Get up!' he orders again, and I can now detect that certain dangerous edge he has to his voice when he's getting all authoritative.

The cocoon of the duvet barely contains my panic until Dad grabs my foot and before I know it I'm out of my cocoon and on the carpet. 'I know you've been bunking off football lately for some reason, and God knows where you go. Matthew's dad said that Matthew thinks you're hanging around with some unsavouries. So I'm telling you now, you get your arse up and get your life back together.'

I've no idea what Dad is talking about, but I can see I'm not going to be able to get out of it.

Ben's words from the night echo in my head: '*You'd never be able to do what I do. You're a girl.*' What a put-down! I can do it. I'll learn a new skill. Not many people can say they learnt a new skill *after* they died.

'It's probably like netball but with feet,' I say out loud, hoping he can hear me.

Having never taken much notice of his various sporting outfits, I get up off the floor and hunt for something footbally to wear. He wore *stuff*, that's about the extent of my knowledge. I choose some shorts, a football shirt that kind of matches, and a tracksuit to keep me warm from the jumble at the bottom of Ben's wardrobe. It's cold outside and I'm not hanging around

148

outside shivering all morning. The tracksuit, grey and soft, pulls easily over the sports clothes I have chosen, and I look in the wardrobe mirror to see what I look like.

The shock is intense.

I'm not ready for the mirror; I didn't mean to do it.

I am Lily, but my reflection tells the truth.

For a second, I don't move at all . . . then I take one step towards the full-length mirror, knowing that what I have done is wrong, that taking over Ben's body isn't really the same as winning a scuffle for the comfy chair.

I inch my way closer towards my guilty secret until I'm staring right into Ben's hazel eyes. Our eyes are almost identical except mine are greener. Nathan once described them as being like a forest floor scattered with moss, after we had finished kissing, when our faces were only inches apart. I think I can actually see myself now beneath the surface of Ben's, if I look very hard, the greener colour shining out through Ben's hazel.

We look so much alike. I reach a hand out and press it against the glass, then I reach the other hand out and press that in the same way until we are joined. 'I don't see why we can't just share . . .' I tell him, a mist cloud forming on the glass between us.

Dad pokes his head round the door again, only to catch my eyes in the reflection of the mirror. 'What on earth are you *doing?* he asks with confusion, but doesn't wait for the answer. 'Stop loving yourself. You've got ten minutes.'

I find Ben's football boots in a plastic bag at the bottom of his wardrobe and put them on. Fumbling fingers struggle with the laces of boots that are stiff and dirty, and it feels strange to walk in them with all those bobble things on the bottom. I glance at Ben in the mirror again, raise my hand in a kind of wave, then leave to make my way downstairs carefully with the boots on, trying to ignore the fact that I am leaving a trail of dry caked mud and grass on the stairs.

The massive Chinese meal from last night has left me with a stretched and empty stomach that needs to be filled. I click my way along the kitchen floor in the football boots, and make an extra-huge bowl of chocolate cereal. I watch the cold milk pour white then turn chocolatey. Crunching, slurping and swallowing, I allow my self-indulgence to help me to forget Ben for a moment. The milk spills from my spoon and down my top, leaving some brown splodges, which I try to wash off after I've eaten. Great, I'm now wearing a tracksuit with dark-grey wet patches and some faded brown splodges.

Matthew knocks on the door, and after shoving my bowl in the sink I shout to anyone listening, 'See you later! Don't worry about me . . . I'll be fine!' then I grab Ben's coat, and shut the front door behind me.

If there is to be any chance that Ben will share himself with me, I need to prove that I'm as good a boy as any girl can be.

'Hi,' I say, grinning nervously, instantly taking note of the fact that Matthew has a green and white team kit on under a warm green fleece, and I know straight away that blue Nike shorts and a black T-shirt with a wet, slightly stained tracksuit over the top is just so embarrassingly not the right outfit. I'm sure Ben would feel really *not cool* but I can't help supressing a slight laugh when I notice that Matthew is staring at me in barely disguised surprise.

It's not going well so far.

'Do you . . . er . . . want to get your kit? It's a match today, you know?' he says, looking me over and searching for the sports bag that I obviously don't have.

I find myself mumbling excuses. 'I knew that. I was in a hurry . . . my stuff is inside . . . I'll go and get it.' I bend down so that I can see Matthew's dad's face behind the wheel of his car, and wave my hand from side to side in my Lily way. 'Hi, Matthew's dad,' I call with the same nervous grin I gave Matthew. 'Nearly ready.' Then I turn and run round the back of the house, almost knocking Mum, who is having a cigarette, off her feet. 'Where's his kit, Mum . . . ? I mean, *mine*. Where's *my* kit?'

Mum tells me where I can find the kit in a voice that questions why I don't already know, as it is under Ben's bed and has been in a proper sports bag all along, everything inside clean and ready, including newer boots. This is so *not* going to be an easy morning, but I'm not going to let Ben win.

'Everything will be fine, little brother,' I tell his reflection as I reach under the bed for his stuff. 'It's all under control.'

I run outside again, clipping and tapping on the path in Ben's old boots, throw the bag in the back of Matthew's dad's huge and shiny black Audi, then slide in on the leather seats.

Dad has followed me outside but as Matthew's dad unwinds the window and looks up at him to say hello, Dad points to the Audi where there's a dent by the offside headlight.

'How did you do that?' Dad asks him without a trace of a smile, and Matthew's dad offers a rueful grin.

'Someone reversed into me,' he answers, but Dad doesn't

151

smile back, and in a heart-stopping moment I know what's coming.

'Dad! It's OK, go inside. It wasn't him.'

But Dad carries on. 'When?' he persists.

'Wednesday. Why?' Matthew's dad answers, and then I see the penny drop. 'Oh . . . Yes . . . it was just three days ago. Sorry, James . . . you know . . . about . . . not finding out who did it.'

I am in the back, looking through the window at my dad, and making urgent cut-throat signals at him to be quiet, while shooing him away with my other hand.

Matthew's dad starts the engine, waving politely as he thankfully drives off, leaving Dad standing at the side of the road. The atmosphere in the car is one of relief, tainted with awkward embarrassment. 'All right?' he asks me, his eyes catching mine in the rear-view mirror as I lean back in the seat, exhaling silently.

'Yeah, thanks,' I say as brightly as possible, as if everything that has just happened is perfectly normal.

Poor Dad.

Matthew is on his phone, tapping away at the screen, but I haven't bothered bringing Ben's and I can't really bring my own. Anyway, I want to look at the world outside where life is a series of houses that belong to people, people that belong to families, cars that are taking people somewhere, people who are walking dogs somewhere. This is the area that I grew up in. I recognise everything: the shops the roads, a girl from school. My face is pressed too close to the window, like a small child, and my breath is causing a cloud of mist to appear on the glass.

Matthew's dad pulls into the car park at the club, and I have to face the fact that all too soon I'm going to be sprinting around the pitch playing a game that I have absolutely no interest in.

The sports field is massive, with several pitches each holding players of varying ages. Team kits in bright colours are everywhere. The edges of the pitches are lined with random supporters hugging themselves from the cold, or sipping hot drinks from travel mugs. Haven't they got anything better to do on a Saturday?

The whole team is ready and some of them laugh at me when they see what I'm wearing. The coach doesn't look too pleased. 'Get changed sharpish, Richardson,' he growls at me, 'and *try* to get it right next week!'

As I jog quickly back from the changing rooms, shivering and miserable, I can see Ben's team starting their exercises, a row of them dancing backwards and forwards in a series of strange muscle-stretching movements like a mad green and white ballet. 'Looks a bit silly to me,' I say under my breath. I can feel the icy air begin to numb my legs and my face, and not for the first time I wonder why on earth anyone would ever want to play this hideous game.

The trouble with 'all too soon' is that it's always too soon. I am placed midfield, marking the Incredible Hulk, an enormous kid who looks down at me with what I can only describe as disdain that only slightly distracts attention from the row of festering spots he has on his forehead and chin. The whistle blows and I start bouncing around, marking him in the same way I know how to in netball, but suddenly guys are running all over the place and I'm left jumping pathetically on my own.

I run madly towards a gap, waving my arms to a boy called

Martin who has just retrieved the ball from the other side. 'Martin. Martin,' I'm shouting. Martin kicks the ball in my direction, but the Hulk appears out of nowhere and intercepts, running down the pitch dribbling the ball. I'm on him in a flash, flinging my leg out to kick the ball away from between his ankles. Then the whistle is blowing and the ref is waving a yellow card at me and shouting 'foul' and the Hulk is hopping about, holding his shin, and calling me an idiot, and Martin is calling me a fucking idiot, and Matthew is yelling 'What the hell are you doing, man?' This isn't going well, and that's an understatement. I hide my pathetic inadequacy by stopping to check that my football socks are neatly pulled over my shin pads.

Ben's words – *'you'll just make me look like an idiot'* – play over and over in my head. For once you're right, Ben. I am making you look like an idiot.

Everyone starts chaotically running around again, while I try to place myself in the clearest position to receive the ball. All around me are male voices yelling and ordering – 'get a move on' or 'shift yer arse' or 'wake up and stop bloody pratting about' – and I hope desperately that the voices are not all aimed at me, but I can't be sure. The ref keeps blowing the whistle and a bloke with a flag is running up and down the edge. I haven't a clue. Not a clue.

About twenty minutes into the game I find the ball heading in my direction again and there's a gap in the field. I can feel my heart pumping. I'm running for it. Here it is. I'm going to kick it. There is a small kid in green and white kit who I can see out of the corner of my eye, so how difficult can this be?

I run up to the ball. I'm there. I'm kicking . . . the air. My foot has only tapped the side of the ball and it is rolling slowly to the right of me. *How could I miss?* I can see someone putting his hands to his face and the coach holding his hands either side of his head as if he is going to self-combust. The Hulk and the rest of his team laugh. 'Oops,' is all I can think of to say, and I grin at Matthew but he is not grinning back.

It gets worse. My team are shouting at me from all angles. I don't know where to be, which direction to run in, and what does this *offside* rule mean? I see some of the others spitting on the field as they run around. Clearing the thick saliva from their mouths. My mouth is thick with it too. I am thirsty and my mouth is all sticky I have never *spat* before. I decide to 'round up' all the gummy saliva from my mouth into a kind of bubblegum-sized globule and go for it. I spit. It doesn't fly out like it does for the others. It hovers briefly near my chin then hangs down in slimy strings. I wipe it on my sleeve quickly. Mental note. Don't try to spit.

Half-time. I suck at a bottle of water, trying to relieve the desperate dehydration going on in my mouth. I can see the others looking at me, and I look back, letting out a huge burp in an attempt to fit in. It is a pretty awesome burp and even surprises me. I congratulate myself. *That's one even you would be proud of, Ben.* But they're still looking at me, and it isn't with any sort of admiration. 'What?' I ask them in a nervous voice that comes out strangely too high-pitched for Ben.

'I know it's been hard for you and all that –' Matthew is looking vaguely embarrassed – 'but what's with all the girl stuff?'

'Yeah,' joins in someone else, who I don't know, and don't

want to now. He starts doing this imitation of me, jumping up and down waving his hands above his head, and shrieking in a high voice. 'Ooh, Martin, Martin, pass the ball to *me*.' Someone else joins in: 'Yes, and . . . I think I've hurt my ankle and my poor knee is bleeding.'

I look around at them all. My knee *is* bleeding and I *did* hurt my ankle. I fell over and no one asked me if I was OK. I realise that football isn't netball. That I am a girl who has never played this ridiculous sport. My eyes are filling and I'm going to cry. 'Oh, stick this game where the sun doesn't shine,' I shout at them and walk off, tears rolling down my face. Even this is a mistake. All I can hear is 'ooooh' coming in a sing-songy way from most of the guys. Then I hear Matthew telling them to back off me in a *don't you know his sister's just died* kind of way.

I spend the rest of the game sitting on a bench on the edge of the football pitch near the play park. I have been replaced.

I watch the game, shivering beneath the green of my team fleece. I notice small things: the 'manly' slap on the back; the body language; friendly banter with a bit of swearing for good measure; taking the mickey out of each other; falling over and getting back up without looking for cuts and bruises or sympathy; sniffing and wiping the snot on their sleeves or hands; not looking at each other when dishing out a compliment about great football skills, but virtually shagging each other if a goal is scored.

There are young kids on the swings and climbing frame, yet most of the older boys are shouting and pushing each other. Their bikes are thrown in a heap nearby. Bottles lie in the grass where they've dropped them. I watch the way they interact because I will not be defeated! I need Ben to let me share.

I realise I'm sitting with my legs crossed, one leg with its bleeding knee hanging over the knee of the other, and I'm swinging my football-clad foot. I uncross. I sit with my legs apart. I move them further apart. I settle on somewhere in between comfortably close together and uncomfortably far apart. I lean back. Doesn't feel right. I lean forward. I lean further forward placing my elbows on my knees. Thinking about what you do every minute is hard work. Being someone you're not is hard work. But living is all-consuming. I want to live. I want to breathe. I want to be.

Two girls walk towards the play area. They're probably about twelve years old, and I notice how they stand nearer each other than the boys do. They are calmer, and look at each other when they talk. They laugh behind their hands or push their hair behind their ears. They sit on the swings and sway slowly backwards and forwards while chatting. A young boy comes sliding down the slide shouting noises that mean nothing in particular and woooo-woos his way to the climbing frame where he yells some more.

I am glad I was a girl.

At the end of the game Ben's dad takes me home and I can hardly wait to get there, to forget the nightmare that is being a girl being a boy playing football. Matthew looks at me in a manner that I can only assume is sympathy, while his dad looks at me in the same way in his rear-view mirror. I guess they believe that bereavement has twisted my poor sad heart into a pathetic version of my former self, that I am to be pitied because I am somehow damaged through losing my twin and that I don't function well without my other half.

If only they knew.

As the car comes to a halt outside our house, and with the engine running for getaway purposes Matthew's dad turns to me and reminds me that he'll be taking me and Matthew to training practice on Wednesday. I try not to look vague while my mind tumbles with the notion of whether I will even be here by then, although my heart sinks at the prospect of having to do this all over again if I am, but 'Yes, OK,' finds its way dutifully out of my mouth as I grab the holdall containing the redundant stained tracksuit and inappropriate sports gear, and I get out of the car.

I tap-tap my way up the garden path, still in Ben's football boots, to be met by Mum, who opens the front door, her eyes quizzing me while giving a thank-you wave to Matthew's dad. I drop the holdall on the floor, kick off the boots, scattering fresh mud and grass on the welcome mat, and make my way to the lounge where I slump.

'Not good?' Mum asks.

'Not good,' I mumble, making it very apparent that I've nothing more to say. She leaves me scowling at nothing, and I hear the kettle being filled and the fridge being opened and shut again. I can hardly elaborate on my awful experience and tell her that I ruined the football match for everyone, especially Ben, because, in his words, I acted like a girl. I can hardly tell her that it's because I am a girl; I *am* Lily.

I want so much to tell someone that being dead isn't easy, that being dead is so terribly lonely and it sucks, but I can't say a thing to anyone, because they'll probably try to organise psychiatric help for Ben and then he'll be labelled a nutter, a freak, that poor boy whose sister died and who went mad.

Mum wordlessly brings me a pint of cold squash, a cheese and jam sandwich and some chocolate biscuits, before sitting in the lounge with me with a cup of tea and her phone.

Shaking the awful morning off my radar, I pick up Ben's tablet, and making sure that Mum isn't looking, I check into all my own social media accounts. It feels just like I've slipped into a familiar room where something has changed but you're not sure what. I scroll through the pages of chat and pictures with a mixture of pleasure and pain. There are hundreds of RIP messages from friends on my sites from February, but the empty weeks that follow are bitter confirmation that both me and my media sites have been laid to rest.

The tiny 'ding' from the tablet alerts me to a message that flashes across the screen and I sit up with excitement. It's Beth!

'Who is this? Is that you, Ben . . . on Lily's account?'

I'm obviously showing up as online, which must be freaking her out. I really want to type back that, yes, it is me, that technology has allowed me to communicate with her through the screen, but even while my fingers hover over the letters, daring myself to open up this virtual can of worms, I know that Beth would never believe it.

'Who's on Lily's account?' Beth types again.

'It's OK, Beth, it's me, Ben,' I type.

'WTF, Ben, you nearly scared the crap out of me.'

'Sorry, I was bored,' I reply, and I *am* sorry, but more because I can't tell her the truth.

'What are you up to? Is the group doing anything?' I type, hoping that perhaps I could meet them, but as her message flashes up – 'What group? Got to go' – she disappears offline. Even though it's just a screen, I feel cut off. What does she mean . . . *what group?* Our group! The me, Beth, Nathan, Matthew and Ben group.

I take a close-up photo of Ben's nostrils and post them on his own Facebook site. His nostrils and his profile picture stare back at me from the screen. Then a sudden guilty thought occurs to me, wrapping its way round me like a tight, stinging vine. If Ben won't agree to sharing, what if I can forcibly live his life for another day . . . several days, or more? What if I just don't lift myself off the bed for a while, so he can't swap back? Admittedly I will have to *be Ben* and do everything that Ben does? Football . . . school . . . *everything*! But that's a small price to pay for having another chance. A sweet, beautiful chance.

The emotions from this morning return full blast. Guilt and excitement hand in hand with each other.

Just for a short while, Ben.

I flick the TV remote until I find some football, then use the tablet to learn about the simple rules of the game, in case my plan works and I have to go to training on Wednesday, or to another match . . . if I'm still here next week! If I'm going to get the most out of this, I need to do it well.

Mum sips her tea and discards her phone to flick through a magazine. At least as far as she is concerned, her son shovelling sandwiches into his mouth with football on the television is a slice of the ordinary.

By the end of the sandwiches, the chocolate biscuits and

juice, a bag of ready salted crisps, a sausage roll, a can of Coke and a packet of Wine Gums, I have discovered all about fouls, penalties, corners and throw-ins, not to mention the fact that boys can eat so much more than girls and that's just not fair.

I have taken note of how, if you collide and slide along the mud for several feet, which leaves your knee hanging off, you just have to get up and get on with it. Unless your team is winning and you want to waste time. Then you have to roll around holding your leg for as long as possible. You mustn't try to wipe the mud off your shorts and examine your nails. You have to spit at the ground and swear at the ref. You must act macho at all times, but if you score a goal you are allowed to climb on top of the nearest bloke, and wrap your arms and legs round him, like an oversexed frog. And finally at the very end you have to swap tops, and you get to wear the sweat of some other bloke next to your skin.

There you go, Ben! It's easy.

I'm going swimming.

Matthew had to ring the landline, complaining that I'm ignoring his messages on Ben's mobile. Mum answered, and I could hear her having a one-sided conversation, arranging something on my behalf, my confidence slowly dropping to my hobbit feet in their boys' socks. 'Yes, he's here. I'm sure he'll go. I'll get him for you.'

'Are the others going?' I ask him, relieved it's only swimming and not another sport and hoping there might be a gang of us.

'No, just me and you. I don't see them much any more. I don't even see you much any more,' he grumbles. 'Anyway, see you in thirty,' he says, before putting the receiver down.

Shutting the front door behind me, and with Ben's bag over my shoulder, I make my way to the street where I've agreed to meet Matthew. I'm pretty sure I've got it right this time, Ben's swimming shorts are on under my clothes, spare boxers and a towel in the bag, and some money.

But I'm not prepared for the changing rooms . . .

Matthew goes into the male group changing room, holding the door open for me to follow, then he basically strips off right in front of me. I feel the red hit my cheeks. 'Don't worry about today,' he says. 'They're all knobs. We're not playing that lot again for a while.' He's standing in front of me with a sympathetic expression on his face, and isn't prepared for the giggle that I reply with and the squeaky 'OK' that comes out.

He's naked. Right here in front of me. Absolutely starko! Completely unaware that he's trying to have a serious conversation with his best friend's sister with everything that he's got to offer on display.

I try to think of something sensible to say to him, but all I can think of is *I can see your willy*, and it makes me splutter before I turn away and share my supressed laugh with the wall, as I slide off my jeans, grateful that I'm already wearing Ben's swimming shorts. I can hear Matthew pulling on his own shorts and sighing loudly in a *why do I bother?* kind of a way, before he leaves the changing room, the door closing heavily behind him.

I hit the water hands first in a dive. I am in the water, under the water and breaking the surface of the water in seconds, and it feels great. My skin registers its coldness and it makes me yelp happily as I shake the water from my eyes. I lie on my back and let the pool, heavy with the scent of chlorine, hold me on its surface, arms and legs weightless, eyes facing the ceiling, eyelashes heavy with bleach-scented droplets. Rolling on to my stomach I push forward, burying my face in the water to swim; push forward, take a breath, push forward, take a breath. After a while I try with my eyes shut, feeling my body sucking in air, my heart pumping, losing myself in a rhythm, like a watery meditation. It feels so good. I am neither boy nor girl. I am neither Lily nor Ben. I am neither guilty nor innocent. I am simply life, breathing, moving, being. Push forward, take a breath, push forward, take a breath.

An elbow in the face from a passing kid stops me mid-swim, and I return. Lily in Ben's body. Guilty.

I'm angry with the kid for ruining my moment, but the two lines of mucus, like insipid slugs, sliding from his nostrils, are a strong contributing factor towards my decision to leave him alone . . . quickly!

'Coming to the top board?' Matthew swims up to me as I'm hurriedly trying to get away from the slugs, convinced that they must now be floating near me, ready to attach themselves to my hair. I look over at the three boards with their varying levels in the diving section, then raise my eyes up to the platform near the ceiling of the pool.

'I don't think so,' I reply without thinking. 'Last time I jumped off the second board I almost lost my bikini!' I immediately realise my error and how ludicrous that just sounded, and Matthew looks confused for a moment before suddenly laughing out loud.

'Yeah right, just before you went to the changing rooms and put on your big girl's blouse.'

I laugh back, but he yells, 'Come on, turd face,' and swims off, as if there isn't any doubt that I would want to fling myself off something that high.

Ben has never been scared of the top board, but I have, and I am now up there, looking down at the pool and wondering why my heart is beating quite so fast. What am I afraid of? I'm already dead!

I can still hear Ben from last night – '*You'd never be able to do what I do*' – as if he's standing right by my shoulder mocking me. The water looks really far away from here, but I reason that it's only ten metres down, and it won't be long before it is over. I try to count the seconds it takes a boy who was standing with us to leave the platform and reach the water, but the telltale slap of skin on water before the enormous splash that rises from the surface makes us both wince. Then Matthew walks to the edge and dives off, straight as an arrow and plunging deep, before breaking the surface and popping successfully up through the crystal-clear water tinted blue from the tiles below.

I hold my nose and jump.

My stomach stays on the platform, and my body drops towards the shiny reflections below, then I feel the water crackle and bubble around my head and ears as I enter it. No slap and sting of skin on water for me. I 'whooo' as my face lurches back out again into the echoey air of the building. Success! Fear, I decide, is a feeling that stops you doing something that might be fun. I have no time for fear.

After five more jumps my stomach starts to join me on the descent, until jumping in becomes something I can do without thinking much about it. It dawns on me that experiencing something each time with the intensity I felt in the beginning is almost impossible. I recall the toddler that I watched out of the window in Ben's bedroom, and realise sadly that this is how we forget each little part of our lives that in the beginning we thought so wonderful.

If I stay in Ben's body forever, will I, again, get used to all the things I have enjoyed in raptures over the last two days? Will delicious food become something I just chew on again? Will loving my mum and dad start to become a feeling I take for granted? Will the very act of living make me complacent once more? I take one more jump. Backwards. I decide that if things get too samey, change them a bit and enjoy it all over again.

'There you go, Ben Richardson. I *can* do what you can do.'

Matthew is sitting on the side of the pool when I eventually swim up to him, the adrenalin pumping round my body, making me feel very much alive, but he looks vaguely fed up. 'You OK?' I ask, shaking the water from my face and hair.

'I thought we were in here together,' he answers with a hint of sarcasm.

'We are,' I answer back, '. . . aren't we?'

'You jumped!' he says, curling his lip.

'Yeah?' I answer and ask, both at the same time.

'You've been running up the stairs and jumping off the board, over and over, like a little girl . . . and holding your nose . . . ? What's *that* about?' He lets go of his nose when he finishes his little mime, letting me know how silly I must have looked. 'We *dive!*' he says, as if he is amazed that Ben could have forgotten. I look up at him from my position in the water, and once again I realise how difficult it is to be someone else. Even if it's my own twin.

'Sorry?' I say weakly, and I know that this barely makes up for anything, as he gets up and makes for the changing rooms.

I'm back in Ben's bed, the scene of the crime, and the place where quite possibly a further and premeditated crime will be committed.

It was an odd day today. I wanted to run at it with my arms open and embrace everything I'd left behind, but in the end all I really did was live a Ben kind of day, doing Ben kind of things, even though I did them badly.

With sadness, I realise that even if I manage to squeeze another day out of Ben, it could never be a Lily kind of day. But even so, all those little things that almost go unnoticed like sunshine, or cake, or the warmth of someone's skin . . . at least I could have those things again.

I know that when I meet Ben in the night I'm not going to want to swap places again. I'm not going to want to lift myself off his bed and give up my chance.

*

I didn't have to make a decision about wrestling Ben.

There was no Ben.

My total relief at waking up for another glorious day is masked by the unsettling reason why Ben didn't appear. 'Where are you?' I ask the empty space in my room. 'I'd have felt better about winning if we had at least fought over it. Not that I was going to let you back, but you could at least have tried.'

Nothing.

'At least let me know you're OK?' I say, getting annoyed. 'Is this hide-and-seek, your idea of payback? Are you trying to put me on some massive guilt trip, Ben . . . because if you are, it's working.'

The stinging vine of guilt that grew yesterday increases its sting. What if my selfishness really has actually pushed him out of limbo and into the afterlife . . . the place where I should have gone?

My teeth bite my wobbling lips, and tears trickle out of Ben's eyes and once more I feel alone. 'I just wanted a bit longer,' I whisper.

I don't know if I am imagining it, but it feels like the softest of cool air is caressing my hand. The very fact that nothing at all is near my hand stops my tears mid-flow. 'Ben?' I whisper. 'Is that you?' I remember the time I put my arms round Fat Lucy, and sat near Ben, and kissed Beth's cheek – they felt it. There is no answer to my whispered questions, but I hope with all my heart that I'm not imagining it, that he is here, holding my hand.

'I'm sorry,' I say, but even as my words of lame apology come out I know that if Ben were to appear right now and ask for his life back, I would still hold out one more time.

Uncle Roger lets himself in through the kitchen door, familiar and territorial, and a little glowing ember of irritation reignites inside me. I'm beginning to wonder if over the last few weeks he has crossed the boundary between being very helpful and becoming a predator. Mum is beginning to turn more to him than she is to Dad, and although he is Dad's brother, I think Uncle Roger is a teeny bit jealous of his relationship with Mum. Who wouldn't be, saddled with the amoeba that is Aunty Ruth? Uncle Roger seems to now be living vicariously off the wreckage that my death had caused, not allowing Dad the chance to find his new place in our family and spending far too much time around Mum. He's like a silver-backed gorilla, muscling his way in and assuming the role of head of our household, while Dad steps down because of his misplaced guilt.

'Your front door needs painting and your car could do with a bit of a clean,' he says, cocking his head towards the front of the house where his two-door sports car is parked next to Dad's old saloon. He winks and smiles at Dad, as if this thin charade will disguise the put-down. 'Cigarette, Amelia?' He waves a package in front of my mum, while Dad mumbles some apologies for not getting around to doing either of those things.

I've heard better ways of saying hello!

'Can you just help me with something, Uncle Roger?' I ask, beckoning him away from my mum.

'Of course,' he answers with the expectant look of sureness that he often has. He follows me to the hallway where I open the front door and look out onto the street; coming up beside me, he looks out too. 'I just wondered if you could, um . . . leave.' I stand holding the door and turn to look at him. His expression is a medley of surprise, superiority and overplayed hurt feelings, and he opens his mouth to say something, but I interrupt. 'Perhaps you could go home to Aunty Ruth and leave Dad to be chief gorilla of his family.' We look at each other eye to eye, the gap between fifteen-year-old and forty-something bridged by the certainty of the knowledge we both share. And after a silent battle of eyeballs, and a slight knowing nod of my head, he eventually leaves.

I head towards the kitchen, clenching my fist and punching the air. 'Uncle Roger remembered something *very* important that he had to do,' I tell them, as I walk back in. Dad looks vaguely relieved that his brother has gone but I wonder if I can detect an ever-so-slight look of disappointment in Mum. I search my mind for something better than Uncle Roger to fill their day and mine.

'Can we go to the seaside?' I ask, and the unexpected randomness of this question causes them both to look over at me with surprise.

'It's going to be pretty chilly today,' Mum says, frowning, while Dad shrugs.

'I was going to wash the car,' he says, but we both know

170

he wasn't. Basically no one can think of a real reason why we shouldn't go.

*

We're in Dad's car on our way to the coast, and I suddenly want to be there very much. It takes a good hour and a half to get there, but the radio is on and there's an atmosphere in the car that isn't despair.

Parking next to the old sea wall, with the wind lifting our hair and catching our breath, we step out of the car and walk slowly along the seafront. A mosaic sea of greys and greens and black stretches out beside us, interrupted only by tilting boats whose bottoms are touching the sands of shallow tide. Seagulls swirl and swoop and call loudly to each other, their screams making the call of the seaside from my childhood, blown here and there by a glorious salty wind.

The seafront is weathered and still sleepy from its long hibernation. Old buildings facing the sea are peeling and cracking from the barrage of cold and salt spray, and the beach is empty apart from a man, warm under hat and scarf and overcoat, throwing a ball for a madly happy dog.

I head down some stone steps leading to the beach, take off my trainers and socks and roll up the jeans I'm wearing. Placing my feet on the sand I remember instantly this feeling of millions of coloured grains tumbling over my skin.

A memory of Ben and me from years ago, playing near this very spot, when we were about ten or eleven years old, appears like a vision in front of me. Ben convinced me to let him bury me in the sand and after helping him dig a deep hole I lay down in it as he piled the sand on top of me, pressing it down as he went. When he was finished, and I couldn't move a single muscle, he turned round to see what Mum and Dad were doing. Dad was asleep on a beach towel, his book over his face, and Mum was engrossed in her book. And then, my darling brother put a bucket over my head and sat down next to me. I remember how I stared at the inside of that bucket while Ben repeated, 'Tell me I'm better than you at everything and the bucket comes off. Tell me you'll give me next week's pocket money and I'll dig you out.'

I was scared, but I never gave in. Each time he repeated his 'offer' I answered a simple 'no' in return.

Despite being grounded for two weeks, he laughed all the way home because apparently it was hilarious when Mum had wandered over to ask where I was and all she could hear was a muffled 'I'm in the bucket, Mum.'

My parents are standing slightly apart near the promenade, focusing all their attention on me. I wonder if they too remember us playing here as children, innocent and carefree. The cold sand, still holding our childhood memories, moves slightly with each step I take towards the edge of the sea, hard stones and sharp shells digging into the soft skin on the soles of my feet, but I don't care.

The briny, exciting scent of sea becomes stronger as I move closer to the water's edge. I step over a heavy line of seaweed where the sea has scooped it along and pushed it into wave-like shapes on the beach, catching pieces of timber and modern treasure: a plastic water bottle, part of a child's dolly, a rotten flip-flop. My feet sting with the intense cold of the winter-chilled water, making me gasp as I stand with the swell and dip of the sea caressing my legs from feet to shin, feet to shin, over and over.

My gaze scans the far, watery horizon where a million wonderful things await in a world of opportunities, and a kind of melancholy stirs inside me with the need to go and explore it, wild and free and young. I wanted to travel the world so desperately all my life, and I want to travel it still.

I *need* to.

Another thought comes into my mind, and again I know it's wrong, but I also know it is *possible*. If I stay in Ben's body . . . if I hijack him, just until the exams are over, and I'm sixteen . . . I could go to Paris with Matthew and go on from there. I could beg, borrow or steal some money and see how far I get. Could I really keep hold of Ben's body until then? My mind dances with vibrant tropical colours and heady spices, of people of all colours and creeds, of mountains and lakes and cities and deserts and *splash* . . . a wave hits my legs, turning the folds on the bottom of my jeans a dark, heavy blue.

I turn my back on the rest of the world but my heart is still out there, flying high with my dreams and with them now are ribbons of hope.

My parents wait patiently while I force on socks, which stick to my damp and sandy skin, as the golden dog comes steaming past us on his way to the ball that his owner has thrown, his fur flying and his paws pounding on the sand. Trotting back he comes by us, dropping the ball from his mouth, letting Mum pat his head with her stretched-out hand. I bob down on my haunches and hold my hand out too. 'Come here, boy.' The dog lowers his head as if he is not sure what to do, wagging but whining at the same time and darting around excitedly.

'It's OK, mate,' the man calls over to me. 'He's not dangerous or anything, but he's never done *this* before.'

'Perhaps he wants to play?' Mum asks, clicking her fingers at the dog, who ignores her and continues to whine and skirt around me, occasionally throwing a bark in my direction. He knows something is not quite right, just like Charlie did when I was in Beth's bedroom.

I laugh to cover up the attention the dog is creating. 'I'll have to stop using that new sausage shower gel,' I say to the man, but even so I turn quickly and start walking towards the pier, away from the dog that knows my secret.

The pier stretches out to sea on its millipede legs, with its old-fashioned white buildings and the slumbering, mechanical bodies of fairground rides, but it is the indoor section and amusement arcades that draw us in.

The chinking and the bells and the lights and the music are addictive. I move from machine to machine having a go with the pot of coins that Dad has passed me, with the memory of Ben and me doing this when we were young, and feeling the pure adrenalin and excitement that is all about winning.

A large woman with her hair scraped back into a straggly ponytail frantically drops coin after coin down a metal shoot, hoping to push the cheap watch with the five-pound note attached to it off the edge and onto the tray. She doesn't know or care that she could buy a nicer watch for the money she's putting in.

Dad is bent over a shotgun, aiming at round targets that pop up randomly, while Mum waits for her go with a smile on her face. I don't care about winning any money; I haven't come here for that, However fake these places, however much of a rip-off, they are still exciting. They are full of beating hearts, adrenalin and, most of all, they are full of hope. And for today that hope is all mine.

Mum and I buy a bag of hot, fresh doughnuts at a nearby stand. Sugar sticks to our lips and we try to lick it off, a mixture of cinnamon and sugar and grease on our fingertips and our tongues burning from eating them before they are cool. They are *so* good. Dad is trying to work his way through an over-large hotdog, getting mustard on the corner of his mouth. Mum points at the mustard and he wipes it off, pointing at the sugar she has on her chin and cheek. She laughs a little bit, then they smile at each other, and I feel good.

Children, grandparents, mums, dads and teenagers are all around us. How many of them will even remember the details of this day by tomorrow? I will. I want to take everything in, so that it might somehow help me feel 'full'. I tell myself that it won't be so bad being dead, if I'm full of life. Like being convinced you're never going to want to eat again after stuffing yourself with a huge meal.

We decide to leave, and as we go we talk about the day and revel in its feel-good factor. If my return can prevent my family from falling through the gaps in the pavement, I have done a good thing.

Dad turns the sound up as a track they both love comes on the radio and I watch the back of their heads knowing what is about to happen. Nodding in time with each other, they begin to sing. I roll my eyeballs and pretend to groan, but my mouth is grinning, and my heart soars as we snatch at some pre-misery madness. Their horrendous singing reaches fever pitch, until they both start headbanging like teenagers from the seventies. I find myself laughing, and the car is full of precious joy. I become strong, and as the music dies I take the plunge. As it turns out, a desperately wrong move.

'Why don't you talk much about me . . . ? I mean, Lily?' I add hastily. They didn't hear my slip-up, but they sure heard my question, because the rainbow-coloured atmosphere in the car changes abruptly back to grey.

'Leave it, Ben,' orders Dad. 'Your mum finds it difficult at the moment, that's all. Give her time.'

I've torn the fragile skin that was forming over my delicately healing family, and I feel my shoulders slump at my fail, while Mum turns her head and stares out of the window and Dad's knuckles whiten against the blackness of his steering wheel. But I don't want to leave it. 'She wouldn't like it you know . . . she would want to be a part of all this. She would want to still be included in your lives . . . In fact . . .' I continue frantically 'I *know* she's right here with us . . . right now.' My insistence is too much. Dad slaps his hands down on the steering wheel, making both me and Mum jump.

'Why do people always say that?' he barks at me, his eyes catching mine in the rear-view mirror, his voice creating a crack in his fortress. 'What the *hell* do we *know*? How would anyone *know* what people would "*want*" once they've . . . they've . . . gone?' I can tell he is really angry; his words come out in staccato bursts.

The conversation stops abruptly and the ugly face of guilt

enters the car. I'm pretty sure Dad still blames himself for not keeping me safe, and Mum blames herself for saying that she wouldn't pick me up from town. My parents can no longer talk about me without releasing the sourness of their own conscience.

If I find myself back in limbo soon, I'll want them to talk about me, to make me still feel part of them, to keep me 'alive' as a happy memory, not one that provokes their own guilt. I really don't want to feel more alone than I already do. I want to watch people talk about me, and to do things because they 'know' I'd like it.

'I just *know* she would . . . *trust* me!' I add several minutes later to the back of their heads.

Twenty minutes later and the scenery is rushing past us, darkening rapidly with the winter evening. Although my eyes are looking out of the window, my mind stays fixated on the fact that they refuse to talk about me. I want them to understand that my death was not the end of me. Ben could be back tonight, or tomorrow night, and then it will all be too late.

'Umm, while we are talking about Lily . . .' I start, but I get no further.

Mum lets out a choking sob. There I go. I have succeeded in actually tipping her off that fragile place.

'Can't you just *stop*?' Dad demands, but I can't . . . and I won't.

'I *need* to tell you things,' I continue. 'I *need* you to know things . . .'

But Mum finds her voice. 'Your dad has asked you to stop, and so . . . am . . . I!' She looks over her shoulder, staring me in the eye. She means it . . . but I don't care.

'You need to stop taking flowers to King's Lane. I'm not . . . *she* isn't still in that ditch; she isn't THERE!' I rush the words out and they increase in volume and they can't understand my desperation, but Mum screams back at me.

'If I want to take BLOODY flowers to BLOODY King's Lane then I BLOODY well will because Lily was my daughter and I BLOODY miss her every single second of every single minute of every single BLOODY FUCKING DAY!'

Dad stares furiously at me through the rear-view mirror. 'Happy?' he asks, before putting his foot down on the throttle, allowing his anger to flow through the engine at breakneck speed. I look out of the window and at the scenery that is now going much faster than it was before.

As soon as we're home, I go to my own bedroom and shut the door.

I was right about how I would feel in my own room. My heart feels ripped open and exposed by everything in here, everything that once defined me.

My ashes on the dressing table taunt me . . . whispering of my stupidity as I walk around examining everything. My room still smells of me, and my perfume; my make-up is still lying on the dressing table; my collection of cuddly toys still lined up on a shelf; photos in frames; and my string of fairy-light lanterns over the headboard. I sit on my blue satin bed cover and run my hands through the black fake fur of my heart-shaped bed cushions. My pyjamas are folded neatly on my pillow. I look at the cute little grey T-shirt and shorts with little white sheep all over them and I so want to put them on and climb into my own bed.

But then I see my phone.

I plug in the charger and press my phone into life and there, on the screen, are lists of people who have sent my phone RIP texts. As I scroll through each and every one of them, tears in my eyes, I remember how yesterday Beth thought that I (Lily) had gone online, and an idea suddenly hits me.

I wipe the blur from my eyes, and, phone still in my hand, I complete my mission, until I'm filled with a delicious sense of revenge that feels so wrong and so right at the same time.

Nathan's mum woke in the morning to find that her phone had a message alert across the screen telling her someone had contacted her through her Facebook site.

'Can you take me to school, Mum?' Nathan called up the stairs before she could read it. 'I'm really late.'

His mum appeared at the top of the stairs looking crumpled and unkempt. Trying to hide her shaking hands and the blinding headache that threatened to pull her eyeballs straight out of their sockets, she croaked, 'No. You're going to have to get your bike out . . . or run, or something, Nathan. I'm not feeling too good at the moment.' Her shift didn't start for another four hours but she couldn't seem to gather herself together in the mornings any more.

'Thanks!' Nathan shouted sarcastically back, and she heard the front door slam angrily behind him, convincing herself that just because she always used to drive him when he was late, didn't mean she should carry on doing it. *He is sixteen for God's sake.*

After sitting in her dressing gown through three cups of coffee and two hours of breakfast television, she remembered the message and picked up her phone to check it. Spotting her reading glasses on the coffee table she put them on, and the words on her screen came into focus.

Lily Richardson: I know what you did.

A foul bitter taste filled her mouth and her fingers dropped the phone as if it was hot, then she picked it up quickly again and erased the message as if that would mean it had never been there.

It's a cruel trick, she thought. *It can't possibly be her. It's him; it must be.* She pictured Ben standing outside her house on Friday, saying the same thing through the gap in the door.

But . . . what if Lily Richardson really is communicating from the other side?

Nathan's mum had never been so terrified in all her life.

No sign of Ben in the night yet again, just the vague impression that he's up to something.

Ben was always up to *something*! Hiding under the bed, or leaping out of the wardrobe after I'd watched a horror film. Or the time he made a body out of his clothes and hung it from my light fitting, which made me almost scream my uvula out. His most favourite thing, however, was to send me cryptic messages that I'd have to decipher to give me a fighting chance before I was pranked. His most recent was when he texted a picture of a honey bee, which I discovered too late was a clue to the honey he'd replaced my shampoo with.

I get dressed in Ben's school uniform and study him in the mirror. 'What are you planning?' I ask him, smoothing his eyebrows into a better shape, but he simply stares quietly back at me through the mirror.

I feel physically sick at the thought of coping with a school day, not the slightest bit confident after the fiasco that was Saturday about how I'll cope around everyone who knows Ben. I'm going to have to put a restraining order on my emotions because I already want to cry at the thought of seeing Nathan and Beth. How am I going to be able to stand back and act all casual, like I'm not that bothered about seeing them? I feel like

I'll be looking at my old life through the prison bars of Ben's body. I just want to be set free and spend the day being Lily.

I give Mum a kiss good morning when I go into the kitchen, and her obvious pleasure at this makes me feel as if I've just thrown a scrap of food to a dog.

Why didn't I do this more often before?

I'm sure she's felt hollow since yesterday when the argument in the car drained the traces of her fragile happiness away. The smoky smell of her hair invades my nose and I don't like it. I blame Uncle Roger once again for denying me the scent of my mother.

Mum can see that I am jittery and she's visibly worried about me.

I lie. 'I've got a revision test today and I haven't studied for it.'

'Like that's ever bothered you before.' She smiles, trailing a hand gently over my shoulder, forgiving me for yesterday at the same time.

*

Walking to the school bus stop, my heart thumps all the way until I think I'm going to pass out with the anticipation. The bus arrives, just as I round the corner, and everyone piles on as I run to catch up with it. My space next to Beth is filled with a new girl chatting and laughing with *my best friend*, and the sight of her causes jealousy to join the resentment that's festering inside me.

That's where I should be.

One of Ben's friends raises his hand when I get on, and I feel I have no option but to go and sit with him, but I'd rather sit with the girls. Not wanting to get involved in more boy-based banter I hunt in Ben's bag for his earphones and I put them in my ears so I can pretend that I'm listening to music instead of eavesdropping on the conversation that my friends are having. They're mainly talking about a party that a girl called Milly is having soon. It's going to be the best one of the year so far apparently and everyone is discussing what they're going to wear. The new girl passes her phone around showing a photo of the dress she's going to wear and I have to physically stop myself leaning over and having a look too. I want to go to the party. I want to choose a dress. I want to be one of them again.

I only realise I'm staring at them when one of them catches my eye. 'Ben?' she calls out. 'What are you looking at?' but I turn and look casually out of the window as if I can't hear her, doing a bit of head-dancing in time to my non-existent music. As their conversation dies down, several kids start sniggering, until my curiosity gets the better of me. I turn round to see what it's all about to find them all staring at me, hiding their laughter behind their hands. '*What?*' I mouth, as if I can't hear anything, still moving my head to the not-music, until one of them leans over and holds up the jack end of the headphones, where it was never attached to the phone.

First fail of the day! Here we go again.

*

When the bus reaches school, we push our way through the doors onto the path and make our way inside as one loud, untidy bundle. There is jostling and yelling and laughing and I am right back in the middle of this living, breathing mass of kids, twisting and turning as each familiar face passes me. I feel as if I am in one of those weird dreams where you're completely naked, walking down the middle of the high street, and you're convinced that everyone can see that you are naked, but no one seems to.

. . . I am Lily, and I'm back!

But, in truth, I am still just as invisible as I was when I was in limbo, and my heart aches with the need to shake off Ben's skin and be *me*. Beth heads off to our form room with all the kids from my class, yet I can't follow because Ben is in a different form from mine. I watch her go, Ben's rucksack slung over my shoulder, his blazer and trousers and shoes an uncomfortable reminder that nothing is the same. Nothing can ever be the same.

I arrive deliberately 'just on time' to Ben's class, when the bell is already ringing so I don't have to participate in any post-weekend chat with his mates and risk exposing my true self. Matthew is already in his seat when I walk in and I hope he's forgiven Ben for the strange Saturday he spent with me, but then it hits me that I don't actually know where Ben sits, because he's in a different tutor group from me. I indulge in a few delaying tactics – examining my bag and searching my pockets for nothing in particular except time – until most of the seats are taken up.

The seat next to Matthew is empty and I slide in next to him; it's a safe bet. He looks oddly at me but moves some of his stuff off the desk to make room. The teacher is calling the register and I feel sick when she calls my name because she's peering at a seat near the back of the class.

'No Ben Richardson again?' she questions, gazing around the rest of the class. 'Do we know why he wasn't here on Friday?' I slowly put my hand up to show where I am, on the wrong side of the room. While she continues calling out names to vaguely disinterested people, I apologise to Matthew for ruining the game on Saturday and acting like a little girl at the swimming pool. 'Sorry, Matt . . . I . . . um . . . haven't been myself lately.' I grin, but the joke, of course, is lost on him.

'You *were* pretty crap,' he answers, and I wait for something else, some banter or conversation like Beth and I would have. But tumbleweed floats invisibly around us when he doesn't say anything else. He clearly has nothing much to say to Ben any more.

Have I destroyed the friendship between my brother and his absolute best friend?

I rummage in Ben's bag for his timetable, my fingers finding all sorts of revolting things that have possibly been in here forever: crisp crumbs, various coins, empty packets of sweets and something really mouldy. There is even a lump of chewed gum clinging to his ruler. His timetable is fixed, like mine, on the inside of his homework book, tattered, highlighted and no doubt memorised by him months ago. Not all of Ben's classes are the same as mine, which is concerning because it presents many more opportunities to, basically . . . fuck up! Ben is in a lower set than me for maths and English, because he is, as I used to tell him often, mathematically mediocre and verbally variant.

I make my way to his class, which is maths, already panicking again about where to sit. I know that in maths both our teachers like everyone to sit boy, girl, boy, girl, but they move us about from time to time. This means that I have to pick the right girl to sit next to. Could be awkward. I try more delaying tactics – *how many times can I tuck my shirt in and examine my bag?* – but thankfully the class is full, apart from one empty desk next to a girl with blonde hair that's been dip-dyed dark brown all along the bottom. It's Hayley or Molly or something like that. I recognise her as one of the girls who hangs around in a bitchy clique of girls, being overconfident in their perfect bitching world, tossing their hair and laughing at the assumed lowlifes around them. On cue she tosses her hair over her shoulder as I sit down and looks at me through heavily made-up eyes.

'Hi,' she says.

'Hi,' I say back, getting my books out, but I can see out of the corner of my eye that she's still looking at me, like she's expecting something.

'You haven't answered any of my texts,' she accuses. I think about Ben's phone and how it must still be in his bedroom with a million messages and missed calls by now.

'I lost my charger. I'm getting another one tonight. Sorry . . . er . . .' I glance quickly at her book where she has printed 'Holly Watts' on the front. 'Holly.'

Thinking of nothing sensible to say she merely replies with an inarticulate, 'Oh . . . awright,' punctuated by a stupid giggle. Instantly I hate her.

The teacher, Miss Wetherly, a weary-looking woman with an ineffectually quiet voice tries to call the class to attention. 'Class . . . CLASS, quieten down, we've got a lot to get done.' Some of the students even listen, but generally the noise levels in Ben's maths class are high, and it would appear that even with the exams coming up most people in this class don't have a clue what's going on.

There is an algebra formula written on the board and Miss Wetherly looks between the board and the class, waiting for hush. 'Is there anyone that can attempt the algebra on the board?' she asks eventually, looking around the room. I slide low in my seat and try to look unnoticeable. 'Ben?' she calls out.

Why me? Don't you know that I'm that naked person in a dream? That I need to see but not be seen?

'Is there any chance at all that you can surprise me today?'

I surprise her.

When I slide back in my seat, Miss Wetherly praises my apparent increase in brain function, which I know has only drawn attention to there being something different about Ben.

'Oooh, Ben, how come you know all this shit all of a sudden?' Holly looks me up and down as if Ben has changed overnight. Which, of course, he has.

'Well . . .' I answer, 'how long have you got?'

She laughs as if I have just said the funniest thing she has ever heard, which causes me to decide that we are talking *vacuous* here. I find myself looking at her for too long, or rather *down* at her for too long, because, well, there's not a *lot* going on behind that over made-up face. Her eyebrows are possibly the largest drawn-on examples I have ever seen in my life, and her eyelashes *must* be false! I peer at the line where she may have glued them, but she flutters them a little and I realise with a sinking heart she is flirting with me. I am not at all prepared for what happens next. She touches my thigh and slides her fingers towards my groin, while looking steadily into my eyes.

'Whoooah,' I call out, finding myself leaping out of my

chair, shrieking in a Lily way. She laughs again, but I can't see *anything* funny about being touched up by Holly Watts, and now the teacher is rapping the desk and yelling at me.

'Get back in your seat, Ben. What are you playing at?' I sit down, scraping the metal legs noisily across the floor, trying to make absolutely sure my body language makes it clear to Holly that I'm one hundred per cent not interested. She sulks but it doesn't last long. She appears overconfident, of herself and of my brother's personal space, and I don't like the way she seems to be taking ownership of him. I decide there and then that I want to shove her, and her chavvy eyelashes, face first into the desk.

At break, I find myself leaning against the wall outside, alone, unable to work out what to do with myself. My eyes scan the playground for my friendship group from the safety of my lookout post. I want to see them, yet I don't think I can trust myself not to be all Lilyish in front of them. There are a multitude of things that can give me away. I'll laugh too loud and I'll fling my arms around when I talk; I'm super-clumsy and far too feminine to be Ben and I'm bound to give it away.

'Do you want to come round mine later?'

A high, treacly voice makes me jump and my heart slides down to my hobbity feet in Ben's scuffed black school shoes. Holly is here, eyes large and dark, circled by jet-black kohl with a huge Latino flick, and she is standing far too close.

I take a large bite out of an apple and talk through it. 'I'm busy, Holly.'

She pouts. 'You don't look busy. You look . . . lonely.' Her boobs are encroaching on my personal space, offering me their company, almost threatening to rest themselves on my chest. I swear to God if they touch me I'm going to shriek, but the wall behind me stops me from taking a step back.

'Go away, Holly, I'm not in the mood,' I growl.

'You were the other day . . . Tomorrow then?' she asks hopefully, not taking the hint, and employing her pathetic whine that is really getting on my nerves.

'I'm busy tomorrow. And the next day, *and* the day after that,' I repeat, noticing how her lips are beginning to pout again.

'You weren't too busy last week.' She cups her hand on my groin, making me jolt back against the wall, hitting my head against the brick. 'You *were* in the *mood* then,' she adds, squeezing her hand.

'What do you think you're *doing*?' I hiss at her, shoving her backwards, but at the same time processing a grossly unappetising thought. *Oh noooo . . . I think we might have had . . . sex!* I'm surprised, horrified and . . . very jealous all at the same time.

When the hell did that happen?

I thought I'd have known if Ben was still a virgin or not, unless it happened after I died. Maybe this is why Ben didn't pull me to him as often as Mum and Dad did. He was busy finding other things to occupy his mind. Although, in this case, it's a very good thing, because seeing my own brother doing the horizontal mambo with Holly Watts would be enough to traumatise me for the rest of my eternity.

I can't exactly ask Holly if we've 'done it', and to be honest I have no idea what Ben was even doing with this girl. Having been pushed away for the second time, Holly's pouty lips contort into a curl. 'Actually you ain't all that special, Ben Richardson,' she snarls.

'And you're pretty chaverage yourself, Holly Watts,' I reply spitefully, breathing a long lungful of relief into the air as she leaves.

Ben . . . how could you . . . ? Holly Watts?

I spend the rest of the morning in Ben's favourite lesson, photography. The droning voice of Mr Meldridge humming on about lenses and stuff fades to the background, while my bland expression hopefully masks the frenzy of sexual contemplation going on in my head. I can't stop thinking about Ben having sex, and why on earth he picked *her* to do it with.

I remember sharing hot kisses with Nathan, his tongue exploring my mouth and his hand bravely wandering under my school blouse. I remember the delicious shivers that rippled across my skin, his body leaning into the hollow of my hips until I could feel how much he wanted me . . .

'Ben!' Mr Meldridge shouts across the room, snapping me out of it and making everyone stare at me. 'I don't know what you're dreaming about but it's not a zoom lens!'

'Oh, it is, sir,' I answer, smirking at his use of metaphor.

*

At lunchtime, with my heart jittering, I make my way to the canteen where Nathan will be, queuing with people who are not me. Will I find him sitting with someone else, another girl, an easy replacement for what we once were?

'Ben!' A brutal slap on the back causes me to fall forward onto my knees.

'Jeez, you idiot,' I yell angrily before I look up to realise that it's Nathan laughing at me.

'Sorry, mate, I didn't think you were going to face-plant the floor,' he says, as he reaches an arm out to pull me up.

It's him. It's my boyfriend, and I know that I am looking far too delighted to see him again. I should be inventing some boy-type reaction in return, such as lumping him with my bag, or smacking him in the head with my fist, but instead, 'Hi, Nate,' comes out of my unwillingly smiley mouth, and my hands fight not to reach for his hand.

He sticks with me, or I stick with him, as we both get trays and load them with all things that are edibly beige, before joining a small group of his friends who are already eating.

I find myself looking for the cute tangle of Nathan's eyelashes that match the slight curl of his hair, and admiring the way his perfect teeth flash white before he scoops each forkful of cheesy chips into his mouth. Now, however, I also notice how little lines and shallow dents have appeared under his eyes that weren't there before, making him look tired and strained, just calling for me to kiss his face happy again. When he catches my eye, it feels so familiar that my fingers keep forgetting to stay planted on the table, automatically stretching towards him until I snatch them back.

'Ben?' he asks.

'Mmmm?' I hum, allowing value pasta coated in some kind of indigestible glue to drop off my fork, as I indulge myself in his pure manly gorgeousness.

'What the hell are you looking at?'

This question, for the second time today, instantly yanks me out of my dream and my fork clatters on the plate. 'Oh, sorry, Nate . . . I was just wondering . . . do you ever think about, um . . . Lily?' I reach for one of his chips, watching the cheese make oily strings between the plate and my hand.

'Pretty much all the time,' he answers.

'YOU DO?' I raise my voice with such gladness that I am unable to hide the delighted pitch of it. 'Oh, do you?' I cough and try to look suitably sad.

'She would have done *this* –' he points at me picking my way through the chips on his plate – 'for a start.'

I pick up my fork again, and wave it aimlessly over my plate. 'Do you think you'll . . . um . . . go to the prom without her . . . you know . . . with anyone else?'

Nathan looks directly into my eyes in a way that convinces me he should be able to see straight inside Ben's skull to me.

'Yeah,' he says.

It comes out of his mouth as if it is the ugliest word I have ever heard, while the telltale blur of tears queue across my eyes, ready to leap like watery suicidal lemmings.

'I might ask Daisy.'

'DAISY?' I say, sounding less than casual. 'Do you *fancy* her?'

My heart is thumping and I'm so jealous I'd be surprised I wasn't turning green.

'She's nice. She's not Lily though . . . your sister is a hard act to follow. But I either go alone, or I ask someone like Daisy.'

A vision of his mum looking at me from the gap through their front door, reminds me that she is the reason behind Nathan having to ask Daisy to the prom instead of me.

'How's your mum?' I ask spitefully, studying his reaction through the flop of Ben's hair, noticing how he flinches at the mention of her. His whole demeanour changes to one of defence.

'Why do you care?' he answers.

Oh, I care, all right!

'Just wondered,' I answer, as casually I can manage. 'She . . . you know . . . wasn't well when I went to your house last week.'

'She . . . she's fine,' he snaps.

'You're not convincing me, Nate. Is there something . . . wrong with her?' Even though I know this is a delicate subject for Nathan, it is just too tempting to know how much his mother is suffering.

Any news about the driver?' he asks, trying, without being aware of the irony, to change the subject.

My mind plays out the answer to this question in loud silence.

Yes, it's your mother! She is the silent hit-and-run criminal that everyone is looking for. Your . . . mother . . . killed . . . me!

'What would you do if you found out it was someone you know?' I ask, tiptoeing my way through the implications of my question.

Nathan looks up from his almost empty plate in surprise. 'It doesn't bear thinking about,' he answers through another mouthful of food.

I play ball with my question, batting it back over the net. 'We live in a village . . . everyone knows everyone else. What if the driver *was* someone we know, or a friend . . . or a family member?'

'I'd kill them. Then make them confess to the police, then kill them again,' he replies, poking his fork in the air, stabbing at his imaginary enemy.

'But if they were *family*, would you . . . *could* you . . . ever forgive them?'

Nathan checks his phone for the time and scrapes his chair back. 'I wouldn't ever want them anywhere near me again! Study club, got to go . . . You're sick, man. Why would you waste your time thinking that shit?' He lifts up his tray, dumps it in the rack and turns away from me.

'Because I died because of that shit!' I answer silently.

*

How do I fit into a life that has moved on without me?

I don't know how to spend the rest of my lunch break, and I'm not even sure where Ben fits into the picture any more. He would normally be doing something sporty or be hanging out with the group, but I can't find anyone to hang out with, and I'm not convinced I should do any more of Ben's sport after Saturday. Beth is spending her lunch break in the art room catching up on her coursework and Matthew is nowhere to be seen.

I wander aimlessly around the school grounds, trying to pretend that I'm simply enjoying being alive and ignoring the fact that in reality I'm feeling awkward and every bit the spare part. Joe, a nasty-looking weasel of a boy, joins me as I pass the edge of the school grounds by the fields.

'Fag?' he asks, as casually as someone who might do this every lunchtime. I look at it for a few seconds, surprised by this random offering, but I try not to show it. I remember how Ben took Uncle Roger's cigarette the night after they found me, and how I begged him not to do it. It is yet another thing I've never done, so I take the cigarette and light it, inhaling gingerly, aware of my total hypocrisy. It catches embarrassingly uncomfortably in my throat, which makes me cough and my eyes water.

Another boy called Graham, all blubber and aggression with a thick neck and a line of black fluff on his lip, joins us, lighting up from his own packet. I'm not sure what's going on, but I'm getting the feeling that I'm being flanked by the main villains in a budget movie. I'm beginning to think Ben has joined some kind of underworld club without me knowing about it.

Joe lets the smoke drift slowly out of his nostrils as if he thinks it makes him look cool but it coils back across his face, causing his small grey eyes to squint through the haze. 'Didn't see you in the park this weekend.' He breathes the last of his fumy breath out and immediately takes another loud drag. Hanging about in the park is the latest craze: drinking beer, smoking cigarettes and seeing if you can stay out most, or possibly all, of the night. Nathan, Beth and I were never interested in this, too cold for a start, and I had been pretty sure Ben wasn't into it either. I wonder if that's what Dad meant on Saturday morning when he made me go to football: 'I know you've been bunking off football lately for some reason, and God knows where you go,' he had said.

'Holly was in the park. She's got a firm grip . . . if you get my meaning,' Joe adds. I get his meaning. Graham's thick shapeless lips draw on his cigarette, followed by a disgusting sucking noise that he makes through his teeth before he laughs indulgently at Joe's sophisticated wit.

'You're welcome to her. Dogs like to sniff around arseholes,' I sneer, preferring the quality of my own humour.

How can I not know this part of Ben's life? I thought his life revolved around decent friends like Matthew. I thought he still loved football and sport . . . not *this*.

Why didn't I know what you were becoming?

Ben has apparently been trying to find a new kind of life. Maybe enjoying all the normal stuff made him feel bad. Maybe the move to an ugly life rather than a sad one was easier, and that's why he only pulled me to him when he was at home.

Oh, Ben! This was no life for you either.

You really need me to manage your affairs. You're obviously incapable!

I flick the hardly touched cigarette at Ben's new friends and walk away.

'Oi, knobhead, we haven't finished our discussion,' Joe shouts, but just at that moment a large group of kids come running round the back of the school building, like wild things tasting sweet freedom, their native call drowning out any more of Joe's interesting description of me as I make my escape.

Nothing they could possibly want to discuss with Ben would interest me.

'How is loneliness shown and what is the writer trying to say about it?'

Mr Venables sits in front of us, tapping his copy of *Of Mice and Men* on his corduroy knees. 'It's highly likely to come up in some form or other in the exams and we need to nail it.' We sit around him in a semicircle with our heavy scuffed bags dumped on the floor by our feet, as he tries to drum up enough enthusiasm for something resembling a debate.

Occasionally someone says something of mild interest that Mr Venables pounces on, trying valiantly to shake it into a viable viewpoint and I try . . . I really try . . . but I just can't keep my mouth shut.

I *have* experienced loneliness. In fact, I reckon I could describe it in a far more interesting way than John bloody Steinbeck has. And, what's more, I'm still lonely, even though I'm alive again and surrounded by people I know. The monosyllabic attempts by the others to describe loneliness is so inadequate that I'm consumed by a need to put them straight, and it inflates inside me, building up pressure until finally it courses its way up my neck, into my mouth, and out in a fountain of vomited personal opinions. A couple of kids in the class start laughing every time I talk because once was OK, twice was a surprise, but having something to say on just about everything is, well, not cool, I guess.

'Ben, this is very . . . *participative* of you,' our English teacher announces, looking almost as shocked as everyone else, then he does that awful thing that teachers do when they use you as a wonderful example of intellectual brilliance in front of all the kids around you.

'Ben Richardson has obviously read this book in great depth,' he says, waving the book at everyone else and nodding appreciatively at me.

'Like fuck he has,' I say silently, placing my hand over the sticky mould stain across the cover, contaminated from whatever that dead thing is in his bag. I catch the tittering looks passed around like a hot brick and my enthusiasm rapidly dwindles, as I realise sadly that not only have I been entirely out of character for Ben, somehow in death I have grown up. My perspective is no longer through the eyes of the teenage girl I used to be, and I can't work out whether it's sad or uplifting. So this must be what old people mean when they say youth is wasted on the young.

I can see Matthew looking at me with one eyebrow raised and I raise an eyebrow back.

'What?' I mouth, frowning my question at him.

'This,' he answers, circling his hand in front of me, as if indicating that the whole of me is very 'wrong'. I realise that in addition to my sudden super-in-depth knowledge of the book I am, again, sitting with my legs crossed swinging my foot, I have tucked Ben's sweeping hair behind my ears and I'm twiddling my pen. My doodle of a flower on the back of Ben's book doesn't help.

I quickly resume a boy-like pose, inking the flower skilfully into an anime cartoon and wait for the red in my cheeks to sink back to where it came from.

*

After school I catch up with Matthew in the place where he chains up his bike. I need to understand where Ben is with his life. I need to stop being selfish to make sure he has a life to come back to, whenever I can bring myself to actually do that. 'Are we still friends?' I ask, putting my hand on his shoulder.

Again he looks at me in an odd way before slowly looking down at my hand. 'Off the cloth!' he orders, his eyebrows almost blending into his hairline.

I snatch my hand away. Girls are so much more tactile than boys. I *must* remember to stop touching everybody!

'If I was *gay* . . .' I joke, 'I wouldn't make *you* my bitch.' I laugh, but Matthew tips his head indicating something behind me.

'No, your new mates would be making you *their* bitch.' He says. I turn to look where his eyes are focused and I see Joe and Graham waiting by the gates, and they're looking my way. 'I need to ditch those lowlifes,' I sigh, looking back at Matthew, but he's already on his bike and slaloming his way between hurrying students.

When I get to the gates, the 'lowlifes' flank me on either side, and usher me up against a side wall, shielding us from the main school and the patrolling teachers, unnoticed by oblivious kids getting the hell out of school. I begin to feel very uneasy and out of my depth as Joe leans in towards my face, his rotten breath exhaling towards my nose.

'I *said*, we haven't finished our discussion.'

'No time.' I try to grin confidently at them, but actually I'm pretty sure I'm offering a strange show of teeth instead. 'Got a bus to catch,' I add quickly, taking a step sideward to dodge their human barricade, but they move their human barricade a step sideward too.

Graham holds his hand out expectantly for money for a small bag of weed that is partially hidden in his other hand. 'That's five pounds, Richardson.'

To my disappointment it becomes obvious to me that this 'meeting' had been pre-arranged and Ben was obviously a willing participant.

I work hard to keep my expression free of the nerves and shock that are dancing behind it but I notice that Joe is not the one trying to hand over money and drugs; he's looking away as if he's not involved, getting Graham to do his dirty work.

'Sorry. I don't want it any more. I'm on a health kick!' I take a deep breath and get ready to leave them to it.

'I don't think so,' Graham mutters. 'This is a regular agreement from now on. You *said* . . . We've made *arrangements* now.'

'That . . .' I tell them loudly, 'is called dealing.' They don't like my words or their volume, causing Graham to glance abruptly at Joe, whose head spins quickly round to see if anyone could have heard me.

'Just shut up and buy it,' hisses Joe.

But I couldn't even if I wanted to.

I show them the eighteen pence I have left over from buying sweets on Friday, and realise now why Ben had exactly five pounds in his pockets that day. 'You seem a little angry,' I say patronisingly and far more bravely than I actually feel. I hold the coins in my hand out towards them. 'Unless you're happy with eighteen pence, you're out of luck.'

He slaps my hand, making the coins fling across the pavement. 'You owe me, Richardson . . . I *will* get my money off you, or you'll regret it.'

I delve into my pockets again, as if I'm searching in them, and eventually hold out an empty hand towards them. 'Guess what? I already gave all my fucks away. I don't have any more to give . . . sorry.' I pull a sad face.

But they don't find me funny.

Trying hard not to cry, as I land on the ground, the smell of concrete and dirt just inches from my nose, I decide that Ben needs to get his real friends back, and I need to find a way to make that happen . . . soon! This is not the brother that I've known my whole life. Graham's shoe in my back as I manoeuvre myself to stand up gets me right in the kidneys, and it is the worst pain I have ever experienced. I fall forward again onto my knees and wait for the next kick while trying to catch my breath. When it doesn't come, I get up painfully to see them both heading off down the road, while the handful of disappointed kids, who'd stopped to see if the fight was going to turn into anything worth hanging around for, turn away too.

Despite everything that has just gone on, I'm glad that it happened to me. I think that Ben would have made sure he had the money for the weed. I think that Ben would have smoked it and ordered the next bag. I know that my lovely sporty brother would have been caught in their vile web if I hadn't been here to save him.

I am doing a good thing.

I catch sight of Beth walking out of the gates with the last of the stragglers and I hurry like a demented injured crab to catch up with her, my arms desperate to link with hers, and do something normal like ask her if she wants to come to my house after school.

'Ben,' she says by way of hello.

'Beth,' I answer.

'Are you OK?' we ask each other at exactly the same time.

'Me first,' Beth says, her eyes looking down at my hunched body. 'You don't look OK. You look like you've been in a fight or something.'

'Oh, it's nothing,' I say, trying to laugh it off, which only causes me to wince with pain. 'Bumped into a couple of arse wipes.' As Ben would say.

'Anyway, how are you doing, Beth . . . you know . . . without Lily?'

She looks at me, as if trying to work out the best answer. It shouldn't be difficult; she should be missing me loads and loads, and her life should hardly be worth living without me in it.

'Shit,' she says finally. 'It's pretty shit actually . . . you know with the group and everything.'

'What about the group?' I ask, not having a clue what she's talking about. Our group, me, Beth, Nathan, Matthew and Ben, did most things together. We were tight.

'There is no group any more. You seem to have *other* things to do; Matthew's pretty pissed at you because you've changed; Nathan is having some kind of breakdown; and I'm –'

A loud horn sounds from the bus, making us look round to see the driver mouthing at us to hurry. Beth leaps onto the bus and makes her way to a seat and I try to move quickly to keep up with her in the hope we can sit together, but it's easier said than done with bruised kidneys and a bladder so full it might burst right here on the pavement in front of the whole school. I couldn't face going to the boys' toilets during the day, and now I find myself huddled in the only vacant seat left, nowhere near my best friend, and nursing my aching body.

Changing out of his school uniform and dropping it on the floor of his bedroom, Matthew looked at a team photo of his football club smiling out from a frame on his wall, next to various sporting trophies.

He stared at himself with Ben, who was standing next to him, aware that somewhere in the room were other photos from other years, probably from ever since they'd met in year seven. Matthew rolled the gum he was chewing into a little ball inside his mouth, then squashed it on Ben's face.

What the fuck was happening to his mate?

He had begged, borrowed and stolen every penny he could lay his hands on to buy all the sunflowers to put on his brother's car; he had texted, Facebooked, Instagrammed, messaged for weeks, even phoned Ben on his house phone when he wouldn't answer his mobile, to lure him back to his normal self. But, man, what was going on?

It was as if Ben had morphed into a weird combination of a lowlife scumbag and an overnight gay!

His mother had said Ben had gone off the rails for a bit, that he'd come back round eventually, time is a healer and all that bollocks, but what did she know? He'd waited quite a long time for Ben to get back on the rails but he not only had gone off them but he seemed to have gone down a very dodgy track indeed. He'd tried to defend Ben at football and he'd offered the hand of friendship one last time by inviting him swimming, but his mate had changed and he was majorly getting on his nerves now. All he could see was there was some serious shit going on with the twin thing, like the Ben he knew had died the same day his sister had, or, even worse, like his sister had never quite left!

What exactly was all that touching about?

He wasn't ready to give up on his best mate quite yet, but it felt like his best mate had given up on him.

Mum lights a cigarette and stands by the back door, the increasing light of new spring evenings triumphing over the winter dark. A mean chill circles its way through the open door and into the kitchen, making me shiver.

'Do you spend *all day* thinking about . . . Lily?' I ask outright, thinking about Ben trying to find his own way down a new and dodgy path.

'Have you forgotten yesterday's little *head to head*?' she replies, indicating that I'd better leave the subject alone.

'Hardly,' I reply. 'Only, you *have* got another child, Mum.'

My words resound around the kitchen for a long while after I've spoken them and as she turns to look at me, as if seeing Ben for the first time, her expression says it all. This is why I didn't know what my friends were doing when I was in limbo; my mother couldn't let me go . . . she still can't.

'She isn't in these things, Mum,' I say, picking up her packet of cigarettes and waving them at her. 'I'm worried about you killing yourself, lungs first.' She looks taken aback, her hand midway between mouth and ashtray. 'It looks . . . ugly . . . and you don't smell like my mum any more. And it won't help anything and I *hate* it.'

Her defence drops and she sighs heavily. 'I used to smoke . . .

once. But I gave it up when I got pregnant with you both and I didn't start again when you were born. I wanted you both to be healthy . . . to set a good example.'

'Then why have you started again?'

'Lily . . . I . . . she . . . I don't know. I *need* it.'

'I'm still here, Mum,' I say, and my voice cracks a little with my double meaning. She looks at me for a long time, and sees only Ben, yet, squashing the butt into a flowerpot, she suddenly rushes over to me.

'I'm so sorry, Ben. I've been forgetting you. I'll try . . . no . . . I will stop. For you . . . I will.' And she presses the palms of her hands against my cheeks before hugging me long after I give up counting past twenty.

I'm doing a good thing.

It's so cold today.

I pull the hood of Ben's coat over my head, shivering at the unexpected drop in temperature, while huge plumes of condensation cloud out of my mouth and nose as I walk to the school bus stop. The edges of my nostrils are freezing and even a few snow flurries blow past me before disappearing into the damp pavement. I raise my shoulders as if tucking my neck into my body and dig my hands deep into my pockets, feeling the bruise on my back pull at me as I do so.

This time, I manage to find a seat on the bus near where I would normally have sat. Obviously *my* seat is taken by the new girl who is still sitting next to Beth, but at least I'm prepared for it this time, and I'm glad Beth doesn't seem that interested her. If I was sitting with her, as Lily, I know we would be laughing at something by now. We used to laugh all the time. But at least being on the bus and sitting near Beth is like a little bit of normal compared to being in limbo.

The timetable this morning is almost manageable with most of Ben's lessons the same as my own, but there is PE this afternoon. This means shivering outside for the best part of an hour while endeavouring to maintain Ben's sports prowess better than I did at football. I groan inwardly at the thought of the changing room.

Going into the form room for registration is easy this time, because I now know where to sit. Matthew looks across at me briefly, and I raise my hand in a greeting, just as it crosses my mind that he might be wondering why I sat next to him yesterday and why now I've moved back. I can't seem to win but I spend registration staring at the back of his head and trying to telepathically tell him not to give up on Ben just yet. The group mustn't fall apart.

I don't even hear my name called on the register until the third attempt apparently, when a ball of screwed-up paper hits me on the side of the head, and the teacher is calling in an exasperated way: 'Richardson . . . ?'

*

Beth is already in science when I get there, sitting alone at the back of the lab instead of in her normal seat, so I join her.

White-coated, and looking part-rat, part-human, Mr Adams the science teacher starts scrawling on the board, telling everybody yet again in his flat northern tones how elements make chemical compounds and something about ions and electrons . . . I can see him and hear him but right now I'm not interested in any of this stuff. All I can think of is why Beth was sitting on her own.

We both used to sit with the girls in the middle, writing notes to each other on the edges of our books or texting under the table, anything to relieve the monotony of the periodic table. But Beth is on the edge of it all now, sitting by the window, looking glorious with the curls of her hair all loose and lit up like a halo by the sunlight forcing its way through the heavy clouds.

'Fancy a quick fuck?' Joe calls to her, just as Mr Adams disappears into the storage room. Beth goes pink and, giving him the middle finger, she tosses her hair and looks away. But her cold shoulder makes Joe sneer. 'I wouldn't be seen dead with you anyway.' Then turning to his mates and looking directly at me, he adds, 'But Lily would.' He laughs loudly at his own joke and I go mad. Suddenly, and without notice even to myself, I push my stool back and stand over him, using Ben's height to intimidate him, my anger causing me to forget the beating I took yesterday.

'Idiot.' I hold my clenched fist in the air.

'Oooh . . . *scary*,' he sings. 'Want a piece of her too? Bored with shagging Holly?' Most of the class are sniggering now, and Joe's horrible face is leering at me with his lopsided smile, and I'm not sure what to do next. I really want to punch him in the face but it's not something I've ever had to do before. I take a swing and . . . he laughs as he ducks and I end up hitting him in the upper arm. It's pathetic.

Joe leans back on his stool in mock terror. 'My gran could have knitted a cardigan in the time it took your fist to reach me . . . That was a right girl's punch.'

He looks over his shoulder to make sure he's getting the appreciation of the entire classroom audience, while swinging on his chair.

Nothing to lose.

Kicking his stool, it tips up easily and the outcome is more spectacular than I was hoping for. Result! He falls backwards, his chair scraping against the floor, his back hitting the desk behind, and his coccyx smashing against the leg of the chair.

The look on his face as he goes over, and the subsequent pain that he's in, is satisfyingly priceless. The whole class laughs again, this time at Joe. 'That's for Beth –' I smile sweetly at him – 'and that –' I kick him between the legs, and watch him groan with pain – 'is for Lily.'

'Ooh . . . man,' says Graham. 'He got you *right* in the sprouts!' Then he cackles with laughter as if I've just made his day. Mr Adams pushes his way between us and his pure anger at me makes his eyes glitter.

'Richardson! How would you like it if I banged *you* against the desk?'

'Thanks, Mr Adams, but you're not my type,' I answer back, and the class breaks out into raucous laughing and wolf-whistling at Mr Adams's expense.

'Show's over!' Mr Adams shouts at us all, and a fat vein on the side of his neck pulsates with fury. He sends a girl out to get the Year Head, while Joe gets up off the floor, trying not to let anyone see him holding his butt in agony.

As I pick up my bag to follow the Year Head out of the classroom, Beth smiles at me and it lights up her face. 'Still in the group,' I mouth at her.

'That sort of behaviour isn't acceptable, Richardson, even if it is in the name of chivalry,' the Year Head says, as he marches me down the corridor, for a morning in isolation outside the Head's office, but I think I can detect the tiniest note of appreciation in his voice. Most of the teachers have had run-ins with Joe; I probably did them a favour.

The morning in isolation is fantastic and not the punishment it's designed to be. It's such a relief not to have to remember every single second how to act like Ben, even if I'm not making too much of a bad job of it today. I even get some study notes completed for him . . . or me – if I'm going to stay.

At lunchtime, I hunt for Matthew, while carefully avoiding Joe and Graham, and eventually track him down playing badminton in the sports hall. The sports teacher greets me as I walk in. 'How are you doing, Ben? Joining in?'

I realise that Ben must have already signed up to this club before I took over his body. I groan inwardly. I can't play badminton.

'I can't play today,' I say and point at my foot, limping slightly. Matthew gives me a hint of a smile as if there may be hope for their friendship yet because I've at least turned up. I need to save Ben's reputation *and* get the group back together.

He smirks. 'I thought you'd gone to the dark side.'

'Oh –' I wave my hand away – 'Joe and Graham are *so* last season.' Hardly a macho expression that I can't take back, and now I can hear myself doing a silly giggle to cover up for it.

I pretend to watch them play for a while, delighted to notice that Nathan is playing too. I can still look, even if I can't touch.

Halfway through his game, he makes his way over to the bench where I'm sitting, picks up his drink bottle, wipes the sweat away from his forehead and takes several deep gulps. As he places the bottle back down, a flop of curls falls over his face that he flicks back before looking down at me with those frothy blue eyes.

'All right, Ben?' he asks, looking down at me. 'You not playing?'

'Foot,' I answer, pointing at both feet, unable to actually

remember which foot I had limped on when I came in and trying at the same time not to smile flirtatiously at him.

He still looks strained and sad, but to me he is beautiful. He's a bigger build than most of the other boys, stronger and absolutely gorgeous, and I watch him with full admiration as he straightens his back, spins his badminton racquet in his hand and places the bottle back on the bench. I can smell an intoxicating mixture of his sweat and deodorant and I like it. I let my eyes take him all in, and I can't stop a powerful desire creeping up inside me, to be a normal girl going out with a boy like him again . . . being in love, perhaps even having sex one day. I smile wistfully, running my fingers along my hair through habit, as he calls 'Later' from his beautiful lips, before running back onto the court.

Something brushes against me and I look down to see what it is. Oh My GOD. I can hardly breathe. My heart is rushing and I can feel the redness of acute embarrassment flooding up my chest to my throat and across my face. Something is going on . . . down below, stirring and moving and feeling very odd. I am having . . . an erection . . . I think I am going to die at the total, absolute, one hundred per cent awfulness of this moment in time and I leave the gym as quickly as my legs will take me.

This is wrong. On many, many levels, this is wrong.

*

At the end of the day, exhausted from trying to hide from Joe and Graham and still flushing repeatedly at my awful experience in the gym, I let myself into an empty house, take off my coat and make a mug of tea before making my way upstairs. I just about coped with PE this afternoon, but I'm not convinced I did Ben any favours again. Basically the whole day was fraught with another catalogue of disasters from start to finish. My head, my body and my heart are all tired . . . so tired.

I just want to live.

I just want to *be*.

I run the taps in the bath and watch the steam rise upwards from the tub, beckoning me into the water and pouring a generous amount of emerald green bath foam into the flow of water. I study the bubbles doubling and mounting and spreading their shiny little bodies across the surface. When I lower myself in, breathing deeply the mixture of herbal essence and steam, the heat of the water does nothing to relax the argument going on in my head.

What am I doing to Ben? What am I doing to *me*?

I think about the moment Nathan's mother killed me, and how this whole awful situation would never have happened if she hadn't had that wine, or driven down King's Lane. The regret that that moment ever happened hurts so much I can hardly bear it. She might be having a hard time, and Nathan might be a bit stressed over it, but frankly they have got the rest of their lives to get over it, while I'm hitch-hiking my brother's body just so that I can spend a few more precious moments on the planet.

'I *hate* you!' I scream at the top of my lungs to Nathan's mum. 'I *fucking* hate you!'

I grab my phone and send another message to her on her Facebook account. 'I'm still watching you . . .'

She deserves it, because she *should* suffer. I spend a moment revelling at the thought of her reading my messages and a cruel satisfaction comes over me. I take a sip of the warm sweet tea, then swap my phone for Ben's.

'I don't know where you are, and I don't know what you're doing, Ben Richardson,' I say out loud, hoping he can hear me having a go at him, 'but if I'm still here tomorrow then I need to know what you've been up to! Something's definitely going on with you, the group . . . Joe and Graham . . . and OMG *Holly Watts*, really?'

I read all the messages on Ben's phone.

Several are from Holly, and despite the warm water I shiver at the thought of her sending them, not to mention feel a little bit sick.

Thursday: Holly – *Wanna do 'that' again baby?*

Friday: Holly – *Let's sext*

Friday evening: Holly – *Going to the park tomorrow?*

There's an emoji with a winking face and I think I'm actually going to have to vomit, but her last text after I told her she was chaverage makes me feel instantly revived.

Monday: Holly – *You're dumped!*

'Good, you're revolting,' I say to the message on the screen, as I text back on behalf of Ben. Ben – *Too slow. I'd dumped you by Friday*

Several messages are from Matthew asking if he could come round to the house and other mundane stuff about football and badminton, plus his last-ditch attempt to invite Ben swimming on Saturday, before they completely peter out to nothing when Ben stopped replying.

I find myself tutting loudly at Ben and grasping at the notion that I could quite possibly make a much better go of his life at the moment than he is. I take another sip of my sweet, satisfying tea.

Then I see one from Joe.

Thursday: Joe – *Hey you good?*

Thursday: Ben – *Yeah good 2moro lunchtime.* As I was in Ben's body by that particular lunchtime and wasn't at school, Joe and Ben hadn't made their transaction.

'Do you think Mum and Dad would be proud of you getting involved with drugs, Ben?' I ask him out loud again, waiting for an answer that I know he can't give. 'Do you think they need that in their lives right now?'

I'm cross with him for doing this to himself and to Mum and Dad, and clearly the fact that I found my way into Ben's body was a gift waiting to happen even if I now have a bruise on my back in the shape of some size elevens.

I'm doing a good thing.

I put his phone on the toilet seat then sink a little lower in the bath to allow the water to warm my shoulders, but my knees poke out into the cool air. As Ben is taller than I was, it is difficult to fit all of me in the bath and I wish he would stop reminding me that I am not in my own Lily body any more. If I had had a twin sister rather than a twin brother, this would have been so much easier. I twist the hot water tap with my toes, allowing more hot water to mingle with the now slightly tepid water, and it warms the bath again. The dying bubbles spring to life and push their way back towards my chest and I hear them snapping and popping around me.

People are surprising me. Their lives are taking ugly turns and my death is responsible. Everything that's happened since then has become so difficult, as if I'm the missing piece in a large and complicated puzzle, and a puzzle with a missing piece is ruined.

A door bangs downstairs and Mum calls out, 'I'm home, Ben!'

'I'm in the bathroom,' I shout back quickly, so that she isn't worried about me, like she was on Friday, and stepping out of the bath I dry myself, feeling the roughness of the cotton towel massaging my squeaky clean skin. I decide that I will never get complacent again about the wonderful sensation of touch, but at that moment I catch sight of Ben's reflection through the steam in the shaving mirror and it spooks me out. For a moment I thought it was actually him. Peering at me from limbo, judging me for casting him aside. Even then I have to take a second glance to make sure it isn't actually him. 'Are you angry?' I ask him, but worryingly, even though it is only a reflection, I am left with the awful realisation that for the first time in my life I have absolutely no idea what Ben thinks.

With damp hair, a loose T-shirt and some shapeless boys' track pants on, I grab some juice from the fridge and chat to Mum, telling her all about my day . . . well, the bits that I want her to hear. If she is surprised Ben is willingly starting a cosy after-school conversation, more like Lily might have done, she doesn't show it. I tell her about school and what Joe said to Beth and how I pushed him off his seat. The school will ring her anyway about my behaviour, so I might as well give my side of the story first.

But she doesn't find any of it funny. 'Well done, Ben, that's at least four behavioural issues in the last few weeks. What are you playing at?' Then as if any annoyance she may have had is draining completely away she sighs. 'I miss Beth . . . I miss her coming round.' Her eyes lower and focus somewhere unremarkable on the carpet, and I realise that Beth is one more person in Mum's life who has left.

That missing piece really does ruin the overall picture of the puzzle. That's for sure.

It's a white world.

It is almost as if snow has come quietly in the night, just for my pleasure and it brings with it a kind of child-like excitement.

Still no Ben in the night, but my concern for him today will have to wait. I *need* to get outside and touch that snow. I get ready for school quickly and keep looking out of the window to make sure it's still there. All the muddy colours of the street have left and been replaced by millions of icy crystals reflecting light and its brightness makes me feel happy.

Mum and Dad are in the kitchen when I dive in there to grab some breakfast. Dad takes the final sips of his coffee and then walks over to the sink, putting his cup in the bowl before stepping towards Mum, his tall strong body stooping a little to kiss her goodbye. As Mum goes up on her toes to kiss him back, Dad gives her a hug, swooping her feet right off the ground. She pretends to get annoyed, her hands trying to push him away but he is too strong, her legs are dangling and it looks funny.

This is what he used to do before I died. I smile at them both, as I push my way past to the toaster, mumbling 'Get a room' as I reach for some bread.

I've decided to walk the three miles to school, listening to the snow squeak beneath my feet, the icy flakes softly landing on my cold face . . . packing my virtual suitcase with memories of this unseasonably Christmassy world. It's not very thick, and it won't last, but it's here now and thanks to Ben I am really going to enjoy it.

Running my hand along a wall, I scoop up a handful of cold, which sparkles in my palm before slowly dissolving, leaving my skin wet and red, and my fingers numb. Then I scoop another handful and eat some, licking at its frosty crystals with the tip of my tongue, tasting nothing but its coldness, while admiring how each leaf and little twig can carry the weight of such a thick burden of snow.

I examine a large spider's web hanging between a high iron gate and a bush. Each thread is thick with tiny shards of white ice; each delicate line is joined to each other to look like little white ladders. It is so strong, so beautiful and so clever. I'm aware that I could tear down the spider's world in an instant, that if I break it, he will eat the web and rebuild it, maybe not exactly the same but just as beautiful.

Nathan's mum tore down my world, breaking the web that belonged to my family and friends, and we haven't managed to rebuild it like the spider can. I want to do the same to her in return. Why should she carry on with life without blame, while I am trapped outside everything, while my parents try desperately to cling to a fragile normality, and my brother messes his life up, and my friendship group falls apart? But what about Nathan if she ever gets to pay penance? Would Nathan heal once his family was broken or would he be like Ben? Finding a new but ugly kind of life?

Is there a difference for our families between accidently dying and accidently killing?

Nathan's mum was, at that moment, driving to the supermarket.

In the boot of her car in a bag were six empty bottles of wine. She was telling herself that she was OK to drive because she had stopped drinking by ten. She would, by now, be under the limit, she was sure, and her shift at the old people's home started at ten in the morning, giving her just enough time to visit the bottle bank and pop into the supermarket. If the Merlot was still on offer, she could get six bottles for the price of four. She would put four in the wine rack and keep two in the garage. She'd run out of wine last night and that wouldn't do!

She had received another message yesterday evening, simply saying '*I'm watching you.*' As a result she'd instantly disabled her Facebook account, switched her phone off and buried it in the back of a drawer.

Yesterday she finally had the courage to replace the smashed terracotta pot on King's Lane. Another large pot in which she planted some sturdy blubs, which were just beginning to push through. And yet, later that same day she got another text. The fear that Lily or her brother or *someone* knew her secret and could really be watching her, had been too much. After consuming all the wine left in the house, she had resorted to the spirits until she'd had to crawl up the stairs on her hands and knees.

Before she got out of the car she turned the collar of her coat up and pulled a brimmed hat low over her brow in the hope that no one would recognise her. *Who was watching her?*

As she returned to her car with an embarrassingly loudly clinking shopping bag, the man in the next car along got out, and she instantly recognised the swollen belly and the dirty overalls of the guy who often washed her car.

'Need another wash, love?' He pointed to her car. 'It's a beauty, this one.' And his head bobbed up and down, causing his glasses to slide down his nose before he pushed them back up, while he ran his fat, dirty hand over the front passenger-side wing of her car.

'Maybe, Fred –' she forced a smile – 'when it's a bit dirtier.'

'Like the last time you came in to have it washed,' he said. 'That was a day that was. The police and everyone was there that day . . . I've been told to look out for anything suspicious . . . to do with that little dead girl . . . you know, the one that was killed down King's Lane. Bloody hit-and-run. I've told the police about every car that could have done it . . . but . . .'

Fred's constant stream of words only faded out when he realised that the lady had closed the door of her beautiful blue Morris Minor and was reversing at speed out of the parking bay.

He squinted through his glasses as she left. 'Nice car,' he called, as he waved goodbye.

I take a photo of the spider's web with Ben's phone, so fragile, so strong, so simple, so vital, and continue on my way to school.

My hood is up again and my hands are shoved deep into my pockets but I wish for a while that I could have put on my own grey hat with its overlarge pompom, and my really big dusky pink woolly scarf.

Stop wishing, Lily. Just enjoy.

The day may be unremarkable for many people, but for me it's a wonder world of enjoyment. I stop and buy sweets on the way to school again: different ones, fruity and chewy. I put them in my mouth, one after the other, barely finishing before unwrapping the next, when Matthew skids beside me on his bike, slowing to meet my walking pace.

'Coming to basketball at lunch . . . or joining the Kray twins?' He asks.

I think of Joe and Graham and shudder. 'I told you, I'm done with them.' I rotate my arm stiffly. 'And I'd love to go to basketball, but I've hurt my elbow.'

When I see Matthew's frown, I realise too late that yesterday I said it was my foot that hurt.

'You'll be drawing your pension next,' he scoffs, and cycles off.

Of course, vermin like Joe and Graham are not always easy

to get rid of.

I think about this fact when my nose gets a snowball smacked into it, which has been packed so hard it has turned to ice. I was too busy enjoying my morning; I forgot to look out for them. I also think about it at lunchtime on my way to the sports hall to watch the basketball, when they find me again, and attempt to push my head down the toilet. And I think about it after lunch while recovering from being shoved face first into the lockers. No one saw, and it can't be proved, but my face hurts all the same. And I really think about it when they corner me round the side of one of the school buildings. 'We're not done with you yet, Richardson,' they hiss in menacing tones, their faces so close to mine that I can smell the cheese and onion crisps they've both been eating.

I find myself rushing for the bus after school so I don't get caught by them. 'You'd better watch yourself, Richardson. We're coming to get you . . .' was the last thing Joe had said quietly into my ear as the final class finished, his breath hot against my ear.

This is how it feels to be bullied.

Shit scared.

The snow, now just dirty slush, melting into dark puddles and running off everything in polluted drops makes me slip, *twice*, in my hurry, finally catapulting me against two girls who fall over at my feet.

'Oh God, I'm sorry,' I apologise, reaching to help them while they shriek obscenities at me, and the Krays laugh from their vantage point by the school gates.

I need to get rid of those two, for good, for both me and Ben, and I need to do it soon.

The green and white kit is still muddy.

I wanted to get out of football practice, but Dad still isn't having any of it. I forgot to put Ben's kit in the laundry and Mum forgot to ask as she normally does. It also smells horrible, like dirty water from a drain. With a sinking feeling, I wipe it desperately with a flannel and spray it with deodorant. It smells better but looks worse. Resignedly I put it on, and tap-tap my way downstairs in Ben's football boots again.

Matthew's dad is already outside, his engine running and I shut the front door behind me, my mind going over all the football information that I've crammed inside it, which can save me from another nightmare session. As I climb into their car my mouth goes dry and I can feel the first wasp stings of panic yet again; Matthew is not wearing green and white.

'It's not a game tonight,' he says, looking down his nose. 'It's training!'

My eyes gloss over Matthew's attire, normal sports shorts and some kind of top under a black hoodie. Now I'm sitting in dirty, smelly team kit looking like a prize loser . . . again.

'Mum's put all my gear in the washing machine,' I mumble.

'What, all of it?' he asks me, surprised, and I think of the numerous sports gear Ben's got.

'All of it,' I repeat.

'I'm surprised you made it at all,' he scoffs, 'with your foot . . . and your elbow . . .'

All things considered, the practice doesn't go too badly. Matthew lends me some of his kit, and I remember a lot of what I learnt. I'm not great, but I'm not disastrous either.

A bright moon casts a blue light across the room through the partially open curtains.

The bedside clock shines 03.10 into the room in red numbers and I am awake, and the same as the other nights . . . there is no Ben.

'You're really freaking me out now,' I call out into the room. 'It's not funny, Ben . . . DO SOMETHING!'

An eerie silence fills the room, but I still can't help but believe that Ben is up to something.

I notice how the moonlight reflects on the little hanging threads of web from the light fitting and how a dead fly dangles from one of them, its legs curled up like a clawed hand.

I tiptoe downstairs to get a cold drink from the fridge, but see that Mum is asleep on the sofa wrapped in a blanket, an empty mug of something beside her. I take a peek at her and her hair is a tangled mess and her mouth is slightly open.

So it is not just for me that in the depths of the night, fear is always greater and sadness is always sadder and guilt is always stronger.

Once more I'm filled with hate over what Nathan's mum has inflicted on us.

Tucking the blanket higher round my mum's shoulders, I

go back to bed, sucking at the straw of a carton of berry fruits, and trying to stop all my worries leaking through the holes in my precious time as a living, breathing person. An image of Beth comes floating forward to join the unhappy party going on in my head.

We did everything together and I miss that so much, the laughs, the shopping, the parties and the late-night messaging. We weren't part of the popular crowd, the perfect kids who are so perfectly perfect they probably never even farted. We were edgy and confident and crazy . . . and now . . . we're not.

I would love to go and see her right now and talk about the fun we could still have now that I'm back! I imagine knocking on the door of her house, and when she answers telling her that I am Lily, then she will hug me and cry with happiness. Then we'll get a couple of Cokes and a huge bowl of popcorn and lie on her bed and talk all night long. I sigh again.

Where do I fit in now?

I feel like that fly. Dead, dangling and suspended.

The most amazing master plan for the disposal of Joe and Graham comes to me when I'm in the shower the next morning. I work out how to ensure their demise, exploring all the scenarios that might make it fail, and as soon as I am dressed I start searching. After looking through all of Ben's pockets and the zipped areas of his bags, I then look in drawers and under the mattress and in all the clutter under his bed. With relief I can find nothing to indicate that he's been doing drugs. It would appear that my brother was about to buy his very first five-pound bag of weed, which makes my plan so much easier.

A rush of nervous anticipation prickles its way through me, bringing with it a thrill at the thought of how this will pan out. It has got to work!

I dress without washing. No time. A mist of deodorant and fresh clothes will do. I am aware that rushing is making time move even more quickly, every time I glance at the clock the numbers have changed and seconds have somehow become minutes, but right now I have to rush to get the most out of this day.

'Have you got any change?' I ask Mum, holding my hand out and jittering in my need to get out of here quickly. She takes her fingers off her cheek, and reaches for her purse to give me a two-pound coin. 'No, *change*,' I repeat. 'Lots of change, maybe pounds, fifties, twenties possibly a couple of tens. Something like that.'

'Please would be nice,' she comments. 'What's it for?'

'Please . . . There's a cake sale at school . . . for charity,' I say, knowing that this will make her dig deep. She routes in her purse for some coins and puts several of them in my hand.

'That's a lot of cake, Ben.'

'I like a lot of cake,' I answer, stooping to give her a quick hug goodbye.

'Bye, love,' she says and kisses me on the cheek.

'I love you,' I yell, as I slam the door behind me.

I take a small detour on the way to the school bus stop, where there's a public telephone, and if I'm quick I will have just enough time. Pulling open the heavy door with its grimy glass panels, I step inside, wrinkling my nose a little at the stale smell of pee and wondering if this thing even works. One of the bottom panels of glass has been smashed and my feet crunch on the shiny cubes scattered on the floor. I study the instructions, as I'm not entirely sure I have ever used a public telephone, except for the time when several of my friends and I tried to see how many of us could fit in one. We got five, until someone complained about the smell.

'Stinks of piss,' I think her exact words were.

I look to see what coins should be used, and put some in the slots and wait. It rings. Thankfully the vandals stopped at kicking in the one window and spray-painting a variety of swear words in black letters across the rest of the glass. Why would anyone even need one of these things? Doesn't

232

everyone have a mobile phone?

A voice on the other end of the line interrupts the ringing tone and talks through the receiver into my right ear. My heart is thumping in my throat but, changing my voice as much as I can to a deeper, more adult tone, I become a member of the public tipping off the school about the possibility of drug dealing within year eleven. I am, of course, asked to give names and reasons for believing this, which I'm prepared for. I give Joe and Graham's names but I also give Ben's, and the name of another boy called Paul, who I know hangs out with them, I don't much like him either with his pale shifty eyes and his contrasting red acne.

The voice on the other end of the phone takes me seriously. 'Thank you for this. An investigation will be conducted as per the school policy, and, if necessary, it will be acted on . . .' I can feel my beating heart change its thump of fear to the thump of elation without even changing rhythm. '. . . if I could just take a few details. Sorry, I missed your name, Mr . . . ?' There is a pause as the person taking the information waits for me to give her my surname.

I slam the receiver down on the cradle. I've said all I need to say, and she said they would investigate it, so there's nothing more I can do; now I just need to pray that Joe and Graham have still got the stuff on them.

My idea to name Ben as a suspect, along with Paul, means I can be pretty sure that Joe and Graham won't suspect me as being the one who exposed them.

As the school day begins I wait in tense anticipation.

I'm jumpy, and do my best not to react each time a member of staff comes within a few feet of me.

And then it happens.

The Year Head comes to our class with his face drawn into a very serious expression and calls the four names that I had given on the phone. We all scrape our chairs back as we stand, the harsh noise breaking the awed silence of the interested kids who remain with their faces turned to the door, watching us troop out. Joe is nervous, I'm sure of it; his body language is over-cool but he hides it from his self-assumed fan base by grabbing his crotch and shoving it towards a girl on his way past.

While we form a line outside the Head Teacher's room, situated at the back of the reception lobby, the rest of us are openly uneasy. The fact that I'm panicking about what I'll do if Joe and Graham *don't* have any evidence on them, is making my behaviour realistically nervy to the others.

Graham is called first, which means that we are going to be interviewed individually. This is a huge disappointment, as it means that I'm not going to be able to see if they've got anything in their bags. I shift in my seat, heart thumping at the thought of this idea going wrong. When Graham eventually comes out, the Year Head escorts him down the corridor and we all watch them go, none of us knowing if he's going back to class or not. The only hint I have that this may be going in the direction I want it to is the fact that his cheeks are too red and he's over-exaggerating the swagger.

When Paul eventually emerges from the room, escorted by the Year Head, he looks slightly green and not at all happy. My hopes rise.

Then Joe is called and after some time, the same thing

234

happens, except he grins an over-confident grin at us as he walks by. Now I'm really beginning to feel sick. It's hard to tell if he's trying to brazen it out or not. Out of all of them, Joe is the one that I need get booted out of school. This plan has *got to work*!

The Head and the Year Head look severe – straight faces, calm, assertive movements – as they ask me to come in and place my bag on the table.

'We've received a call this morning suggesting there may be drugs on the premises, and due to the serious nature of this call, we are conducting an immediate search of the bags of the students in question. If anything suspicious is found, your parents will be notified and we shall deal with it according to the school policy.' There is an uncomfortable silence while they let me digest the seriousness of the situation, but in truth all I care about is that they found stuff in the others' bags.

'I don't have anything, sir. I don't do drugs,' I say, defending myself.

'That is great to hear, Ben. But if you could just help us by turning out your pockets and your bag,' the Head says, using her *I'm not accusing you but really I am accusing you* tone of voice.

In my bag there is nothing, and in my pockets there is nothing. I am obviously completely, wonderfully squeaky clean. I have deliberately only got the remaining change that Mum gave me for the public telephone, £1.90, not enough to be planning to buy anything more than a drink or some chocolate.

I'm asked a few questions but I tell them Joe and Graham gave me a cigarette on Monday and later, tried to sell me some stuff after school, but I wasn't interested. I also tell them that they cornered me and tried to get money off me, desperately hoping that if they *have* found anything on them, my embellished story will confirm that they are not only dealing but trying to exhort money out of defenceless kids. They give me a lecture on smoking and drugs anyway, then thank me for being helpful with the search and, to my huge, lung-collapsing relief, I'm allowed to return to class . . . un-escorted. Surely the fact that the others were escorted and I'm not must mean something. Entering Ben's class, I force a massive rush of euphoria inwards, displaying a talent for acting that I didn't know I had when I realise that the other three are not at their seats.

The resulting rumours that are circulating year eleven are incredibly pleasing to my beautifully innocent ears. The corridors are ringing with the drama of it all. Someone saw the police turn up, someone else saw their parents arriving, and everyone thinks they'll get expelled . . . this is FANTASTIC! Stories are swapped, such as what happened to the brother of a friend of a friend in another school and so on, each story getting more adventurous than the last. I feel a tiny bit sorry for Paul because he did nothing to me, but then perhaps it will teach him not to hang around with Joe and Graham, but to take his shifty eyes and spots elsewhere. A group of friends, including Beth, Nathan and Matthew, corner me in the break.

'Why were you searched, Ben?' Beth asks.

'Oh, I haven't done anything . . . I was just stupid enough to take a cigarette off Joe the other day. Whoever tipped off the school must have seen me and thought I was taking something else.'

'So you smoke now?' Matthew asks, and Nathan joins in. 'Tell me you don't smoke?' They look pretty disgusted at me.

'No, I don't. It was a one-off. They made me do it . . .' I know I sound pathetic and my voice trails off.

'Nice friends,' Beth scoffs, and I hate the way she's looking at me.

'They're not my friends,' I answer. 'I was stupid. Like, really stupid.' Then I add, '*You're* my friends . . . you know . . . we're a *group*.'

I watch them all looking at each other, trying to gauge what is going through their heads, so when after a long drawn out silence, Beth eventually says, 'Yeah, we're a group. Welcome back to the group, Ben.' I almost squeal in my Lily way with relief.

My step is lighter now. I am free to move around the school without fear, and I'm loving this feeling of safety. I feel confident that I've completed a mission, to save both me and Ben from Joe and Graham.

Even so, the rest of the day is difficult as Thursday is another day when Ben and I had totally different subjects. I am not at all sure where to sit, and I keep getting it wrong. I have to check how the other boys are sitting, talking, acting in class. I even have to constantly remind myself to write like Ben. The only other bright spot is that Holly Watts ignores me through our entire maths class, texting some other victim on her mobile phone.

Not a bad effort. I've got rid of three prize idiots in one day! *I'm doing a good thing.*

Lily's mum prepared to go out, carefully putting on her make-up and choosing the right lipstick for her dress.

It suddenly dawned on her, as if someone was spitefully poking her with a sharp-nailed finger, that for once she had not been thinking about Lily. For a short while, perhaps even minutes, she'd been thinking only of going to meet her friend and after she'd carefully applied her make-up at the dressing-table mirror it was the first time she'd not seen a bereaved mother looking back at her.

She had come to accept that her family as she knew it had died the day Lily had, yet the other day, when she found herself in James's arms as he lifted her off her feet to kiss her, a tiny fragment of who she used to be had lifted too. The guilt that threatened to envelop her and suffocate her in those terrible hours in the middle of the night was her penance, but in her waking hours could there could ever be a time when Lily's death would not hurt her so much?

The sharp-nailed finger continued to jab at her, accusing her of daring to even try to enjoy her life, when she was to blame for Lily making her own way home that night.

I need to see Beth. I don't want to spend another day without doing something that a regular teenage girl would do. That Lily would do.

I find myself standing at her cheery red front door, a cheery colour for a cheery house. I'm familiar with every part of this door, arched at the top with a letter box and knocker in yellow brass. The porch is painted white with a plaque showing a circle of flowers surrounding the number ten. Beth's house is white, and clean, and small, and familiar, and I clatter the knocker, calming myself, and stilling my nerves, reminding myself that I must not march in as soon as the door is opened, as I would have done before, like part of the family, reaching for the cookie jar, sharing half of my biscuit with Charlie, and chatting to Beth's mum. Now I'm a visitor and have to stand at the door, being Ben, with whatever reason he may have for being here.

Beth's mum opens the door, a mug of something steaming in her hand and a pair of rabbit slippers on her feet.

'Hi, Ben.' If she's surprised to see me she doesn't show it and she greets me in her normal cool, casual way. Her naturally pale skin looks fresh against the sky blue of her jumper, and her shoulder-length hair has the amber that lightens the wiry curls of Beth's Jamaican hair. She points to the stairs for me to go on up, calling, 'Beth, Ben's here.'

I kick off my shoes and make my way upstairs, two at a time, with my new slightly longer legs, knowing that I haven't asked which direction Beth's room is, and I can't be bothered to pretend. Knocking at the same time as I open the door, I slip inside her neat, pretty and familiar room, where she's lying on her bed with her earphones in. She's curled up on top of the duvet, facing the wall. She clearly didn't hear her mum calling up and is watching something on her phone, totally unaware that I'm here.

Her bed is double, in white cream ornate metal, and her duvet is cream with enormous magenta roses all over it. She has a magenta fluffy rug beside the bed, and a host of pretty things pinned to the wall above her head. Hanging hearts on strings, with pearls, glittery crystals and mirrors with ribbons; a string of little flags from each country she has visited; some peacock feathers and some wooden flowers. Large dark purple, fake flowers reach into the room from a tall black vase, and a string of coloured lantern lights hang from the curtain pole. I know her room so well, yet I can't stop looking at everything as if it is the first time. As I make my way over to Beth, I notice a new collection of photos on the wall above her dressing table, and they are mainly of me and her. I stop to look at each one.

Beth pulls the earphones out of her ears and sits up. 'Ben . . . ? What are you doing here?' For a second, I can't read the strange look on her face, but eventually a smile breaks through. Even so, there's something else in her expression and I don't know what it is.

'How are you doing, Beth?' I ask as casually as I can, even

240

though my head is ringing with the questions that I really want to ask. *How are you doing without me? Do you miss me?*

'I should be asking how you're doing,' she says.

'Well, better for seeing you,' I answer, wondering if that sounds a bit odd, coming from my brother. 'Shove up,' I order, pushing her legs over and flopping on the bed as I would have done as Lily. I reach my hand into a half-eaten bag of wine gums and pull a few out, putting one in my mouth and chewing on it. 'What are you watching?' I ask. It feels so perfect to be here.

'Just a video on YouTube,' she answers. 'It's supposed to be funny.' She plays it, and it *is* funny. We both start sniggering at it, and when a really funny bit happens we both laugh loudly at the same time.

'We used to do this a lot. Endless funny videos that made us laugh,' Beth says when it comes to an end and I have to stop myself from saying 'I know!' Instead I ask her a question.

'What do you miss the most about Lily?'

'This,' she answers quickly. 'Hanging round each other's houses. Having a laugh.' Again I have to stop myself adding 'Me too' at the end of her sentence.

'What do you miss most?' she asks.

'Having a body,' I nearly answer, but I manage to contain myself. It's a hard question, wondering what you miss most about yourself. 'Umm, everything,' I answer truthfully.

I want so much to tell her my secret but I know she won't believe me and I'll probably frighten her off.

'Do you know what's really sad?' Beth continues. 'Lily won't ever get to do her trip round the world. She wanted that more than anything else, didn't she?'

'Yes,' I answer, feeling my throat constrict.

'She planned to save up to go, then work her way across the globe.' Beth stares at a distant point across her room as if imaging the miles that I wanted to travel.

'I know! I might go anyway,' I announce brazenly. 'In the summer . . . instead of Lily,' I add quickly, but Beth laughs at me.

'What with, Ben? It will cost a fortune, and you haven't got a job yet *and* you have to come back for sixth-form college in September. Lily was going to get a part-time job when she was sixteen and save every penny for two years until she finished her A levels so she could sail off into the sunset when she was eighteen.'

Beth stating the obvious like this is almost unbearable. The summer is so close, almost touchable. But Beth is right. I don't have any money and I can't steal Ben away from the chance of doing his qualifications so that he can get a career in his precious photography. 'I'll go for the summer . . . maybe just Europe . . . I'll get a loan from the bank of mum and dad.'

'You're beginning to sound as desperate as Lily was,' Beth says. 'She was hell-bent on climbing mountains, or scuba diving . . .'

'In the Great Barrier Reef.' We say these last five words together at exactly the same time, because I know exactly where I was hell-bent on scuba diving.

'. . . and she wanted to go on safari, and visit Alaska, and . . .' Beth is halted by the strange gurgle my throat makes, and the big fat tear that drops off my face. I reach across her for one of her pink tissues and carefully fold it, using the edges to wipe carefully under my lashes, dabbing delicately before I remember that I'm not wearing any make-up to smudge.

'I think . . . it was my fault,' she says suddenly, shutting her eyes as if by looking at me she might see something that's too painful to bear.

'What was?' I ask her, quickly wiping at my face and taking another wine gum to distract myself from breaking down completely.

Her eyes open again but she looks away and her gaze travels over the field of roses and out into the evening sky. 'I suggested she could use her . . . bus money . . . that day . . . for some earrings.'

'*Your* fault? The only person who spent the bus money was me. Nobody forced me to do it.' I pick at the wine gum that's stuck to my teeth, and as she frowns I realise too late my mistake. It's so hard referring to yourself as *she*.

'You weren't there. What are you talking about?' She is looking at me as if I've gone mad.

'I mean Lily . . .' I hurriedly correct myself. It's almost harder being Ben around Beth than anyone else. She is like my second skin. 'You know Lily as well as I do, Beth, she did a million stupid things and one of those stupid things went wrong.'

'You don't blame me?' she asks hopefully.

She doesn't really understand why I'm here, why Ben is sitting in her bedroom. They were friends, of course they were, but we either hung about in a big group or we did our separate things.

'I blame the driver of that car, that's who I blame. Anyway . . .' I leap off the bed to change the subject. 'That's boring. I don't want to talk about it.'

243

I stand up to study the photos pinned to the wall where I look happy and carefree. Beth and I in the park, with friends, at sleepovers, at parties, each snap holding a precious second in time when I was alive. My eyes sting again and my nostrils quiver, and the unexpected bitterness of resentment that floods my body from the soles of my feet to the top of my head is almost physically painful.

Charlie comes bursting into the room and he starts his frantic whining and dancing around me in the same way he did last time.

'Hey,' I say brightly, chasing away the next bout of threatening tears, 'Charlie!'

'What's wrong with him?' Beth asks me and I shrug theatrically.

'Perhaps he's cross with me for not being Lily.'

Beth thinks about this for a while. 'Do you ever get cross with Lily?' she asks me. 'You know . . . angry with her for leaving?'

'Yes, I get angry with her for leaving. Apparently it's all part of the process . . . you know, disbelief, blame, anger et cetera . . . the seven stages of grief and all that.'

'And what is the last stage?' she asks

'Acceptance,' I reply.

'I'm nowhere near that yet,' she says.

'Nor am I,' I tell her truthfully.

'You have her eyes,' she points out by way of an answer, peering closely at me. 'Strange, I never noticed before.'

I certainly do.

And as she carries on peering for quite a long time, I wonder if I'm experiencing a slightly awkward moment, where my best friend is flirting with my brother.

'Do you want to stay for dinner?' Beth's mum asks, poking her head round the door and thankfully diverting Beth's attention. Beth and I look at each other, sharing our answer with our eyes and saying 'Yes' at the same time.

Normality . . . at last!

At the end of the evening, placing my plate by the sink, I thank Beth's mum for my meal and with a newfound confidence, I go to a shelf on the other side of the kitchen. Lifting the lid of a cream ceramic jar, I put my hand in and pull out a homemade white chocolate and raspberry biscuit. 'My favourite,' I say, taking a large bite out of it. Beth's mum always said to help myself, and for years that's exactly what. Now I can't help but note the look of surprise on her face, that Ben, who has never been to their house before, knows where the biscuits are kept. Just like his sister.

I'm going to Milly's party!

I'm so excited about it that I feel like dancing to every track that comes on my phone, although I have to confess that I'm less enthusiastic about what to wear. As Lily I would have been trying a million outfits on, my wardrobe doors wide open, hangers and clothes on the bed or the floor, and Beth on the other end of Skype doing the same thing. I would have dressed to impress, spending hours on my hair and my make-up, Nathan admiring me making all my efforts worthwhile.

But now I find myself showering and shaving off the random patches of dark hair on Ben's chin, taking care not to remove any skin this time. I threaten the reflection in the mirror to pluck his eyebrows, which should never have been allowed to grow that big, and I imagine him snatching the tweezers off me. I spray liberally with his deodorant whose packaging tells me it is warm, sensual and spicy, then I try to work his hair into a suitable style.

I dress in Ben's clothes, listening through the silence for him to tell me what he would like to wear, but I can't hear him. We are no longer tuned in to each other like before and another stab of guilt threatens to ruin my moment. I run my hands over his clothes until they stop on a particular T-shirt.

From experience, I know what he would like, and imagine him telling me, *If you're taking me to a party, you had better make me look good*. If only I knew what he was really thinking.

I change the music to my favourite track and fill my head with thoughts of the evening ahead. I think Ben looks pretty nice in what I've picked out, and I admire us in the bedroom mirror.

*

I get Dad to take me to the party via the shop, insisting that I can't turn up without something to drink, and, no, I won't get drunk, and I won't be irresponsible, and I won't disrespect Milly's house and, yes, her parents are definitely going to be there, and, finally, that I will ring when I want to come home, but not to expect it to be early.

We pick Matthew up on the way but when I knock on his door he's not ready. His mum tells me to go on up and dig him out of his room, but unlike in Beth's house I don't know which is Matthew's room. Making a choice to open the one with dirt round the handle and stickers on the door, I breathe a combination of disgust and relief that I got the right room. Apart from Matthew, who's only wearing socks and a T-shirt, there's a single bed with biscuit-thin pillows; walls covered in photos and posters of semi-naked women; a waste bin that is full to overflowing; books; clothes; dirty socks; and even a pair of worn underpants on his bed. His room is littered with sweet wrappers, a couple of empty plastic drink bottles and a half-finished bowl of cereal, growing mould. 'Nice,' I find myself saying sarcastically, screwing my nose up at the faint sweaty smell before it occurs to me that Ben would have seen it all before.

Matthew grins, as he pulls on his underpants and reaches for his jeans. 'Home sweet home.'

He removes the gum he's been chewing and adds it to a sculpture he seems to be creating on his wall. Two large breasts fashioned entirely out of gum are staring me in the face.

'You're making boobs out of gum?' I ask him with an element of disgust and forgetting that I'm not supposed to be surprised at anything I see.

'Yeah, you know I am; you helped me start them off!' He looks at me as if he can't understand why I don't remember. 'My bubblegum tits.' He says this fondly as if he's in love with them. 'Already a B but a bit more work and I reckon they'll be a C soon.'

'I see you've spared one piece of gum for other things,' I say, looking at the photo of the football team with his chewed gum on Ben's face.

'I had to sacrifice it,' he says, turning to look at the photo. 'You deserved more. I should have shaped it into a dick and put it on your head. I might do that with the next one, if you go back to hanging around with scum.' But before I can answer he carries on. 'So, Holly . . .' He grins. 'I hear you've been doing the dance with no pants . . .'

'Yeah, OK, Matt, give me a break.' I look away and run my hand along his collection of DVDs, obviously unwilling to talk about that particular subject.

'So you DID . . . you bastard. You won. Fair dos mate.' He whistles, his appreciation, indicating that the loss of his and my brother's virginity was a competition, then he grabs his jacket and he's off down the stairs and through the front

248

door, leaving me to run after him.

'So, are you going to throw some shapes at the party?' Dad asks as he pulls out onto the main road towards Milly's house.

Matthew laughs into his T-shirt. 'Yeah, that's right, Mr R, we're going to . . . *throw some shapes.*'

'No one says that any more, Dad.' I sigh. 'No point trying to pretend you're not old.'

I try to detract from the slightly embarrassing dad situation by opening the bag by my feet, so that Matthew can see the cider in there, then I have to squash my mouth together to stop it giving away exactly how excited I am about tonight. Matt winks at me and partially reveals a bottle of vodka tucked inside his coat. I assume my *jeeez, how did you pull that one off?* look of appreciation and glance at Dad's reflection in the rear-view mirror, but his eyes are thankfully focused on the road ahead while he gives up on us and tunes into something awful on Radio Two or an equivalent old fart channel.

When we arrive, there are a few people going into the house and Milly's parents are in the dining room, visible behind closed glass-panelled doors, but thankfully out of the way. There's some music playing inside and outside, and the kitchen is littered with beers, ciders and soft drinks and snacks. Milly takes the drinks off us and puts them on the table but I notice that Matthew hasn't given her the vodka, just the cola.

'Tight git, Matt. Where's the booze?' she demands, beckoning knowingly with her fingers, and reluctantly he produces the bottle from his jacket, with Milly taking it off him with a flourish. As she walks back to the table, I happen to look down and notice that she is wearing the most fabulous pair of shoes, and before I know that it's happened I'm shrieking.

'Oh my GOD, Milly, your shoes . . . they're GORGEOUS!' to which she looks down and squeals with delight back. 'I know, right?'

Matthew looks at us both and rolls his eyes.

'What the fuck?' he mouths at me as he takes a glass to make a drink with the vodka that he brought, but I grab a cider, pull the ring and drink straight from the can, trying to hide my Lilyness behind it.

Milly shows us where to find the toilet and points to the garden where there is a big gazebo and several people, including her older sister and some of her friends. 'If you're going to have a fag, do it out there,' she yells, then rushes back inside as the front doorbell rings.

As both Ben and I know most of the people invited to this party, apart from the older ones, it means I can mingle freely with anyone, boy or girl. The house and the garden gradually fills up with bodies. Some have obviously got themselves high before arriving, some are on a mission to fill themselves full of any alcohol they can get their hands on, and some just want to be there because it's going to be a great night. There is expectation in the air and it is met; I am a teenager at a party and I'm sure as hell going to have a good time.

The navy blue of an evening sky gives in to the infinite darkness of night and the lights around the gazebo offer a magical effect to the garden. The glow from the fire pit highlights everybody's faces with orange, and reflects a flicker of flame in their eyes, while the few smokers intermittently share their lighters or flick their cigarette ends into the coals.

I love everything. The cider I'm drinking has untied the knots inside me and I feel euphoric. It's like the whole of teenage life as it should be in one single wonderful point in time: music, dancing, friends, attraction and energy. I wanted so much to feel life again, and it is here.

As the evening wears on, everyone is getting louder and beginning to show the effects of the alcohol that they are managing to hide from Milly's parents, or that Milly's parents are managing to ignore. Several people are kissing, one couple are going for it in a big way, and someone has vomited near a flower bed, leaving an interesting splatter worthy of an impressionist artist on the garden path. Some of the older kids keep having to turn people away who weren't even invited because the glow from the fire and the music are advertising to the outside world what a great party this is.

The sound of Matthew talking endlessly in my ear about the hot girls that are here begins to fade into a buzz as I pretend to look at each one he points out, but my peripheral vision is concentrating on Nathan. He looks so good in his designer jeans with a new expensive-looking T-shirt clinging to his chest. I feel my heart crank up its beat. He moves to the side of the gazebo where I am, and I pretend for a few seconds that I'm in my own Lily body, and he's going to walk up to me as if everything is normal, and put his arms round me, pulling me to him.

Daisy steps out in front of him and puts her hand on his chest. On *my* boyfriend's chest. She looks up at him and he looks down at her and something in the pit of my stomach feels hotter than the burning wood in the fire pit. She throws her head back and laughs at something he says, then flicks her hair over her shoulder in a seductive manner, and I can't bear it. He leans down further to hear what she's saying and from where I'm standing it looks too close.

I wander over towards them as casually as possible, forcing my legs to move slower than they want to but in the end I can't help myself. I rush over and manage to pop up between the two of them, almost skidding to a halt.

'Great party,' I shout to Nathan, turning my back slightly and rudely to Daisy, who tries to move round between us again. I unkindly carry on this little charade, until she thankfully wanders off to find another victim.

Nathan holds his drink and points vaguely towards a group of girls dancing. 'Anyone for you?' he asks me, and although I'm supposed to be searching the group of girls for any possible fit ones I look up at him and can't help reacting to the fact that he is dangerously, touchably close. I feel a flush invade my face, and I'm glad the garden lights are too dim to show it.

'No. There isn't a girl here for me,' I say, and my head screams, *but there is a boy and you're right here, and you should be mine* . . . 'You?' I ask instead and hold my breath. I don't want his answer, but he dips his face towards me to shout over the music.

'This is my date tonight.' The music has stopped between tracks and Nathan is left holding up his bottle of beer, and shouting so that everyone can hear that alcohol is his only date. A few people laugh at him, but we both ignore them. I can smell his scent, a woody and warm perfume that fills my nose, and I shut my mouth, leaning towards him, breathing in, so my nostrils get the full benefit. I almost hug him – *You're still mine, Nathan Peterson, and I love you* – but I raise my cider to him, as if it is my date too, while continuing to take him in through my eyes and breathe him in through my nose. 'To the love of our lives,' I toast, and take a drink.

Nathan tips his head back and takes several gulps from his bottle, before waving it in front of my face to show that it's empty, and as he turns and walks away from me I can see that he's swaying as he aims back up the garden towards the kitchen, presumably for another bottle.

I watch him go, then wander over to Beth and the group she is standing with, just as a track comes on that we all love. All the girls start dancing and with the cider that I've drunk and the party atmosphere all around me, I decide I don't care about what anyone thinks, and I start dancing, hands in the air, circling hips and flicking hair, just like the others, and when the track finishes Beth takes my hand, laughing. 'You're so funny, Ben.' Fortunately for me, everyone thinks I'm trying to be deliberately funny so I give them all a wiggle of my butt and exit the gazebo to get another drink. Beth follows me and we are still holding hands. As we get outside she pulls me back and as I stop to see what she wants, I feel her other hand on my waist and she stands on tiptoe to kiss me. *So Beth likes my brother now?* I pull my face away from her and I see the hurt instantly in her face.

'Er . . . I . . . it's not you, it's me.' Lame, I know, but it is all I can think of to explain why Ben won't kiss her. 'Can we keep it like this for now?' I ask. 'Just friends?' Equally as lame!

After searching my eyes for a minute, looking for reasons why she should be rejected, but seeing the genuine love I have for my best friend, she thankfully links my brother's arm and we make our way to get another drink.

*

It's already past one in the morning and some people are beginning to leave; some have crawled into sleeping bags on the lounge carpet and a few are clinging to the seats in the garden around the still-glowing fire pit. Nathan is staggering his way to a garden chair but when he tries to sit down, he catches the edge of it, falling off and pushing the girl next to him into her friend, spilling both their drinks. He sprawls on the grass dangerously close to the fire pit, and all I can hear is a combination of people swearing at him or laughing at him until I haul him off the damp grass, with my brother's strength, into a semi-standing position. I've had quite a few ciders myself, and as a result the world is tilting sidewards and he almost yanks me back down with him. We both end up unsteadily weaving our way up the garden until I somehow manage to get him onto a sturdier chair in the house.

'I mish Lily,' he slurs at me with a forlorn expression.

'You and me both,' I say. In the cool light of the kitchen I can see that he looks like shit.

'I can't believe that she has gone . . . in the blink of an eye,' he says, pronouncing the word 'gone' in a high theatrical tone while flicking his hand into the air like an explosion.

'Oh, I'm absolutely positive she's still around,' I tell him, stooping to look him in the eye. 'You've just got to believe.'

'Believe,' he repeats slowly, then waves a finger at me. 'I'm waiting for a sign from her. I loved her you know.'

'Yes, Nathan,' I say, 'I loved her as well. I still do.'

'I still do too,' he echoes, and I'm so glad he said it.

'I love you too,' I whisper.

'And there's something wrong with my mum . . . really, really, really wrong.' He repeats each word in a sing-song way.

'Oh,' I say, thinking, *What could possibly be wrong with your secret-keeping, child-murdering, police-dodging mother?* But my heart goes out to him, as he looks so totally awful and not like the Nathan I know.

He grips my hand and looks into my face. 'I'm losing her too,' he says and his eyes are glassy with unshed tears, and I now understand how shattered and lonely Nathan's life has become.

*

When Dad turns up to take me and Matt home, he finds me shoving Nathan in the car as well.

'Good party?' he asks, getting several slurred grunts as his answer. I fix the seat belt round Nathan, and as we drive away from Milly's house, I'm trying to talk extremely carefully to convince Dad that I'm sober, compared to the other two, but he turns to where I am sitting in the rear passenger seat, looking pretty fed up. 'You're drunk,' he accuses me.

'Yep.' I grin stupidly, just as Matthew starts singing a string of rugby songs out of tune. He won't let up, even when a stink fills the car, like a cross between vinegar and cheese, and Nathan has been sick. Dad groans and hands me a cloth from the glove compartment, saying, 'He's only gone and bloody vomited,' and I lean over Nathan to wipe it from his seat belt and his clothes. But there's just too much for

Dad's cloth to cope with as it slops all over my hand and Nathan's clothes. Dad indicates to pull over, panicking. 'Is he going to do it again?' And he does do it again, only this time some of it lands in my lap. Whatever Nathan ate at the party is now all over both us and the back of Dad's car in multicoloured lumps. It makes me gag and for a minute I think I'm going to join him, but Dad has stopped the car and he's pulling Nathan out.

Liquid and lumps withdraw inside the roller of the inertia mechanism from the seat belt and Dad swears, '*Jeeesus Christ, Nathan!* Get out of my bloody car!' Nathan heaves more of the beery contents of his stomach over the pavement, while Dad holds a fistful of his T-shirt to stop him falling forward. 'There's a big bottle of water in the boot, wash what you can off my car,' he orders.

I use some of the water to wash the sick off the lap of my jeans first, then do what I can on Nathan's side of the car and the seat belt while Matt continues to sing.

When we eventually reach Nathan's house, Dad and I get out of the car and knock on the big wooden door of his beautiful house. His mum opens the door and visibly twitches at the sight of Dad and me in front of her, clamps her hand over her mouth and says absolutely nothing. Despite the fact that she looks worse than I have ever seen her, the fact that I'm drunk is making this whole scene look pretty funny as far as I'm concerned.

Dad is trying to apologise profusely while also trying to prop up Nathan, who is swaying all over the place, with sick on his chin and all down his front. My own jeans are damp all round my crotch as if I've wet myself, and Matthew can be heard singing tunelessly from the car.

'. . . never let your bollocks dangle in the dust . . .'

And I laugh. I laugh so hard that I'm bent double and tears are running down my face. Nathan's mum isn't laughing, she simply reaches for him, pulling him roughly into the house, and without looking at the rest of us she shuts the door, leaving Dad and me on the step.

Nathan's mum was having a panic attack.

Her heart had swelled like the airbag in a car, and was threatening to explode through her chest cavity and land in her lap.

The sight of that poor girl's father on her doorstep, unaware that he was staring the killer of his daughter in the face was almost more than she could handle. She had virtually disintegrated on the spot and the effort it took to keep her own legs propping her up while Nathan staggered inside was monumental.

She could still hear Ben laughing. Was he laughing at her? Did he really know? If he knew it was her, why had he still not told the police? Was he playing with her? Stretching her to her limit until she literally broke into a million pieces as revenge?

Well, it was working!

Each day was even more difficult than the last, like climbing a mountain and never succeeding. She kept forgetting things. Meals would have a fundamental ingredient missing; wet clothes were left in the washing machine or not washed at all; milk would run out; bread would run out; and people at the care home were beginning to notice that her 'illness' was affecting her work.

Her overwhelming tiredness was becoming too hard to fight and the person she used to be had ebbed into nothing but a distant memory. She ached to be left alone to sleep, or evaporate into nothingness.

She woke Alex up, partly so he could drag her son up the stairs and get him out of his stinking clothes, but mainly because she couldn't stand to listen to Nathan's drunken slurrings. 'I love you, Mummm, and I love Daaaad, and I love Lileeey,' he'd said over and over as he sat on the hall floor before he moaned loudly and added, 'Oh yeah . . . I forgot . . . my Lily's not alive any more . . . She's dead . . . dead, dead, dead.'

For some reason, the day after the party is the most difficult
one so far.

I've had a whole week without any contact from Ben. Even
when I was in limbo I had more contact than this. The guilt
over what I've done to him feels like a heavier burden now
and the wonderful feeling that took me over at the party last
night has changed shape. With the music and the cider and all
my friends around me I'd felt vibrant and happy and a part of
it all. Yet, today, I know that all of it was just an illusion. That
really I'm an ugly imposter who doesn't belong anywhere.
Even heaven doesn't want me.

After a long, tiring day just trying to be Ben, when I really
don't want to have to be a boy any more, I creep, like last
Sunday, into my own room to be with everything that is mine:
my clothes, my ornaments and all the familiar treasures I've
gathered over the years. The blue urn that contains my ashes
continues to mock me from the dressing table. The carrier bag
containing the things I bought on the day I died catches my
eye; the earrings, still in their box, have never been worn and
never will be. I take them out and study them.

'Well, they are nice,' I say, trying to justify them to myself
and holding them up to my ears, but suddenly, without knowing

I'm going to do it, I find I'm squeezing them in my fingers before throwing them against the mirror. 'Silly bitch,' I say out loud in the words of my brother. Ben stares back at me from the mirror, wrenching at my conscience, reminding me of the parasite that I am.

I take the T-shirt out of the bag and suddenly I want to try it on. I want to be me. I want to dress up in my own things and feel like Lily one more time. I search in the drawer and put on one of my bras, a pretty one with pink hearts all over it, clipping it on the widest setting and stuffing it with tissue from the box by my bed. I quickly put the T-shirt on and try not to notice that it is tight on Ben's shoulders or the fact that it's cropped, which exposes the hair round his belly button. I then rummage in my make-up for foundation and eyeliner, and some fabulous purple and lilac shimmering eye shadow that picks out colours in the T-shirt. Ben and I look so much like each other that this is going to be quite easy. I take a big breath and look in the mirror, painting my own face back on as carefully as I can. My eyes transform into my own again, and I finish by tying a spotted ribbon round my head to hide the short sides of Ben's hair.

My reflection has become Lily and I touch the mirror with my hand.

'Hello . . . I've missed you,' I say to myself.

'Ben?' Dad is standing in the doorway with a puzzled expression, 'I-I . . . thought I could hear someone in here,' he says, stuttering slightly, while his eyes travel all over me, questioning what he's seeing. A deep frown is wedged between his eyebrows.

'What's going on?' he asks eventually . . . and predictably.

I can only stare back at him, wondering if there is any possible way to bluff this one out. My poor father can't work out whether to be very angry, or very sad or just plain freaked out, and I can't blame him.

'Are you . . . um . . . all right?' He waits for my answer, but I continue to gape at him for a few moments, until I decide that humour tactics are the only way to go. I try to laugh it off, not really sure how that's going to help, or how it's going to convince my dad that Ben dressed in my clothes could, in any way, be amusing. But instead of forming the shape of a smile, my mouth starts moving all on its own, I can feel it coming. My lips are kind of dancing from side to side, my throat tightens until it really hurts, and finally I cry. My head is bowed, and my shoulders shake, and suddenly I feel him next to me, his arms round me holding me so tightly.

I know he thinks I am Ben missing Lily, but I am not; I am Lily missing Lily, and I really can't keep it to myself any longer.

I drop the lip gloss I'm holding, and I put my arms round my dad and shut my eyes. I am a little girl again in my daddy's arms and he's going to make it all right, because that is what they do. For these few precious minutes, I know what it is to be hugged and held and loved again. And I hug and hold and love him right back.

I don't know how long we stand here like this, but I think it's long enough for Dad to feel better prepared for what I might tell him. I think he believes I'll talk to him man to man and then he can provide the answer. We drop our arms and look at each other. I can see his gaze travel along my lashes, taking in the heavy mascara and the eye shadow and there is such deep sadness in his eyes that I feel my own eyes fill with tears again, making me squeeze my lids together before looking up at the ceiling in a bid to try to stop it from happening again, but I can't.

When Ben cries, which is hardly ever, he always pretends he isn't, brushing the tears roughly away from his face and maintaining his cool as much as possible, getting a little bit angry with himself for letting go. When I cry, I have to run a folded tissue, the tip of a finger or the side of my thumb along the lower edge of my eyes to carefully wipe at any wet make-up that's threatening to trickle darkly down my foundation, and I also bite my bottom lip to stop it wobbling.

I realise I'm doing that now.

Dad is staring intently at me with a range of emotions travelling over his face, and his eyes hover over my mouth, where my teeth are still pinning my lip down, then they move to my fingers that are carefully folding a tissue to dab under my mascaraed lashes. Having carefully observed the display in front of him, his focus rests on my eyes and delves deep inside them.

He can see me.

The seconds tick past.

Suddenly Dad exhales sharply. 'You know, you really have to get out of this gear, Ben. If your mother sees you like that, it will destroy her. You look too much like your sister . . . and it's ridiculous.' He turns to leave the room, no longer able to cope with this strange image in front of him, which is neither son, nor daughter.

'What if I told you I *am* Lily?' I call out. Those three words, *I am Lily*, sound so wrong in Ben's deep voice. He stops with his back to me, his shoulders visibly slumped, before he turns slowly back round to face me, making me feel so sorry for him.

'Then I would think that you aren't very well,' he says, sitting down on the edge of the bed, deflating before my very eyes, despair coming through the pores in his skin.

'But I am . . . Lily,' I whisper deeply.

'Don't do this, Ben,' he begs me, and he wraps his arms round his own body, as if to hold himself in.

I sit on the bed next to him, disturbing the air with the scent of peach and vanilla that I'd sprayed on my body, and I hold my arms round him too, trying to help him keep himself together.

'I don't know how to make you believe it, Dad,' I say into his shoulder, my voice choked and too whiny for Ben, as I try to explain. 'The conscious part of me didn't die with my body. I've been here all the time. Not in Ben's body . . . that didn't happen until recently, but I've been around . . . I never left.' I can hear myself rambling but my dad just keeps hugging himself, unable to bring himself to look at me.

He eventually sucks in a huge shaky breath while staring ahead at the urn on the dressing table. 'I think you just want to kind of . . . recreate Lily.' He says. I can hardly bear the way his face seems to have lost its shape, and now hangs in loose folds around his skull and jaw. 'Remember, Ben, I *know* you –' his hand moves until his outstretched fingers are held over his heart – 'in here. I know you both *in here*. I met you when you were seconds old, studied you, breathed you in and watched you grow day by day. I know more about you both than you even know about yourselves. I am so proud of who you have become. You don't have to be Lily as well; you are just fine being Ben.'

I feel the tightness in my throat again. He is such a good dad, and I was so lucky to have him, but how do you make someone believe that what they see in front of them isn't everything? I search around in my mind for a while, but I realise that I've just given myself the answer. I sit forward and look right into his eyes. 'Dad? If you know your children so well, look *past* what you see and remember what you know.'

He frowns and sighs as if he has given up understanding me, but I carry on, 'I know you could see me just now. Look at me, Dad. I *am* your sleeping beauty. I have woken up . . . *please*!' We sit like this, motionless, almost nose to nose, staring right inside each other until suddenly I know that he can see the green forest floor of my eyes beneath the hazel of Ben's.

He has found me.

'. . . Lily?'

The tears, greasy and grey from make-up, drop off the end of my jaw, and this time, I let them go. I nod my head slowly. 'Lily?' he repeats again. Then in a whisper: 'Oh my God . . . it *is* you . . . but it can't be!' He twists and turns between acceptance and denial. 'Oh no, this is mad . . . I'm mad. This isn't real, Ben. It can't be real.'

I simply sit and let him continue to work it out for himself. I know that I look a ridiculous sight, a boy in a tissue-paper-stuffed bra with make-up running all down my face.

Gently cupping my chin in his big hands, he holds my face

before him again, and breathes, 'I . . . *can* . . . see you,' and I
nod my head with relief beneath his gaze.

'Thank you,' I whisper. 'I'm so tired . . . so tired of trying to
be Ben, and I . . . I've been so scared . . .'

'But where is Ben?' he asks. The question that I am dreading
hangs suspiciously in the air between us.

'I . . . don't exactly know,' I answer honestly, noticing a look
of shock come into his expression. 'I think he is in the same
place I was,' I add, hardly daring to think about the fact that
Ben disappeared from the side of his bed in the middle of the
night and hasn't been seen since.

'Was it you or Ben at the party?' he asks.

'It was me,' I answer simply.

'And the trip to the beach?' he asks.

'Yes,' I confirm.

'So how long?' he asks, trying to compute what has been
going on under his very nose. My guilt and my shame burns
inside me and I try to make it better. 'No further back than
that . . . really. He's sharing himself with me . . . being a good
twin . . . and . . . stuff . . .' My voice trails off, as I realise how
insufficient that reasoning really is.

After what seems like hours sitting side by side, simply being
confused, he eventually yawns deeply, then stands up. 'I don't
understand anything right now, and my brain can't take any
more, but I know one thing . . . you'd better not let Mum see
you like this. It will kill her.' He gives me an extra hug, squeezing
me for a long time, before taking his poor tired face out of my
bedroom and into his. 'We'll sleep on it and work out what to
do tomorrow.' Then he closes the door quietly behind him.

I know it is unfair but part of me feels a massive sense of relief. I've shared my burden.

I catch sight of myself in the mirror again. Once upon a time, I would have taken a photo of Ben like this and made it go viral, but now this vision in the mirror is just a pathetic reminder of what I am doing . . . to the both of us.

I return to Ben's bedroom, and thankfully I sleep, leaving traces of make-up and sadness all over his pillow.

Six o'clock came and went over two hours ago and Mum, curled on the sofa, has been getting more fidgety and cross with each passing minute.

Dad is late home today and she's been unable to get hold of him. I wonder if it is like the day I didn't go to school, or whether the shock of a sudden death in the family makes you think the grim reaper could be round any corner, waiting to take your loved ones away from you at any moment. Poor Mum, there are so many stains on her once-perfect life.

When Dad eventually comes in, she pushes her phone aside angrily and gives the television her full interest as if she's been casually watching a programme all evening, and hasn't the slightest interest in what time he's come home.

Before I died, my dad was always so dependable and funny, and my mum was fairly chilled, but my death seems to have eaten away at the best parts of all of my family, leaving festering wounds too easily opened. He forgot to tell Mum he was running late tonight and he hasn't even noticed that she's pretending not to care.

We can hear him getting his dinner out of the microwave, which he then brings into the living room to eat off his lap while Mum concentrates rigidly at the screen, saying nothing.

Dad searches my eyes for evidence of Lily . . . *I am here*, but then he completely forgets to say hello to Mum. I believe that she feels lonelier now that he's in the room than before he came home.

Although I am so tired from the strain of another school day and of trying to be Ben, I'm so glad that, at least with him, I can relax and be Lily.

A crime programme comes on and Mum reaches for the remote. It's like a televisual conspiracy every day, with programmes sneaking in scenes about dead people, or pathologists, or funerals, which pop up on the screen like a cruel, mocking joke. Mum flicks the TV over to a comedy and laughter instantly fills the room but her face doesn't change its fixed defiant expression, and the space around her is invisibly spiky.

We continue to just stare at the television, letting it pretend for us that our lives are normal.

As soon as the credits mercifully roll at the end of the programme, Mum withdraws almost unnoticed out of the room. We can hear her in the kitchen for a few minutes, crockery banging, water running, the general sounds of clearing up, then silently and alone she goes upstairs to bed. It's only 21.35, but she's already given up on the day.

We both sit looking at the ceiling, listening to Mum shedding the day, and when it all goes quiet I leave my armchair to join Dad on the sofa. 'Where were you?' I ask him. 'Why were you so long?'

'In the office. I lost track of time . . . I've been trying to come up with a solution.' He immediately looks aghast. 'I . . . I didn't mean . . .'

269

My relief at sharing my burden is instantly swapped for the bruising feeling of deceit that he has been trying to think of a way to make me leave.

'A *solution*? I don't want a solution! This is between me and Ben. He's letting me live. He'll come back!'

Do I believe what I have just said?

Dad bows his head as if the entire weight of the world has just landed on his shoulders, and I can hear him loudly swallowing as if he is trying not to cry.

'I'm sorry, Ben . . . er . . . Lily, but you have to be shown how to . . . leave again.' He focuses on the green in my eyes. 'You can't stay. It isn't fair to Ben.'

'I didn't tell you so that you could *get rid* of me.' My heart is racing and tears are threatening to cascade down my face. 'What are you going to do? Get the church round with flowing gowns and a huge cross to order me out of my brother's body . . . as if I'm the devil?' I hardly give him time to answer. 'I'm not going to rotate my head and shout rude things like in *The Exorcist* you know. Ben can come back any time he likes.' There is total silence in the room apart from the ticking of the clock on the shelf.

'Can he?' Dad asks. 'It's been several days.'

'He's only got to find me in the night . . . like I did with him . . . It's easy.'

Why hasn't he found me in the night? Why can't I feel Ben any more?

My teeth find their way to pin my bottom lip down and my hands reach up in my Lily way to carefully wipe my eyes as they spill with tears. Dad puts his arms round me tightly for several minutes until he eventually clears his throat. 'I never thought I would hear myself say this, but we need some advice from someone who knows about this stuff, like one of those mediums . . . Mystic Meg or Septic Peg, or something. We just need to find one that isn't a rip-off con artist.'

I don't want to own up about One Shoe Sue. What if she has the power to banish me from Ben?

'What about that strange woman . . . you know, the mother of that boy in your class? The one with the limp?'

My heart sinks; this is going to move forward whether I want it to or not, I guess. 'One Shoe Sue? . . . She was at my funeral . . . she knew I was there.'

He looks surprised. 'You were there?'

'Yes, but not in Ben's body. I've told you. I was around you all the time. Kind of floating. Thank you for saying I was like a sunflower.' I smile at him and squeeze his arm.

'She might have been guessing, I suppose?' he suggests, going back to One Shoe Sue. 'After all, it's not the most stunning feat of psychic ability to *sense* the departed at their own funeral.'

'She turned her head just as I walked past her, and she told her husband that I was there. She couldn't see me, but she knew I was standing beside her.'

Considering Dad has spent his whole life believing that anything to do with the afterlife is a massive pile of horse shit, he's holding up quite well. 'Well . . . if you really think that Voodoo Sue, or One Shoe Sue or whoever she is, is the real deal, then we should at least go and see her. Perhaps she can actually talk to people like you . . .' He pats my knee and gives me a sad smile. 'People like you,' he repeats for lack of any better description.

I tell him about the wisps of smoke that were hanging around in the crematorium, and that Mum had one around her and he even had one around him. 'I guess they were all ghosts of people we knew, who came back because my funeral made people think about them.'

'Perhaps the one around me was my mum?' he says, and I realise that deep within his disbelief there must have been a desperate longing all this time.

I tuck my knees and feet onto the couch, curl my spine over and lean my forehead on his shoulder. Almost foetal. My hands are holding his arm but one hand slides down until it is inside his warm fingers.

We fall silent for a while and find ourselves pretending to stare at the images of current news events on the television, the voices of the presenters just a noise in the background of our heads. 'Dad?' I ask him eventually, breaking the silence.

'Mmm?' he answers.

'Don't make me go too soon,' I say, unable to tell him that I need to stay long enough to reach summer. I *need* to see at least something of the world.

He turns to me but I can't see him clearly; my eyes are full of tears again and my throat hurts.

James stayed slumped on the sofa, long after his son . . . who it would appear was also his daughter caught within the body of his son, had gone to bed.

Listening to the deep voice of Ben speaking the words of Lily had been so confusing, an impossible situation. His brain had tumbled over and over again since Sunday night, whirling with the madness of it all and from trying to keep that madness all to himself.

Contacting Sue was probably his only lifeline, even though he'd always struggled to believe that there was such a thing as a real psychic. Lily believed that Sue had definitely sensed her at the funeral. It was worth a try, because otherwise he was at a total loss.

He so badly wanted to tell Amelia what was going on, but until he had some answers he also needed to protect her, because Lily coming back through Ben would pick at the fragile scab that was forming over her grief. They were both struggling with it so much; one day they would almost be OK and the next they were back in the bowels of despair. It seemed disloyal to try to enjoy life in the same way they had before, but he had faith. The heart of his family had been broken, and it was a very long way from being mended, but he loved them and time would be a healer. He believed that.

For now he was more worried about *why* Lily had returned and where the hell Ben was. Although he felt a traitor to his daughter, his son must have his life back. Ben could not be a vessel for her soul any longer.

I feel naked again.

I'm walking through the school, feeling exposed, like I did on my first day back here as Ben. Having told Dad that it is really me in here, I felt his eyes on me this morning when I was getting my breakfast, taking Ben's skin away to reveal me underneath. The initial relief I felt at telling him has morphed into something else, like when you believe that it's almost OK doing something wrong as long as no one knows about it.

I'm finding it easier to act like Ben as each day goes on and I make less Lilyish mistakes than I did in the beginning, but now Dad knows about me I feel *condemned* and somehow *dirty*.

Even being with Beth is different after the party. She obviously fancies Ben now, which feels like I'm deceiving her in a worse way. I can't even convince myself that I'm just a friend to her, because she not only sees Ben . . . but she also *wants* Ben.

And Nathan? He is dying inside as surely as his mother is, and although I know the secret of his misery, there is nothing I can do about it.

And Ben doesn't appear in the night, so even if I *could* bring myself to step back into that awful lonely place, he isn't there to swap with anyway.

* * *

On the way home I find myself outside Nathan's house. He's
stayed after school for a sports thing so he's not here, and I
don't know why I'm here either, but I am. Their house makes
me feel sad. It could have all been so different if that day in
February had never happened. I could be making plans to go
there tonight and sit with my boyfriend while his mum cooked
us something lovely to eat. We could hold hands on the sofa
and kiss on the doorstep and make plans for the prom and for
summer. I wonder what part of her thinks that it's OK to let
my family spend the rest of their lives never getting justice
for my death by not confessing. Why does she think that it's
OK to be here, making everyone's lives miserable, including
Nathan's, when she should be in prison? No one would believe
me, but they would believe her. She is the only key to giving
everyone involved in this nightmare some peace.

When Dad comes home the next day, thankfully on time, he looks at me, winking in a way that is not really a cheery wink but more of a knowing one.

After dinner, we go into the living room again and wait for Mum to go to bed, the same as last night

When finally she says goodnight and disappears upstairs, I get up and close the door, then sit down next to him to hear what he has to say.

'I've managed to contact Sue. I went into work early so that I could spare the time to go and see her during the day . . . She's a strange old thing.'

'But what did she say about me?' I ask, wondering what her reaction would have been to hearing that Dad had his very own spiritual possession going on in his house.

'I didn't tell her exactly what is going on with you, but she said to go to her house on Thursday after school.'

'Do you think she'll make me . . . move on *there and then?*' I ask, my fear spiralling about the fact that Thursday isn't very far away and I'm not prepared to leave yet.

'I don't know,' he says honestly, looking into the mossy flecks of my Lily eyes. 'I think we just need to see what she says first.'

My breath catches and swells in my throat. 'Tomorrow is Wednesday . . . that's only two more days to go . . .'

He doesn't understand my panic, or he's ignoring it. 'Yes. She couldn't see us any earlier, and we need answers as soon as possible, for both you and Ben.'

We fall into silence while the blue light of the television screen flickers around the room.

'Dad . . . ?' I say eventually and he turns to look at me, and I think he expects me to be crying again but I'm not. He doesn't expect me to say what I say. 'I don't think I should leave too quickly . . . You and Mum . . . you're going down separate paths.'

He puts the television onto mute and takes a breath. 'You mean since you left?'

I nod. 'Yes . . . maybe that is why I'm here . . . you know, to help.'

He exhales before he talks, as if he isn't sure exactly what he is going to say. 'It's not that we're going along different paths from each other, Lily, just that we're going along *difficult* paths. That's all.'

'No! You're not like you were . . . before.' His face is sad as he looks at me and I reach over to give him a hug. 'Me not being here . . . has pulled you all apart, so maybe . . . I'm here to put you together again.'

His big shoulders hunch and his expression is one that I can't quite determine. He reaches for my hand and strokes it. 'Lily, I don't think that's why you're here. Yes, our paths are . . . *difficult*, but that is normal. Any change, like a death in the family, will always blow everyone apart for a while, but –' he pauses as if trying to find the most delicate way of saying what he wants to say – 'time *does* heal, Lily. We are a bit self-absorbed at the moment . . . all of us . . . that's all . . . but we're strong. We *will* be OK.'

An unexpected stab of hurt gets me right between the ribs. He wasn't supposed to say . . . that! They will be OK? *But they can't be OK . . . if I'm not with them.*

I recall how my parents sang to the music in the car on the way home from the beach, and the time when Dad swooped Mum off her feet in the kitchen.

So, they aren't falling apart without me . . . ? They are . . . *healing*!

Her door was once a shiny bottle green.

I can tell because in patches it's still shiny. The majority of the door, however, is covered by a dull sheen that is beginning to crack and fade. There is no glass in the door, just a little peephole to scrutinise unwanted visitors. There's black gathering in the corners of the porch and it's difficult to tell if it's mould or dirt, but by contrast there's a thriving array of lovingly tended pot plants, mostly green herbs and ferns, but there are also some daffodils and primroses, exposing their sweet, colourful faces to spring. Petals and leaves reach skywards from metal or terracotta pots of different sizes; a chimney pot billows an evergreen plant aptly labelled 'angel eyes', and a cracked floral teapot pours ivy from its spout. It all looks so pretty and very Mother Earth.

It's a bit dispiriting trying to slow down time when it won't listen. We are at One Shoe Sue's house and it is as if the minutes and hours since I first told Dad who I really was have slipped away in the blink of an eye.

Dad is straightening his shoulders in a bid to feel braver than he does. I try to settle the swarm of nerves in the pit of my stomach as I hear someone approaching the faded door. One Shoe Sue opens it, and stands framed by the opening like a picture. 'Thomas isn't here.' She smiles kindly to reassure me that her son from my school is out. 'I'm always confidential.'

Her hair is very long for her age and coloured a strawberry blonde, held back by a fat flowery headband. Her clothes are flowy, slightly hippy. Two shoes poke out from beneath her multicoloured skirt.

She welcomes us in, turning and limping noticeably down the narrow hallway into a kitchen. There's an old-fashioned dark green kettle on her hob, which is beginning to whistle. I can hear the sounds of sport coming from the television in the next room and, through the gap in the door, I can see Ted squashed into their old brown sofa, his face turned to the screen.

The kitchen is big and warm and very green with a coffee table in the corner and a green two-seater sofa beside it. Sue tells us to make ourselves comfortable, while lifting off a fat stripy cat with an emerald velvet collar, several magazines and a random black sock from the jade-coloured cushions, which are dotted with tiny yellow flowers. She offers us a hot drink.

'Only herbal or soft drinks I'm afraid,' she says with a smile. 'Caffeine isn't good for anxiety levels.' She looks briefly at us both with her blue eyes that have light shining out of them, a light that makes me feel comforted.

'I'll have forest fruit please,' says Dad, after looking through her little basket full of flavoured tea sachets.

'I'll have the same,' I say and she turns to get four cups down from an old-fashioned dresser. She gives Ted a drink, then returns from the lounge, quietly closing the door behind her with a click. She has already placed a large glass jug containing water, ice and some sliced lemon on the table along with three tumblers. Sue picks up the mugs of steaming herbal tea, and places them on the coffee table before sitting down on the single armchair, which she has moved closer to the sofa and to us.

Dad looks around, studying the room. There is nothing particularly 'hocus-pocus' about Sue's house. It feels lived in and comfortable. My own eyes travel along the windowsill and its array of clutter, a photo of Thomas squinting at the camera, glass ornaments of various shapes and sizes, a flower vase. 'It's very . . . green . . .' I comment, 'your kitchen.'

Her wide mouth smiles again. 'Oh, thank you,' she says, although I was unaware I was paying a compliment. 'Green is the colour of birth and renewal,' her wide mouth informs us. 'It is also a great balancer, creating an equilibrium between the head and the heart.' Dad and I find ourselves scanning the room once again to see if we can *get* the equilibrium. We both nod, as if we know exactly what she's talking about, but neither of us do.

She continues to smile at us both, particularly at me. Her eyes hold the reflections of the yellow flames of three candles, all green of course, and scented with honeysuckle, which are on the coffee table in front of us. Neither Dad nor I can find much of a smile to return; we're too busy wondering how this session is going to progress. 'Is there anything you'd like to ask me or would you like to just start?'

Dad clears his throat. 'Oh, we're not here for that . . . reading stuff.'

But Sue keeps smiling and inclining her head slightly, as if agreeing to something we haven't actually asked yet. Her serene expression and aura of all things spiritual make me believe that she will understand if we just tell it how it is.

282

So we both begin at exactly the same time, then give an embarrassed laugh at the same time.

Sue laughs with us and suggests that I should be the one to ask her what it is we want to know.

'I'm Lily,' I say, and those two words hang in the room expectantly. Dad and I both look emphatically at Sue to see what her reaction might be. If Sue is slightly shaken, she manages very successfully to keep calm.

'Now, dear –' Sue looks me in the eye – 'explain to me exactly what you mean.' I tell her exactly what I mean, and at the end of my full explanation, Dad chips in.

'She . . . er . . . he . . . really is Lily you know. You *have* to tell us what to do.'

Sue looks questioningly at me. 'Do you always feel like Lily or only sometimes?' she asks me, trying to be sensitive, but I answer abruptly and slightly annoyed.

'I don't *feel* like Lily. I *am* Lily.'

Sue reaches out and presses my arm lightly in order to get my full attention while explaining what she really meant.

'What I mean, dear, is that sometimes it is possible for a person to be possessed by a spirit, or the ghost of a relative, for a short while . . .'

'It's not a short while. This isn't a half-hearted possession . . . I *am* Lily, and I'm using Ben's body. One hundred per cent.'

I shuffle slightly in my seat and take a jade-coloured cushion with tiny yellow flowers from behind me, so I can hug it to my stomach.

The more Sue listens to me, and the way I describe what has

happened to me, the more intrigued she looks. She tells us gently and sensitively, and in my opinion somewhat patronisingly, that she doesn't doubt that I'm Lily, but that she still needs to determine exactly what I mean.

'I'm not doubting you, dear, but can you give me any piece of information that will help me understand what you mean.' In my book that *is* doubt, but I suppose, like Dad, she needs some proof.

I try to rack my brains.

'Well . . .' I begin, 'when I was at my own funeral, I could see everything and I could wander around the audience –'

'Mourners,' she corrects with a huge smile that makes the crow's feet around her eyes show deeper and wider.

I giggle nervously while Dad remains completely poker-faced.

'Mourners,' I repeat, and I continue to tell her that I know she felt my presence behind her and that she even told Ted I was in the crematorium. I'm able to repeat exactly what happened at the time, and what Ted said back to her, when he pointed over at my coffin and told her that I was in it. When I tell this part of my story, Sue seems to get quite excited and sits forward still clasping her tea. Her fingers are surprisingly short and wide and adorned by several large rings encrusted with pretty gemstones. A straggle of strawberry blonde hair has fallen over her shoulders and she flicks it back eagerly, while placing her mug back down on the coffee table. She is completely alert.

'I knew I could sense something . . . you.' She jiggles excitedly in her seat. 'I can do that.' Sue nods her head to confirm her own talent.

'And then one night I just . . . kind of . . . got into Ben.' I add, omitting the part about not seeing him since our fight over his body.

'I've never met a spirit inside someone's body before.' Sue says as she gets up and makes her way over to a bookshelf crammed with magazines and books of all shapes and colours. Running her finger along the back of each book she stops at one and lifts it out. As she flips through the pages, I reach for my cup and take a sip. I find myself being very glad that Sue is preoccupied, because the tea tastes like something scooped out of a puddle. I let the liquid run out of my mouth and back into the cup while she isn't looking, then wipe the back of my hand over my mouth. I look at Dad and pull a face, sticking my tongue out as if there is poison on it.

Eventually, after some tutting and some 'mmm'-ing, Sue speaks up. 'Well, I'm pretty sure that you've somehow got "stuck" between life and death and this is allowing you to "use" Ben for the moment.'

I experience a fleeting desire to say, 'No *shit*, Sherlock,' but I catch it before it becomes audible.

'If you can, dear, I need you to tell me in detail what happened at the time that you departed from this world.' Dad starts shuffling in his seat and clearing his throat and I'm very aware that he probably doesn't want to hear me talk about the moment that I died in such great detail, but at the same time he doesn't stop us. I can see the muscle in his jaw working again as I describe to Sue how I found myself sitting on the grassy bank of King's Lane and that I didn't even realise my body was in the ditch until the police showed up.

She asks me delicately if I knew whether my death was sudden and, recalling the fact that my head was on backwards, I tell her that I'm pretty damn sure it was. She nods slowly. 'Yes, yes, then that's what happened, you simply died so quickly that you didn't know you had.'

I look at the clock. We have been here nearly an hour already and we haven't talked about what *will* happen to me, we've only talked about what *did* happen to me, but I don't have to wait long.

'You must move on, dear,' she says, and I think I can detect the slightest nod of Dad's head, '. . . not just for Ben's sake, but so that you can find peace in the next life . . .'

'He's not appearing in the night . . . you know . . . to swap back,' I say in my defence, trying to avoid looking directly at Dad.

'Mmm,' Sue mutters thoughtfully. 'You probably have to be "ready" to go. I can *make* it happen but it will be a difficult process and not altogether very nice.' She doesn't go into detail, and we don't particularly want her to.

'Do you feel ready, dear?' she asks me, reaching out to press my arm gently again.

'Of course she bloody doesn't,' Dad intervenes, when he sees my eyes glistening, but Sue calmly takes a moment to get some tissues, which have a pleasant lilac scent to them. I bury my nose into the smell and breathe in slowly, then she waits as I blow loudly into the tissue, aware that Dad is sitting next to me, silent, upright and uncomfortable as he has been the whole time. He reaches out for my hand and I release it from the lilac tissue, wiping the dampness away on Ben's school trousers, before we clasp our fingers together. After a few minutes, I feel composed enough to look back up at Sue. 'Don't make me leave right now!' I beg, and she looks back at me with her calm, blue eyes, radiating light and a kind of feeling of peace. I like how reassuring they are.

'I won't *make* you go, dear . . . unless we need to do it the messy way –' she presses my arm – 'but there's no need for that. I can help you go when you're ready,' she says, looking purposely at both of us, then abruptly and unexpectedly she inhales deeply, forcing air up through her nostrils, closing her eyes, and sitting bolt upright in her chair. Dad and I look at each other. Our eyelids widen and slide back to focus on Sue. Despite how traumatic this is, both of us feel a strong urge to laugh and I purse my lips together to prevent one bursting out.

Sue snaps open her eyes, making us jump a little, and she looks at us.

'I think Ben is here,' she says in her serene and very believable way.

'Oh, thank God,' I burst out, slumping over, as if I had been previously inflated with guilt-laden air. I avoid Dad's gaze again, as my reaction confirms that I didn't really know where Ben was all this time. 'Is he mad at me?' I ask her.

'No, dear . . . no, I don't get that vibe from him . . .' But a fat T-shaped crease appears on her brow as she screws the muscles of her forehead tightly together. 'I can see purple . . . purple flowers . . . they look like hyacinths. Does this mean anything to you, dear?' she asks me.

'No,' I answer simply. 'I doubt Ben even knows what a hyacinth is.'

'Well, he's waving them at me as if you should know what they mean . . . but I can't get any more . . . I can't . . . stay connected.' She looks a little unnerved, and my fear and guilt over what I've done to Ben returns. If that was supposed to be a reading, it was crap. Ben would never give me flowers especially after I'd pulled a stunt like this.

'Why can't you stay connected?' I ask, wondering yet again what Ben was playing at, if indeed he was playing at anything.

The fingers of my right hand are squeezing Dad's so tightly, and my other hand is gripping the lilac tissue, all crumpled now. All trace of nervous laughter has left me.

Sue continues to sit, tuning in, with her eyes shut. Dad leans forward as if that will help him hear what she might say. We stay silent. Expectant. Her face is tilted at an angle and she stays like this for so long I begin to think she's passed into some kind of catatonic state.

'He *is* here, but he's not giving me anything else . . . just the hyacinths.' She breathes out noisily through her nose. 'Sorry.'

Suddenly Sue is released from her trance, becoming unpinned from the furniture, allowing her to pick up her tea to swallow the last of the puddle water liquid.

Dad and I look at each other and then at Sue.

'Er . . . is he . . . OK?' Dad asks her. I hear the anguish and worry in his voice and now I understand that he must have been really worried about Ben all this time. My heart twists with the childlike sense of unfairness Ben and I used to get if one of us had something better than the other. I can almost hear my six-year-old inner self complaining it isn't fair while I stamp my foot. *Worry about me too. I'm the one you are trying to get rid of!*

288

'Yes, Mr Richardson. Ben is OK. History has come across many cases of possession and I am confident he will be able to return to his body, when Lily leaves it.'

Dad breathes out a visible lungful of relief.

'I think it is as I've already said, dear, that you need to be ready before you can cross over.' I am so relieved that Ben will be OK, but I've no idea how I'll know when I'm ready or if I'll ever actually be ready.

'How will she *ever* be ready exactly?' Dad asks, verbalising my inner worry, employing a frown that brings his greying eyebrows together until they almost touch. He has a note of disbelief in his voice. 'How can a child *ever* make themselves ready to . . . you know . . . ?'

'Die?' we both chorus at him quietly, using the one word that he has been unable to utter since the day they found me in a ditch.

Sue places her mug back on the coffee table and leans back in her chair. She crosses one leg over the other and I can now see them quite clearly. One shoe is creased across the top where the natural shape of her foot bends, and the other looks almost brand new wedged on the end of her stiff-looking artificial leg. Even though she has tights on, which pick out the maroon in her multicoloured hippy skirt, and the ends of her legs are hidden in those horrible shoes, I can easily tell that only one leg is real.

She sees me looking at it but is not embarrassed. 'Accident,' she announces, patting her leg as if it's an old friend. 'A long time ago now.'

She returns to the point. 'So, I have faith. I believe that

one day soon you will work out when it's time, then Ben will be able to return. Look *deep* within yourself and you will know, dear.' She smiles reassuringly and gives a funny jiggle of the head.

'How can you be sure of all this?' asks Dad, still with his frown and more than a hint of disbelief. 'You have to admit, this is pretty weird.'

'I've been doing this for years. I can *feel* it; the spirit world tells me things.' I can see that Dad can't think of a valid argument because this whole situation is, as he says, weird . . . totally bonkers in fact. 'But,' she adds, 'if you feel ready but Ben doesn't come to you, I *must* urge you to contact me when the time is right. Do *not leave* his body to look for him in your dreams, if he isn't waiting for you.' Her smile is gone and her face is serious.

'Why not?' Dad and I ask at the same time, confused now, because it was in our sleep that we managed to do the whole swapping thing in the first place.

We are not prepared for her answer.

'Because if neither of you are in Ben's body, it will eventually die. It cannot survive for long without a soul.' I know we are both staring at her with our mouths slightly open, very grateful that she remembered to tell us this stunningly crucial bit of info, but Sue carries on as if what she's just told us is completely normal.

'It could be anything . . . you know . . . that has stopped you passing over completely . . . regret, guilt, anger . . .'

I think about this for a while. I led a perfectly normal life until Nathan's mum snuffed it out.

'I can't think of anything . . . really . . . but if there is anything, I suppose it is guilt.'

Sue waits, and Dad leans in towards me. 'You're guilty?' he asks me in surprise.

I shrug my shoulders. 'I saw things when I was in limbo –' I look between them both – 'I could see all the people I knew before I died, and their lives are different now.'

Sue tilts her head to the side in a sympathetic manner.

'In what way, dear?' I pour some of the clear cold water into a glass. A cube of ice plops in, and a lemon slice follows. I take a sip. Tasteless but beautifully cold and with a lemony smell. It helps my hot throat, which is tired from my anticipation of what this day would bring.

'People's lives have changed, and it isn't for the better. I suppose I feel responsible.'

'You blame yourself? For your own death?' Dad says.

'Well, no, I blame the driver for that. But stuff is going wrong. Ben's life is going astray for a start; he's getting into all sorts –'

'I didn't realise,' Dad interrupts mournfully.

'Exactly,' I continue. 'He's trying to make his own way through all this. Matthew misses Ben, Beth blames herself, whatever you say, you and Mum are not the same, Nathan is without a girlfriend, and, as for his . . . for the driver of the car, well –'

'Wait!' Dad interrupts again, raising his voice in amazement. 'You *know* who *did* it? Tell me who the bastard is, right *now* . . .' He pulls his phone out of his pocket. 'I'm not entirely sure *how* we tell Brian that we know but I'll figure that out later . . .'

'Stop!' I snatch his phone away and switch it off. 'I'm not ready to tell anyone who did it yet.'

'Why?' Dad asks, completely incredulous.

I picture Nathan with his mother. What do I say? *My boyfriend would be upset?*

'I just . . . can't. That's all I can tell you.'

'But he *killed* you! Why would you protect him?' He waves his hands in the air, unable to contain himself. 'That bastard *killed* you and didn't hang about long enough to face what he did.' I let him continue to believe that the driver is a man and wait for him to pause.

I reach out for one of Dad's hands again, until I'm holding it with both of mine and look him in the eye with what I hope is a determined expression. 'It's . . . complicated.'

But Dad is beside himself. 'He'll be bloody complicated when I go and beat his brains out,' he shouts. 'Tell me. Tell me now!'

And here it is. The full anger from my father's raw grief, finally finding its way out of his head and out of his heart. He paces the room and smacks at the walls, and tells me over and over that I absolutely have to tell him who did it until Ted pops his head round the door.

'Is everything OK?' he asks.

'Of course it bloody isn't.' Dad turns to him, some spittle shooting out of his mouth, leaving a little bunch of bubbles on Ted's shirt. Ted ignores the spit and retreats, after getting a wink and a slight raise of the hand from Sue, who reaches out to press my arm again. I have no idea why she keeps doing that, but it has the effect of making me feel grounded, reassured.

I search my mind for anything that will stop him losing control in this way. 'Dad!' I snap at him. 'I shouldn't really have been there anyway. I shouldn't have spent my money. I should have been on the bus.'

He stops briefly in a moment of disbelief, before exploding again. 'What the *hell* do you mean . . . you shouldn't have been there? You *were* there; you just shouldn't have been run over and killed by a moron. Perhaps you could have been saved. Perhaps if he hadn't driven away and left you out there, you would still be alive.' He bites his fist.

'No, Dad,' I tell him gently. 'You know I wouldn't have been. You read the coroner's report; it was in black and white. You know how it was.' He punches the wall again, immediately bringing his hand to his chest and holding it with other hand. I'm pretty sure that *really* hurt.

Dad deflates in front of me and Sue, and sobs as if his heart is going to break. 'But you wouldn't have been left there . . . in the cold . . . all night.' It is one of the most painful sights I have ever seen. Sue passes him some of the lilac-scented tissues and he takes about five at once, blowing his nose loudly. 'Please?' he begs in an almost child-like way, and even though he can see I won't change my mind he adds with a tight throat, 'You were my little girl.'

I notice how he says that I *was* his little girl, even though I am right here, and although he doesn't know it my heart is wounded.

The black oil that is staining the beautiful sea of our lives is spreading further, and again I think of Nathan's mum and my anger flares at how I can get my revenge, other than my spooky messaging tactics, and without ruining Nathan's life in the process. If I could do that, then maybe my dad wouldn't have to suffer with *his* anger any more.

'So, Lily,' Sue says calmly, changing the subject, 'I think you should contact me when you think you are ready. But don't be scared, dear,' she adds, 'don't ever be scared. If you want to come back and talk any time, please do.' I look at her and think about her complete and utter peace with the world. I think it must be because she is so sure that death is not the end. It is sad, that's for sure, but perhaps not as tragic as it is when you don't believe.

'Sue?' I ask, and she inclines her head in her strange way. 'The wisps of smoke I told you about . . . at my funeral. You had two, do you know what they were?'

'I know *who* they *are*.' She smiles and leans back in her seat as if she has just eaten a satisfyingly good meal. 'They are my first husband and my first boy, Andrew. The accident.' She pats her amputated stump. 'I've never *seen* them since they passed over, but I know they are around me when I need them. The spirit world tells me,' she says confidently. Then she laughs. 'They have my leg with them for now, and when it is my turn to go, they can have the rest of me.'

'Oh.' I laugh a little too, sort of. 'I see . . . What happened?' But she presses my arm again as she gently leads me to the front door, giving me a look that I don't understand.

'What happened is no longer relevant. It's how we move on that counts.' She opens the door for us and my dad steps over the threshold to the world outside, looking somehow smaller than he did when he went in. I link arms with him and we leave her, closing the green door behind us until another day.

Climbing into the car, I can see Dad's hand beginning to get puffy and purple where he smacked it but I try to hide my

294

pure joy at not being expelled from Ben's body tonight, as I had feared might happen.

I have more time.

We are both silent as Dad drives us home. I think about what Sue said, about being ready, and I try not to entertain the idea of what should happen if I never decide to be ready. I remember what I said to him the night we swapped places, that my whole life was unfinished business. How do I finish living quickly when I'm only fifteen? And why couldn't she talk to Ben properly? She's supposed to be a medium, and as his twin sister between us we should have got some sense out of him. Perhaps he isn't strong enough to come forward . . . or perhaps I'm preventing him.

I suddenly notice the clock on the dashboard: ten past seven! Mum will be demented, to say the least, that we're so late.

'Dad?' He takes his eyes off the road for a second to look at me. 'We have to tell Mum. If I'm going to be here for a while, she really ought to know.'

'I think you're right,' he agrees, 'but you'll have to be more convincing about Ben. Tell her that he's in there with you.' He indicates to pull into our road, and the engine makes a quieter sound as he slows down. I'm almost excited at the thought that in a short while I won't have to pretend with either of my parents.

'This is really going to blow her bananas though,' he says, and we share a nervous glance.

'Pretty much,' I agree.

Nathan's mum held a second bottle of wine in her hands. She had had another bad day. One of the old people at the residential home had grabbed her arm as she walked past. 'I know your secret,' she had said with a shaky voice and watery eyes. She'd prised the lady's gnarled fingers from her grip, telling her that she *didn't* have a secret. Her eyes had scanned the other residents and staff to see if anyone had noticed, to see if any other eyes were upon her, questioning her.

But of course she did have a secret and that boy knew it. She'd seen him standing outside her house only the other day, staring through the windows, silently accusing her. She was clinging on to every day, yet every day was proving too hard.

Thankfully everyone at the home was busy in their own way, or in their own heads, or deaf. Rows of comfortable shoes with thick tights or trousers hitched high and almost under armpits lined the edges of the communal room. The elderly residents whiled away their days in comfortable chairs, under crocheted blankets, with rheumy eyes and idle hands. All they knew was that their favourite member of staff, the lady who always brought a touch of loveliness, and colour, and humour, to their shrinking days, had, over the last few weeks, become faded and mechanical.

The kind lady who had once stroked a cheek or held a hand, joking and laughing with them, reminding them that they were still alive, who left a trail of beautiful perfume in the air as she walked around their home, which otherwise smelled of wee and cabbage, was now just another person who got paid to see to their basic needs.

Nathan's mum poured another glass from the second bottle and tried to shut out the penetrating and accusing eyes of the old lady, *and* the brother of the girl she'd killed. '*I know what you did,*' he had said, but neither of them could possibly know, she told herself, and she swallowed her thoughts with the dark red and slightly sour liquid. She looked at the clock. Ten past seven. Alex was out and Nathan was at a friend's house.

She looked into her glass for a solution to her troubled mind. Alex was beginning to notice that she was drinking more than usual, but he wouldn't know if she had one more glass. It was just for tonight; she was sure tomorrow she wouldn't have anything at all. As she made her way back to the sofa, the glass jolted from her hand as she sat down, spilling on her skirt and the arm of the beautiful cream sofa, but she didn't notice.

Then, picking up the remote control, she curled up on the sofa in front of a television programme that she would neither see nor hear.

Nathan's mum was killing herself softly.

Mum is curled up on the sofa when we finally let ourselves in, a glass of wine in her hand and the television blaring a notch too loud. She can hardly bear to look at us. She'd gone to the effort of cooking tonight and the house smells rich with the juices of chicken and garlic, but a broken dish lies on the kitchen floor amongst the vegetables and chicken pieces that are scattered around, and gravy is splashed up the kitchen cupboards and the door. We look at each other and again our eye widen before our eyes return to take in the view. We stand together in the doorway like two partners in crime, while Mum calls out sarcastically from the living room. 'Your dinner's in the kitchen.'

'Shall we tell her tomorrow?' Dad whispers, as the weight of Mum's anger and dejection hangs in the atmosphere, but as difficult as this is, if I'm going to stay for a while, she needs to know. Besides, I'm tired of pretending to be a boy in my own home.

We clear the mess silently and make a snack each, eating in the kitchen, staring at each other. When our plates are empty we take a breath of courage and make our way into the lounge, as if we're two conspirators going into battle, only we don't have a strategy. Mum rigidly faces the television as if we are not even there, as we stand pathetically in the centre of the room, clearing our throats and waiting for her to look up.

Dad picks up the remote from the cushion beside her and switches the power off. In a flash she leaps out of her chair, clawing for the remote like a cat snatching at its prey, and her anger is barely contained. 'Give it back!' she shouts at him.

'Calm down, Mum . . . please?' I beg her, hating to see her like this, as Dad continues to hold the remote too high for her to reach. Her anger is as bad as the day I came home after taking the day off school last week. She is going ballistic, as if all the emotion from my death is only just below the surface, like when Dad lost it tonight in One Shoe Sue's house.

When she finally gives up and tries to push past him to get out of the room, he uses his height and weight to block her way, then gently leads her back to the sofa.

'Mum? Listen, I need to tell you something.' She turns her face towards me, a single blink causing one fat tear to spill down her cheek. Her expression is one of expectation for the damn good reason that could possibly cause Dad and me to join ranks this evening and think that it was OK to leave her at home alone, cooking for us and waiting for us to not show.

'Ummm,' I begin tentatively. 'We're late because we've been sorting something out. It's something that you really need to know . . . but I just don't know where to start.' I take a breath and watch the confusion grow on her face, along with a hint of fear over what this could be about, etching several more years into her face.

'Well, *find* somewhere to start,' she suggests aggressively.

I kneel down next to her and my words come out in a muddle.

I tell her what I told Dad and Sue, about Ben's dream and how I managed to come 'through' and that I am actually . . . Lily. There, I've said it. 'I am Lily.'

I watch a strange activity take place on her face, like a kind of facial dance: confusion followed by complete and utter disgust.

'How *could* you?' she shouts.

'Well, I don't really understand it myself . . . I think it must be because I'm not ready . . .'

But, out of the blue, she slaps my face.

'How *could* you be so insensitive and . . . and . . . STUPID?' Her eyes flick angrily between me and Dad. 'What do you think you're *doing*?' My hand reaches for my face and I hold it against my cheek, and the fact that my own mother did this hurts so much more than the pain. My eyes fill with so many tears that I can't see anything apart from a merging of colours and for a moment I'm too shocked to blink.

'I *am*, Mum. You have to believe me. I'm not playing a cruel trick.' Then I do blink and my fingers that are still against my cheek become damp with tears. 'I really am . . . Lily.'

Mum tries to get up from the sofa again and I grab her, pulling her back down by the hand.

'Get . . . *off* . . . me,' she says deeply between clenched teeth. The way her nostrils flare and the way her staccato words are forced out frightens me.

Suddenly she gasps a little, and she holds both hands in the air with her palms facing me, as if halting any ridiculous notion of what I have just told her. 'You're not well, Ben . . . He's not well, James. We need to get him a doctor.' She looks from me to Dad, waiting for him to agree with her, but he doesn't move.

'Why are you just standing there? Do something. Ben, you've been under a lot of stress lately; we all have, but –'

'Mum, I'm perfectly sane.' I look at Dad for support.

'It's true, Amelia. I didn't believe it at first either. It's a very . . . *unusual* thing –'

'Listen,' I interrupt desperately, 'I can tell you things. I . . . I know that you wore a brown jacket to the hospital the day I died; I know you had sunflowers at my funeral and I know that you had a Chinese takeaway on the weekend . . . and we ordered a meal for six.' I sit back, breathing quickly, waiting for her reaction, expecting a flicker of recognition, a flash of joy, a hug. Her reaction comes. Her eyes stare widely at me for a few seconds, then her brow furrows, and an almost musical mixture of perplexed and furious tones play up and down in her voice . . .

'Of *course* you do! You were *there*, Ben!'

None of us makes a sound for a few seconds as it takes a while for the penny to drop, and Dad, who is now sitting forward on a chair he's pushed up in front of us both, taps my knee.

'*Ben* was there . . . for all of those. Think of something else.'

'Oh,' I say. A small word for such a huge realisation of my own stupidity. 'Of course, *Ben* was there . . . Ummm . . .' I think quickly, then speak in rapid-fire sentences in my hurry to get Mum to understand. 'I know that you went to my room when everyone else was out. I know that you took my hairbrush and ran my hair across your cheek; I know that you smelled my pillow and said you would always love me.' I pause to catch my breath and to see if any of it is sinking in. Mum sits perfectly still, eyes on me all the time, trying to work out how

301

Ben might know these things, recollecting the moment she had braved going into my room.

'I know you kissed my glass where the lip balm left the shape of my lips on the edge of the rim.' As I mention the lip balm, her lips start to quiver and the colour around her nostrils becomes red. 'You put your hand on my urn and sang a few lines of my funeral song before Uncle Roger interrupted you by calling up the stairs.

'And I know you told my pillow that you feel guilty for telling me not to spend all my money . . . because if I couldn't pay for the bus, you wouldn't come and get me.' A little gasp comes out of her mouth, and tears fall down both our faces when I hear myself say that out loud. Still kneeling in front of her, I take my hand away from my cheek and put both my hands on her knees. I didn't mean it to sound like blame; it just came out that way. She *had* said she wouldn't come and get me. Mum's guilt is laid bare in the room and I did that to her, and I feel bad. She struggles to breathe evenly, as the reason for her torment since my death is exposed. 'I'm not blaming you, Mum. It was never your fault.'

She stays completely still, staring into her lap. 'Mum?' I lean my face towards her. 'I shouldn't have spent my money, Mum. It wasn't your fault.'

She fiddles with her fingers in mine, processing everything.

'I don't understand. I don't understand what you're trying to tell me. How *could* you think you're Lily? It isn't possible.' Every part of my mother's face shows layers of varying emotions, which I think, if she hadn't reached for my hands in her lap, might suck her under and never let go. She lets a trail of mucus

302

leave her nose and travel towards her lips unchecked and Dad fumbles about for a tissue. When he can't find one, I produce a small wad of damp lilac tissues from my pocket and I reach up to wipe her face with them.

I do my absolute best to describe, yet again, how it all happened, my words sounding unbelievable and inadequate. I start from the beginning and describe the man with the ridiculously large forehead and how he handed Mum the tissues when she was crying in the morgue. I describe some of the moments that she's experienced when neither Ben nor Dad were anywhere around her, and how I watched over our various friends and families and could see everything that was going on in their lives too.

'You used to watch all the supernatural stuff on television, Mum,' I remind her. 'You believe in life after death. Why should *my* death be any different?'

'I've been waiting desperately for a sign from Lily but nothing ever happened. I've been hoping so hard for something, *anything*, that would tell me that she's OK . . . but nothing.'

'Well, here I am, and I'd say I'm a pretty big sign, Mum. It *is* me. I have come back through Ben . . . he is letting me.'

'How is he letting you?' Mum peers at me with a look of pure incomprehension.

'He's kind of . . . stepped aside. He's still here . . .' I add hastily, tapping myself to indicate that the Ben she can see is still here as well, but trying to hide the fact that actually he isn't.

'So . . . he *is* here too?' she clarifies.

Dad and I shoot a look at each other.

'Yes, but he's allowing me to use him . . . for a while . . . sort of.'

Mum rubs at the swollen veins on her temples as if a massive headache is pounding through her head. 'So what are you saying? That you'll keep switching places?' she asks. It occurs to me that for Mum, if I could use my brother's body as some sort of visitors lounge, it would mean never having to say goodbye.

'I don't really know, Mum. I don't think so. I don't know how long I'm here for, but I'm here now.'

The room goes quiet and no one moves. I can see Mum turning this information over in her head, trying to make sense of it.

'Then . . . tell me . . . what was the surprise present that Lily was going to get you for your birthday?'

'The surprise present *I* was going to get *Ben* was a sport multi day,' I reply.

Mum nods slowly, still thinking hard, in case I couldn't keep the surprise to myself and had already told Ben.

'What boots did you try on before buying the purple Converse shoes?'

This is easy. 'A really high pair of pink heels with a little bow on the back . . . You said they were too high.'

'What's your bra size?'

'34B,' I answer, looking down at Ben's chest. 'Well, it was.'

I suddenly think of something that is so obvious, I have no idea why it didn't occur to me before. 'Wait there,' I order them both and try to unravel my legs from my kneeling position. The pins and needles work their way up my feet as I attempt to run from the room and up the stairs. Rummaging in my bedroom I find what I'm looking for, abandoned months ago for a far more interesting teenage life, and as I slowly walk down the stairs towards my waiting, expectant parents I begin to play.

My brother's lips take a moment to adjust against my flute, but finally I sort them out, and the haunting notes of their favourite classical piece, 'Stranger on the Shore', float around me and into the room where my parents are sitting. When I appear in the doorway, still playing, I almost struggle to keep going. They are both sitting and facing me with a look I can't even describe. It's like the deepest joy, the saddest pain and the pure amazement of new birth all in one.

Ben wasn't musical, he was sporty. Ben couldn't play the flute, he couldn't blow a single note, and here I am, making soft music come from beyond the grave and turning melancholy into a strangely beautiful thing.

I almost get to the end before I drop to my knees again in front of my mother, and look her in the face, imploring her to find me as I'd asked Dad to do on Sunday night. She stares for a long time; the clock on the shelf ticking away the seconds slowly, and heavily, and inevitably. Her brain tries to ignore the face of her son, the body of a boy, the instinct of a mother reaching through these windows of the soul to the daughter I am within. 'There *is* life after death,' I whisper and I know she can now see what Dad sees in my eyes, and what I can see, when I look carefully at Ben in the mirror, like a river running clear exposing the green moss beneath.

I am here.

Mum starts shaking, shoulders, knees, teeth and hands, like a physical earthquake within her own body. She continues to look closely at me as if I'm looking up from just below the watery surface of a lake. Her face moves closer to mine, until we're staring only inches apart through these windows, like we used to do when I was a very young child. We try not to blink and therefore break the spell, but the spell is not broken; I *am* here. Suddenly Mum leans towards me, her arms reaching round me and pulling me to her. Squeezing me tighter and tighter. Squashing me back inside her empty heart.

'Oh, and by the way, when Ben couldn't find his football shirt the other day, the one signed by David Beckham, I took it ages ago and sold it on eBay. He will go ballistic!'

'Yes, he *will* go ballistic,' they both say together.

'I guess he knows now . . . don't you, Ben?' Mum adds, looking at my chest as if Ben is inside, reclining in an internal armchair and watching the action.

'I guess he does,' I answer, and sit beside her to hug her, hoping that she won't question me any more about Ben.

She wearily leans against the body of her son to be comforted by the soul of her daughter, and Dad joins in for the all-American hug. For those few minutes our heartbeats are in time with each other.

'But what do we do now?' she asks us both, cheeks stained with drying tears, eyes bloodshot and fingers stroking my back.

Dad and I tell her how we've just been to see One Shoe Sue and what she told us about me needing to be ready to leave.

'But I'm here now,' I say, omitting the fact that as time goes by I'm becoming less and less willing to leave.

Mum looks at Dad and he looks back at her, and they share a secret look that I can't read, but I choose to let it go.

'I'm here now,' I repeat silently to myself.

Nathan's dad and Nathan cleared the glass and the empty bottle of wine away, and dabbed a cloth at the red stain on the sofa. Nathan fetched a blanket and wrapped it round his once glamorous and sparkling mother.

There was a ladder in her tights and her glorious auburn hair was being drowned by the tide of mousy brown, silver-flecked roots. Her make-up had smudged as if she had rubbed her eyes and the fact that something had gone very wrong with her was obvious to both of them.

The figurehead on the Peterson ship was a mess.

The sweet smell of hot chocolate floats up from our mugs and for a short while there is a beautiful sense of belief.

Belief that the essence of my family and who we are will never change, whether we can be seen or not. But then Mum clears her throat and I can see that her lips are dancing with emotion. 'I would have come to get you . . .' I know instantly that she's referring to the shopping trip again, to her claim that she wouldn't drive me home if I spent all my money.

I reach over and squeeze her hand quickly. 'I know that, but I was a big girl and I thought I knew what I was doing . . . It was not your fault, and besides, I shouldn't have lied.' Mum doesn't let go of my hand.

'And the bloody driver's got away scot-free,' Dad pipes up again. He can't help himself. 'She knows, you know,' he says, staring at Mum, while tipping his head in my direction, and I groan. 'She knows who did it, but she won't tell.'

I roll my eyes heavenwards and prepare to say the same things I said to Ben in the night and to go through the same battle that I've just had with Dad at Sue's house. 'Did you have to mention it now, Dad?' I'm annoyed with him for bringing it up again. 'You know it's not that simple. The police are hardly likely to believe me . . . or you. And we certainly can't tell them I've returned from the dead to put the blame on someone. There isn't a shred of evidence to prove it.'

'Their car. The police will take his car in and examine it. They have ways . . .' Mum looks hopeful. 'It won't matter how we know, as long as he's found –'

'There isn't any evidence on the car,' I interrupt. 'There isn't a single mark.'

'You've *seen* it?' Mum asks. 'Do . . . do we know him?'

I think quickly, anxious not to have Dad running madly amongst everyone we know blaming their husbands and sons. I lie. 'You don't know him. Like I said, it's complicated . . . The police won't be able to solve the case unless *he* confesses.'

I run my fingers across my lips, like pulling a zip. 'I can't say anything yet. But as soon as I can, I will.'

Dad glances at the clock on the wall. 'We're going round in circles now; it's very late.' And he stands up, nudging at Mum to do the same, and sharing that same secret look that they had earlier.

'Can I sleep in my own room?' I ask them. 'Would you find it a bit freaky?'

Dad smiles ruefully. 'Yes. It would be very freaky, but I expect you'll do it anyway.' And within ten minutes I find myself squeezed, slightly uncomfortably but happily familiar, into my own pyjamas, snuggling under my own duvet, and looking at the shapes of my own room. Taking my phone I go on the Internet and search 'purple hyacinths' and their meanings.

'It's a clue, isn't it?' I say out loud to Ben, finally understanding what happened at Sue's. 'One of your cryptic specials. Like the honey-bee clue and all the other stuff you've ever done.'

I scroll through the answers online and come across one that I think fits.

'The purple hyacinth . . . it means . . . I'm sorry, please forgive me.'

Ben was trying to tell Sue that he forgives me for using his body. That's it! Ben is giving me time, because he forgives me.

As tiredness gets the better of me, I ignore myself in my urn and turn the light off, feeling confident that Ben won't come and get me tonight.

I am most definitely not ready.

After only a few minutes, Mum creeps out of their bedroom and into mine. She doesn't turn the light on. 'Shhhh,' she whispers into the darkness before I can speak. 'Don't say anything. I came to kiss you goodnight . . . like when you were a little girl.' She kneels by my bed and leans over me, burying her face in my hair, breathes in really slowly as if absorbing the very essence of me deep into her soul, then she kisses me on the forehead and creeps out. 'I love you,' she murmurs, as she briefly hesitates by the open doorway, before withdrawing to her own room. I guess with the light off it was easier for her to know that I am Lily.

James and Amelia undressed for bed in silence, clicking the door shut behind them before freely sharing the same furtive glances they hoped their child or *children* couldn't see.

Climbing into bed, they met in the middle and clung on to each other as if the bed beneath them was not enough to support the weight of their concerns.

'I . . . I don't know where to begin . . .' Amelia said, her breath warm against her husband's chest. 'I don't know if this is fantastic or awful. I can't process the idea that Lily can talk to us through Ben. And I don't understand how they can both be in his body at the same time. If you ask me, Ben seemed . . . absent.'

Her husband sighed into the dark and tried to arrange his words as carefully as possible. 'I think Ben is stepping aside . . . you know, to let Lily do this.'

'Like a medium who allows someone who's passed over to talk through them?' Amelia rationalised.

'Exactly,' James confirmed, relieved that she thought it could be as simple as that.

'So what do we do now, James? How do we save them both?' she asked.

'By helping Lily move on,' he replied. 'Sue said she'll know when she's ready, and I don't know how she will but we need to do our best to show her the way, as soon as possible.'

'To show her how to leave us . . . again,' Amelia echoed sadly.

'They can't share the same body, Ames; Ben needs his life back.'

'At least we know now . . . at least we know there is something more . . .' whispered Amelia, 'even if she won't tell us who did it yet.'

They both fell silent, contemplating everything that was happening to their family, until sleep thankfully overtook them both.

The clock's red numbers shine 09.50. I have overslept.

I can already hear the sounds of morning coming from downstairs. The coffee machine makes its rumbling death rattle, and I can hear the clinks of cutlery on china. When I enter the kitchen, Mum's at the sink in her faded blue dressing gown, the colour of ragged forget-me-nots at the end of their time, and Dad is next to her in his favourite blue T-shirt with the slogan 'My idea of a balanced life is a beer in each hand' printed on the front. This T-shirt used to stretch slightly over his stomach, but this morning I notice how the letters stay in shape, and the material hangs in folds where the telltale pounds, which used to cling to his belly, have slipped away over the last few weeks. His jeans fit better as well, as if at first glance he's somehow become younger from the neck downwards, but in order to compensate, the years have now crept up to his face.

They both look different from yesterday. I can't rationalise it because it isn't happy and it isn't sad. I suppose it must be the promise of something intangible that will replace the absolute certainty that was, until yesterday, their previously bleak lives. The skin on their faces looks as if it has shrunk a little in the night. It now nearly fits.

They both look up at the same time and I notice identically

startled expressions, which they instantly try to hide. I don't know what they were expecting this morning, but I don't suppose it was to see their son, wearing my cute PJs and my pink dressing gown, and I can see how difficult it is for them to translate this vision in front of them.

Mum pushes orange juice towards me, the expensive kind, bits clinging to the tall glass, promising the freshness of Mediterranean landscapes. The toaster releases its springs, sending the golden slices upwards until their crusty edges poke out, and Mum puts them on a plate and hands me a knife and some peanut butter, finally understanding why I was eating the dreaded spread the other day. Dad pours them both a coffee and they sit down opposite me, nursing their mugs, ignoring their toast, and trying to pretend that this situation is in any way normal.

The late night with its jumbled and bizarre discussion hangs noisily in the air.

'I guess you're not expecting me to go to school today then?' I ask, surprised that they let me sleep in, and that neither of them have got ready for the day either.

'We thought we could have a sort of . . . snow day?' Mum replies.

'Abandon the normal and seize the exceptional,' Dad adds.

'You mean bunk off . . . in real English,' I tell them.

The unseasonal snow only lasted one day, and the ever-changing spring weather is now casting alternate splashes of sun and shade on everything outside the window.

'Sounds cool.' I smile at them and notice how they share that look again.

Mum clears her throat. 'When did you know . . . that . . . that you weren't . . . ?'

'Alive any more?' I say it for her. 'To be honest, the first thing that worried me was that my new Converse shoes were ruined.' I laugh at this and watch them try to laugh too, because they know that this is so Lily. 'I cottoned on quite quickly . . . I couldn't touch anything . . . feel anything.' I omit to tell them about the actual moment I saw my own body in the ditch.

As I talk, I try to figure out the expressions on their faces. I really don't know if I have ever seen such a look. It is as if their eyes show the pain of loss, a flicker of hope and the pure amazement of a brain trying to reason that there is massively more to life than it has always understood.

'And after you got over the shoes?' Dad asks.

'Well, I suppose it was almost like normal, except without all the workings of a live body. I didn't feel fear, or anger any more. It was like a kind of . . . peace. Imagine you're standing completely alone in a beautiful place.' I give them a moment to think of somewhere nice. 'You can't, in reality, see it, smell it, taste it, feel it or hear it, other than in your mind; you just know that it's lovely.' I take a bite of peanut butter and toast and talk thickly through it. 'That is a bit of what it's like to view the world from limbo.'

Dad leaves his chair and turns to make more of his never-ending supply of coffee. The scent of the ground beans reaches my nose, the clink and the chink of the cups, and the machine, choking and gurgling, sounds so . . . normal. Mum picks up her empty cup and waves it at him. It happily occurs to me that no cigarettes have touched the lips of my mother since she said she would stop; the scent of her has returned and I am so glad. Dad rejoins us at the table with another two steaming mugs, a notebook and a pen, and places his glasses on his nose.

'We've come up with an idea, Lily,' he says confidently, obviously relieved to have an element of control over the situation. I notice how Mum nods her agreement, even though he hasn't said what it is yet. 'One Shoe Sue said that the reason you're here is because you aren't ready to leave. I can only think that it's because you haven't done enough yet, being only fifteen. I think that you should write down all the things that you would like to do . . . you know . . . before –' his newfound confidence falters and threatens to snuff itself out completely – 'er, the most,' he finishes.

We all know what he means but only I can voice it.

'You want me to write a bucket list?' I reply, but he pulls a wry smile and takes a deep breath.

'Well . . . technically it's an *after* bucket list.'

We all giggle a bit at how daft that sounds, then look silently at the blank lines of the notebook, line after line, which offer the opportunity for me to do a thousand and more things.

Dad coughs, and his cheeks flush a little. 'The only trouble is –' he looks embarrassed – 'is that I can't afford to . . . you know . . . send you to the Moon, so to speak.' He looks at me with apology but I *do* know. His ten-year-old car in the drive and his obsession with websites promising to compare and compete with other companies for the cheapest deals has told me that.

I look at them both and smile indulgently. 'I like it!' I say bravely, even though I totally get what is really behind his idea, and what it means. If I do enough, I'll feel as if I have lived enough, and then I should go. Then I silently add, *I'm not going until I've done some travelling in the summer.* 'I'll put down everything that I would love to do, expensive or not.' I flick the blank pages. 'We can still dream. Besides . . . it doesn't matter if I don't do half of it, you two or Ben can finish it for me . . . when . . . if you can. It will be my legacy.' I give them my 'brave' smile. The reality of me putting dreams on paper that will never get fulfilled is horribly painful, but I refuse to put a price label on my hopes and wishes. A dark and silent part of me, however, wonders, if my after bucket list is very long, perhaps it will mean I won't have to leave for a really long time.

I begin immediately because it's quite nice to dream. Chewing my nails and thinking hard, twiddling the pen in my fingers, my eyes are searching around the room, as if for ideas hidden in corners or behind ornaments, but really my eyes can only see buildings, and beaches, and horses, and ships, and a host of sensations that the world has to offer past our own front door. My inner mind swirls with colour, and water, and mountains; the fabric of landscapes and far-flung places.

'Number one – travel the world.' I don't look up at my parents. I don't want to see it mirrored in their eyes that they believe this would never happen for me. If I was doing a real bucket list instead of an after bucket list, I would stop at number one. For me, there is nothing I want more. My second entry on the list raises their eyebrows. 'Number two – get a tattoo.' I talk in a slow sing-songy way, as I write each word.

I look up and remind them that it is *my* after bucket list, and that the moral ethics of each item is not open for discussion.

Mum touches Dad's arm and I hear her say 'Look, James . . . Lily's handwriting,' as the blue pen releases its ink in my rounded and neat style.

As my enthusiasm and ability to think of things grows, so does the list. 'Number three – stay up all night. Number four – dine out in a really expensive restaurant. Number five – learn to ride a horse, and ride it along a beach. Is that one or two items? Never mind. Number six – learn to ski.' I stress to them both that these things are most definitely not an order of preference. 'Seven – go in a hot-air balloon; eight – go Zorb balling; nine – learn to scuba dive . . .' I wonder how many people die without ever doing the things that would make them really feel as if they'd lived. I look at my parents. 'Have you ever done any of these things?'

They look at each other as if asking themselves the same question.

'Not many, although we've been skiing and we both used to stay up all night when we were younger, at parties or nightclubs.' I look at them from a different angle and it makes me smile, my parents partying all night, that's cool.

'Number ten – learn to drive; eleven – bungee jump; twelve – get drunk.'

'You got drunk, at the party,' Dad reminds me.

'Oh yes.' I snigger, and put a little tick by number twelve.

'I got so drunk once that my friends had to wheel me to the taxi rank in a shopping trolley,' Mum pipes up, and I laugh at the image; it's easy to forget your parents were ever young.

'Dad?'

'Er . . . yes. I got on the wrong train home from London after a heavy night out and ended up in Wales. I *was* twenty-two!' he added in his own defence. I laugh and tut as if I'm totally disgusted, but secretly I'm enjoying it. I continue. Scribbling and thinking, thinking and scribbling.

'Number thirteen – put gum on the Seattle Gum Wall.' Again their eyebrows shoot up. They haven't heard of the Seattle Gum Wall. 'It's a wall . . . in Seattle obviously, with a million bits of chewed gum stuck to it. They tried to clean it but everyone's sticking their gum back on. I look at their astonished faces. 'It's art!' I add.

The list grows. I put everything down that I once thought would be part of my memories to share with my grandchildren as a little old lady.

When, after what seems like a very long time, and a very long list, I sigh and add, 'Fall in love, have sex, and have children. Not necessarily in that order.' They share a glance. 'Don't panic,' I reassure them – I don't have to put it in words that this isn't possible – 'but,' I add, pleased with myself for thinking of this, 'you two did meet, fall in love and have children. And for that I would like to thank you. Just for the record, I'm glad that I am . . . *was* Lily Richardson, even if it wasn't for long.' I drop the pen and reach out to squeeze their hands. It is a sad fact that several weeks ago, I wouldn't have thought to hold their hands this easily. Now I want to hold on forever.

'Number four,' Dad announces, clearing his throat, looking down the list, 'and number seventeen. That's what we'll do for our snow day. We will have a bloody expensive meal and drink champagne!'

And there it is. My after bucket list is about to commence.

*

Dad appears wearing a jacket and tie, and Mum is wearing heels and a dress that now hangs off her, both ready to dine out at a restaurant they can't afford.

Due to Ben's extremely casual wardrobe, I'm wearing the only smart clothes he has, his funeral clothes. I try to imagine how he felt when he was wearing them. Did he feel uncomfortable on the day, or did the smart clothes give him some protection, as if dressing like this was like stepping aside from normal life? Like armour for battle or a wetsuit for diving. I feel that wearing them for this occasion will be like washing them clean of death, and I hope that the next time Mum and Dad see Ben wearing these clothes, if there is a next time, they will not think of my funeral but of numbers four and seventeen on my list.

*

We all feel like whispering. The tables are pristine and the waiter is serious. We move carefully and behave very well, as if expensive eating should be enjoyed as quietly as possible. Dad orders champagne and the waiter brings a shiny ice bucket, in a shiny stand, and places it beside the table. When we're ready he pours some into each glass, believing me to be sixteen, which I nearly am, if that even counts when you're dead, and I watch the pale cold liquid change the reflections in the glass to gold. It looks exciting. He places the bottle back in the bucket and I hear the ice clunk loosely around it. As I take the glass, Mum tells me to hold the stalk of the glass not the bowl.

'It must stay cold,' she says. 'Your hands will warm it up if you don't hold the stalk.'

So I hold the stalk. We take a sip together and I let it wash over my tongue, and it feels cold and bubbly. It makes me shiver and tastes sharp with just a hint of sweetness. I prefer cola but I'm not going to admit that to anyone. I smile blissfully. 'To number seventeen,' I say and lift my glass to my lips and we drink.

So, is this a life-changing experience? Not really. Don't get me wrong, it's a lovely thing to do, and adds another thread to life's rich tapestry, so to speak, but do I feel even the slightest bit as if I have taken a step towards being 'ready'?

No.

*

When we eventually close the front door on the dark cold evening that has finally descended upon us, conceding that we are all very tired from lack of sleep, and the emotional peaks and dips we've all been riding for the past twenty-four hours we head up to bed. Again we all troop up the stairs one behind the other, and as I walk sleepily into my own room I call out, 'Number one hundred and twenty-six – go to a drive-through movie . . . in America.'

Lily's parents couldn't put into words what was happening.

Before Lily had died, life had been so black and white. They had always followed a basic formula: work, eat, provide, protect.

Discovering their daughter had broken all the rules they ever believed in, and that she'd found a way to come back from the nothingness that was death, had distorted their outlook on everything. It was like looking through a kaleidoscope: toppling and turning fragments of life, creating a spectacularly beautiful yet darkly worrying picture.

It was going to be so hard watching Lily trying to grab each day by the horns in order to get the very best out of her time, and yet they were both beginning to wonder how on earth she was going to ever find a point when she could honestly say she was ready to bow out and give Ben back his rightful turn.

Each item that she could experience on the after bucket list would come with a cascade of mixed blessings. Which one, if any, would be the catalyst that might make her feel complete and ready to go?

'I'm doing my best to believe in this *thing* Ben and Lily are doing,' Amelia had said in the quiet of the night, 'but it's hard to know what is right.'

James had turned on his side to face her, trying to make out the outline of her beautiful face in the dull light of the room. 'We have to keep doing what we are doing, Ames. We have to keep giving her some experiences, while making sure Ben isn't compromised. I'm sure she'll work it out soon. If not . . .' He hesitated. 'If not . . . there is always the other way.'

Amelia turned on her side to face James until their faces were only inches apart. 'The other way?'

'Sue said there was another way . . . where we could kind of *make* Lily go.' He avoided using Sue's words. The '*messy way*' she had said. 'But let's give them a few days longer. Something will happen . . . it has to.'

They lay quietly together, not speaking, in their mirror-image positions, until eventually, heavy with unspoken worries, their eyes closed and they slept.

My dreams are muddled. Fragments of twisted images: notebooks and lists; Ben standing in the shadows shaking a bunch of purple hyacinths at me and calling me 'dumb arse'; Uncle Roger laughing at me and holding his belly like a mechanical, coin-operated clown; One Shoe Sue pressing my arm and telling me not to be scared just before I bungee jump off the school science block towards the deepest darkest hole in the ground, the stretched bungee catapulting me in and out of the hole repeatedly in front of everyone I know.

These images start spinning around a giant hourglass, their colours merging, faces twisted and mocking. The sands of the glass are trickling downwards, the words on my list disappearing through the gap between the two halves before I can experience any of them. I haven't got time. I haven't got time. I haven't got time. I start to panic, and as the very last grain of sand falls, my eyes snap open and I sit up in bed. My forehead is sweaty and I am gasping for breath.

I lie back, feeling my heart pump inside my chest until I can visualise turning the hourglass round, so that the sands can begin again.

I will *make* time.

Nathan's mum had got up really late, even for a Saturday. It was 11.45 and she was even later than Nathan, and that hardly ever happened.

Yesterday's shift at the care home had been awful. Old George had tried to take her hand, asking sadly, 'Where's your lovely smile, my darling? You used to light up this place for us oldies.' She'd given him a tight smile, knowing that her 'lovely' smile had died along with Lily Richardson and moved on to Isabelle, the old lady who kept mumbling accusing words at her.

'You *know* nothing,' she'd whispered spitefully into Isabelle's ear, and kept out of her way for the rest of the day.

Nathan's dad was sitting on the sofa, catching up with the news when his wife poked her head round the door to ask if he wanted a cup of tea. 'Yes, please,' he answered, taking in the vision in front of him. Her face looked grey, and her hair was flat, pressed to her head where she'd slept on it. Even through the folds of her slightly grubby dressing gown, he could see the weight she'd lost. She came back in, bringing two mugs with her, and gave him one, the steam from the amber liquid rising into the air. She settled on the sofa, moving a cushion that was now half covering the red stain on the arm of the chair. She cupped one hand round her tea while the other massaged her temple, as if she had a headache.

Alex paused the television with the remote control. 'You've got a hangover, haven't you?' he asked, and when no answer came, he added, 'I'm worried about how much you're drinking . . .'

As soon as the words left his lips, he knew he'd chosen them badly. She fired gunshot words back at him, the level of her voice increasing rapidly as she informed him that she'd had a lot last night but only because she'd a particularly bad day.

'*You* went out,' she retaliated. '*You* had a couple of pints after squash. What's the difference?'

Alex tried again. 'I went out and had a few pints but you've been drinking every night for a long time. I'm worried you'll become an alcoholic at this rate.'

She pounced. 'If you think that having a few extra drinks makes me an alcoholic, then so are you and so are all our friends.' Nathan could hear the shouting from his position on the stairs. He'd been making his way down when the argument had started, and found himself sitting there nervously straining to hear. When he had tried to ask her what was wrong the other night, she'd told him to mind his own business, then she'd cried and cried. Now he listened to his dad quizzing her – obviously he was worried too. At one point he had thought his dad was having an affair or something, or that they were splitting up, but he could hear the care in his dad's voice and believed with a huge sense of relief, that it wasn't that. No, there was something else wrong with his mum. So wrong that the lovely, funny, kind and loving person she had always been had almost completely disappeared.

Alex held the palms of his hands up as if to deflect the blows of her words, and tried a different tack.

'I don't like who you are at the moment, that's all.' His voice was as soft as a caressing hand, and there was anguish in his eyes. 'You are . . . different . . . and I am worried.'

He waited. The silence in the room filled it entirely, resonating with expectation. His wife stared into her mug, as if the words of her answer were unfurling with the minuscule drops of water rising cloudily out of it.

She finally looked up, placed the mug carefully down and rushed out of the room.

A few moments later Nathan and Alex Peterson could hear her violently throwing up.

*

Later that day she had found herself back at work for the evening shift, without even remembering how she got there.

Swallowing the telltale headache tablets she now kept in her bag permanently, she knew it was her turn to get Isabelle from her room and help her into the lounge area. Today, a team of hatefully cheerful people from the local theatre group were coming to sing for everybody.

Isabelle looked up from where she sat in the chair beside her bed.

'I know, you know,' she started again in the same way that she had a couple of days ago.

Nathan's mum avoided her stare, heart pounding, the image of Lily Richardson smiling at her from the pages of the newspaper, swimming in her line of vision.

'I don't know what you mean,' she said as brightly as she

could, stepping into the room, helping the old lady out of her seat, and propping her against her walking frame, half waiting for a gnarled finger to point its accusation at her, denouncing her as a murderer. She felt faint. But the image of Lily evaporated when Isabelle spoke next.

'You drink.'

Nathan's mum was so relieved that she almost laughed.

'It's not funny . . . you're heading down a slope made slippery by alcohol, my dear.'

But Nathan's mum didn't really find anything funny at all. This was what Alex had said to her only that morning. She felt tired, and scared, and ugly, and twisted inside.

'I can always spot someone who is in the grip of the stuff,' Isabelle continued, her face now showing nothing more than her many years of wisdom. 'You don't get to be ancient without learning a lot about life . . . the only trouble is that by the time you know everything most people don't stop long enough to listen any more.'

Nathan's mum's heart was beating in two different ways: with relief that her most awful secret was still safe, and with anxiety that there was now a new ugly secret to consider. Alex's words replayed in her head as Isabelle told the story of her own alcoholism.

'. . . and when I somehow managed to swim to the surface of the vat of alcohol I'd been in for years I discovered that no bugger had waited long enough to pull me out,' she said, cackling with a kind of mirthless laughter.

'Don't let that happen to you, dear.' She gripped hold of Nathan's mum's hand. 'There's no tragedy that can't be overcome, you know.' And her old, dull eyes looked into younger, dull eyes, as she pulled herself back up onto her frame. 'We'd better go and listen to all that singing.' She tutted on her dentures and sighed. 'Though why they can't just bring us those sexy Chip 'n' eggs, or Chip 'n' dales, whatever they're called, I'll never know.'

Nathan's mum forced a tired laugh, suffocated by the knowledge that her own tragedy could not be overcome.

My parents keep arranging stuff for me to do on my after bucket list at every opportunity, then studying me closely, as if each time I tick something off, I'll be saying 'toodle-pip' as easily as Granddad Colin does when he's off out to the shop for some tobacco.

In a few short days I've been to the opera and not understood a thing, yawning 'number forty-eight' from the balcony; seen a West End show, clapping 'number thirty-two'; had a number seventy-one night bus tour of London; fed an elephant by hand at the zoo, breathing 'number thirty-six' against his trunk; driven a Land Rover in a figure of eight in the middle of a farmer's field, calling 'number ten' out of the window; skied down an artificial ski slope, shouting 'number six' to the onlookers; and climbed Snowdon where I stood at the highest point, arms outstretched and yelling 'number fourteen' to the sky.

The world is a beautiful place.

But I'm not sure I will ever be ready.

*

Now the coastal air blows in from the sea and fills my nose with scents of salt and seaweed and the anticipation of number five.

Harrison, the guy at the riding centre we are at, has spent a fast-track morning teaching me the basics of riding and now we are ready with two beautiful horses to make our way to the beach. His horse, a huge black and white Irish Cob called Paddy, nuzzles me with his fat white lips, brushing their softness across my hand, before nodding his head and tossing his long wild mane. Mine is the most beautiful horse, dappled in greys and blacks, like an old-fashioned rocking horse, with white ears and a pink nose. Her name is Arizona and she looks down at me with soft, patient eyes.

We head towards the beach, along a well-worn path, interspersed by leafy green trees and bushes that separate occasionally, revealing an expanse of sea beyond. We make our way slowly downwards into the never-ending landscape of an unspoilt world, where occasional bursts of sun break through patchy clouds to splash on the ground and reflect off the twinkling sea.

Arizona carries me safely past rock and ditch until we reach the sand where the beach is wide and flat and edged with sloping hills dotted with the occasional farm building. Seagulls call all about us, screaming above the wind to each other, and as I sniff at the salt in the air and watch the waves lapping at the sand another burst of sunlight spills around us, and I am flooded with such a rush to be doing this that I wonder if this moment is all I need.

Am I ready?

'Is there anything better than this?' Harrison shouts through the wind. 'Couldn't you just do this forever?'

'Forever . . .' I echo, knowing that he has no idea exactly how good *forever* would feel.

Harrison confidently nudges the horses into a canter, their

hooves splashing through the foamy-edged water, with shining droplets dancing from sea to sky all around me as I cling tightly to my saddle.

I am flying.

But in my heart I know that still I can't let go.

James found Amelia listening over and over again to the greeting Lily had left on her phone.

Their daughter's voice, sweet and young, said, 'Hi, this is Lily, say something nice after the tone and I'll get back to you.'

'I love you,' Amelia had said into the hole at the bottom of the blue diamanté phone cover.

When she caught sight of James watching her she smiled, making a kind of sadness spread across her face. 'There must be so many *I love you*s inside this phone,' she said, studying the picture of Lily and Beth on the screen saver. 'It's difficult listening to Lily talk with Ben's deep voice . . . I worry that I will forget –' she sniffed, as the threat of tears caused her nose to go pink, and her eyes to water – 'that I will forget what she sounded like.'

James sat down beside her, ran his hand over her hair then let it rest on her shoulder. 'We have to believe she is here for a reason, and that the reason *will* unravel itself.'

'I thought I knew what the reason was . . . when Lily said she forgave me for saying I wouldn't come and get her if she spent that money; it was like barbed wire had been untangled from inside me. I thought . . . maybe . . . she'd come back to release me.' She rested her head on his arm and sighed.

'When someone dies, blame is handed around like a bag of chips,' he said, remembering his own guilt at not keeping his precious daughter safe. 'I'm glad you feel easier about it, although it wasn't your fault. It wasn't anyone's fault except that bloody driver. We just have to keep on the way we are for a bit longer.'

Amelia looked up at him, now feeling guilty for what she was about to say. 'As much as I will be eternally grateful for this chance with Lily, I worry about Ben all the time. I miss him . . . I miss the *boyishness* of him . . . and I miss . . .'

'. . . the way he can burp whole sentences at you?' James added and they both laughed.

'Even that,' she said.

After a long silence, James took a breath. 'She's finding it easier, you know . . . to live Ben's life.'

'I know,' she answered, and the awful truth found a spot between them and nestled there.

It was over.

Life wasn't just about living and breathing. Everything was heavy, dragging at her skin and her muscles and her lungs. The air burned her eyes and buzzed in her ears, drying her mouth and stealing her oxygen.

Confessing wasn't the difficult bit, owning up to being *the one* and facing the nuclear fallout that would change and disfigure every single part of her life to follow from that moment, no, the difficult bit would be never being able to look in the eyes of Nathan or Alex again.

To live without her family would be impossible, and even if Alex did stand by her, she believed that Nathan would never love her in the same way again. She would lose him.

She used to be scared, but now she was nothing. There was, quite literally, nothing left of her except skin and the need for it all to end.

'There is no tragedy that can't be overcome, you know,' Isabelle had said. But she had lied. This cannot be overcome, it cannot be changed, it cannot get better.

Nathan's mum accepted that soon it would be over . . . for everyone, and it brought a bitter sense of relief.

We stand in King's Lane surrounded by a countryside that is no longer winter bleak.

The criss-cross hedgerows budding with the green of blackthorn and gorse and dog rose interlace their way between hawthorns, weaving a tapestry of spring.

I have brought us here because I hate it. It is stained by the memory of the way I died and I want to change that. This is what I wanted to tell my parents in the car on the way back from the beach and now, finally they are trying to understand. I want this place to become the place 'where Lily last lived' rather than 'where Lily got run over and ended up with her head on backwards'.

'Oh, Lily, why did you walk home this way that day?' Mum asks sadly, as she scoops some dead bunches of flowers into one of the black sacks I'm holding. My fingers clench round the bag that crackles as the flowers are placed inside, the musty odour of dying petals mixing with the sharp smell of plastic. It's pretty embarrassing having to keep on explaining my stupidity and I want to snap at her, but I make do with a vaguely annoyed sigh and remind myself of One Shoe Sue's moral code about moving forward. 'This isn't about what I did; this is about what you're going to do from now on.'

After an hour we have moved everything, except a wooden wreath that Mum and Dad laid there weeks ago, and a large terracotta pot with sturdy flowering plants. I guess Nathan's mum put it here to replace the pot I smashed and now we've managed to get rid of all stuff here except that sodding thing. It is ironic watching Mum run her fingers across the terracotta.

'Aren't they lovely?' Mum says, admiring the sturdy plants each carrying a host of opening florets.

'Hyacinths,' Dad adds, before I can tell them to get rid of it, my words catching in my open mouth.

I look between the pot and my dad who is happily repositioning it now that the rest of the area is clear, blissfully unaware of how they got there. And in that precise moment something shifts deep inside me.

It's as if the world has suddenly stopped revolving and I am the one who is turning. The tiny opening florets carried by the sturdy stems of those hyacinths . . . are purple.

Purple hyacinths . . .

Ben's cryptic message from One Shoe Sue's house becomes as clear as a light switching on and I know that Ben is back beside me saying into my ear, 'Dumb arse slowcoach! You took your time.'

'It means I'm sorry,' I say quietly.

'What does?' he answers.

'The purple hyacinths . . . It means sorry. That pot is a message and it says "please forgive me" . . . in the language of flowers.'

It takes a minute for my words to register, but when they do, Dad grabs the side of the pot, 'You mean . . . ?' he says with a

337

dangerously angry look on his face, and I can tell that just as I smashed the first pot he is about to do the same with this one.

'Don't!' I hold my hands up, to stop him. An image of Nathan's mum comes to my mind and as clearly as if she were actually standing in front of me I can see her ragged decline. I can see clearly now how my death has destroyed Nathan and his family as much has destroyed mine, yet unlike mine, they cannot move on. 'It should stay here. I know it doesn't make it any better, but it's all they have to offer . . . I . . . I think . . . we should let them say sorry and forgive them.' As I say it out loud, I realise that what I've just said is true.

'Say sorry?' He almost screams. 'Forgive them?? They *should* confess, that's what they should do; they *should* go to prison or pay a fine, or whatever the punishment is,' Dad says, dumbfounded, swinging his gaze angrily between me and the flowers.

'And what if the person who did it has a family? And what if someone in that family will be destroyed by finding out . . . ?'

'And what about our family?' Mum asks.

'It's too late for our family, Mum, but it will ruin his life.' I don't think I should say it, but I know it's going to come out despite what I think. '. . . It will ruin Nathan's life.'

'NATHAN's father ran you over and never owned up?' Dad shouts, and Mum looks horrified that it could be someone they knew that well all this time.

'Nathan's mother,' I correct him, as he pauses for breath, and the stunned silence that follows stretches before us for a very long time while they both look wide-eyed and slack-jawed at me. 'She didn't know it was a person, she thought it was an animal, and, to be fair, it wouldn't have made any difference if she had stopped and found me . . . would it?'

'But if she had been looking where she was going, she wouldn't have hit you in the first place,' says Mum, while Dad opens and shuts his mouth, repeating, 'Nathan's *mother*?' as if saying it over and over might make him believe it.

'I told you it was complicated.'

Dad whistles. 'You don't say.'

It takes a while to come to an agreement. It takes a while for them to convince me that the course of justice is the only solution, and it takes a while for me to convince them not to phone the police immediately, and especially not to go to Nathan's house and deal with the matter themselves.

'Give me some time, and promise me you won't do anything for the moment. I think I know what to do,' I say.

*

Leaving the terracotta pot, we place all the surviving notes and pictures in a shoebox and bury it in the soil with the wreath on top, and in amongst the grass, all the way down the lane, we dig little holes where we drop the seeds of sunflowers and cover them over. We also plant some primroses and sweet william in little patches to give instant colour against the spring green.

I've spent all my savings, which wasn't a lot, and bought packets of seeds and bulbs to be planted in late September. Daffodils, snowdrops, bluebells and crocuses will now spend their winter here, tucked beneath the surface of the roadside, and in February next year they will begin to stretch and yawn, and eventually colour the edges of this road with their new life. Wildflowers will emerge at various times and surprise anyone coming past with their beauty.

I'm delighted with my own idea. 'OK, you two,' I announce, covered in mud, and straightening up to look at them both, I make my demand. 'This is my living gift. From now on it will be a place to remember my life not my death . . . agreed?'

'Agreed,' they answer together.

On Friday afternoon, I walk out of school leaving everyone to their lessons.

I walk out through the iron gates where bunches of flowers were once threaded through, like a guard of honour in respect of my untimely death. I pass the point where Joe and Graham pushed me to the ground and kicked me in the kidneys, and I can't help give a grim smile at the trouble they found themselves in. I walk along the road where the buses will line up to take home the approaching tide of children released from the confines of education. A yellow sun hangs in the sky like a disc of thin tissue paper, and I make a phone call.

I know where I am going.

I'm back at the wooden door of Nathan's very nice house. The beautifully restored Morris Minor is parked outside and I walk past it, running my hands over the paintwork of this car, built in a time before crumple zones, in a time where even the body of a teenage girl couldn't make a dent in the fine curves of its dense bodywork.

Nathan's mum opens the door and as she registers who it is she immediately tries to slam it shut, to remove the vision of the twin brother of the girl she killed, standing right in front of her. This time I'm ready and I put my foot in the gap between the door and the frame and everything that she ever used to be – a loving wife, a loving mother, a great cook, a glamorous lady and, above all, a genuinely kind person – has gone. She is weak, and she is no match for me.

She turns away and walks back inside the house, as if she's now past caring if I stay on the step or follow her in. So I follow her, leaving the door deliberately open behind me.

In her dining room she sits slowly down on one of the chairs in front of three sealed envelopes, which are addressed to the police, and my parents, and to Nathan and his dad. It doesn't take me long to realise what is in these letters, but the one that bothers me is the one to Nathan and his dad, as to my mind there could only be one reason why whatever is in that letter couldn't be told in person. She pushes the letter addressed to my parents towards me, and with an expression that is so empty, as if she has already left, she quietly murmurs, 'It's probably best you're here . . . I . . . I can't live with myself any more.'

I recall how she had once held the dark curl of my hair in her hand and told me that I was beautiful, and how she had looked at Nathan at his party with such love.

'I'll take this,' I say, putting the letter to my parents in my pocket, but I also reach for the one addressed to Nathan and his dad and tear it up, leaving the pieces on the table, 'but you can tell your family yourself.'

I pull a chair out from under the table and sit on it, feeling the slight give of the soft cushion beneath me, and I notice how a tiny flicker moves across her empty expression as she looks briefly up at me.

'In a few minutes,' I tell her, 'there will be a knock on the door because I've invited someone here to talk to you.' Nathan's mum nods as if she is expecting me to bring in the entire British police force, although her terrified hand reaches for her lips.

When the knock comes, she flinches, but her anticipation of an immediate arrest turns to surprise when One Shoe Sue walks lopsidedly in through the open door and presses her arm in her peculiarly reassuring way.

I tell her the reason I am here clearly so there is no mistaking my words.

'Mrs Peterson? I have come to give you your life back.'

Sue pulls out another chair and heaves herself down, stretching her false leg out beneath the table before eventually introducing herself.

'I'm Sue, a clairvoyant . . . I can talk to those who have passed on and I have come to tell you that I have a message for you from Lily Richardson . . .' As soon as my name is mentioned, Nathan's mum flutters with the movements of someone who is trying to contain an anguish that is so much bigger than she is. I see a weak flush of red creep up her neck and clash with the grey of fear that has been her pallor since I walked in. Her shaking hands hold each other for comfort and her eyes dart between us under a frown that gives away her confusion.

'We know how Lily died,' she continues, and her head nods gently in agreement with herself, 'and we are not here to judge, but to give you Lily's message.' I glance at Nathan's mum and wonder if she is going to pass out any second. The minuscule shred of colour that she had previously has drained away,

343

although I think her need to know what Lily's message might be is the only thing preventing her from sinking slowly under the table.

'Er . . . would you like to give Lily's message to Mrs Peterson?' One Shoe Sue says, looking directly at me.

Nathan's mum does not move an inch, save for the continuous stream of saline that dribbles down her cheeks and drips off her chin as she tries to process what she is hearing.

Ben had given me a clue . . . and then . . . nothing else! He had stepped back and left me to it, like we were playing one last game.

I clear my throat, picturing the purple hyacinths. 'Yes . . . she forgives you, Mrs Peterson . . . *I* forgive you.' And as I say those words, it feels unexpectedly good.

I no longer hate Nathan's mum.

As the word 'forgive' comes out of my mouth, Nathan's mum gives up her grief. It pours out of her mouth, her eyes, her nose, her skin. It is audible, and visible, and painful. I reach out for her hand, and she leaves it within my fingers, believing that I am Ben, gripping back at me as if holding on to her own life through mine.

After some time, she tries to talk. The words burst out in staccato jumps. 'I'm . . . so . . . sorry,' she says over and over. 'I thought I'd hit a deer . . . I'm so sorry. I would never have meant to hurt her.' Her eyes bravely lift until they meet mine.

'I believe you,' I say. And I do.

'But how do you know all this?' she asks us. 'Has . . . she . . . really come . . . back? Has she really been watching me??' She looks at Sue who smiles her lovely, calming smile.

'Those who have passed on are often around us when we need them most. Sometimes we can see them, or feel them, but we often dismiss it as a puff of wind, or a glint of sun,' she explains, and, bending the truth a little, she adds, 'I have been given a special gift and because of that I have been able to communicate with Lily.'

'But how can *you* forgive me?' she asks Ben, and although I don't know exactly what Ben would do in this situation I'm going to give it a pretty good guess. I think back to the evening in the posh restaurant and how Dad had two glasses of champagne, and a coffee liqueur and then the waiter brought complimentary drinks for them both at the end of the meal, which he felt obliged to drink, and yet he still drove home.

'I'd say something about only throwing stones if you're perfect,' I answer.

'Let he who is without sin cast the first stone,' Sue clarifies.

'Yes –' I point a knowing finger at Sue – 'that one.'

'This blame . . . from that single moment in time,' I add. 'It's destroying too many people. My parents know it was you now, and they'll come to accept it in time,' I say, 'but I *will* give them this.' I pat my pocket with the letter in it.

I push the letter that she's addressed to the police towards her. 'Do this –' then I point to the letter I tore up – 'but absolutely don't do this.'

'I think Alex might . . . just . . . understand, but Nathan . . . how could a boy ever understand this?' she whispers.

She has a point. Me forgiving her is not enough but I have an idea. Nathan needs to forgive her too.

'Don't tell them tonight . . . tell them tomorrow evening . . .

there's something I need to do.' I wait until I have her promise, then add, 'Just so you know, it was me that sent you the Facebook messages . . . sorry.' I think it's fairer to let her think that Ben sent them, than let her believe that Lily did it, even though I did. 'And one last thing . . . the pilgrimage to King's Lane . . . ? Make it right in a different way.' I have no idea how she should make it right in a different way, but that's her challenge, not mine.

As we leave, Nathan's mum stands by the front door, looking as if she's just been turned inside out and dragged through a hedge backwards, but there is something in her eyes that wasn't there before. Her hand briefly touches mine as I move past her, and she simply says, 'Thank you . . . You have saved me . . . and . . . I hope . . . my family.'

As Sue and I walk down the path, the sun slides out from behind a white cloud, spilling over everything I can see, and I tilt my face upwards to its warmth and light, and somehow, inside, I feel the same. I am finally free of the burden of hate I've been carrying around and it feels good.

Sunlight glints off windows and cars, and a lawnmower buzzes in the distance and the air smells of the promise of summer to come.

I love summer so much. That wonderful feeling of being outside, letting the warmth soak into my skin and inhaling the scent of fresh-cut grass carried along on breaths of cool breeze, of picnics and barbeques and light, lazy evenings. I breathe deeply through my nose, absorbing every single trace of the season to come, and suddenly I know that it is no longer mine to have.

As Sue's car pulls away from Nathan's house, I realise that, like the spider, I have repaired my web.

'It's time,' I say, staring at the road ahead, and as Sue indicates to turn left out of Nathan's road, she simply says. 'Yes, dear.'

Back home, I take the after bucket list and go to my own room.

I study everything on it, my eyes travelling along the lines and down the list. I look only for the numbers that I've managed to tick, remembering everything: the delicious and luxurious meal with Mum and Dad, and the taste of champagne on my tongue; the wind in my hair and the salt up my nose on the beach, feeling the strength and the beauty of Arizona as she carried me safely along the edge of a foamy sea. I can feel my face lifting to the cool blue sky at the top of Snowdon, and my sense of achievement at sliding down a ski slope without falling over, and I smile with pride when I think of the wildflowers that will nod their heads all the way down King's Lane. Before closing the book, I tick one more item on the list.

I go to my drawer and get out my own stationery and begin to write to the people I love. One for my mum and dad, and one for Ben. My writing is my own, round and pretty and familiar, not the elongated scrawl of Ben's hand that I have perfected over the last few weeks. It takes a long time, writing a message for the ones you love, which has to last them a lifetime until you meet again. I sign the end of their letters with the loopy way I write 'Lily' and place a tiny heart above the 'i' as always.

I put the after bucket list carefully alongside the letter for Ben and push them into an envelope.

Finally I lie back on my own bed looking at my own things and thinking of the people in my life who have made me what I am. In everything, I wish I could have enjoyed it more. I wish I had not taken anything for granted.

The emotions and sensations that were missing from my time in limbo stir inside me. These feelings that made up who I was, feelings that helped me decide what was wrong or right, good or bad, lovely or nasty. Although I need these physical reminders in the living world in order to make the right decisions, in limbo they were not necessary. I remember that kind of *knowing* and the kind of peace that I felt. In a way it was lovely and I try to hold on to that thought.

When all the pieces of my mind feel as though they are in order as much as they will ever be, I go downstairs. Mum is finishing off the trimmings of a savoury pie; there is music and she is singing and it feels like home. I give her a hug and she smiles at me. 'Hello, dear,' she says absentmindedly and carries the pie over to the oven. I find Dad in the lounge, catching up on the day's newspaper and I sit next to him, leaning my head on his shoulder as I reach for his hand. We sit like that for a few minutes and Dad asks me if I'm OK, but I can't answer. I swallow the saliva that is building in my mouth and the sound of it is noisy in the room, yet I still don't move. Dad folds the paper clumsily with one hand, and places it on the wooden coffee table beside him, squeezing my fingers between his large warm hands.

'You're leaving, aren't you?' he says, already knowing the answer. 'Is it time?' The words come softly out of his mouth.

I nod and the movement of it shakes tears over the edge of my eyes and sends them down my cheek.

Mum comes bustling into the room with a smile on her face, a question on her lips and a tea towel in her hand. She stops short and her smile drops, as the tea towel falls to the floor, and she knows too. She comes towards us and sits down until the three of us are squashed on our familiar soft sofa, my left hand in Dad's and my right hand in Mum's. We must sit like that for a long time and no one says a word, and no one moves until the timer from the kitchen rings loudly to tell us that the pie is ready.

At dinner, we sit quietly and united round the table. The food is delicious, but we eat very little of it. A cherry-red candle flickers in the centre of the table, and our eyes focus on it through the meal. This time I haven't shuffled the seat to the middle to disguise the space. This time I sit in my own seat and leave Ben's vacant, so that the chairs round our table show that we are a family of four and always will be, whether we're in the same room or not.

'I have forgiven Nathan's mum,' I say quietly into the silence, and this time they say nothing in return. I hand them the letter she wrote to them. 'Tomorrow she will tell the police and they can sort it out from there. You will get your justice . . . And now I can go . . .'

And finally they understand what I needed to do to leave.

Mum excuses herself for a moment and we hear her blowing her nose in the downstairs toilet. When she comes back to the table only the bravery of a mother shows on her face.

It's Saturday. My second-to-last day.

In my own room with the clear light of a blue sky coming through the window and a soft breeze promising a warm day that feels delicious on my skin, I look at Ben's phone and there is a line of replies, each saying 'OK.' Matthew, Beth and Nathan have made a last-minute agreement to meet me here at 09.30, for an early sixteenth birthday present to myself. I put on my own soft and cosy dressing gown and go downstairs.

Mum and Dad are up and dressed and bacon is on the grill. I breathe in that familiar smell and there is nothing like it. Morning in our house is really quite nice; it is such a shame I didn't enjoy it more when I was Lily. I try to make a mental note of every sight and smell and taste and touch, because I know that by tomorrow it will all be just a memory. I pour myself some juice and sit at the table watching them both, and I love them.

*

We are going to a theme park, my hurriedly decided early birthday present to myself, courtesy of Dad's wallet. As I will no longer be around on our sixteenth birthday I have decided to bring mine forward. Today shall be all about the thrill of speed and fun that belongs to the joy of living and not the fear of

351

dying. Four teenagers spending the whole day on thrill-seeking rides; perfect.

For Beth, I can see a glow in her golden eyes that tells me she is having fun and that there is a bright future for her. I know she will be OK.

With Matthew I can see that as the day unfolds he's amazed at the relationship Ben seems to have with his parents, and I hope that he takes a little bit of today home with him to his own mum and dad. I hug both of them openly in front of Ben's mates and I hope Ben does the same when he's back. But when you know that this is your last day everything is different. The expression about living each day as if it is your last could never be truer.

I persuade Nathan to sit next to me on the rollercoaster and as we climb in and wait for everyone to take their seats, I grab my chance. 'You know Lily loved you, right?' and he looks hard at me.

'We were only together for seven weeks and one day and but I loved her too. She was a beautiful girl and for a while she was mine.' My heart skips a massive beat with joy. 'If she was still here we would have been going out for . . .'

'Fifteen weeks today!' we say at exactly the same time, and I know I have the widest grin all over my face.

He looks at me with total confusion. 'Why have *you* been counting?' he asks me.

'Oh, just good at maths . . . I know you asked her out on New Year's Day, that's all.'

And as the rollercoaster jolts and begins its slow climb, I suddenly realise that for Nathan it must be time to stop counting.

'Are you going to take Daisy to the prom?' The words push their way round the lump forming in my throat.

'I don't know. I keep changing my mind.' Tiny spikes of jealousy play a sword fight with my bravery.

'You should . . . Lily won't mind . . .' The lump, now the size of a melon, prevents me from saying anything else.

'Is that your twin thing?' he asks. 'The *I know my twin without words* thing?'

The top of the ride is looming, which means I have to ditch that melon and speak before it's too late. 'Yeah, it's the twin thing. I also know that when you get home your mum will have some news for you.'

'Whoa, that's cryptic, man.' He balks at the mention of his mother. The rollercoaster creeps upwards and I don't have much time.

'I'm serious, Nate. Promise me that whatever she tells you, you'll stand by her, for Lily's sake . . . Family is the most important thing . . . trust me.' He looks confused and the knot in his forehead asks what the hell Lily has got to do with his mother. 'The person who was driving the car that day . . . ? Lily has forgiven them . . .' Nathan continues staring at me, but nervously now with an *I don't know what the fuck you're talking about* look, as the carts keep shifting upwards, but I tap my nose knowingly. 'It's the twin thing . . . you HAVE to promise!' The rollercoaster has now reached a point where we feel as if we are almost vertical, our bodies pressed into our seats and our stomachs balancing on our spines.

'I'll believe it if I get a sign from her to tell me she's OK,' he says, looking down at the park way below us. 'I asked her for a sign and I got nothing. You say you *know* what she wants but why is she always telling *you* and never *me* any of this stuff?'

I look ahead at the sky. In a few seconds we will be hurtling down and around, twisting and turning, and I anticipate the huge rush that we're about to experience.

'You just need to believe in her, Nathan,' I yell at him right before we drop. 'BELIEVE.'

*

The rest of the day is full. We laugh, and scream, and eat candyfloss, and hot dogs. Mum and Dad turn shades of green or pink depending on the ride, and we all laugh at them, deeply admiring them for not joining the other older people on the benches, viewing the young living their lives and never being sure at what point they had stopped wanting to join in.

When it's finally over, I look at my friends who still have all of their tomorrows and the seed of resentment that grew shoots and became a plant withers and recedes. I don't resent them for what they have; I just wish I could have it too. I say my goodbyes, hugging Beth and whispering in her ear, 'Keep laughing.' Then I punch Matthew on the shoulder, as I know Ben would, but mainly because he thinks I'm leaning in to hug him too, so he hops back exclaiming, 'Off the cloth, man!' in case I'm going to get all mushy with him.

'You're a good mate,' I say and watch him squirm at the compliment.

'Whoa, that's intense, man,' he answers with what my female instincts detect as a hint of gratitude not to mention relief. And, finally, in an effort not to kiss Nathan, I hug him as the next best thing, and being so much more relaxed than Matthew he lets me. 'Promise me you'll do what I said?' I remind him, and he nods his agreement, but this time I make him actually say the words.

'Promise,' he answers before we shake on it.

'You're acting like you're leaving us,' Beth laughs, and I turn quickly away so that none of them hear me say, 'I am.'

Sleep did not happen for Nathan that night.

He'd walked home from Ben's house wondering what he'd been going on about on the rollercoaster. It was so confusing.

And when, later that evening, his mother had told him and his dad that she had been behind the wheel on the day Lily had died, Ben's urgent words to *promise* to stand by her had been more than difficult to keep hold of.

How had Ben known? Had his mother told him first? Why would Ben and his family protect her, and how had they managed to stop themselves going to the police, or even coming round and tearing his family limb from limb themselves?

Ben had insisted that for Lily's sake, whatever happened, he *must* keep his promise, but as his mother was escorted to a waiting police car, Nathan and his father struggled to believe that the family as they knew it would ever be the same.

As Nathan lay on his bed churning over the events of the day with words and images going round and round in his head, a splash of colour caught his eye, starkly bold against the cloth of the jacket he had worn earlier. His heart accelerating rapidly, he sat up and reached over to where his jacket was hooked on the back of his door. A prickle began on his skin and worked its way up his whole body until it played with the hair on the back of his neck. There, just peeking out of the pocket was a spray of pink. He pinched the end of it and pulled until a feather uncurled in his hand in all its bright-pink glory. 'No one knew,' he whispered to the space in the room, staring at what he held in the palm of his hand. 'No one *knew*!' he shouted, louder this time, as if the volume would help him know it was true. Then he sat back down on his bed and stared at his pink gift, his very own personal sign, until finally he understood that, in time, it would all be OK.

'I believe!' he shouted out to the air above his head, and without realising it he gently let go of the girlfriend he used to have. Life would move on. Never quite the same, but it would eventually repair itself.

'Thank you,' he sighed. 'I'll never forget you, Lily Richardson.'

As the hands of the clock slide inevitably past twelve into a new and final day, we all make our way up the stairs. I want to spend the remainder of the night in my own room for the very last time, around the things that I once believed had defined me. The photos, the diary, the tickets to concerts, souvenirs from various places, jewellery, make-up and posters. These things are pieces of the fifteen-year-old girl's life that I once had. I touch them and hold them to me and remember how I came to have each one.

At the back of my wardrobe, slightly battered now, is the old chocolate box, the picket fence now cream, and the colours of the garden faded. I find that I'm holding my breath as I lift the lid. There, hidden delightfully amid the crushed pink tissue, are the little silver memories of my gran, dulled now with age.

Taking the ancient silver cleaning cloth, I return the little treasures to their former glory and feel sorrow that I won't have a child of my own to pass the memories on to. Tearing a sheet off my notebook that has a winking smiley face at the top of each page, I write a letter to the children that Ben will one day have. In my own handwriting I ask them to look after my things because they contain a love that has spanned decades and generations, then I fold it carefully, kissing the folded paper square, before tucking it inside the box.

This is really it, the absolute end of my life.

I don't want to go.

I reach for my urn and place my hand upon the remains of what I used to be. The mourning for myself that I've held inside since I came back through Ben's body finally comes out. A whirling range of emotions spin inside me, scraping and grazing their way through me, hurting yet healing at the same time.

I stay up all night, 'number three,' and as the anger, and hurt, and rage, and fear gradually works its way out, and as the sky changes from black to navy to pewter and finally to the light blue-grey of a brand-new day I know that I too must accept.

I take the little box to Ben's room, take my clothes from the drawers, the last picture off my wall and ornaments off my shelves, and place them in neat piles against the wall. I don't want Mum sitting in here any more, keeping my room as a shrine, trying to avoid getting rid of my stuff as if that would somehow mean she was getting rid of me. Keeping it all just as it was on the day I left . . . *hurts* her.

These things are not me.

I am me.

I am Lily.

Amelia and James listened to the sounds of anger coming from Lily's bedroom and it was all they could do to stop themselves from going in there and joining in. They had a lifetime ahead of them to adjust to losing their beautiful girl, but Lily had only one night. Amelia had begged Sue if it was possible to give her own body to Lily and let her daughter live for longer, but of course that's not how life should work. Lily could not live in anyone's body; she had to be shown how to move on. Amelia knew this to be true, but a good mother would lay down her own life for her child if at all possible, and Amelia was a good mother.

They knew they had been given a true gift. Lily had to leave them, but this time she would not have to do it alone.

The soft music from Lily's flute that had floated through the air and into their very core would haunt them – in a beautiful way – for the rest of their lives. It was the moment they had both known that what was once lost had been found.

Tomorrow they would help their daughter to find her way to move on.

Tomorrow, thankfully, they would help their son find his way back.

Tonight they would lie tight within each other's arms and know that their family, whether near or very far away, would always love each other, in fact, love each other more than life itself.

Knowing that this last day will all end in a few short hours makes me feel as if I am somehow slowly disappearing even before the moment that I actually have to go.

Sue has promised that, this time, I'll find my way out of here without floating around forever on my own, and I'm really hoping she's right, because the temptation to keep coming back will be too much, and I'm sure that Ben will get fed up with me gate-crashing his life all the time.

'Ben!' I say out loud. 'I don't know what you've been doing these past few weeks, but you'd better be ready to jump back in.'

The deep breath that I take before I leave my dismantled bedroom this morning is just enough, though barely, for me to convince my parents I am most definitely, without a doubt . . . ready!

I should win an Oscar.

A cursory attempt at breakfast is made then left. Hot cups of tea go cold, and the day trickles past in agonising suspense, an atmosphere of anticipation growing, like in a dentist's waiting room.

When the knock finally comes at the door we all jump and my heart thumps with the adrenalin that is released into my system by fear, and it feels as if the very ground beneath me is shaking. Sue comes limping heavily into the house, wafting the air around her with the scent of lavender and calmness, as far removed from the Grim Reaper as you can get. She is more like a beacon, as if her very insides are alight with her surety that what is about to happen is a natural and good thing. Her warm hands touch each of us as she passes, busily making her way to the lounge as if she's as comfortable as she would be in her own house.

Mum hovers in the doorway, anxiously out of her depth.

'Would you like a drink, One . . . I mean . . . Sue?'

'No, thank you, dear. We should just get on. Ben will be waiting,' Sue answers, as if Mum is holding up a game of rounders. I'm about to be caught out and Ben is waiting to bat.

While our hearts do loops in our chests, Sue talks to us in a tone that's almost musical, and which is lighter than her meaning, cleverly disguising the horrific outcome of not doing exactly what she says.

'Now that you're ready to leave, Ben will be waiting for you. At the same time, you must look for the wisps that you described at the funeral . . . They will be people who have gone before and they will be coming to help you over. When they reach out for you, reach back, don't be afraid. And don't forget, dear, that you must let Ben back into his body as *quickly* as possible because his body cannot survive for long without its soul.' I guiltily find myself entertaining the idea that I would rather spend eternity in limbo with Ben than without him, but Mum interrupts this temptingly unfair idea.

'What are you saying?' she asks. Her face is a stricken shade of puce.

'It's fine, Mum,' I say convincingly, as if anything about this could be fine. 'He'll be right back, annoying the pants off both of you before you know it.'

Sue brings three chairs round to the sofa, and she sits on one, asking Mum and Dad to have the others, but me to lie on the sofa. She really isn't wasting any time.

Out of her bag she produces a small docking station, which she sets beside us all so that it can fill the air with the softness of her atmospheric music. 'OK, Lily,' she begins, 'I am going to show you how to meditate until you experience a trance-like state, or even sleep. Mum and Dad, could you kiss Lily and tell her that you will see her when it is your own time to move on.' They dutifully do this and it's not lost on us that we don't have to say goodbye. Dad has to pull Mum gently away, as he did that day in the morgue, and her fingertips caress my hair, until with Dad's protective arm firmly round her shoulders her fingers cannot reach me any more.

Sue begins to allow her words to form a steady line, like a verbal slipstream in amongst her music, encouraging me to breathe deeply and relax. 'Don't be scared, dear. You are warm, you are comfortable, you are looking for a bright light, and when you find it you must move towards it.' Her words go on, and on, and I know I'm supposed to find some sort of meditative state in all this, but really? That music is doing my head in.

Suddenly I snap open my eyes and make everyone jolt slightly, and I know they are all looking intently at me to see if I am Ben. 'It's still me,' I say, looking at each one of them. 'Can one of you get my phone? Sorry, Sue, but this is not my kind of music; It's for old people. I want something to remind me I am a teenager and I have lived.'

Dad gets my phone and hands it to me and I scroll through for something. I find a track that was played at Milly's party and I set it to play on a loop, settling myself back on the sofa and sucking in a deep breath. 'OK, ready!'

'Close your eyes, Lily . . . you are warm . . . you are comfortable . . .' Sue's words become a drone again, and I let them fade into the background as my music floats into my head, the lyrics and the soft beat reminding me of that one single brilliant night, of dancing and friends and music. I want to tell Mum and Dad to let Ben be the one to decide what to do with my ashes but when I open my eyes again it is Ben that I see standing next to me.

He takes a step forward and holds his hand out to help me up. This time, I do take his hand, my arms and legs and body becoming Lily again, my hair long and black. His arms round my shoulders feel so good, and I know, without him saying anything, that he's OK. We are one again, arms entwined, tied forever by the twin thing. I turn to look into the room and I see Ben's body lying on the sofa as if he's asleep. Mum and Dad are watching him intently. They cannot see their children hugging each other so close beside them. I wish they could.

Sue is not looking at the sofa. She has that strange look she gets, as if tuning in to something 'She has left his body,' she whispers. 'They are together.'

I see a wisp of smoke curling around us, and some more in the corner of the room. I know then that they have come to get me, these wisps that belong to people who have gone before, and now there is nothing holding me back.

Sue is still talking. Her words are filtering through and she is asking Ben to let me go and to come back to his family.

'Hyacinths? You jerk! At a time like this, you gave me a *clue*?' I ask. 'Why didn't you just tell me to go and forgive her?'

'Because you needed to work it out yourself,' he answers. 'I could have tried to find you in the night on several occasions but I wanted to give you a bit of time to find your way.'

'How long would you have given me?' I ask, wondering if I could have at least made it to Paris.

He shrugs. 'I don't know. Not enough to make it to Paris. I just knew you needed to sort some stuff out before you could let go of everything. Thankfully your superiorness worked it out reasonably swiftly.'

Who knew? My brother is a wise old thing and not an idiot after all. But I have to say it. 'Superiority! "Superiorness" isn't a word.' We both laugh one final time.

'I left you a letter,' I add.

'I know,' he says and his look says a thousand words as a smile plays on the corner of his mouth. He has seen everything. I didn't steal him, I just used his body for a while, and he let me. He gave me the greatest of gifts and I will literally be grateful for eternity.

'Thank you, Ben.'

'What for?' He grins, acting, as if these lost weeks in his life were nothing.

'Allowing me to . . . climb back on my perch for a while.' I grin back. 'And letting me make an idiot of you.'

'Yeah, you did make an idiot of me . . . several times over . . . but you saved me too.'

A vision of Joe and Graham comes to mind and I know Ben saw all of this. 'Yeah, I did, didn't I . . . ? So we're even?' I ask.

'We're even,' he answers.

I did a good thing.

'You'd better go.' I point to his body, as Sue calls him back, and the wisps of smoke begin to take form, beckoning me towards them. 'Can't have you dying on Mum and Dad too.'

'You'd better go too,' he says. 'I think someone is waiting.'

A wisp beckons me like it did in the crematorium, but I now can see the shape of our lovely gran, her gentle, timeless face that I remember so well, emerging through the beckoning forms. In an instant all the difficult emotions that I have felt over the last few weeks, anger, fear, regret and guilt, slip away; I am warm, and I am peaceful.

I am so glad to see her, and as I move towards her open arms I am overwhelmed by the most amazing feeling, like peanut butter, riding Arizona through the salty sea, and the twenty-second hug with my mum and dad. The other wisps take shape and reach their arms towards me too, I don't remember who they all are – our other gran from long ago, I think, and other faces from the family album, but I know I want to go with them. I know now that I will no longer be alone. It's as if the sun has come out, its warmth and brightness leading the way, and that to follow them towards it will be the most wonderful thing to do.

'Tell Dad Gran came for me,' I say, but as I turn back to look at Ben, he is already lying down in his own body. I wanted to tell him I love him, but I guess he already knows. It's a twin thing.

When my brother opens his own eyes, in his own house, with his parents beside him, ready to live the rest of his life, I am gone.

I can see the tops of distant buildings, a patchwork of countryside and the beetling of cars along tiny grey threads of road becoming smaller and smaller, masked occasionally by the mists of rushing clouds, until they have gone, and there is nothing but blue. I lean back, breathing with satisfaction, letting the brightness of a foreign sun flooding through the oval window bathe me in its light.

I use this time, as I always do, to reflect. It is a time with no agenda except the hours between taking off and landing. As the aeroplane banks I think of the tiny seeds I've just planted in a patch of ground belonging to a small village, now nestled in the African soil that I'm flying over. I picture their golden heads waving under the orange African sunshine in a few months' time, watered by my new good friend with conker-brown skin and the whitest of teeth. I hope that his smiling face, beaming out from his copy of the *World Traveller* magazine I am photographer for, will encourage him to remember his task. I trust him, as I do the many other friends I have made around the world, to care for my seeds. I think of their feet, and their children's feet, treading the ground beneath them, perhaps in the very place where some of the ashes of my sister have settled.

My camera equipment is stowed safely in the hold, having captured all the photographs of this particular adventure, and as always, I'm so grateful that my amazing job means I get to travel the world. Lucky, lucky me.

I still have the urn. The ashes within are steadily reducing as I take my sister on her much-wanted trip around the world, number one on her long-ago list. The ashes settle in sand, or grass, or dust, undetected by my glossy photographs submitted to the magazine, but very much there even so. Every summer I imagine Lily and her sunflowers rising out of unusual places, an old wooden boat filled with soil or a tractor tyre in a junk yard, on hills sweeping down to the sea, or small front yards in drab urban corners, or on the rooftop gardens of city buildings. It makes me smile.

I think of the first adventure when I took Lily's ashes to Paris in the summer of our sixteenth birthday, when I went with Matthew and his family. At the highest pinnacle of what was once the tallest building in the world, I took a tiny bag out of my pocket and scattered the ashes to the wind. I imagined Lily floating over Paris and eventually coming to land in gardens, on buildings or on an open-topped boat on the River Seine. I snapped a picture with the camera on my phone and that was the moment I knew what my future would be.

When she used my body, when we were just fifteen, I watched her every moment. I watched her every night from the shadows of her sleep while I waited, keeping a safe distance away, so that the power of my own body couldn't draw me back to itself. Because after that first time, when she wouldn't let go of the duvet, I realised that I couldn't push her aside, leaving her on her own with her unfinished life. She wasn't ready.

I knew that my sister needed to work out how to let go, and in the few short weeks that Lily had her second chance, she learnt to forgive, to accept and to die. I watched her mend the rips and tears that had appeared in everyone's lives from that one fateful moment on a February day. *She did a good thing.*

I also thank her for every single day that I've missed her. And on Nathan and Alex Peterson's behalf, for giving them back their wife and mother, the very lovely Alice Peterson. The world is definitely a better place with her in it.

I hope that from wherever she is Lily can see the faces of the old people where Alice still works. She kept her promise too, and honoured Lily in a different way; tired but peaceful eyes now spend their last days lingering on an anonymously donated courtyard garden, with raised planters, hanging sun catchers and carefully arranged bird feeders, and an old terracotta pot with ever-changing flowers.

I also hope that she can see that Mum and Dad honoured her wish to revisit King's Lane in September, planting a host of wildflowers all along the lane where they grow still, returning year after year, flourishing where death once lingered, waving their colourful heads at all who drive down that road.

As glamorous as my job is, there is only one place for me at the end of it, with my own family. My wife, with her beautiful warm, copper-coloured skin, and the wild black hair of my daughter, with its untamed curls that dance around cheeks spilt with cinnamon freckles, and those eyes, those big green eyes. I love them both.

Beth and I tasted the sweetness of a brief wild fling when I first returned, healing the wound that was life without Lily, until our lives, as they needed to, went their own separate ways. A quirky burst of rain found us running for the same doorway of a warm London cafe eight years later, pearls of water clinging to our hair and clothes as our lives unfolded over frothy cappuccinos and blueberry muffins. So much to tell . . . university, her promised world travel, and mine, of loves found and lost, memories of who we used to be and who we had become, until in the hour and a half it took for the rain to stop, love found its way.

The steward's trolley stops by my aisle and I order one of their tiny bottles of white wine. The stewardess with the reddest of lipstick applied to perfection asks me if there is anything else that I need. But I have it all. I make a toast, as I do on every trip, to everything that is good, and sip from my plastic glass, as I read Lily's long-ago letter, which was left with an old chocolate box of silver memories.

Dear Ben.

With this letter you will find my after bucket list and all the many things that I would do if I could. Now you have to do them for me. All of them, if possible, and more.

I know you wanted to take my ashes and do something crazy with them. Well, here is a clue. In the wrappers inside the envelope are two pieces of gum. I have chewed one (I cleaned my teeth first) and you must chew the other, preferably not after eating pizza!

After you have done that, put a teeny tiny bit of my ash inside, then merge them together and stick them on the Seattle Gum Wall. I don't care how you find the money for the trip, or when. Do it! Our bits of gum will have the craziest story out of all the other bits of gum. How cool is that?

Do you like the tattoo? It is number two on my list. Sue took me to have it done on Friday after I saw Nathan's mum. Pretty, isn't it? Payback for the potty photo! I wanted the tattoo but you are the one who has to live with it. My final work of sabotage . . . Hurrah for me!

Well, I had better sign off. It just isn't possible to fit a lifetime of words on this small page. All I can do is thank you for all time – my fabulous brother.

Lily x

The cabin feels warm and I roll the sleeves of my white shirt up past my elbows. The skin on my arms is tanned and shows up the scattering of grey amongst the once-black hairs. My shirt hides the tattoo on my arm of a lily. It's not very discrete, and not very manly, but this also makes me smile every time I see it. I thought we were even, but she won!

There is a pocket in my heart where all the jokes and pranks, the flicking of tea towels and the firing of elastic bands now lie dormant. This pocket belongs exclusively to me and my twin sister and our fabulous childhood years.

I fold the letter, finish the wine, and sigh with pure satisfaction. Lily is everywhere. In dust, in cities, in fields and rivers and even on the Seattle Gum Wall.

And sometimes, out of the corner of my eye, I think I can see wisps, like clouds in a summer sky, changing shape with the breeze.

Acknowledgements

My sincere gratitude to the author Anthony Riches for believing this book had legs and for pushing it under the nose of Broo Docherty, Literary Agent.

Thank you from the bottom of my heart to the very lovely Broo Docherty, for having faith in and for making it happen.

Thank you to Emma Matthewson and all the staff from Hot Key Books for your amazing enthusiasm.

Thank you to Geraldine Davey who was always ready for brainstorming sessions, suffered my endless ups and downs, queries and self doubts, whilst tirelessly sliding delicious homemade cakes and cups of tea in my general direction.

A big thank-you to my life-long friend Della Ray and the late Josie McDonagh for sharing the most wonderful bottle of 1982 Veuve Clicquot to celebrate my book deal. I feel honoured that you shared this with me.

Thank you to Lisa Cherry – speaker, trainer, author – for giving me the push I needed to believe I could write a book.

Thank you to all my friends and family for their ongoing support and to the friends who read the first drafts and gave me the confidence to keep going: Helen Riches, Antoinette

Wilcox, Barbara Drummond and Marti Scott-Lee.

Thank you also to my Dutch family, Carla Meijer and Marjon and Bert Bakker for encouraging me to write and for always being so positive.

Thank you to my stepdaughter, Christina O'Sullivan, Paramedic Education and Training Officer, East of England, and to Garrett Gloyn, Gloucestershire Police for their advice.

And last but not least to David Mooney, my wonderful husband, for supporting me in every way while I wrote this book.

Phyllida Shrimpton

Phyllida Shrimpton is a full-time mother of a teenage daughter and currently lives in Essex with her husband, their rescued Newfoundland and small badly behaved Jack Russell.

She achieved a postgraduate degree in Human Resource Management, but soon jumped ship to work with teenagers, including students with Asperger's syndrome, on an Essex-based agricultural college farm before eventually moving to live temporarily in the Netherlands. She is also an artist. *Sunflowers in February* is her first novel.